# Bloodlines

Born in Durban, South Africa, Elleke Boehmer is the author of *Colonial and Postcolonial Literature* (1995) and of two novels, *Screens against the Sky* (1990) and *An Immaculate Figure* (1993). She taught in the School of English at the University of Leeds for a number of years, and is currently Professor of Colonial and Postcolonial Studies at the Nottingham Trent University. Her recent research interests include the relationship of Ireland and South Africa during the Anglo–Boer War.

# Bloodlines

## Elleke Boehmer

**dp** DAVID PHILIP PUBLISHERS   Cape Town

First published in 2000 in Southern Africa by
David Philip Publishers (Pty) Ltd,
208 Werdmuller Centre, Newry Street, Claremont, 7708, South Africa

© Elleke Boehmer 2000

ISBN  0-86486-361-6

Printed and bound by Clyson Printers,
11th Avenue, Maitland, Cape Town

# Acknowledgements

I am grateful to the Arts Council of England Writers' Awards, the Centre for Creative Arts, University of Natal, Durban, and the School of English, University of Leeds, for support while working on this book.

I am indebted, too, to the imagined but nonetheless keenly felt 'hands' of WB Yeats, and Maud Gonne, on pp. 22–23 and 188–190, and am grateful for the snatches of Yeats's *The Wind Among the Reeds*, and *Last Poems*, that run through the second half of this book, as I am to the presence, throughout, of Bessie Head.

TO STEVEN MATTHEWS

A black-and-white postcard, 'Natal 1899', shows a strip of beach, a building under broad awnings, the Jetty Tea Room, a background of dense bush. Three women and two men in black stand in a group beside a tethered horse. Anthea Hardy knows this postcard, so does Mrs Dora Makken. It lies in a glass case in the hallway of the local history museum next to a bullet stained at the tip 'with Boer blood', so the label says. The message scrawled in faint ink on the back of the card is not revealed to the public.

Dear Family,
      You can't imagine how we long to be back at the coast with you. We are always hungry though in relatively good spirits. The siege is by and large peaceful and can even be dramatic. Did you hear that it is the Irish rebels and not the Dutch who are most successful at lobbing bombs into the town?
      We hope very much to have been relieved by Christmas. More at this stage we are not permitted to say.

'All of us', the card is signed.

# 1

The bomb exploded at 11.10 in the morning, outside the main entrance to the small beach-front supermarket called the Right Now Superette.

It was a searing white instant. And a sudden hurtling and falling of debris, which was already the bomb's aftermath. Wrenched window frames and bits of shelving smashed on to exploded cans, split bags of rice, crumpled avocado boxes and pineapple crates, a tumbling rubble of broken plaster, bottles, plate glass, refrigerator doors, red and blue buckets and spades, cracked tiles, mangled tills.

Breaking the barrier of skin, metal shredded by the bomb tore into flesh, ripped veins. The rubble crushed bone. The head of a man was pulled from his body. On the concrete floor next to the toppled pik-'n'-mix sweet counter the scattered sweets drifted along the flow of his blood. A shard of flying plate glass sliced a left arm from its shoulder. Before she died of severe abdominal wounds the victim tried to clutch it to her side with her other arm.

It was just before the Easter Weekend, a Thursday. Easter was early this year but even so it was unseasonably hot. Larger crowds than usual had driven the eight hundred kilometres and more to the coast to enjoy the still-warm waves, the baking sea air, the cool melt of ice-cream down peeling chins. It was so hot that from about ten o'clock the sand was scorching feet, skin burned under clothes. Long lines of children and their parents queued outside the air-conditioned South Clacton aquarium, *Biggest in the Southern Hemisphere*, where even the seals performing their tricks seemed testier than usual. In the shopping centre and the beach-hotel bars, flushed sun-puckered faces clustered in search of shelter and an early lunch.

The bomb was home-made, a lump of explosive and household nails, compact and portable. It was carried to the site of the explosion in a sports bag which also held a pair of muddy trainers and the sludgy remains of a beef burger. Disguised by burger wrappings the bomb was slipped out of the bag and activated. As though the food in the grease-proof paper was hot or slippery with mayonnaise the parcel was gingerly placed in a refuse bin on the arcade side of the Right Now Superette.

Before going over to the bin the man carrying the sports bag had bought himself a corrugated plastic bottle of guava juice at the Superette. He left the shopping arcade drinking the juice, the gold foil top pinched back, and turned in the direction of the post office to make a telephone call.

At about 11.06 a.m. a child raised her hand to the shiny tubes of Smarties on display at the Express till in the Superette. The blue glitter reflected off the Indian Ocean danced across the ceiling above her head. The child's mother, who had been prising sand from under her fingernails while waiting for her change, slapped down the child's hand and shoved a hot cross bun into it. The Superette baked glazed Home Made hot cross buns on site. The mother had just bought half a dozen.

At 11.10 a.m. a block away a man put his hands to his ears and screamed but couldn't hear his own voice. Later he dusted down his shirt and trousers and walked away hurriedly, moving through a surging of police cars, ambulances, yelling children, people running with their heads down. As he walked the dinning in his ears grew louder. He did not hear the crunching of the glass that covered the pavement like a carpet of diamonds. He did not hear the man who came running past him screaming, 'Fuck them, fuck them, bloody terrorists, nothing ever changes, fuck them.' He saw the lips mouthing but he could not hear.

About three days later the crescendo of noise in his ears reached its peak and at the same time his hearing, thank God, partially returned. There was a call for witnesses to come forward. The man lay low and practised telling himself aloud in English that he had been in the area to visit Victoria Mahlangu his girlfriend who worked as a cleaner in a block of holiday flats. This story was true. He wanted to have it off by heart just in case someone had spotted him. OK, maybe the country was turning itself round, the Old Man was free, rumours of big change dusted the air, heating your eyes like curry powder – but still you couldn't trust the situation. If they knew about him, Phineas Mdlalose, a black man in the near vicinity of a bomb, the police would certainly want to take him for questioning.

In gaol a guy could still be choked close to death with a bit of hose-pipe for having shouted no more than 'Power!' in a crowd of protest-ers.

At about 11.10 a.m. an elderly man pruning roses in a garden up the hill from the beach front felt a thud. An earthquake, he wondered, or underground mining works? But no, there weren't any underground workings down here at the coast, of course. He made his way to the garden gate and looked down the hill towards the centre of town. Nothing the matter. About an hour ago the lady who lived next door had set off for the shops. He hoped she'd be all right. From the gate he could see a thin blue line of ocean between the bougainvillaea hedges and the trees. Would the sea rise and suddenly fold if there'd been an earthquake? he asked himself.

A bomb. Suddenly. Then. The torsion of a moment produces a tin-nitus, dinning across lifetimes.

When past and future collide together and foil-wrapped sweets float on pulsing blood.

The bomb at South Clacton beach that Maundy Thursday in the early nineties claimed six lives. There were 67 injured. Wounds were caused mainly by pieces of flying glass and shredded metal. For an emergency situation – and the newspapers said it sadly looked more than ever like an emergency situation – the fatalities were relatively low. They were also as it happened all of them white. White people more than any other community could afford holidays down at the coast in the scorching African sun.

# 2

In the normal run of things the day would have brought Anthea Hardy only the one story.

*Yesterday Olive Swann, our oldest resident, celebrated her 100th birthday in the heart of her family.*

Anthea leant her long, narrow body away from the writing pad and squinted through pale eyelashes at the sentence. No – no good. Blandly factual, far too flat.

*Presiding over a canary-yellow birthday cake blazing with ten large candles (think 10 x 10), Olive Swann our oldest resident yesterday welcomed in her 101st year. She was surrounded by her four children, eleven grandchildren, and seven –*

But this stuff ballooned off the mark in the other direction, the way of housekeeping magazines. Anthea tore off the page and picked up the photograph of Olive Swann straining one of her great grandchildren to a baggy pink angora cardigan intended for someone not so reduced by age. The child bore the star imprints of the cardigan buttons on her cheeks. Anthea yawned, blew her thin blonde fringe off her forehead.

The office this noon was quiet and steamy. In a corner an electric fan pulsed softly, sunlight burned on the blue-tinted windows. As if, Anthea liked to think, they were suspended in the centre of a strong blue flame.

At a neighbouring desk Arthur Naidoo rested his head against his out-tray, a mass of smooth black hair spilled over spread fingers. The other journalists were on lunch. Anthea had stayed behind to finish the Olive Swann story. It was, as Arthur had fussily pointed out, her one project of the day so she needn't kill herself over it. But then she was new to this kind of thing, as was clear to see, she told him, from the way the words were hardly flowing out of her Bic.

A few short paragraphs on a 100th birthday. There were two reasons why, in the normal run of things, that Thursday would have produced only these scribbled-over paragraphs in Anthea's notebook. One reason was that it was the start of the Easter season. Though snug and chatty, *provincial in the true sense of the word*, the *Natal Times* generally tried to mount two pages of serious local news, but over a holiday period the editors lowered their sights. Stories were lighter in weight, so was the paper. 'Let's face it, we must go where our readers want to be.' Journalists, especially new recruits, were sent out in search of holiday interest snippets: Beauty Queen's Game Reserve Visit; Boy Surfer's Big Wave; War Veteran Moto-X in the Mountains. Stories that would get attention though pinned under sandy elbows, and bottles of Everysun and Ambre Solaire.

The other and main reason why the day would normally have brought Anthea Hardy just the one story was that she was the new trainee journalist and at twenty-three among the paper's youngest. She had been accepted earlier in the year on the strength of a lively and determined, even brisk, letter to the editor-in-chief. *Writing the news, bringing it home to people, is what I have a mind to do.* The letter came supported by a warm reference from her MA supervisor Dr Nicholas Griffiths at the University of Natal.

*Anthea Hardy demonstrates a searching and steady insight that would have been of immense value to her were she to have wanted to continue as a scholar of turn-of-the-century poetry. However, as she, to her credit, cannot bring herself to focus where her heart does not lie, where, as she says, words seem remote from the world we live in, I trust that she will find her talents to be of great value in a very different field of letters.*

Anthea Hardy's eagerness to abandon the university and bring home the news quickly communicated itself to her new employers. In a letter the editors had given her a starting date; in a telephone call she now asked to be taken on a month earlier, at half-pay if necessary. 'I'm really serious about this. I'd like to start as soon as I can.' You'll have little to do, they warned, and it'll have to be no pay. She said less confidently that she didn't mind. Pink with heat and agitation she appeared in the editor-in-chief's office to present her case, her elongated shape absurdly slight in a baggy Indian skirt, her freshly washed and high-lit hair bristling on her shoulders.

Still they hesitated and hung back. A fortnight later one of their journalists disappeared overnight. Trouble about the consumer boycott, his friends said, he had to split into Mozambique. Nah, said his wife when called, he couldn't face me after I found out about the girlfriend, the cupboard full of sex toys and new Jet clothes.

Anthea was taken on as a replacement, at half-pay for the first month, to teach herself on the job. Ask questions, they said, but make sure not to bother anyone.

She tried not to. Though it didn't feel entirely natural – shouldn't journalism feel more rushed? especially now, amidst these incredible political changes? – even so she tiptoed with care through the first slow weeks, keeping to herself, muddling quietly through her stories, not quite believing her luck, her thin lips compressed in concentration. Transported from scansion and metre to columns and inches – to converting days into stories, voices into instant paragraphs, two halting but at least printable paragraphs a day, and at this time in the country's history – it was astonishing good luck.

Now she again pulled her notebook towards her. Tearing off a page she decided to go back to the first plain sentence about Olive Swann. It was early days yet, best not overstrain for effect.

*Yesterday*, she wrote, and having got so far, put down her pen, gazed into the blue of the windows.

In the close heat her thoughts blurred, dulled, began to drift. She noticed as if from another room a phone on a nearby desk ringing. The whirring coiled lazily through the humid air, wound itself round the rhythmic fizzing of the fan. Arthur stirred but didn't wake. How easy it would be to doze right here alongside him, the relaxing beat of his breath in her ears, her forehead on her story, skin against cool paper – she shook her head. Just over a month into this, forty days, forty-one, and sleeping on the job.

Abruptly the whirring ended, then almost immediately started up at a phone on another desk.

'Shall I answer it?'

Arthur slept on. Twenty or more rings, now drilling into her. She picked up the phone. The voice of the news editor.

'Hello, who's that? Hello? Oh right. Anthea. Who's with you?'

There were background traffic noises. He'd be in a public phone booth somewhere in town.

'Listen, I've just heard on the radio. There's been some action, terrorist work or something, at the beach front. It's south – South Clacton. I want someone to get down there a.s.a.p. Why not Arthur? You go together, right away. Leave now, it's a big story. I want the eye-witness point of view. I want it on tomorrow's front page.'

Earlier this morning, even half an hour ago, forty-one fun stories like the one about Olive Swann on, Anthea couldn't believe her luck. And now this had happened, a Big Event, the Real Thing – she felt winded, almost dazed. From poetry to a Story, here, right now, driving down a crowded East Street in the direction of an explosion, Arthur Naidoo at the wheel beside her sweating – she couldn't believe this massive swoop of good fortune engulfing her.

All that time studying late Victorian poetry, she saw so clearly now, it just hadn't enough to do with this – this drama, this world out here. No doubt she'd made the wrong choice of subject two years ago, should've picked something less obviously exhausted and vaporous. Those twilit poems of the fin-de-siècle, their pale glimmering moons, slow processions, diffused yearnings – they seemed so very distant from everything, though at the time this was oddly what had attracted her. The carved shapes of the poems created a pathway to somewhere else – a misty obscurity, a place of suspended responsibility that was supremely peaceful, worlds apart.

They reached the end of East Street. Sunlight glinted on the barrels of machine guns. Soldiers stationed at the entrance of Greenacres department store were making sure well-groomed women in ostrich-leather shoes could shop in peace. This was the world out here, this pressured present moment, a state of red alert in which the opposed sides in the old apartheid struggle, tongue-lashing each other in public, had begun to talk about sitting down together to talk. Political prisoners of twenty-five years' standing were being photographed blinking delightedly at the light of day, daily new 24-hour multi-racial discos were opening on the beach front. Poetry; distance and misty obscurity: was what could have been. Pointless to reflect back on this now. When she was more than happy to be here. In fact nervous with excitement.

Arthur drove through a stop sign. Up at the top of South Esplanade the traffic started to thicken. They could see blue police flashes in the direction of the docks. Arthur tried taking a loop around South Clacton by way of the main road, approaching the beach area through the old suburbs. But here too the roads were blocked by cars parked higgledy-piggledy, hooting frantically or abandoned. Still they could see nothing unusual in the direction of the beach front. Seagulls screamed overhead.

'This won't work,' said Arthur. The long lines of his face looked drawn down and deeply grooved but his voice was surprisingly measured. 'Let's park and make a run for it. Write down whatever you see, it doesn't matter what. If it's big we'll get the official story from Reuters. If we're separated, take a taxi back.'

But they weren't separated. The end of the road was blocked by a police cordon. People stood up against the orange plastic ribbon huddled close as if cold, their sandals and beach shirts looking disconnected from their set, sullen faces. Away to the side a rickshaw runner in a plastic rhino-horn head-dress leaned up against his beaded cart, stopped on his route to the beach front like everyone else. Despite his taking care, the strings of charms and Coke bottle-top amulets hung round his ankles occasionally clinked. Each time this happened the clucking and whispered rumours moving through the crowd were turned in his direction.

'Just troublemakers.'

'Our new comrades, like hell!'

'No understanding, no bloody brains. "No, baas, me no understan." '

'Give an inch and see what happens.' A man's face horribly contorted by a faked whine. 'An eye for an eye, I say. Fuck peace. Let them feel our force.'

'Kill the fuckers, why not grill them alive?'

Arthur ducked to see past the bulk of the two policemen squeezed arm to arm supervising the cordon. The afternoon breeze blew in from the sea, gritty with dust.

'Can you smell it?' said Anthea. 'Bomb debris. Like breathing the insides of a building.'

'I don't want to think about it,' said Arthur. 'Shall we move on? The mood of this crowd isn't good.'

As he spoke a white woman in front turned as if to shush him. Then she saw his colour and her face convulsed. She heaved herself forwards.

Arthur stepped to the side and simultaneously, neatly, swivelled round. Anthea followed. She felt the woman's huff of breath on her neck.

Next they tried the hospital, 'the casualty list,' said Arthur, but here were more orange cordons and gathering crowds. He showed his press pass to a security officer. The man pretended not to notice him, his eyes slid away from Arthur's face.

'But he's Indian,' Anthea whispered.

'What do you mean? Black like me? Anthea, man, even weirder stuff happens. Since I wrote a feature article for the *Times* criticising over-crowding in the Coloured township, my mother hardly speaks to me.'

They waited another hour. Four police cars skidded up in convoy. They heard the sirens of ambulances arriving and fading out. A security entrance must be hidden somewhere round the side of the building.

'This looks a really serious hit,' Anthea said.

'It could be a major fuck-up, it could be planned retaliation, God knows. Maybe someone's impatient with the pace of change. The veteran prisoners are free but we're a way from voting yet. In many respects our situation's still hyper-toxic. I suspect this is someone striking out on their own. I say we head to the office, hear what's on the radio news. Write what we can.'

The office remained quiet and sultry. The day staff had gone home. The news editor had left a note on Arthur's desk. *Out for a quick snack. What have you got? Rick.*

On the filing cabinet behind Arthur's desk the transistor repeated the same news snatches between every two hit tunes. 'Major casualties. Ten suspected dead. Nearly a hundred wounded.'

There was a brittle, stagey excitement in the presenter's voice. 'A random terrorist bomb, police say.'

Arthur paced the aisle between the desks, plucking at his shirt where the sweat patches clung to his skin. The buzzing fan craned left, craned right, like an attentive spectator.

'You try to start,' he said, jabbing his finger at Anthea's pad. 'I've got to wind down. I don't know what to think. This looks a major change-around, if the Movement's involved, that is. It's not like them, it's not how they've fought their war so far. And why this bomb now? They're not callous. Maybe the civilians were caught in the cross-fire of a bomb meant for somewhere else. It's bad this, I don't know what the fuck.'

Anthea tried taking her keynote from the people's comments at the street cordon.

She tried *Anger and confusion*. Paused.

Then, *Anger and confusion broke out yesterday in response to the bomb explosion at the beach front.*

Anger and confusion? She stopped. She pushed the pen away, shocked at herself. It was suddenly repulsive to be writing this with the same Bic as she'd been using this morning for the 100th birthday. Using the same kind of sentences. *Yesterday –*

What did she have to say? What did she in fact know? Ten were suspected dead. Anger and confusion. The words were shambling, pallid, so clumsily weak. Even a careful sympathiser and seasoned journalist like Arthur couldn't think what to write. Injustice, seeming retaliation, and ten suspected dead. At university last year as well as down here at the paper, the struggle against oppression was the ideal no one questioned. The paths which led to justice sometimes diverged, but even so, people agreed, Anthea agreed, certain rights had to be defended with arms. It is scandalous – she used loudly to exclaim, nod vigorously when others spoke – scandalous that activists are beaten, starved, electrocuted, poisoned, for pleading no more than this.

And then a bomb exploded and ten were suspected dead.

It was the timing, not the violence only but the timing of the thing that hit so hard. The dust of his prison cell had barely been brushed from the Old Man's shoes. The blue sky had burned brilliantly overhead as he had walked painstakingly, unstoppably, down that tarred road into his freedom. It had been barely a week before she had started this job, the blue sky blazing the future open. And then ten victims fell at the beach front. Their deaths, now, had an especially harsh quality, like murder. *Anger and confusion broke out.*

Arthur read her sentence over her shoulder. His smile started as a grimace but then grew kindly, softening his face.

'Look, you're probably dead tired. You head off home. I'll finish this – it's more my kind of thing. I won't say very much. Can't. I'll mention the wall of silence at the hospital, the high security. The cloud of dust, though that could be overdoing it. Reuters'll give us the rest.'

# 3

There was Glenda Hart, a newly retired school teacher with a firm voice and shy eyes who had lived in a small bungalow a few roads up from the beach. 'Granny,' said her daughter Mrs Darlene Cross, 'liked to smoke Benson and Hedges Gold. We will always remember her for the posh way she smoked her cigarettes. Like this, you know. With straight fingers.'

Glenda Hart was smoking that morning when she popped her head over the jasmine hedge and told her neighbour Peter Marlow, also retired, that she would be walking down to the shops to buy Easter eggs for the grandchildren.

'I was pruning the roses when she came past,' said Mr Marlow. 'I was surprised she had her shopping bag with her. She normally drove to the Checkers out of town. I don't like those shops on the beach front, she used to say. I agreed with her about that. She told me there were too many beggars these days for her taste and they spit and do their business on the pavement. "But there, it can't be helped," she said, "I forgot the eggs, my fault."'

Solomon Makatini, a beggar, sustained light shrapnel wounds to the back during the blast but was not interviewed by any newspaper. Had he been asked, he might have spoken of 'being looked after' that day. The spirits of his ancestors, he told his friend, a newspaper seller down the street, were 'kind' to him. Had he not been walking away from the shopping centre, had he not covered some distance already – 'you know me, I can go fast on this bad leg when I want to' – had he not walked some distance he would have been *ngalimala,* far more seriously hurt. And had the old missus smoking Benson and Hedges not given him money, 'man, a two whole rands', and two Benson and Hedges

Gold on top of that, had he not had money in his hand, and his eye on the bottle store across the road, he would not have walked some distance already when the bomb went off.

There were Sally Long and Chantal Stone, girlfriends, best friends, fourteen and fourteen-and-a-half, 'not that the difference matters, feels like we were born on the same day'. Chantal and Sally were in Standard 8B at the Girls' High School, and went to clubs together, read magazines, teased boys, giggled relentlessly, smoked secretly and tanned together. On the beach Chantal and Sally did each other's makeup, perfecting a way of putting on lipstick that they knew would drive boys mad. One drew the colour on her own lips and then slowly smooched the other. Both kept sidelong eyes fixed on nearby sunbathers while doing this, watching out for the shocked stares which, predictably, they always received.

That morning Chantal and Sally went to the Right Now Superette to find tampons. Both girls were dying to menstruate, grow proper breasts, start a real life. Chantal's elder sister had told her that using tampons you could lose your virginity to yourself and in this way prepare generally for what followed, namely, boys. Boys and how to deal with them. Sally was trying to squeeze a box of Lil-lets into the belt of her shorts, Chantal was keeping look-out, when the bomb struck.

'It was me who wanted to go for the ice-cream and hot cross buns,' said Andries Cronje, motor mechanic, of Florida, Transvaal. 'I said I'd go, but Martie said she was feeling too lazy and needed the exercise, so she went, taking our little girl. Luanne, our little girl. I wish it was me and not them that went to the shops. But most of all I wish for justice. I wish for whoever put that thing there to hang by the neck, and I pray for his parents.'

Martie and Luanne, wife and child. Bomb victim father would have given his life for wife and child. This sentiment, catching people's approval, was widely quoted in the papers.

There was a sixth victim, the last to be identified and, as chance would have it, the only man. His briefcase full of tennis socks samples and a big carryall holding new rugby shirts in plastic envelopes were found intact beside his shattered body. A side compartment in the briefcase held the passport photograph of a smiling blonde woman. *With Love, A. xx*

It was thought the male victim had been having his lunch, a hot cross bun and juice, standing just outside the Superette entrance when the bomb went off. His proximity to the bomb – his having perhaps faced it – explained why his body was so badly damaged. Torn apart if the truth be told, his skull sliced in two like a cake. It might even be that he had seen the terrorist drinking his juice over the refuse bin opposite, just after dumping his fateful load of grease-proof paper.

At the trial the prosecution pressed the accused to confirm whether this might have been so. Was there a tall white man with a big bag standing anywhere close to him? Could this man have been eating a bun, as he himself had recently been?

'Did you at all allow yourself to think, Mr Makken, did you at any time allow yourself to think that these people, like that man who was standing there, will soon be dead?'

As chance would have it. A bun and juice. The idea about the shared, or at least parallel, lunch caught on. During the trial a stringer for the *Irish Independent* noticed that the bomber and his one male victim had that morning bought almost exactly the same items for their lunch and had bought them at the shop that was hit. A local journalist contradicted this, arguing that while the detail about the juice might be correct, the matter of both men eating buns was uncertain. True, the victim was found holding the corrugated plastic bottle, and, yes, the bomber himself mentioned guava juice as part of his reconstruction of events. Yet earlier that morning the accused had bought himself a Wimpy hamburger, which of course comes in a roll. The bomb had in fact been covered by the burger wrappings when he placed it in the refuse bin. The accused, a confirmed liar, could be muddled about having eaten a second bun.

The *Irish Independent* stringer did not take up the question again. It was enough to have pointed to it. It was enough that there was the guava juice connection, that ironic suggestion of summer cocktails as opposed to Easter sacrifice.

As fate would have it. People mentioned the shared lunch in their talk about the bomb. Building these frail links was a way of coming to terms with the senselessness. There seemed to be some pattern behind the random horror, even though it soon collapsed when handled. That day fate, God, the spirits of the ancestors, decided to single out those who were best friends, and smoked, and were female. But why smokers, why women? Well it was fated, predestined in some way, mysteriously related perhaps to the immense transformations moving through the land. It couldn't be up to blind chance alone that these people died, those lived.

As design would have it. It was discovered too that Mrs Hart attended the same Women's Institute as Sally Long's grandmother, though old Mrs Long couldn't for the life of her bring Mrs Hart's face to mind even when she closed her eyes tight and concentrated. Mrs Hart did beautiful tiny crotchet work using a magnifying glass, a friend told her. Mrs Long shook her head.

Many people also pointed out that the majority of victims, two-thirds, were local, which was surprising because of the numbers of tourists around at the time, and again underlined how criminal and senseless this thing had been. The bomber wanted to strike at the heart of rich peoples' tourism, at the troubled heart of the dying white state, and instead he hit these locals, and half of them children.

Hart. Long. Stone. Cronje. The Harts and the Crosses, the Stones, the Longs, and the widowed Andries Cronje. For weeks after the bomb, family members of those killed were pictured together in the papers. They stood side by side, white-faced, on the steps of coroners' offices. Holding hands they visited the gutted Superette. Where possible they attended the funerals of all their dead. Andries Cronje and Darlene Cross, whose articulate pushiness and disgust were considered under the circumstances acceptable, appeared on the television news demanding tougher security in shopping centres, denouncing the monsters who had planned this outrage.

For each one, the ritual of these events was soothing. But even so, just now and then, if it happened that the interviewer was running late, the conversation petered out, the photo shoot took time – all at once like a rush of vertigo the complete randomness of the disaster would strike at them again. And at the same time, shockingly, they would see what their shared grief had masked, how generally ill-dressed or red-faced, snobbish, liberal, or bad-tempered, yes, even thick-headed, pimpled, rude, these other bereaved really were. We have nothing in common with them, they thought, why in God's name have we been thrown together like this, at the whim of the media, and politicians trying to make a point? What is the point? And sometimes they went so far as to allow themselves to think, they are total strangers to us, these people, it's impossible their loss has the depth of ours.

But these were hidden thoughts, and weighed against them was the sad relief of mourning together. The shameful feeling of superiority soon passed till after a while it was as though they had always been connected in this fateful way. Forever their names would be linked together, and the names of their loved ones, soldered together by the heat of destruction. Martie Cronje, Luanne Cronje, Sally Long, Chantal Stone, Glenda Hart, and the last to be identified, Duncan Ferguson. Thrown into the arms of strangers and, see, the strangers were in the same pitiful trough as them, and because of it were transformed completely, just as they were.

# 4

As soon as Anthea Hardy got back to her flat that night she made herself a cup of tea, a tomato salad and a toasted cheese sandwich. Food without forethought, she called it, the same as on any other evening when she worked late. She switched on the television as an automatic aside to spreading the sandwich. The eight o'clock news. The scene in front of the hospital, the rows of illuminated windows and the police cordon. Taken from the same position as where they'd been standing a few hours before.

'Uncontrolled terrorism,' frowned a reporter.

She switched the television off.

She went to stand at the window. The electric light hummed, seemed incredibly loud. It was difficult to get used to this quiet. Arthur's pacing and blunt words back at the office had made her feel on edge, silly and superficial and on edge. But now she wanted to be back there, enclosed by that buzz of things, working on the story. The drop in intensity, this sudden peace, gonged in her ears.

From the livingroom window there was a view through palm trees down the Berea to the beach front. There were no curtains at the window because she hadn't yet hung them. The beach front was a blaze of lights, winking as the trees moved, as usual. There'd been a massive explosion down there. Things had smashed, burned, changed irreparably, and for no obvious reason, Arthur's reaction if nothing else confirmed it. She felt there should be some more widespread, thorough response. There should at least be a deeper reaction inside her. The flat should be affected, the windows showing cracks, the phone disconnected. And see her hands, the smooth clear-varnished fingernails, her thin, straight-up body, feet snug in her shoes – they appeared totally unshocked. Why weren't things more marked, more thrown about? Why wasn't she more touched? *Anger and confusion broke out yesterday.* This was what she had thought of to say.

She moved in the direction of the phone. Try calling Duncan, see how things were going. She thought of his slow, low-pitched voice, the gentle rising and falling she liked to listen to, sometimes without concentrating on the words. 'How's it Anthea, my girlfriend, my girl?' Calming Duncan. This evening though, on second thoughts, he might be too much so, too undisturbing. Duncan's belief was that in the long run – 'and I mean, Anthea, in the *long* run' – a person had better plant a cabbage or a row of mealies than organise a political meeting, write a pamphlet. It depended of course on *where* you planted your cabbage. But in the long run it helped more people, produced more good.

Anthea walked away from the phone. It wasn't one of Duncan's nights to come round to the flat, maybe just as well. As it was the Good Friday holiday tomorrow he'd either be at his own flat now or home with his mother, having a meat-and-potatoes meal. He still spent every second weekend including long weekends at his mother's. This Easter her own parents were on holiday, but Anthea usually timed her trips home to coincide with these weekend visits of his. She and Duncan hadn't quite been together long enough – just under six months it was – for this to change in any way, for them to develop the settled confidence in the relationship, was it that? to insist on time for themselves as against family habit.

Along the wall opposite the window, cardboard apple-boxes were piled full of her books, a reminder of her recent transition. She now walked the row. When she had started at the *Natal Times* earlier this year she had moved flats, to be closer to work but mainly to put student life behind her. On moving day, after she and Duncan had carried in the last box, they had unrolled the big floral carpet donated by her granny in Newcastle, which temporarily but emphatically filled up the room. Then because it was late they had left things at that, had gone out for fried polony and chips. Since that day, it was ridiculous but true, there hadn't seemed to be time to sort the place out.

She picked a book off one of the piles at random, rubbed at its light coating of white dust, trying to find something that would reply to her mood. Pater's *The Renaissance*, a Collected WB Yeats, a volume of verse with Irish themes by Lionel Johnson. Achebe's *Things Fall Apart*, the university's gesture to the present context. But a bomb? This act of extreme resistance *now*? Six, ten, twenty people dead, unsuspecting shoppers? Where were the adequate responses to that? Set the leaders free and see what discipline they keep, the white man-on-the-street would say. And could he be right? How could she begin to get a grasp of this shattering fury that had taken place?

People driven to extremity resorted to extreme measures to get their say said. She understood that, even if remotely, in theory. She imagined expounding this later to Duncan, his expression of tolerant boredom. Once the oppressor blocks all avenues of non-violent resistance, the armed seizure of power by the people is justified. At what over-indulgent length hadn't she and her friends talked about these things in the Student Union canteen? They had distilled the energy of their talk into inky slogans printed on t-shirts and posters. *End Oppression Now. Fight for your Rights.* The t-shirts sold briskly in the Union shop.

Always easier to print than to carry out those ideals, she thought, making another cup of tea. Easier to shout than to bomb, be bombed. But this explosion today, that was different again, wasn't so much difficult as senseless. This act grabbed the new signs of hope and smashed them underfoot at the very moment of their emergence. 'I greet all of you, my people, here and in exile,' the Old Man had said on that magical day in the late summer. And from what anyone could tell – from the spontaneous street celebrations everywhere, the singing troops returning from the border, the way pedestrians were exuberantly greeting each other while waiting at crossings – the world was to be painted over again. And now? Now that new world, like the Superette, was crushed to pieces.

*The Renaissance* dropped open to one of its last pages as she shifted it for the second time from one pile of books to another. *To burn always with this hard gem-like flame,* she read, *is success in life.* It was a sentence she had underlined. The thick pencil betrayed the pressure she'd used marking the words.

As she turned the page a couple of gum-tree leaves fell out of the book on to the floor. She picked them up, put them back, same page. A slight indentation there. The leaves from the river picnic they had been on with friends late last year, she and Duncan, when they had decided to go out together. It was just before she quit her studies, a time of several changes. The friends, her supervisor Nick and his wife Marjorie, had introduced the two of them at a dinner party. She remembered taking the book with her to the picnic as a kind of visual aid, a prop to her concerns about quitting. She was carrying it as she and Duncan walked away from the group to sit under the sparse shade of the gum tree, Nick and Marjorie smiling in their good-natured way. 'Let's keep on going, going out,' Duncan had said, pulling her to him.

It wasn't his first time saying this but it was then under the tree, within the warm cloak of its eucalyptus smell, that she had agreed. They were talking about other things – Marjorie's powerful fruit punch, an alienated university, how Nick was mail-ordering his own piece of the Berlin Wall at vast expense – and then Duncan slipped the suggestion in, just by-the-way. It thrilled her a man could be that gentle.

She tried dialling his flat number after all. She let the phone ring, he might not think it was her. She wondered what he might be doing to avoid noticing the phone. After work he often lay on the carpet for hours with his hands behind his head and a bottle of beer at his side, listening to difficult music, sounds as contorted as the names that composed them, Penderecki, Lutoslawski, others. He would blame his inertia on his job. When she tried dragging him upright, tickling him into fetching her a beer from the fridge, all he would do was slowly unclasp his hands, hold hers.

'Anthea, Anthea, I know it's hardly as if I need to wind down, having sat in a car for eight hours nursing my samples. But you've got to understand. When a guy has spent his day trying unsuccessfully to sell his wares and then having a two-hour nap in a car park, he likes to think how else he might've used his time. Look, maybe movement just isn't my line, I'm trained to be slow.'

She couldn't deny it. Deathly dull as his sales job might be, there was a hard edge to his self-mockery. Representing a sportswear factory wasn't exactly on the line from a good degree in Fine Art, which Duncan had. And yet in the search for work after graduating he had found very little in fact lay in his line. '*Oh yes, a BA, but can you type? So no, I had to say, no not really.*'

His support for her decision last year, Anthea knew, rested on this matter of typing. To him a newspaper job signified being practically disposed to the world. He said so over their first meal together, vegetable samosas in coconut gravy that he had prepared. 'I mean, when these sports people offered me the job, say what you like but I personally put everything about *plein air* and the abstract Cézanne out of my mind. That's one thing you can hold on to, Anthea. Even if it doesn't change society, journalism teaches you to type.'

Anthea tried calling him once more, then let the phone ring twice at his mother's, then stopped. It was late and, besides, his mother watched jealously over the time Duncan gave her. Once, picking him up for a Sunday movie, Anthea had caught her at it, the mother's lips silently counting the hours her son had spent at home that day. It didn't yet feel right somehow, not quite yet, to interfere in this closeness.

Not quite yet, but very nearly. Not together long enough for the pattern of their lives to change? Anthea thought back to her reasoning earlier. Well yes, probably – But even so, just lately, ever since starting at the paper, but especially now, tonight, there were moments when the feeling came to her – elbowed her with a jab of discomfort – that their relationship which was after all so new, had in some way skipped several stages of development. They hadn't been going out half a year, but already their companionability was beginning to exhibit what was, well, in essence like an autumnal glow. As if, she caught herself thinking, they had rubbed along together ages, could face out times apart, differences of opinion, whatever, with an unspoken understanding and a quiet word, an almost whispered 'never mind'.

Most of the time she didn't of course mind this. It was a reflection of what she most valued about Duncan himself, his studied quiet, his understated scepticism, the pacifism she liked and respected, that made such a stabilising contrast to her own confused compulsion to be involved. But on a day like today, when she felt hammered by that compulsion, it did seem a lack, a real loss, that the relationship had taken on, so soon, the subdued tones of his internal calm. That it had come to this premature passivity – later she was to say this foreclosing, this fateful passivity.

She poured herself a glass of water and walked over to the window. A sea wind was whipping at the palm trees and the lights down along the esplanade and at the docks beyond twinkled and changed colour continually. White, yellow, white, white, blue. Injustice and confusion, Anthea thought, anger and yet more anger. She closed her eyes and saw rows of illuminated windows. She remembered the grit in the wind.

She left the glass on the window ledge and went to bed, taking a book with her. A book of letters. She opened to a random page. *My dear Mrs Shakespear*, she read but had to put the book down. The words were crinkling and dissolving in front of her eyes. She held her head steady in the clasp of her cupped hands, propped the book against her knees, but still the lines on the page would not settle. Just like Duncan does, she thought giving up, sinking back. His head in his hands. His head in my hands, her thoughts spun on, my head in his, my hands in his hands, his in mine, in mine, mine his.

# 5

My dear Mrs Shakespear,

I have been laid up with some kind of influenza, but yesterday, despite the gloominess of our political life, emerged into fairly good spirits – the best in a while. I seem to have evoked this state when, late last night, there appeared to me the vision of a hopeful but ailing man who claimed he had just, by alchemical means, made the Elixir of Life.

This new tragedy has been a great grief & anxiety. Will our literature I wonder now be much changed? Will poetry once more be shackled to politics and used to incite? As I have not seen a paper for days I do not know how far we have plunged into trouble, though across Ireland it seems the future grows dark. The one sign of disturbance I notice is that everybody speaks with caution for no one knows who will be master tomorrow.

All we can see from our windows is beautiful & quiet and has been so; yet two miles off close to a main-road, British soldiers flogged two young men and then tied them to their lorries by the heels and dragged them along the road till their bodies were torn to pieces. 'There was nothing for the mother but the head,' said a countryman and the head he spoke of was found on the roadside.

I write daily & find I write better for the uncertainty. The one enlivening truth that starts out of it all is that we may eventually learn charity after mutual contempt.

Tomorrow I shall fish for pike on Coole lake. Is not that a medieval way of getting a meal? I stay out till I catch four fish, enough for a dinner.

Your cousin Lionel Johnson's book is, as you say, very stately.

That you like my poems is a great pleasure, the greatest of joys.

Yours ever
WB Yeats

# 6

The call came at ten past nine, a few minutes after Anthea had arrived at work. By now everyone had heard the names of the bomb victims because they had listened to the morning news. Anthea however had overslept and felt harried. It was Good Friday so the paper was operating on a skeleton staff and she was late. Almost as soon as she sat down and folded open the fresh paper lying on her desk – Big Bomb in Shopping Centre – the phone began to ring.

Later she would say that she had expected it all along. There was something about the slowness of the holiday traffic on the way to work, and her skirt caught in the car door when she locked it. Something about having overslept too, that suggested a reluctance in the day, a resistance, as if there was a force in things holding her back from what had happened, from hearing of this fate.

But it was later that she said this. At the time, when the ringing began, she jumped.

Though she was sitting she had to hold on to the side of the desk so as not to fall over. She was aware of the wooden edge cutting into her palm. She was aware of the mouthpiece lying upturned and adrift on the newspaper, murmuring to itself. There was a moment of dispassionate interest in which she opened her hand to see the livid red mark left on her skin by the desk edge.

'Anthea, are you all right?'

Arthur came over and took her by the shoulder. She wondered why he was doing this. It was now that the dreadful sound began, coming as if from a distance, a sound of choked dry sobbing and someone crying in a strange, high-pitched sing-song, No, No, No.

*　*　*

Mrs Ferguson had asked her daughter to notify Anthea and Duncan's other friends. She herself had been under sedation since the early morning. She lay in a private hospital ward and studied the patterns of sea salt crystals that fanned out from a top corner of the window. She wondered to herself how long it would take for the crystals to edge across the surfaces of the entire hospital. She imagined them radiating along the floors, the operating tables, the stainless steel cabinets, sinks, scalpels, up the walls, across the ceilings, across the marble top of the morgue table on the ground floor where her son lay. She saw the crystals stretch their cool delicate angles across his face, his wide open eyes, open wide as when he was a baby. She liked thinking of him this way, encrusted, silvered over, iced. This way she could think of him as a whole body, a headed body, not torn up.

# 7

The accused Joseph Makken said in his speech of self-defence from the dock that he had first aimed to hit the post office.

'I wanted to do my job well. I carefully picked the government structures to target. When I worked in groups, before, the other comrades got impatient with me. It was me who targeted the post office at South Clacton beach.'

'So you say, Mr Makken, so you say.' When the state prosecutor made a point he ground his right heel into the carpet. 'But might you not equally have chosen the police station further up the main road? Or the magistrate's court that lies right beside the post office? Were these not sufficient to *engage the enemy*, to use your words? Why not these, Mr Makken? Why not the city hall for that matter, with the nice big statue of a great white queen sitting in the middle of her bed of canna lilies at the front?'

'I was part of the successful operation some years back at the post office out at Elmtree,' said Joseph Makken, refusing to be shaken by this taunting. He was twenty-two, his voice sounded light but convinced. 'The land mine explosion at midnight, I was involved in that operation. I wanted to continue in the very same fashion. The post office was off the beaten track but powerful. I targeted the post office at South Clacton beach.'

'*To continue in the very same fashion?*' the prosecutor wondered in a loud whisper. 'Is the promise of majority rule then so lightly dismissed? Is the post office such a very vexing symbol?'

But Joseph Makken rightly did not take these as questions. He stared ahead of him and said nothing. He heard the fan overhead wobbling in its socket as it turned. He felt a fly settle on his forearm and his skin twitch in response.

The South Clacton post office was long and narrow and had a low roof. He could still conjure up exactly how the building looked. He had spent hours walking the street in front of it, hours pretending to make phone calls, drinking from empty cans of Coke. There were the four windows, the brick archway over the main entrance, the jacaranda tree that shaded the roof and dropped soft purple flowers the colour of early morning dreams on people's heads as they waited for the telephones. Those five phone boxes out in front. There was the side door that once had the sign *Non-Europeans/Nie-Blankes*. He remembered from when he was a boy. He had come with his oupa to draw his pension and oupa had always been careful to choose the right door. *Non-Europeans*. They didn't put up those things any more though now it didn't matter to him either way what they did. That kind of little stuff, little insults, weren't his concern.

The post office was a small, modest building, 'fetchingly rural,' the prosecutor said, but that also didn't matter. The building could have been even smaller, with no archway, no phones. The post office at Elmtree had been a converted butcher's shop. It could also have been bigger, it could have been a lot bigger with tall windows and huge pillars in front, same as the city hall. It could have been made of shiny white marble just like the statue the prosecutor talked about. Joseph Makken had sat on the benches next to the statue. His ma had taken him there on Sunday outings when he was a boy. He had seen how the bottom of the statue, the woman's stony skirts, were stained betel-yellow with piss.

None of this though made any difference. What was important was how people went to the post office, that they went, trudging powerlessly in and out of that archway like cattle. Rain or sun, paid or skint, almost every week people had to use the post office. His mother, his aunt, everyone stopped in there, met each other, posted parcels, dealt with pensions, licences, passes, stamps, things they needed to live. And every time, as part of getting on with things, they were reminded who was boss, even now. Even now that the leaders were free, the white state still was boss. It wasn't the same for a magistrates' court. You didn't go there in the same way, as often, along with every other man and woman you knew. At the post office you licked stamps and felt the government's thick glue on your tongue. You lined up for the phones, you just wanted to speak to your comrade, your girlfriend, and your voice travelled along wires the state had laid down. And then later, when maybe you kissed your girlfriend or had your lunch, you still could taste that sweet glue taste of the stamps on your tongue.

Held inside the machinery and kicking.

The Movement was directed against the repressive machinery of state? Yes, Joseph Makken agreed when the prosecution put it that way. Armed propaganda was his own preferred term. But the thing with post offices, he added, as with hospitals, say, or clinics, state crèches, was that you found yourself right inside the machinery, unable to change anything, unable to get out. Often, as part of your daily life, you found yourself caught inside. Held in the fist of the state just like comrades of his were being held by its unofficial death squads even now, held tight and kicking.

Here Joseph threw back his chin.

'In this country the situation happens to us,' he said. 'Those Boers can fight dirty, history shows. They haven't given up fighting yet. I tried to make things happen. I was striking back. The powerless don't yet have power.'

This then, suggested the state prosecution, justified bombing these buildings at any time of day, with the people inside them? 'Come on now, Mr Makken, think, think. Innocent people in holiday gear, citizens of an altered country, this then justified blasting them to pieces?'

'No,' said Joseph Makken, his voice rising, breaking. 'Sorry no. That isn't what I was meaning.'

In the end the problem with the post office was that it stood on a piece of land that jutted into the street. He'd need help for something so exposed. He calculated minutes, he thought of metres, numbers of paces. Second best was the shopping centre where white people on holiday went to buy their ice-creams. Across the arcade from the Right Now Superette were the offices of the national airlines. All through the years its sunshine logo had shone stubbornly on the people's suffering. Hitting the airlines, that was local beach tourism and rich state-aided tourism in one go.

But the post office remained on his route. There was the bank of five public phones outside the main entrance.

'What was on my mind was a call box will be free when the time comes.'

He kept on saying it but the judge had his head in his hands, seemed not to be listening.

'I wanted to continue in the very same fashion,' Joseph Makken said. 'I intended to do it when the shops were closed. I intended to make a warning call. But it was the incident at the Movement's offices that derailed me. I said this yesterday also. It was that incident some days before. The so-called pre-emptive operation to preserve law and order. Maybe it was the extreme element and not the state led it, but I know the extreme element is everywhere inside the state. I know they loaded that place with enough explosive to bring down a water-tower. And they hit the office crèche. To preserve the peace, they later said, the recent unbannings, the freeing of black leaders, may disturb the peace. There was no choice but hitting back. I worked it out carefully but this incident some days before was bad. The news of the crèche especially. I thought what my mother will do if it was me as a small boy caught in that place. The papers had a photo, the baby that was hit. The wound to the head. That photo especially derailed me. That photo said to me, we're still at war.'

He stopped, out of breath.

'You may pause and rest if you wish, Mr Makken.'

He had been warned. There are problems with presenting your own testimony. They might not listen, said the defence lawyer who was also advising his mother. You might get anxious, your voice might go. 'We believe you have refused the use of an interpreter, Mr Makken?' That was at the start of the trial. He had nodded yes. Of course he didn't need the services of an interpreter, just as he didn't need their *pro deo* counsel. His mother's legal-aid lawyer could help him if necessary, no court in the land would fairly represent him. He was a soldier, a prisoner of war, if only they could see it. And English was the only language he had.

'I would like to go on,' he said.

He gripped the wooden railing of the witness box more tightly.

'I calculated the details but things quickly went wrong. I picked up the bomb late, the taxi got caught in a jam. I was working alone, these days I'm operating alone. When I arrived there it was getting on for lunch time. I decided to do it straight away, quarter to eleven, it would be more crowded later. I had chosen the red blade, the red time-fuse that is. The red time-fuse allows twenty-five minutes before detonation. There was also a yellow blade which allows only ten. I knew I had twenty-five minutes to make my call. I was sweating, moving too fast. Events worked against me. When I got to the phones in each and every one was one person. In each and every one. So I cannot approach to tell them please may I phone. I will draw attention. I try to walk slowly up and down, I cannot. I wait for ten minutes and after ten minutes, it was around eleven, I can see there will be panic if I phone.'

*A lump of nails, late taxis, occupied telephones,* the state lawyer wrote on his scratch pad, *The mechanisms of slaughter are mundane indeed.* He was thinking of putting together his memoirs for his grandchildren. He had served in magistrates' courts up and down this coast for nearly forty years. Forty years, a ruby occasion. During that time he had pursued, as far as he was able, criminal elements like this one, though Makken, he would wager, probably took the cake. The story of this trial's triumph – and triumph it couldn't but be – would provide a fitting close to his career.

'I did not want to make an error,' said Joseph Makken. 'And I didn't want to do wrong. I wanted to do the post office at 4.30 a.m. In training they told us people are our friends, white people too. I did not want to act like a racist. I was a soldier. I was always careful.'

He said he was always careful, his mother said he was a good son. Yet, as the prosecution took pains to emphasise, the one and only film-star the accused could remember from the four or five movies he had seen in his adult life was Sylvester Stallone. A big man blowing things apart. Despite his mother's efforts as underlined by the defence lawyer, the accused knew few books – Amilcar Cabral's writing, *What is to be done?* by VI Lenin, the life-story of the Irish radical Joseph Connolly, revolutionary texts such as these. He sometimes read the papers, tellingly cut out stories about the Brighton Bomber, about Irish and Libyan terrorist cells, the links between them. By his own admission, mistrusting school books, he had stopped reading more widely when he was still a teenager. And besides, as the Makken defence counsel must agree, he had been too busy and too angry to read. He therefore had no convincing models to set beside Connolly's dream of permanent revolutionary sabotage, Stallone's soldier of fortune. Rambo silhouetted in flames, and the bricks and pillars of a Victorian post-office building raining down around his head.

However, if this was his role model, the counsel for the defence noted, the words with which Joseph Makken ended his testimony from the dock were curious.

'I know what I have done and my heart is sore now. People say my insides are stone but this is not true. If ever I can cut off a piece of flesh of my own and give it to those who remain after the bomb, I will do it with pleasure.'

But fah, said the prosecutor grinding his heel. Could the defence not tell he had been fed these lines by the student counsellor advising him and, moreover, that he had fluffed them?

# 8

She insists on it. Walking. Already she can feel her thighs chafe against each other, an annoying, moist scraping. Tonight she will have to put on Elastoplast. But she insists. She must walk. Walking, Dora Makken believes, steadies the brain.

Only just past eight thirty, and the sun glare on the cars in the makeshift car park across the road from the court building is already fierce. When she squeezes her eyelids shut and then opens them again, the world is rose-coloured. The azalea flowers over the road go a deeper pink, their leaves are bright red.

She picks her way slowly between the crooked rows of cars, squinting. The familiar prickle of sweat in her armpits. Shouldn't have worn this red nylon blouse today, too tight and shiny, though Joseph likes it. He likes red, used to like red, the colour of struggle. All three of her nice blouses seem too tight nowadays, even this baggy ruched one. She tried the church sale last week but there was nothing smart, not smart enough, courtroom smart. Obviously white ladies don't give their best old clothes to charity, they don't know where the stuff will end up. Imagine seeing some black woman in the street wearing last year's best dress. Or for that matter on the TV. Can't bear it darling, the mother of that bomber in my John Orrs coat.

And there, the chafe between her thighs has started for real. She has to walk with her legs further apart and it looks so stupid. Nowadays she feels fat, she feels like she's put on mountains of fat. It's there on her back and wrists, round parcels of fat on her shoulders even, trembling when she so much as irons a dress, writes her name, she doesn't need these tight shirts to tell her how fat she's got.

But then it's only to be expected, isn't it, having to go into that court every day and hear the endless questions that aren't really questions but nets of words to catch Joseph in? It's to be expected, with Joseph in there, and John on the bottle as usual, but that's understandable too, and Bernice the only one bringing in proper money. What can you expect? When she goes home to their two-roomed prefab she eats. Eating fills up the time, gets you through the hours, food strengthens you inside. She makes bredie with plenty of good bone stock and a thick eggy custard, or brinjal curry, the brinjals fried to perfect purple shininess in real Bombay ghee, and then Bernice brings out the packets of biscuits.

'Dor, you need it, you can walk it off tomorrow,' she lays out Eet Sum Mor shortbread, Boudoir Biscuits, Nutti-krusts, sweet Lemon Wafers, almondy Royal Delights, and best of all Romany Creams, and Marie Biscuits with the chocolate vermicelli and butter paste spread on when the other packets are finished.

Bernice works in a discount store warehouse and knows what Dora needs to feel a bit better. Bernice herself can't face going to court.

'I'm your sister I know, Dor, and I love to support you, but I mos can't go. If I'd hear their lies, and what they're doing to him, I'd scream. He says he did it, man, I'd say, why don't you leave it at that?'

'He did it, he did it, that's the thing,' Dora says each evening eating biscuits. If Bernice isn't there she talks to herself, or to the picture of Albert Luthuli as a young man in a panama hat prestiked to the dresser, or to John lying on the sofa by the front door with his mug of Old Brown Sherry beside him, which is a lot like talking to herself. 'That's the thing I think about as I sit in court. I try to look at this thing straight on. He did it. Those people died.'

The glare today makes her head feel hot and swollen. Every evening the lawyer Daniel Moodey offers to come pick her up in the morning, to save her the trek to the Northville court, first the early township bus, then another bus, and only then the walk along the main road past the park and the cricket pavilion. But she wants to walk. As she walks she can think of Joseph. There are so many pictures she carries with her. She tries to remember them, put them side by side, clear in her mind, before allowing her eyes to meet his, very briefly, a quick confirming glance, in court.

His feverish eyes and shaven head.

There is Joseph as a little boy playing in the back yard in the mud puddles. And how he could magically fix broken fuses, light bulbs, such a clever boy, moody at school but clever, Joseph hunched over the kitchen table and winding the tiny silver fibres together so that they could use the bulbs again, bright lights without the glass globes.

There is Joseph the last Christmas he was home, pretending not to have bought her a present, making himself look guilty by offering to sweep the back yard and stoep, and then carrying in the biggest box of chocolates OK Bazaars could supply. The same Joseph who would the same day have some of his friends round, even on Christmas day, to talk girls and politics and whatever. She brought them orange squash at three o'clock, stayed a few minutes, asked about their studies, their plans. She was pleased to see how they seemed to like him, made jokes about how he was always telling them what to do.

She settles these pictures of Joseph in her mind because she knows once she's in there, between the peppermint-green court walls and the big fan thumping overhead, inside the smell of damp and floor polish, she won't be able to look at him properly. He is over there in his usual place with the thick-necked minders like bouncer men on either side of him, handcuffed as if he was some dangerous beast. He's over there, close, and helpless and accused, but after greeting him she can't meet his eyes.

Earlier this year, around the time he must have been planning all that's happened, he began to drop his gaze to speak to her. Joe was always an honest boy, said things straight out, so it was then she knew some sort of big trouble was stirring, bigger than anything he'd been involved in before.

And now she is the one to look away. The difference is she has nothing to hide, nothing except she can't stand seeing him like this.

Joseph accused, her son.

It isn't that she's ashamed of him. She hopes it doesn't look that way. She doesn't reject him, not at all. He has been so brave, he has come straight out and said, I'm a soldier, I did it. She respects how he has always felt his people's trouble. And he's offering his own speech in defence, something like the sixties men themselves did, and on top of that suffering all their questions, 'Come on now, Mr Makken, think. Why this, why now, why *now*?' But she doesn't want to see him accused.

What does it mean for a mother to rear her child, and tell him right from wrong, and then hear him branded a murderer who took life without thought or scruple, reddening the country's new horizons with blood? She puts her hand to her mouth with the pain.

A crowd of people is blocking the stone steps leading up to the court door. She turns to one side, fishes in her handbag, checks her face in her compact mirror. The strong square nose, nicely powdered, her medium-full lips, 'half-fat' Bernice calls them, she presses them together to spread the red lipstick more evenly. She turns back. Light flashes on polaroid glasses. A sound boom held by a man in dungarees swings in her direction. There are the TV people with their glittering arsenal of camera equipment, the foreign journalists in a noisy huddle, the bystanders who have come for the show. The State v. its Opposition. The State v. a Madman. It is eight days into the trial and they have learned to recognise her, 'Mrs Makken, please, a word.' 'One comment, Mrs Makken.' The journalists jostle forwards, the bystanders remain where they are. 'Death to terrorists!' 'Let him vrek like a dog.' Their hard voices roughened by shouting.

This is when she most wishes she'd accepted the lawyer's lift.

And they could use some manners these journalists. They crowd in close, the closest of them is about to crush her blouse. But she believes that somehow she's doing it for Joseph, facing them out like this. People say killer, murderer, she listens for every spat-out cry, as he would, but even as they're shouting and staring they can be seeing for themselves what kind of nest this murderer comes from. She forces her shoulders back, the blouse stretches tight around her arms. She is his mother, yes, a decent upstanding woman, an educated person, nicely dressed, how hard she hasn't worked to raise her family, pull and tug them upwards through this cut-throat and closed-in society. What would drive a son of hers to take lives? Wouldn't it have to be something huge — huge, scheming, and ghastly? Something that doesn't change its character overnight with the sweep of a president's blunt hand?

She presses her lips together and walks on, her arms held out like a sleepwalker's to make a passage for herself between the bodies. They have to step back, every day up till now they have. But today there is a young white woman still standing in her path. She has the blind hunted look of a journalist but isn't carrying the notebook. She's light-skinned and blonde, blonde with highlights. Funny how so many of them want to look even paler than they are.

'Please,' this girl says.

She grabs her wrist, not hard but tight. Dora pulls back. Can the girl have begun to think what it means, coming forward like this, snatching into her private space? You'd think the apartness laws would have safe-guarded this at least. Take care not to broach my brown skin. No, the girl can't have begun to think – how her expression gives her away. The shrinking in her face, that strange, quick wince, even as she's forcing herself on.

'Please,' she says again, 'Could I meet you somewhere after court today? Could we speak together?'

Dora shakes her head.

'It's not for a paper, it's for myself.' The girl stops short.

Dora presses forward. She feels the girl's damp warmth on her skin. Her face is unhealthily red and now that she's closer Dora can see the thick veins in her bloodshot eyes.

'Isn't it terrible, this thing that your son's done?' the girl asks on an undertone. Her eyes don't let go.

Dora speaks her first words on the steps of the court. She says, 'It's wrong, it's not wrong.'

'Do you support him in what he's done?'

'There's no question. To him the country's still at war. Events began to squeeze him. I see why he did what he did, I weep for him.'

'Please,' says the girl, 'I really need to talk with you. Please can we meet?'

# 9

*A handwritten sheet of good vellum paper lines the bottom of the small wooden chest stored on Dora Makken's back stoep. The chest she calls her odds-and-ends* kas. *The paper, lying face down, she has never bothered to lift up or read.*

KATHLEEN GORT
PERSONAL ESSENTIALS FOR AFRICA

A Dublin mackintosh
Laced boots
A panama hat
Four holland skirts (unbleached brown, for camouflaging mud)
One smart crêpe de Chine blouse (pure silk rots in the heat, says
Aunt Margaret)
Two flannel blouses
My nun's veiling tea-gown (sea voyage occasions?)
One dark silk umbrella (green-lined, advises *The Colonial Companion*)

A supply of green Celtic Society pamphlets. *For the Irish Republic and the Boers*

Two flannelette nightdresses
Seven pairs of cambric knickers, four cotton shifts
Three pairs of corsets (one to hold in reserve)
A traveller's comb and brush set (tortoise-shell is light)
A notebook, marbled, and a writing pad (this one)
Soap

*Etceteras*
A book of needles and thread
Six pairs of boot laces
A light strong box for pro-Transvaal Donations

*Emergency supplies*
Three boxes of Dover's Powders
Candles

*Note*
Papier poudre?
Aunt Margaret's advice: a hot climate gives a tendency to greasiness
even in the best complexions. I am aware my complexion is far from
good. But *this* remedy? One thinks of the middle-aged.
Papier poudre, Aunt says, leaves no white streaks.

# 10

*Duncan Ferguson. His friends will remember him for the way he cherished the objects he liked to work with. The wood he used to make strong bookcases and big box beds. The soft stone that the young Zulu boys on his grandparents' farm taught him how to carve. The great variety of tools he used with such fine skill. The favourite mahogany spirit level with its 'watchful and demanding' green eye, also egg-whisks, spatulas: he was a perfectionist wizard of a soufflé maker. Standing up from his work, his expression quietly welcoming, his hands absorbed, the fingers curled around whatever piece of wood or metal it might be. This is how his friends will remember him.*

But she was those *friends*, as the editor-in-chief Robert Meyer plainly saw when a pinched and white-faced Anthea Hardy showed him the article about the bomb dead she had spent that week following Duncan's funeral completing. Robert read no further than the long middle paragraph, then pushed the sheets of paper away.

Anthea's writing confronted her upside down on the page. She had been dumb to think her proposal would work out, the awareness now came to her too late. Stupid, self-pitying, was how it looked. Putting Duncan centre-stage in a story of remembrance featuring all the victims, how had that happened? It had happened because she wasn't thinking, because nothing made sense. Since that dreadful Good Friday something inside her, her thoughts, her bones, had turned heavy, dank. Grief enfolded her in a clinging embrace, wherever she turned she felt the terrifying chill of its touch. Duncan? Duncan was where? – He was not there, nowhere she could reach him. *Not anywhere.* She spoke out loud to him not believing – But there was no reply, no reply. Only this deafening, obliterating silence.

She tried using work to distract herself, this memorial article. The young girls' story would work well as a cameo piece, she had decided, a collage of memories told by classmates. She had made some effort in this direction, called a Salome Stone, Naomi Stone, an aunt referred by a mother reduced to monosyllables.

'Chantal was the best crawl swimmer in the school,' Naomi Stone had said. 'But she let Sally Long win the races because the boy she liked was House Swimming Captain.'

When Anthea had put the phone down after that, she had been weeping and clutching her arms to herself so tightly her nails drew blood. It's not true, not true, they'll be back, she had wept. They walked out of the other side of that explosion as if through a cracked mirror, they are resting somewhere bruised but alive on the other side. But the dusty rubble of the Right Now produced no echoes, no further movement. Chantal's name, Duncan's name, were not among the injured.

I should have pursued the young girls' story, Anthea told herself, unable to meet Robert's eye.

What had now emerged looked like an imposition. Grieving in public, by one of the paper's own journalists. How had it happened? Of course it had to happen, of course Duncan would figure centre-stage in a story of remembrance. She *loved* him, didn't she? missed him, no, *lacked* him, so badly. At moments it seemed as if her chest would burst with the weight of this grief. Maybe the relationship had sometimes felt too settled, too staid? – but her former discomfort now reminded her only of her loss. Because she wanted exactly that, his quietness, the solace of his settledness. She wanted him back here beside her, listening to his music, holding her hands. The inhuman violence of his end, for one so gentle, his body the most damaged of all the victims – it was so bad, unspeakable. So unspeakably unfair.

She should have looked out. Of course she'd write him into the centre of her piece. His age was the average age of the group of victims; he was the everyman, to her. She was his *friends*. His manner of dying was a contradiction of everything he stood for.

Her article slid across the desk. Robert had touched the papers again, his fingers flicking them this second time a degree too briskly to match his sympathy. That restrained politeness which set the tone for the whole office. Nowadays in the vicinity of Anthea's desk colleagues held whispered conversations as if they were apologising for getting on with their work, a job in which tragedy was politics, bereavement news, in a world seemingly laden with sorrowing.

Within days of the bomb the Movement had sent a terse but kindly-worded statement of condolence. *We pray the time is not far off when our land will be free of slaughter and reprisals ...* This, and individual politicians' expressions of disquiet, had featured on the *Times* front page every day since the event, printed in a highlighted column along-side colleagues' stories about vast funerals and flower-bedecked coffins, hysterical cortèges and racially-mixed congregations, and the police hunt for the Right Now Killer.

Anthea blocked the skimming of her rejected article with the side of her wrist.

Coffins like corsages, she thought, squaring her papers, tapping them together. Corsages and cortèges. Hysterical corsages, carnationed cortèges. She had made the slip in one of the first articles she had written here, not long before the Olive Swann piece. *The bride of fifty years wore an orchid cortège flown in from Mauritius by her still-doting husband.* She felt herself smile, a silly automaton, separate from her own expressions, feeling her lips performing their functions. The grimace of weeping, of smiling. Cortèges, corsages. Arthur, reading upside down as he walked past that day, had laughed till the tears came.

'It was a positive suggestion, Anthea.' Robert was encouraged by her smile. 'An article tracing the biographies of the dead. Obviously I took a risk agreeing to it. But I thought it might be interesting, might give a sense of the background, the pathos, the survivors' endurance. What we didn't want was a – ,' he looked away, he looked back at her frozen smile, 'a personal obituary, if you see what I mean.'

Her dried-out lips stuck to her front teeth. She raised a hand to hide this, loosen them.

He waited in silence for her reply but his fingers on the desk-top were bunched, impatient. This was a job where writing wasn't therapy, and, yes, of course she knew it. Duncan himself had once said some-thing along these lines. Remember, Anthea, journalism is practical but it isn't any kind of solution, it doesn't build houses. Hearts and minds stay pretty much fixed.

Duncan. Duncan's voice. She missed it, how she missed it. Suddenly, as on so many occasions during these past two weeks, it seemed to Anthea impossible that her single body could contain this quantity of longing and regret and not fragment. It was clear Robert wanted to end their conversation but if she moved right now, she was sure, she would fall down and break into pieces, give way to some form of violent public lamentation.

Duncan, she thought, Duncan's voice. She was trying to breathe more calmly, folding her arms tight as if to encircle the chaos of emptiness inside her. Duncan spoke as if words were objects to be handled carefully, cupped roundly. That slow voice like a hum, gently, steadily, carrying his words.

'What was that you said?' Her call from the kitchen table where she liked to work on her articles, from distant points of the flat when he was helping her move in. 'Did you say yes or no? Coffee or tea? What was that you said?'

'I said, my girlfriend, my girl, I said I love you.'

His voice coming back intermittently, like a haunting, appearing unannounced as it had now, while she sat moulding her lips for a discreetly irked though forbearing editor. That hum in Duncan's throat, a burr of static on late night radio, 'I love you.'

'I love you,' she wanted to say in reply, 'I need you here.'

It was ten days after the bomb, the day after Duncan's funeral, when the article idea had crystallised. Anthea was standing at the uncurtained livingroom window and saw it clearly. A story about the bomb dead, an article offering short biographies of the Superette Six, favourite memories cherished by loved ones. It would respond to the *Times*'s emphasis on human interest yet would be sensitive, engaged. It would point up the true catastrophic horror of the event, would show how much the dead had been valued, how deeply they were now missed.

The first picture of the Superette Relatives visiting the mashed wreckage of the Right Now had already appeared in the paper. An upturned trolley, a crude tribute, was posed at their feet.

A memoir article, Anthea put it to Robert, not only offers a more considerate means of forging links between the victims, it also gives a sense of stabilizing context to the devastating instant of the bomb. It demonstrates the impact of the event on people's lives: regardless of who they were, their race or age, their lives were brutally shattered by this violence.

Over those ten long days after the explosion, she had made attempts to attend the other funerals, to lift the dragging weight of her grief in this way, by meeting and talking to her fellow-bereaved. Once she had showered, put on a dress, a grey one, 'your school uniform' Duncan had called it, then found she was out of light-coloured stockings. To go bare-legged, with the press cameras there ... She decided no.

Another time she had driven down the street and begun to weep, breaking into the dry sobs that possessed her without warning, tearing through her chest, aching in her throat. There was her face in the rear-view mirror, twisted, make-up askew, a cartoon of grief.

The last time she nearly got there, the Catholic church up beyond Island beach, but some joker had twisted round a sign, she took a wrong turning. Within minutes she gave up, drove back home.

Duncan's mother must have gone to that funeral, the girls', because standing at her own son's coffin in the funeral home the next morning she had been wearing a bunch of the yellow rosebuds that the Catholic church was decorated with, so the *Times* reported.

Corsages, cortèges.

'Lovely yellow,' said Anthea lightly putting a finger to the petals, longing for the mother to embrace her. But Mrs Ferguson, tiny, wizened by grief, seemed not to hear.

A story in memory of the South Clacton Six, Anthea decided that day at the window looking out to sea, a collage story of remembrance. To offer something – it had become an almost physical need. Build something solid against the chilling ache and emptiness inside her.

As far as she could tell there was a pact of silence about this aspect of loss, the slow hours of painful vacancy, hours broken by spontaneous bursts of tears which then died away again into the enveloping numbness, each familiar room in the flat, each one of her footfalls, echoing with absence.

Every morning for ten days she had gone out shopping for basic necessities, bread, milk, coffee; by ten thirty every day she had showered, dressed, eaten, she had cried; she had taken her place at the window. She listened to the stillness; emptiness within and without.

Now and then phone calls came from family, friends, Nick and Marjorie. 'We're going to the beach, Anthea. We'll understand if you don't – '

'Be well, dear Anthea, we're thinking of you.'

She stood at the window, wept, tightly folded her arms.

The second, or maybe the third day, her parents had called from their golfing holiday in the Cape.

'Darling, we'll come back straight away if you want us to. How terrible this is, unbearable. Our poor, poor Duncan.'

'Are you there, darling? Look, I really will come back if you want. There's a flight today – '

'I'm all right, mum, I think I'm all right.'

She tried speaking firmly. Her parents had barely known Duncan; there had been, after all, so little time. Worse than coping on her own would be their feeling obliged to participate in her mourning.

'I'm keeping myself busy, thinking about unpacking boxes at last. It'll be good to see you when you do get back. Here's awful anyway. Roadblocks down every main street, you can imagine. They're trying to get the man. The – terrorist.'

*Terrorist.* She had slurred it. The word used in police reports. *Activist, freedom fighter,* were what you said privately amongst colleagues, friends from university days. Freedom fighters, guerrillas, newspapers increasingly recognised, fought for a just cause.

That language now stopped in her throat.

'Kill the fuckers, bloody terrorists.' The man shouting at the scene of the bomb.

Anthea said the word again under her breath. *Terrorist.* She was surprised how powerful and calm this made her feel.

That same day – the third day it must have been, Easter Sunday – Duncan's sister had phoned to invite her round to their house. She was his only sister, Louise, ten years older, broad and freckly.

'Just be with us, Anthea, if you like. We can't offer much, food, some wine. Mother's under heavy sedation. But we feel it's important to be together. Duncan would have wanted it.'

Anthea made it over on the Thursday, two days before the funeral, a week since the bomb. Under a clear bright sky autumn leaves spun in the swimming pool. The warmth diffused the overripe watermelon smell of late-season pool water across the garden. Two children, Louise's, flushed with looted chocolate, played catch on the lawn.

People stood in small groups. Louise stayed at her mother's side so there was no one to make introductions.

A bent man with Duncan's fleshy nose, wearing a military cross, leaned up against the French windows and told anecdotes of army life. His copper-blonde wife mimed the movements of his lips.

Anthea steered past them, thought of Duncan. Duncan throwing his shredded, green call-up papers into the sea late last year, just before Christmas Eve.

'What's there to defend here?' Shouting through blown-back hair. 'Prejudice and poverty.'

For their loyal love, nought less,
Than the stress of death, sufficed:
Now with their souls in blessedness,
Triumph they, imparadised.

Anthea stowed a photocopy of the Lionel Johnson poem under Louise's cake plate at the plastic table where she sat beside her mother. She pressed her arm and pointed. Something she had found yesterday, to recite at the funeral perhaps?

Louise smiled vaguely, rolled the silver bracelet on her mother's wrist.

In the shade of a banana hedge, two tall men, Duncan's colleagues, were stationed on either side of a tin bath clunking with beer cans.

'I've heard. In a blast like that. Fillings are violently dislodged. Literally fly out of your mouth.'

And Duncan had bad teeth, a mouth full of fillings.

An hour later Anthea was helping the Fergusons' maid Evangeline wash up. She dropped a pottery bowl, a muddy-looking creation of Mrs Ferguson's which didn't break, and the shock released her laugh, a strange hacking laugh that collapsed into coughing. She thought of fillings hailing from Duncan's torn-open mouth.

An exploding shout.

Evangeline patted her forearm. Nails bleached by No-name

washing-up liquid.

'Quiet now, Miss Anthea. That Master Duncan. We'll miss him.'
Even in death. *Master.*

And then she was collecting soiled glasses, then handing round
scones, bumping into Louise and Mrs Ferguson at a sideboard massed
with flowers.

Mrs Ferguson fretfully tweaking arum lily stems.

'I said no flowers. *No* flowers. Louise, Anthea, what was the name of
that organisation? I said donations to – what was it? Grass-roots, the
approach he preferred.'

'Operation Hunger?' said Louise.

'The Gandhi Ashram Fund?' said Anthea, and caught herself yawning.

As though her hysterical laughter had unlocked a catch inside her,
from that moment she couldn't seem to gasp in enough air. She opened
her mouth as if to gulp or weep and instead she yawned. She sniffed
away the tears wrung out by these unstoppable, gaping yawns till
Louise looked at her in alarmed concern. She decided to leave the party
before dark.

That night, and the next day, and at the funeral the day after that,
the gasping and yawning wrung her face. At the funeral were more
arum lilies, larger crowds of people with stale alcohol on their sweat,
more trestle tables covered with casseroles and margarined rolls and
folded paper napkins. Evangeline worked as hard as ever covering,
spreading and folding, and Mrs Ferguson smiled evenly through her
sedation.

To begin the service Anthea read the Prayer of St Francis because
Louise had asked for it, not the Lionel Johnson. Which went to show,
she thought while reading, poetry fascinated with ceremonials of death
didn't suit real-life ceremonies. It was warm in the chapel, she felt her
colour rise. She tried thinking of Duncan, his low-pitched voice, but
she heard only the organ thumping out the hymn, Louise's thin, sweet
soprano straining in solo to keep up. She hugged herself tightly, feeling
once again entirely desolate, her throat thick with unexpressed sobs. In
the front row the military relative snored gustily.

And so it happened that, standing at the window the day after the

46

funeral, her arms twisted together, Anthea decided it must be time to return to work, try to occupy herself somehow. She couldn't go over to the Fergusons' again, join the mourners standing about on their own, couldn't bear it. The memorial article, she said to herself, was a gentle way of beginning again appropriate to Duncan's memory, a compromise between mourning and work routine.

The wind thudded against the window. Far out she saw the sea was mottled, must be rough. She remembered a boy in her class at school, the 'ace surfer' who had lost his girlfriend in a weekend car crash during their final year. That Monday after the crash he had come to school, stood by himself in the cafeteria looking self-conscious, his tanned surfer's body and dyed white hair made ludicrously cheerful accessories to his pain.

Anthea thought of his expression and recognised herself in it. Uncomfortable, helplessly unhappy, hugging his arms to his chest.

The first day back at work – the fourteenth day after the bomb – she began by calling Andries Cronje, the self-appointed spokesman for the relatives' group. She intended to explain who she was, a bereaved friend and a journalist. But she didn't get round to saying journalist, he was already talking.

'I don't know about you, ja, but this I know for myself. A tooth for a tooth, Miss Hardy, that's what I say. Justice only will wipe out injustice. Forget reform. This is God-cursed savagery.'

Time passed, he talked.

'Thank you, Mr Cronje, we'll be in touch,' she said.

She wasn't sure if she had cut him off or if he had simply stopped talking.

Apart from her conversation with Naomi Stone, this call was the one piece of telephone research she did.

Robert Meyer now walked her to the door of his office, his hand on her shoulder, the lightly lingering touch of condolence.

'It's that this whole bomb affair must be so tactfully handled, Anthea. You'd be the first to see that. As one of the few independents, this paper doesn't necessarily support the institutions the bomb was aimed at.'

'A supermarket and unsuspecting passers-by. A mother and child. A pacifist. Six dead altogether, hundreds terrorized, as if the victims of some IRA fanatic.'

She stopped, surprised at her own vehemence. The same way she was surprised at her attacks of weeping.

*Terrorized* – that word again. Catching Robert's blink, she glanced away embarrassed. The politics she herself had once warmly supported had crashed into her life and so far she was able to offer no more forceful response than these petty one-word lunges, *terrorist, IRA fanatic* —

'Yes, OK, terrorized,' Robert was saying, 'But maybe not intentionally. We've got to allow for that still. The error or the rationale. Was the bomber forced to do this? We've got to retain perspective, steer clear of sentimentality. No civilian targets. That's what the Movement has always maintained, and so far they disclaim responsibility. Arrests are being made countrywide but no one has yet been charged. The last thing we want is to play into the hands of those who are all too ready to brand what's happened as simple barbarity and regression to an earlier political state. I'm thinking for example of some of the victims' relatives.'

Neither a victim's relative nor at present a working journalist, Anthea packed her briefcase and went home again on compassionate leave. In a formal letter he had his secretary type while she waited, Robert suggested she take two more weeks, and thereafter a discretionary six weeks on half-time, May to late June. Arthur met her in the foyer to Robert's office and offered a coffee, 'The canteen.' She walked down with him but at the swing-doors had to turn back. She saw raised eyes, stopped jaws, people in rows looking up from their lunch. At her, she was sure. Feeling sorry. Her throat clamped tight.

Arthur accompanied her to the car park, at least saying nothing. He didn't impose a consoling hand.

The renewed leave passed slowly: she ticked off the days on her calendar each morning at 11.10. But she had stopped yawning and, more gradually, her attacks of weeping subsided. Instead she filled the pages of a new notebook. The new notebook was green, the one she kept for journalism was red. She wrote to keep her hand in, finish what she had begun. She wrote because the hours were long and empty and she wanted Duncan around and this was a way of lifting him into her memory.

*Writing, Duncan, makes things happen after all.*

*Unaware I began to write up the story of your death in the paper and you were dead.*

> *Go from me: I am one of those, who fall.*
> *What! hath no cold wind swept your heart at all,*
> *In my sad company?*

*In the Johnson collection I read before the funeral I found I had marked the page at these lines. Was it a premonition? a warning from the dead?*

*'Anthea, the guilt of the bereaved.' I see your concentrated frown.*

*And yet – I want to put it down – how it's at once an agony, and also at times almost too natural, to think of you as past. That too settled quality to us being together. What might have been between us – now unimaginable. Always it will be – always my regret.*

*I seemed to write you into death and now I write you into my memory, your own personal obituary. Writing as healing, Duncan, after all.*

Writing as restoring, she thought, putting things together to make a living retrospect: a piece here, a piece there.

Beside her notebook she placed the miniature cactus he had given her on Valentine's Day two months ago. A frail purple flower bloomed between spines. 'Look on this and think of me,' Duncan had said. 'Be glad it wasn't a cabbage.' They had laughed, hugged.

Throw-away lines that boomeranged.

She wrote

*A man of quiet. A death so violent could not have happened to someone as filled with quiet as he was.*

*Whatever you do, don't expect, he'd say. Never enter a competition, run for a bus. The higher you hope, the more dissatisfied you are.*

*His hands locked on his chest or behind his head.*

*How he felt for surfaces as he passed, savouring their textures. Edges of furniture, the sharp twists of a newly-cut hedge. How he held me, his hands intently circling, winding, rounding. As if it was always for the last time, to feel exactly.*

Anthea turned a page, stretched her arms. And what if, she thought. What if, as that newspaper had suggested, this man of quiet had in fact met the bomber on the way to the Right Now Superette? Fallen into conversation with him as he could with strangers? Any strangers, in this country with its deeply grooved degrees of strangeness.

What if, by chance, he'd seen a glint of the stuff carried in the bag as well as lunch wrappings and trainers?

*He said talking did not prevent horror. But it could create delay. And delay could create a changed point of view.*

But when a detonator has been set?

There was no close to this writing, which was why she liked it, leaned on it. It was a day-to-day gradually unfolding exercise, it moved time along. She was aware of the half-hours passing, paragraph by paragraph. She showered, dressed. She sat at the kitchen table with her notebook, sometimes shivering, rubbing her arms, sometimes smiling and weeping at once. The cactus stood beside her papers. Putting the lines together, word by word, she began to feel more continuous with herself, of a piece, growing used not so much to her loss as her uneasy regret, as if it had become a sensitive scar, healed but tender, she would always carry with her. Matters with Duncan would now remain always – painfully yet in some peculiarly appropriate way – unfinished, uncommitted, suspended in time.

Then, ten days into her leave, as she was beginning to tire, a kind of resolution came. A point of culmination was reached that drew her gradually out of the confined and bitter space of her sorrow.

*Writing, Duncan, gives the effect of making things happen.*

A photograph appeared on the front page of the *Times. City Late.* Nothing but the photograph trailing tomorrow's story. CLACTON SUSPECT CHARGED. A middle-aged woman in a floral dress and apron held closed fingers over her eyes, snapped before slamming her front door on the camera. The mother of the bomber.

*Joseph Makken, Coloured, is 22.*

Anthea stared. Bent over the paper at her kitchen table she couldn't stop staring. There was something about the floral design and the shape of the woman's dress – sensible straight lines, home-made, a McCalls pattern. Something about the calves, slightly apart, unsurprised, as when you open a door expecting nothing alarming. There was something also about that gesture of instinctive protection. Not unlike any woman responding to a sudden shock, her own mother, herself.

The mouth behind the hand beginning to contort but still half unastonished.

The picture so familiar that for some moments she very nearly did not see, overlooked, the difference, now becoming sharper in this stark black-and-white photograph, the difference of skin. The mother of the bomber, of course, coloured dark.

Throughout that evening she kept returning to the picture, looking again at that expression. As if by looking she might lift the hand and see the face whole. Never mind the grey or black colouring, look at it whole. The mother of the bomber, the source of her pain, standing at her front door in her apron like any other township woman. Like any other woman. How to make sense of this? place a piece here, a piece there? How to attach things together: this stricken figure, her own private grief?

*When shock cracked open an ordinary day.*

*But from the other side of the story.*

A buzz then seemed to come into her fingers, a pressure in her forehead. No, this was not a perverse or voyeuristic gloating – see, the other side is afflicted also. Something could emerge from this, she was suddenly sure, a new understanding, a seeing differently. She had the opportunity, this half-time leave. The paper wanted soft stories, more of the Olive Swann variety. There would be time to attend the trial, there was the chance to approach this Mrs Dora Makken, this woman standing on her concrete doorstep, shocked beyond speech.

*There was an ordinary woman who opened her front door one day to find her son named a bomber.*

That night, for the first time since the bomb, Anthea, pacing her livingroom floor, puzzling, did not weep.

# 11

Starting at the beginning again, Dora Makken thinks, bottom rung of the ladder.

She lays the quartered sheet lengthways along the board and leans on its creases with the iron. The steam brings the comforting smell of lightly scalded cotton.

Amazing that no matter how hard you struggle, pull yourself up, read and learn, learn your kids, you can land up at the bottom of the ladder again. After leaving school she began like this. Never mind getting her Shakespeare off by heart, never mind the accountancy correspondence course. Bright but black, her father Sam said, our lowliness depends on our blackness, you can't change the system. So house work it was at first, house work and nanny work, waking dizzy-headed at four in the morning, rocking with back pain, seven days a week.

What Joe would say when she told him about the job.

'A luta continua, mama.'

Committed to the extent of joking.

'Bright and black, ma, that's our future.'

When she complained of her bunions burnt raw by the second-hand shoes. When she stuck pictures of thin white women cut out of magazines on the food cupboard door, he'd toss the lines from the side of his mouth. 'Mama, remember, always the struggle.'

Dora puts the ironed sheet in an empty basket and draws another out of the tangled pile of clean laundry on the bed.

Stash away a kitty for the rainy day that will be Joseph's trial, that's why she took this no-hope extra work. Bernice saw it advertised in the canteen at her discount warehouse.

*Washing and Ironing. Afternoons only. Phone Mrs Arnold.* If she did the early shift at the factory Dora could fit it in.

But within days the extra became the necessity. The factory manager matched a name on his payroll to a name in the papers. The call came down to the table where she sat checking toothpaste tubes, where for years she'd dreamed of other, better jobs, a sudden breakthrough, *Mrs Makken, I'm writing to offer you, despite your lack of qualifications, the post of Library Assistant …* This table where the women she supervised knew anyway but said nothing.

'Mrs Makken?' The manager looked worried, whether on his account or hers was difficult to say. His eyes smalled by his glasses were not unkind.

She had never seen such a dusty office.

He said, 'Any relation?'

And she, no use dodging, 'Can I please work out the month?'

'I'd rather you left at the end of the week, Mrs Makken. We'd want to avoid associations.'

In spite of how carefully she does her job, of how she was working for the supervisor's diploma, sitting up past midnight studying – her name sticking out like a sore thumb.

'Makken. Mak-ken. Sounds like nothing, mama.' Joe home from school, thirteen and sulky, kicking the table leg. 'The teacher says, McConnell, McKenna? McKen? Now is that meant to be Scottish? Irish? *Maak* it, Makken, *Maak* it, the boys say. Like they're asking me to roll a spliff.'

'You be proud, my Joseph.' Watching his blunt foot hammer the table leg. 'That's one unique name. It was your oupa Sam's name, and his mother's, my ouma, a strong fighting lady who loved songs. She had it from a fighting man she knew, her man. So be proud.'

Half making it up. The family story full of fuzzy patches, puzzles, snags. But a soldier in it somehow, she remembered hearing. Bernice definitely remembered their father saying. Now Dora said it for Joe's benefit.

'A soldier in our family. Like you, a fighting man. Who's to worry what people he belonged to? And the Irish anyway, what about them? What a nation of battlers.'

Joe kicking the table.

Around the time his voice broke he could go sullen on her like that.

Shuffling about and pouting when John was on the drink. Scowling at her for asking why he was out late.

'Hai Joey, I'm your ma, remember!'

It's that he's proud like she's proud.

The ugly Saturday night he was about sixteen and, on the way out to the toilet, surprised John squelching drunkenly in the mud along the fence. One of the teenage *hoers* from the shebeen up the road with her mouth in John's trousers.

Joseph running straight back into the house, fisting his side.

'Now you see why they pull their front teeth,' Dora shrugged. 'Like Bernice says, make more room.'

For a week then he didn't speak to her.

Proud like she's proud, struggling for better things just like she has struggled.

Dora holds the second cubed and warmed sheet to her cheek before putting it in the basket. Nice to see the heap of ironed things grow, the pile of sheets like a stack of coins. Martha the new Coloured ironing girl works neatly, Mrs Arnold helpfully tells her neighbours in her young, so tired voice. If they pay the extra, Martha'll stay behind on Fridays. There will be a small charge for the use of the Arnolds' ironing board and electricity.

Martha Christian, that was Bernice's idea. Her manager's name at the discount warehouse, an alias meant in good faith, 'And a more unchristian cow, Dor, you've never seen. You take her name and make it different.'

Outside the sunlight strikes the swimming pool, flashes a bright diamond star on the crystal swan standing in the window. Dora squints. She angles the ironing board away from the light.

But she can't say it isn't beautiful though, this glittery house, the thousands of gleamy things Mrs Arnold has in it. The first days on the job she had enough to do taking it in. Letting her hands do the ironing and taking it all in. The enamel doorknobs, the light switches made of brass, the bronze animal pictures, that silver rose-bowl glinting on the polished chest of drawers. Looking at these things she can forget herself, for minutes at a time she can forget even about Joe.

Joe detained. Joe charged.

These days, these weeks, over a month now, of no real news, no messages. What do they do to him in there? The one time she took him clean clothes, they told her he could wash and wear the two sets he had and sent her home.

Looking at the sky-blue pool under the frangipani trees she can sometimes forget.

The broken handle on her front door, still broken. Joe's mattress vomiting its stuffing into the red mud in the back yard. The day the three policemen kicked open the door and roughed her to one side, shrieking for him, a bomb suspect.

Their voices go up high with their anger and excitement.

Two days later they found him. Easter Monday. A safe house in the north, Ladysmith maybe. She heard it on the radio. Three weeks later she heard the news that he was charged on the radio.

'Bernice, what do they do to them inside?'

'Better not think, Dor, better not think.'

'The violence done to us, mama.' How many times Joe said this. Late at night sitting on the odds-and-ends *kas* on the back stoep talking. 'The violence done to us, mama, the violence they go on doing, the cowered existence we lead.'

Mrs Arnold's house shines. Dora takes time each ironing afternoon to gaze at the fancy-frame mirrors, the Tiffany lamps, the low-slung glass chandelier in the hallway, the spotless white skirting boards everywhere. These bright shining gymkhana and angling trophies clustered here on their special shelf in the guest room. Thinking how glad she is her job isn't Grace's. Wherever she goes in the house is Grace's bent back, her right hand rubbing like a pendulum. Grace the Zulu woman who says few words, *Hamba kahle*, Go well, at the end of the day.

Probably doesn't have much schooling, Dora suspects, nothing like what she herself has got. She hopes that's not a bad thought.

Would Joe put her right?

'So divide and rule, ma? Here's Grace in the kitchen who can't write. And you with your Standard Nine Certificate, perfect English and old school books wrapped in plastic, ironing in a quiet back room. Divide and rule as always, take care to keep those different blacks apart.'

But how is he? she wanted to ask.

When the police came for her to sign his detention papers, calmer this second time, she wanted to ask, How is he, my son? Do you know?

Are you the ones who took him?

His soft amazed eyes in the morning.

Did he look up from sleep, confused where he was, when you broke into his safe house? I'm asking you as a mother. How is he, my son?

Dora shakes out a last piece for today. Silky nylon panties with lace insets there in front. Right *there*, true's true. She turns the iron to low.

'Bernice, you can't imagine.' Chatting at the end of the first day. 'Even her undies. Ironed smooth she wants them. Extra shiny. How can she take it? Someone else fiddling with her smalls. And the panties themselves! Show more than cover.'

But Bernice was already grinning, her skirt hitched up, what a fast one. Standing there with nothing but a string of lace arched tight across her coffee-cream hip.

'And what's this then, Dora? Now tell me, doesn't this beat what Mrs Arnold has to brag about?'

'But to let another woman, I mean, *see, touch*. I don't know, Bernice.'

Giggling so hard they had to hold on to each other. And giggling again yesterday evening, when Bernice showed Dora the washing line hung across the back yard loaded with clothes, Dora's big cotton knickers flapping at one end.

'I did it while you were at work. Don't say a thing, my sister. You need all the help you can get.'

Dora arranges the panties in their drawer in the main bedroom. Pink and beige, red, black. A special favour for Mrs Arnold, a rainbow pattern, so in the morning she can reach straight for what she wants.

She leans against the chest of drawers a moment resting, smooths a fold in a doily. Mrs Arnold's make-up is laid out in little baskets and enamel bowls floating on crocheted doilies. Tubes, sticks, tubs of make-up, all new, gleamy. Strawberry Glacé. Pearl Ice. Names like sweeties. The Crimson Smoulder lipstick Mrs Arnold has promised her at the end of the month. 'Doesn't go with my light skin, Martha.'

Good war paint for the trial, put up a fighting show.

Mrs Arnold on the phone, Dora has noticed, traces the tip of her tongue along her top lip. Tirelessly tests and retouches her make-up even without a mirror, even when talking to Dora about the ironing. Stroking her eyelashes against a finger held like a mascara stick. Dora recognises that technique.

Years ago she didn't worry too much about trying out the missus's make-up on the quiet. See how the stuff felt on. Doing her lashes and glossing her lips by touch, the missus in the next room. See how blue shadow looked on brown skin.

A lot like a bruise.

Now it would be the fridge only. That only, if she had a choice, she'd want to take home. On these warm autumn days whenever Grace is having her tea, Dora goes to stand in front of the big white monument of the fridge and opens both doors, freezer and main section. Feeling first the cool freezer smoke brushing her cheeks, then a heavy wave of cold air tumbling on to her bare feet.

She'd like to do that at home, cool burning cheeks. She'd like the food too. The deep-frozen fresh meat to fry up late at night when the sudden hunger comes. In bed, after biscuits, any odd time since Joe was charged. Fresh meat, brisket chunks, offal, she'd take old off-cuts even, as long as fresh, brown-fried in cardamom, Maggi sauce. It's only meat fills this gnawing space inside.

She walks down the long passage, past closed doors, shiny door-knobs, pale pictures of flowers and horses, dust-free skirting boards, untying her apron, feeling a heaviness in her legs. Pity you can't sit down to iron, to dust. This work that never ends, Grace's, Martha's.

'Throw the things away if you've always got to clean.' Joe said that more than once.

At home she doesn't mind dusting though. Doing her own things, just the few bits, the bed with its curly plastic mouldings they took three years paying for, the orange jug and glasses set on the front room dresser, and next to that her treasured books, the Standard Nine Reader, her tatty schoolroom *Macbeth*, *Coriolanus* underlined in at least four different ballpoints, a *Great Expectations*, the jumble-sale copy of *Jane Eyre* she's read so many times she's lost count, the books arranged large to small and supported between varnished bricks. And the framed pictures of Joseph, they're the best things for dusting, the ten of them all over the house, that she does very slowly. And worst, worst for dusting, is the soft leather hat hung on its hook that draws the dust like a licked ice-cream on a windy day.

'Throw it away, ma. What are we doing with that thing anyway? A Boer hat?'

'It's in the family, Joseph, somehow. Since when didn't us Coloureds have a bit of Boer inside?'

But each time she says it she feels her cheeks grow hot. Doesn't know for sure anyway, the family story full of those twists and snags. The past's a sleeping beast that's best left undisturbed.

The television is muttering in the lounge. She waits at the door collecting herself. Mr Arnold is by himself this evening, Mrs Arnold is at tennis. Not looking in the mirror opposite Dora straightens her apron, her collar, strokes back her hair.

'La lutta continua, ma.'

So proud. So proudly brought up.

'What a good speaker,' his friends said. 'He made us feel good about ourselves. His words were big. He made us want to get up, organise and fight.'

It paid off. Joe sitting on the sofa with his blunt bare feet sticking out in front of him, any number of weekday afternoons.

'Now listen carefully, Joey, and say it again. I don't know what they must be teaching you at that fifth-class *skollie* school. Reading and learning is the only way to get on, yes, even for a black person, even for a Coloured. I myself, your own ma, read everything I could lay hands on. Everything I've done, the correspondence course, the supervisor's position, I got it on my own, on my own steam. Now say after me. Brown as a berry, busy as a bee, drunk as a lord, happy as Larry.'

'Brown as a berry, busy as a bee – Hey, ma, have you ever seen a brown berry?'

'Now Joey, no backchat.' But smiling at him for noticing. 'I said listen carefully. Learn good sentences. Good sentences open doors, proverbs are handles for speaking with, berries are brown in cloudy England. England is where education and laws come from. Foul can be fair and fair can be foul, that's what people over there say. Now let's begin again. Busy as a bee, drunk as a lord, happy as Larry.'

'Ma, why a lord? As in Lord God?'

The bip-bip of the evening news.

Dora knocks and quickly goes in.

'Martha?' says Mr Arnold fixed on the screen.

News pictures. What Bernice has been saying she mustn't see, mustn't hear.

'It's poisoned, Dora, what they put on the news.'

And it does look poisoned, that face. A police mug-shot glaring from the screen.

No.

'First picture of the man charged with the Clacton bombing. Further evidence has emerged linking the self-confessed bomber suspect to the crime.'

Joey.

But they must've done something to his face. He's not that dark, he's too purple around the eyes. They've bruised him. The helicopter, she's heard people whisper, is it that? Blood to the head. They hang political suspects upside down, spin them round, smash at them, spin them round, smash at them even harder since they heard their authority would one day be coming to an end. Blood to the brain.

Dora can taste her spit thick and sour in the back of her throat. The first sight of him since he walked out of the house with his sports bag that Saturday two weekends before Easter. 'I'll be gone a fortnight, maybe a month, ma. Don't worry.'

Blood to the head.

They're talking about shredded trainers. Football youths, members of the team he played in, have recognised the shredded trainers carried in the bomber's bag. But does it matter? Haven't they beaten and twisted enough evidence out of him?

And to think that all afternoon she's been living in another world – the world before they caught him. Living on memories of him, pictures, like then. When he walked out the door he could be gone weeks. She had her framed photos on the dresser, on the wall, beside the bed.

'Bernice, what do they do to them inside?'

'Better not think, Dor, better not think.'

The mug-shot is still there, flickering.

Force must be answered with force must be answered with force, Joey's words. We must keep them to the mark, burn them out of power, and when a fire's burning who's to stop it? She feels she wants to lie down. She puts her hand on the door frame. Good sentences, good speech, learn your books, that's what she taught him. *If it were done when it's done.* Maybe he stopped studying when he got more political, or studied in a different way, but still she's proud of how he's turned out, yes she is, of how he cares, how he presses on, of his determination. If the bomb was his, it was sabotage, the deaths were accidental. The anger in this country, it infects everyone. She believes in him. All the victims were white, it's a sad pity, but usually the victims are black. She's said it to those journalists who crowd at the front door.

Wouldn't it have to be something huge that would drive a son of hers to take lives? A huge, life-long wrong?

His eyes, his wounded eyes.

My son.

The image is suddenly gone. She hears herself say no, hard, like a cough. She notices her hand on the door frame. She brings the hand to her side. Thank God Mr Arnold doesn't turn around. He has found a comfortable angle to the side of the sun's reflection, a square of late evening light lying on the screen.

The newsreader begins another story. Galloping interest rates; a soaring rate of rape, both of women and of minors. Dora sees a thin film of dust on the screen that has escaped Grace.

Mr Arnold holds up an envelope weighted on the one side with coins. Still without turning.

'Thank you, Martha. See you next week.'

Dora backs out. She doesn't trust herself to speak. She wants to cry in a high voice to release the choking taste at the back of her throat. She's sure she still sees the after-image there, behind the golden film of the sun's reflection.

That bruised face.

It was on television. My son, how they beat him.

# 12

*A letter folded into fours is stored undisturbed under the old vellum lining of the odds-and-ends chest that stands on Dora's back stoep.*

Shoreditch Guest House,
Estcourt
Monday Jany 22nd 1900

My dear Aunt Margaret

We arrived here yesterday evening by bullock cart. The Shoreditch Guest House, a shack built of boards between which the wind is at liberty to enter, is surprisingly comfortable, the beds soft and wonderfully stable after these weeks of travel. Altho' you will justly find it a poor excuse for my silence, this is, believe me, the first time since leaving Cherbourg that either mountainous seas or stony tracks have not persisted in jerking my pen from the page. I trust you will have received my wire from Capetown.

From the Azores till we rounded the Cape it was an extraordinarily rough voyage. However I can say without exaggeration that the sea voyage was as nothing compared with the wild knocking, shaking and bruising that the three days' ride in the bullock cart from Durban inflicted. Natal is a rolling country that appears to slope smoothly from the coast, tho' in fact the land is broken up everywhere by outcrops of red rock. With hindsight we might have waited for the sprung equipage which was promised us upon disembarking, but as so many four-wheeled conveniences are requisitioned to carry troops inland, this seemed too hopeful a policy.

Signs of the hostilities are visible all around us, the battle zone having penetrated deep into this sleepy colony. Trenches and wire obstructions encircle the towns, all men bear arms, and fresh bread and meat are hard to come by. Yesterday Brid O'Donnell, the Belfast nurse who joined our ambulance detachment in Paris, traded her panama hat for a single small pineapple. Just to the north of here, I am told, the heliograph balloon used by the besieged is clearly visible on a clear day, a brown speck in the sky.

Estcourt itself is a one-storied hamlet built along two wide streets which peter into the wide grasslands, or veldt, round about. I am at moments quite overwhelmed by the great space, the sheer *breadth* of the blue sky, the numbers of stars at night, their foreign configurations. The sky in particular impresses upon me how far I am from home and all that is familiar. At such moments I try quickly to remind myself of the great purpose that brings us here. Our collective efforts to withstand if possible the terrible, cruel folly of an empire making war upon a mere fifty thousand republican souls.

There are rumours in town that the trains waiting beyond Ladysmith where the Afrikaners are dug in, are chalked with the legend *To Durban*. A great spirit indeed moves this freedom-loving people. The foreign volunteers speak as one man of their resolved courage and strategy.

To the untrained ear the sound of their cannon does seem surprisingly brave and large. This sound, which has been proceeding since cock-crow in the direction of the besieged town, is like the strangest noiseless thudding and shuddering, seeming to leave an impression on the body rather than on the ear. In response to my question my host at breakfast said, very gloomily, Maxim shells.

It is an unfamiliar world, and yet not entirely so, for today not long after breakfast a detachment of Dublin Fusiliers passed through town to the north. They marched wearing their embroidered waistbands and singing some ballad I did not quite catch, it could have been Donal O'Mullen. They are of course imperial troops, honoured and sent on their way by 'our monarch Victoria', yet the rumble of their Irish voices lifted my heart.

As I write here on my dusty knee I imagine you at the big table in the Celtic Society Rooms on Lower Abbey Street, doubtless deep in some plan or labour, our Ireland-wide protest at Victoria's visit to Dublin perhaps, some such task. In your hands, my dear Aunt, the campaign will I am sure be enthusiastic and successful. It is comforting to think that the two of us are still connected by our work tho' so many miles lie between us.

For my part I have now studied the entire series of Red Cross medical handbooks and feel I have some good advice for my hands, and some background on cleaning wounds and lifting patients for when we reach the chief stationary hospital near Colenso town. The co-ordinating Red Cross commandant in Paris had no doubt there would be a role to play even for an inexperienced volunteer such as myself.

I shall leave you on a patriotic note. This morning my host (a European with white features tho' exceedingly *brown*) proudly served the breakfast tea in 1897 Jubilee mugs. This gilt-edged chinaware, evidently reserved for guests from far-flung regions of the Empire, you in Dublin were in the habit of breaking on the flagstones not so long ago. Immediately I resolved I could on no account drink with the head of the monarch at my lips. And yet, could I risk rudeness? I steeled myself to ask, quaveringly, might I have another mug? Much as I valued the gesture, I said, coming from so great a distance I should appreciate sampling some local plate or pottery. The man withdrew discomfited but soon reappeared, his expression much relieved tho' sheepish. He was carrying a small clay pot marked out in a pattern of speckled lines. He would not usually …, he demurred, it could look so uncivilised, but as I'd asked … I gratefully accepted this bush cup, I suppose a form of *calabash*, and, much relieved myself, drank deep of a tea bearing the distinct flavour of dried grass.

My dear aunt I remain
Your loving and faithful
Kathleen

# 13

Anthea Hardy suggests a café known for its 'improbably chic' break-fast-nook decor and its short distance from the court buildings. But even so there's the whole breadth of the park to walk across. Looking overheated she waits for Dora Makken in the court foyer, then doesn't meet her eyes. 'I've a car. Do you want a ride?' The misery she must be feeling, Dora thinks, but still she can't stop herself from noticing her rudeness, that stiff, unyielding rudeness, as if, you might say, the high-and-mighty expression was in-built. Dora says, 'I'll make it on my own steam.' The walk takes her fifteen minutes. The court gives an hour for lunch.

In the café the sun burns on the raspberry walls.

'I repeat, I don't think I can help you, Miss Hardy.' Dora looks bowed and thick-set in a red hound's-tooth pattern shirt. She chases a piece of scone round her plate with a knife.

'I hoped we could simply talk. I wish we could just talk to each other.'

'Just talk? I said no questions.'

'Simply talk.'

They've said all this before. Dora attempts to sit at a more oblique angle to the table, a tight fit in here. The leg of the chair, nothing but a twice-crooked chrome bar, creaks and sways.

She looks round at the glass tables, the clever drinks gadgets. Coffee, cigarettes, chat, what the young white things who can afford these places must do. Smoke and live on diet. But for herself and this high-lighted sad young woman, the tendons in her neck poking out like bones, her flush radiating through her bleached fringe, well, all chat ends here. Sorry but no, with regret, no thanks. Couldn't be further apart, a victim's girlfriend, a bomber's mother. Dora glances at her, past her, and gives way to a strong impulse of distaste. This white girl, relation of a victim, sitting here fairly and squarely – doesn't she see it herself? – like a reminder, a charge against Joseph. No, it's very clear, there's no common language between them, nothing to say. History hangs too heavily over the three of them. Monday when the girl first bothered her, yesterday on the court steps when Daniel Moodey was so kind as to whisper about the boyfriend, she told her, keeps telling her, I support my son. I'm aware of the agony people have been through, my dreams are still dark with it, but it's him I mainly weep for now.

Where mine has caused the death of yours, we're symbols of ourselves.

She looks at her watch. Fifteen more minutes. The girl makes a small, hopeless gesture and crumbles her roll into pieces. As little appetite as Dora herself.

'Soon it'll be time to get back.' A bitten-in grimace. 'That wasn't a very good beginning.'

'Miss Hardy, it wasn't a beginning, it wasn't an end. Nothing started between us here today. I don't want to be cruel, you understand. You're obviously in pain. Obviously. I just want to get my point across. All I can repeat is what I already said to our lawyer and the journalists. What my son did was an act of political sabotage. Maybe he acted alone but he had no personal motive. He believes the race war here isn't won yet but he's not a racist. The deaths were a tragedy, your boyfriend's death was a tragedy, Joseph got sucked in by events, but it's not for me to say these things. Black people have died and still die every day in this country for demanding no more than what whites have.'

The girl leans forward and Dora can smell the hot anguish of her sweat, deodorant mixed with sweat. For an instant a pent-in eagerness replaces that shrunken, lost look in the girl's eyes.

Dora shivers, she's unsettled by that expression, that change in her, can't help but feel affected by it. She's a mother after all, isn't she? Something in what she just said had the power to shift the girl's sorrow, even if for a moment, no doubt about it. So young she is too, she also can't help noticing, too young to be this stricken, so very violently – so violently bereaved. The horrible crushing of that shopping centre, Dora thinks for an instant, feels chilly inside. A bad mistake to come, she reminds herself. Joseph, she thinks, it's him I weep for now.

'I agree with what you just said, Mrs Makken. Yes, in my mind I agree.' She becomes aware the girl's talking. 'Acts of retaliation are justified within situations of extreme oppression. But these recent events, they've undermined my feelings. This bomb blast on what was going to be an ordinary day, the random deaths, the violent transformation of people's lives, and at a time of real change. Something inside me can't come to terms with these things, I don't know what I feel about them any more. That's why I want to understand the bombing better. I want to find out about the individual circumstances of this particular bombing.'

She presses a piece of roll into her mouth, is unsure what to do with it. A white paste lies on her tongue.

Dora looks away. Oh dear, she sighs to herself, oh dear girl, this is too much, too sore, too sore. You shouldn't be here, I don't want to be here, don't want to be reminded, to notice the pleading in your eyes. And at the same time she can't not see it. Alongside her aversion to everything she represents, Dora can't suppress how the girl's loss is chafing her. Her huge, devastating loss. The longer she stays here, the more it affects her. That dreadful crashing, of rubble powdering bone. How emptied Anthea Hardy's life must be for her to have come to sit here today, across the table from herself, Dora Makken. What strength of will that must take. She remembers her waiting on the court steps, the grip on her arm, the belief packed into that strength. Her confidence she'll be taken on trust, not saying a word about the boyfriend. Her white girl's confidence, Dora thinks, but, even so, she does respect that kind of determination, that pushfulness.

'I realise what it means, Mrs Makken, for you to come here today,' the girl goes on, 'I do realise. That's why I don't want to ask questions, I don't want answers. I'm just hoping you could tell me, well, anything – anything about your son. What moves him. I'm not interested in blame. I'm looking for a story that will bring things together, create a pattern I can understand.'

'But that means giving an explanation, and how's that possible? Miss Hardy, it's not possible to look at anything in this country as a special case. Even with the recent releases and so on, many non-whites identified with the bomber on that day of the bomb. And all whites were hit.

If you kick a dog enough times, one day it'll bite back.'

'Yes, one day it will bite back. That's it. It's that *one day* I keep coming back to. One day rather than another day, the chance of it. Why *then*? Why did these people, black or white, have to carry this thing for the rest of us? Why *this* shopping centre? What was it that took Joseph Makken into the Right Now at South Clacton beach? What was it driving him, what rage, disgust?'

But no, this is unbearable, this comes too close, she's had more than she can take. Dora pushes away from the table. The salt and pepper cellars knock together, tea slops into saucers. She drags herself up by holding on to the chair back.

And the desperate girl is immediately at her side, just about bumping into her, blushing bright red. So clumsy her distress, her untidy hungry need. And that dull pain in her face – but Dora doesn't want to see her pain.

She talks to the extractor fan above Anthea Hardy's right shoulder. The patient deadpan tone of the prepared statement is harder when the audience is this nearby and insistent.

'Miss Hardy,' she says so low the girl bends even closer, 'Again I repeat. For you standing there, me here, the only way of looking at this is as a general problem. My sorrow is not your sorrow. Justice in this country has always been white justice. Joseph'll likely still be badly hurt for this so-called crime. But even a life sentence won't bring your boyfriend back. Joseph's sorry to have taken lives, but being sorry won't bring the victims back. He's paying the price for being black in this system. He was striking out at years of extreme prejudice. Eventually the bomb got the better of him. That's what I have to say.'

This time Dora feels the sigh shake through her whole body. Her shoulders, thighs, take the tremor, slacken. She feels suddenly leaden, turns heavily towards the door.

'But I'm not contradicting you, Mrs Makken, please!'

Still the girl's talking, almost a hissing. Still she's close and pleading and humidly warm. The hand now clutching Dora's wrist is sopping.

'What I'm saying is, if I understood your son's motives better, I might be able to see Duncan as – not a random fatality but part of a larger process. Not a death in vain but a sacrifice towards something bigger, a changing country, part of secret talks in Viennese hotels and pop songs coming true, part of this difficult shift in things, like your son himself is. That's what I meant, that's what I think I meant.'

The door bursts open in front of them. A waitress, a blur in a starched cotton frill, has acted out of an excess of zeal. She flattens herself against the door frame to let them through. As white light confronts them, they catch their breath. The heat grasps them like a sock.

Anthea Hardy's mouth is a pale open circle.

'What you're saying, Miss Hardy, is that you're asking a lot. It's a lot, talking about my son. As I said, I'm here and you're there and between us lies this terrible event that happened. You're asking for my sympathy to weigh in against my support for my son. Does sympathy work like that? I don't know, I'm afraid I can't say. Probably my sympathy must stay on my side of the fence with me.'

But even as she's speaking their movements are countering her words. They are having to weave together through the late lunch-hour crowd moving along the pavement. Together they look up at the city hall clock to confirm how late it is. Ten to two. Anthea points in the direction of her white Fiat, pulling down the corners of her mouth, an exaggerated resignation, might as well? Dora nods back. They help each other with seats too sunbaked to sit on. 'Try spreading tissues.' 'This scarf.' The parking space is tight. Dora leans out of the window, twists around again. 'Turn sharply, small reverse. OK now.'

As the humming silence of the moving car encloses them, they come apart again. The physical closeness separates them, creates the opportunity to steal glances at each other, though it is only Anthea who allows herself this.

She is concentrating on timing the car's acceleration to the changing of the traffic lights. Dora Makken shouldn't be late, the mother of the accused sitting here in her car, spread hips pressed against the seatbelt socket, shouldn't be late. And still she can't stop looking, checking Dora's face, her skin, the grain of her colour. Before, of course, she'd have tried to see Dora free of race, this was what she believed in. She'd have worked to strip away her colour, see her as some kind of inner self or core person. But because of the bomb – the black bomber versus his white victims – this has become impossible. Dora's race is vividly visible, indelible, and Anthea wants to see it, confront it … Confront directly this difference that's virtually pressed against her arm, her hip.

Would Dora for example leave a patch on the headrest, like a stain? She can't cut off the thought, the shuddery fascination, once she gives way to it. That shiny skin. When Mrs Makken sits forward, check to see if her neck, hair, has left a mark. Can't help this. No black person was ever in this car before, ever this close. Something near to a catch of panic comes into Anthea's breathing. Paying the price for being white in this system. She has to ease her shoulders by pushing up on the steering wheel. She looks away, looks back again almost immediately, corner of her eye.

This time she begins to notice the dense network of tiny lines marking Dora Makken's throat and cheek. The lines shirring the skin around her ear, gathering in a deep fold under the chin, as though hands wiping away tiredness, tears, have been endlessly dragged across her face, discomposing its surface tension. And the hands too. Veins like exposed grass roots knot across the backs of the hands lying in the broad lap. This white-person ignorance about dark skin. Thinking it must offer a mask, a smooth oily mask, a protection against such strain.

Looking into the rear view mirror to overtake, Anthea feels embarrassed to have taken advantage of this closeness. But then does it over again. Mother of the bomber up close, up close her worn dry skin, marked by worry. She slides her eyes over to look at Dora Makken again.

From a distance, on the steps of the court, in the newspapers, Mrs Makken is full-figured, solid, a mother in an illustrated children's book, a rock. But a rock that's crumbling. Face powder packed into the wrinkles running across her cheeks.

'I like that dress you're wearing.'

Anthea grates the gear stick as if caught in a guilty act.

'Yes, I did say something.'

Mrs Makken comes close to smiling.

They have reached the long road approaching the court buildings. On their left, beyond the temporary car park, is the cricket pavilion. A party of schoolboys in motley sports gear fans across the oval.

'I said I like that grey dress you're wearing. I noticed it the first day in court. It suits you.'

Another sigh heaves through Dora's body, pushing her belly against her bosom, closing her throat. Under a cupped palm she licks a finger, tests the sour smell of her spit, a stale unpleasant mouth, should've eaten more at lunchtime.

The girl parks. For some reason she's blushing madly again. Red patches flare in her throat. That strange effect of her blushes, as though they puff her body heat into the atmosphere, a faint odour of spoiled flowers, which Dora doesn't mind.

She turns towards her, almost she touches her arm with her fingers. Ah, but she must ache for him, she thinks. If she's feeling anything like what I'm feeling, anything like this hunger for the loved one who's absent, for his closeness, she must sometimes want to wail, cry out in a loud voice. She wonders, should I give her arm, wrist, the back of her hand there, just the smallest touch? the passing breath of an acknowledgement, we've met, I see you? But her hand lies limp in her lap.

Instead she says, 'You should watch the sun over the next few days. You shouldn't stand so long on the court steps.' She almost smiles again. 'You're looking very burned if I may say so. Take a mother's advice.'

Seeing Dora's buried smile, Anthea smiles. She switches off the engine.

'I have thin skin, I know, prone to moles. It's irritating. Sun-sensitive but not a real blonde. Pale skin without the benefits.'

Speaking without thinking, Dora suspects.

They sit staring ahead. The car holds them comfortably within its snug space.

'Skin, skin, skin,' Dora suddenly says. 'When will we ever be rid of that subject, hm, Miss Hardy? Here's a thing about skin difference you'll be interested in. As a non-blonde mole-suffering person. I also have moles. And so does my sister. When she drives she has to wear long white gloves for protection. And my son Joseph has moles across his back and forearms where the sun's caught him. Those hot-headed redheads in our background, believe it or not, make our so-called coloured skin get moles.'

Joseph. The name's spoken before she has time to think what she's giving away. Playing to the girl's request. *I'm just hoping you could tell me –*

'My mother had a mole cut out,' Anthea says. 'In the small of her back. It left an angry pink scar.'

'That I haven't seen before,' Dora says, withholds the obvious point that minor skin ailments don't get attention in township clinics.

But now that it's begun she wouldn't want to cut this talking short. It's the girl's happy chance to have muddled with her into a chat, the kind that drifts, settles, knits across gaps. Webby, all-over-the-place chat like she has with Bernice. It's been nearly a whole fortnight now with no chance to chat unless late at night and the two of them, her and Bernice, both blinking with exhaustion.

Anthea keeps still. Mustn't move, she says to herself, mustn't move in case Mrs Dora Makken, startled, will stop speaking. From the corner of her straining eyes she catches sight of Dora's knees, legs, so very dark under the black tights, and those veined hands also deep brown, so surprising, and the black flecks, yes, scattered across the skin. It's the more surprising the more they talk – that difference, that shiny dark brown skin.

Her fingers make red marks in her thighs. Until she goes to bed that night, her hands released from the clamped grasp on her legs will not stop shaking.

'We have a good method in our family for getting rid of moles, the raised ones. This one here on my left side.' Dora's hand goes up to her neck. 'You take a thin piece of thread. Tie it round the foot of the mole, then pull the thread tight. You need to feel a sharp pain, then wait. Within days the mole disappears.'

She opens the car door.

'It shrivels away like magic, leaves no scar.'

The plock-plock of the boys' cricket game, the rush of traffic.

'Look how late it is. Thank you for the lift, Miss Hardy. You not coming along?'

Anthea shakes her head.

'You OK?'

'Yes, OK. Tired. It could be the sun like you said. I might go home, have a rest. I'm glad we – '

'Maybe the lunch turned out better than expected?' Dora begins to move away, halts. 'You can cover that mole with an Elastoplast by the way. For a few days the big ones look quite angry.'

She walks away, resting gripped fists on her hips. And resists the urge to turn back and wave. It's not like that between them, can't be. But she feels happy with herself and so less annoyed with the girl. She made it through the hour, there was no scene. No scene or quarrel, feelings left no harder than before, no more agitated. Except, that is, for her sense of the girl's sorrow, that memory of the moist clutch of her hand on her wrist, which she can't shrug off. That plea in the girl's eyes she couldn't answer, her impossible request to understand.

Later that afternoon it strikes her differently again. The court is hearing the testimony of a stammering state witness, the taxi driver who drove Joseph Makken from the beach front to the first of the three buses he used to get to his safe house. It's then that she thinks, Ah, I was slow, that's why she went off home. To write down everything that was said between us. *Looking for a story, a pattern I can understand.*

But in the end these are distant thoughts. Here in the green paint and dark wood interior of the courtroom the outside world feels thin and vague. Her stomach groans. She clenches her folded arms and tries to ignore it.

The last witness of the day, of the week, is Joseph's high school head-master Bram Meintjies. He delivers a prepared speech about his now-famous past pupil. But although it's the state prosecution who have summoned him to discuss Joseph's truancy and alleged emotional instability, this development excites the Makken defence counsel. As Mr Meintjies, whether intentionally or not, builds into his statement a supportive testimonial for Joseph, Dora begins to see why.

'Here was a person, a serious, driven person,' Mr Meintjies says, 'who couldn't believe the sickness in the country would fix itself overnight. At school, throughout his time with us, he was diligent, trustworthy and helpful to others, until the day he disappeared for good.'

True, true, Dora nods to herself, he can't help but say it. Diligent, driven. Certainly, like Mr Moodey says, this will cushion the strain of next Monday.

The head's words give her the courage to glance over at Joseph pressed between his minders. She sends a silent goodbye across to him. For two days he'll be put away in some place she can't imagine. Friday evening till Monday morning, in dirt, damp, 24-hour lighting. John, imprisoned once for disturbing the peace, has mentioned rats.

For two days she'll be counting the hours. And dreading them.

On Monday Joseph will begin to give his own special speech, the beginning of his evidence in extenuation.

There where the accused stands: Joe her son.

His unblinking feverish eyes.

# 14

Anthea did not go home to write up her interview with Dora Makken. As she had said, she went home to sleep. She went to bed and slept for fourteen hours, and when she woke the sunrise washing over the sea was soaking pink into the bedroom walls. Stretching she went to the bathroom and put up her hair. She angled the mirrors of the cabinet so as to see her neck and upper back. Scrutinise the moles.

Her first thought was to suspect Dora Makken of delivering some veiled insult. That talk about skin and moles, what was that about? She see-sawed her shoulders. Had she sprouted fresh moles or sickly blemishes across the two weeks of the trial, baking in that sun? Some cancer nourished by recent stresses now rising to the skin?

What she saw in the mirror was the red-brown half-circle of her collar burn and a mole, two moles, nothing angry. A familiar aspect of her body since childhood summers, wearing the garment of her white skin.

So was it some sly moral? An oblique joke? Moles as concentrations of melanin, nuggets of darkness bedded deep in skin whatever its colour or sheen. We all carry a blackness inside us, Dora Makken was saying? A treacherous blackness to boot.

Anthea checked the armpits of her grey dress for sweat marks, began to pull it over her head, stopped. It was Saturday, not a trial day. Must still be half-asleep. She tugged the dress off again and put on shorts and a shirt. She made instant coffee, went to sit at the kitchen table. She heard the shove of the newspaper under the front door and a bicycle clatter down the street.

Six in the morning on a Saturday, near-perfect stillness. All day to sit and think, about skin difference, skin conflict. Dora Makken in the restaurant, her eyes glazed with distraction and anger. *Not a death in vain.* And Dora changed, her profile softened and in motion, talking in the car as if they had all day. Her fingers, her wrinkled, work-worn knuckles, suddenly delicate, miming how to tie a thread around a mole.

Moles like mushrooms, like molehills. Anthea traced a finger down her forearm, around the big sunspots and freckles and the familiar mole to the side of the wrist, a small mound like a molehill. 'You can cover that mole with an Elastoplast.' Mrs Makken herself used thick make-up to cover her skin, her face almost rosy-brown with it. There was that other possibility. She'd given simple advice, just that, no dig or attack.

Anthea remembered Dora stretching her pantihosed legs into the space under the glove compartment, neatly smoothing her skirt. She took care about how she looked, Dora did. Her lipstick was a rich garnet, flattering against her brown skin, her red hound's-tooth shirt. She liked to exchange tips about looking your best. Home remedies against blemishes, moles.

Remedies against moles, Anthea swung on her chair. Petrol and sulphur had been the one at home. Countless Saturday mornings, she and her father picking their way through the networks of freshly turned mounds on the lawn.

'Softly now, they feel the slightest tremor.' Her father breaking the heaped clay to find the mole's burrow.

Working side by side, equipped with a spade each, a can of petrol, a box of sulphur pellets to spike the petrol.

'Pack the earth in tight. They die a slow death.' Her father with satisfaction. 'If the pellets don't kill them the petrol will poison them good and dead.'

But the moles succeeded in breeding before suffocating. The garden on Saturday mornings was always bumpy with molehills. Right the way across the white suburbs moles infested the lush lawns.

'Smooth grass at all costs for your golfing dad,' Duncan's sour remark, which crumbled into a chuckle.

'There's a different method against moles I've heard. You'll love it. Best method against moles. Get a squeaker button off a commercial birthday card. Winkle the squeaker out of the card and stick it into the soil close to the molehill. OK, it's not a cut-price method, but the moles don't like the intrusion. All that latent squeaking buried round them.

They leave your garden in a hurry.'

'Come off it Duncan.'

'What do you mean?' The chuckle shaking through him. 'The secretary at work swears by it. You should tell your dad.'

She should tell Dora Makken, a wacky tip to make her smile. Anthea shuffled newspapers, notebooks, sympathy cards, to find her purse, noticing as she did so one of the cards, pink and grey, from Nick and Marjorie, glide to the floor and flop open.

*Duncan – we'll remember him always.*

Duncan's name descending, she thought uneasily, suddenly conscious of how this interest in Dora had for the past several minutes displaced – not thoughts of Duncan, this was his joke after all – but any awareness of her grief. *Anthea, the guilt of the bereaved*, she remembered writing out his words. And yet it was true, she leaned against the table, knitting her hands behind her neck, as he used to do. She couldn't deny that her curiosity about Dora's remarks had for moments completely lifted the heaviness of her loss. Did she no longer then miss Duncan as before? She tried reminding herself that this encounter with Dora was in his name, part of working through what had happened to him. But was this all? Didn't her disquiet also connect with the definite sense that missing him was no longer as acute a pain? Her grief was turning into a thinner shadow, a shadow that she mainly became aware of, as now, because of its sudden absence, but that had otherwise resolved itself into something more subdued and continuous, an uninsistent wistfulness underlying the activities of her day.

That thing about the cards and squeaker buttons, Duncan, she thought fondly, gratefully, it was an infectious joke.

Anthea rescued the grey-and-pink sympathy card and put it up on the windowsill. There, behind a flower pot, she found her purse.

The café down the hill sold dog-eared greeting cards in a dusty box alongside the wheezing fridge of cool-drink. The proprietor thumbing sleep out of his eyes came over to help with the search. They spotted what she wanted at the back of the box, *Congratulations* in silver glitter arched across a squeaker insert disguised as a bunch of red balloons.

'I remember unpacking that one. Careful, he's sensitive.'

'Just the thing.'

At the first touch of opening the card began to whirr. A fast, slurred

*For he's a jolly good fellow.*

In her kitchen Anthea cut around the musical device keeping the balloon picture intact. She put it in an envelope with a note.

*We mentioned moles. This is another anti-mole remedy. If ever you're plagued –*

She addressed the envelope care of Mrs Makken's lawyer. Should reach her on Monday afternoon, at the latest Tuesday.

But on Monday morning as Joseph Makken stood for his testimony in extenuation Anthea realised her mistake.

He began quietly, the judge occasionally interrupting or prodding him. She could see from the gallery where she was sitting, the stretch of his knuckles around the spindled railing of the witness box, the working of his Adam's apple, the sweat on his neck, and the pulse there, she could just see it, stirring under the skin.

And now she too had done damage. Sulphur pellets packed in tight.

Sending a silly card to a woman whose son is in the dock – who would do that to an enemy? What had she been thinking of? What was this self-frustrating need to forge some sort of exchange? Like a fool she herself had now made contact impossible.

She rested her chin on the gallery barrier, feeling the polished coolness of the wood, as Joseph Makken must be feeling it. She furtively glanced over at Dora, wearing that red blouse again, freshly ironed. Her face giving away nothing but a set endurance. Her make-up thick and neat.

'The incident at the Movement office's crèche derailed me,' said Joseph Makken. 'The Boers' so-called pre-emptive strike to preserve law and order. They loaded that place with enough explosive to bring down a high-rise. It was the news of the crèche especially derailed me. I thought what my mother would do if it was me as a small boy caught in that place.'

Unbudged by the reference Mrs Makken looked straight ahead.

'The papers had a photo, the baby that was hit. The wound to her head. That photo especially derailed me. That photo said to me, we're still at war.'

Joseph hunched his shoulders. He seemed to swallow hard. His knuckles on the railing were pale with tension.

'Of what use is a crèche for bombing? I was thinking how babies can't run away. I was thinking of the nappies and baby food exploded across the streets. I nearly had to laugh when I was thinking of that.'

Mrs Makken coughed, took out a tissue, coughed a second time behind the tissue, touched it to the corners of her mouth. She checked the tissue for lipstick stains.

'You nearly had to laugh?' said the judge.

'I nearly had to laugh,' said Joseph Makken. 'It felt so bad.'

At lunchtime Dora and the defence lawyer left by a side door. Anthea walked about in the foyer but Dora did not reappear. She found a bench not far from the car park to eat her sandwiches. The plastic wrap resisted her fingers, she tore at it.

What for fuck's sake had she been thinking of? She swallowed big mouthfuls of the bread, eating without tasting. That envelope, its ridiculous squeaker contents. Certainly she hadn't been thinking enough about Dora, what it must mean surviving the trial from day to day, what today must mean. Sitting there helpless as her son damned himself, inevitably damned himself. 'Like Mandela I want to give my own speech in self-defence. I am a soldier, a prisoner of war.'

*My sorrow is not your sorrow, Miss Hardy*, said Dora. *Justice in this country has always been white justice.*

Somehow she must contrive to get the envelope back.

She tried calling the lawyer's chambers but there was no reply. Lunch hour. She returned to the foyer early, she hung about. If she could get a message to Dora, a second message to cancel the first. She found herself inside a gathering group at the court room door. Faces from the newspaper pictures, several more than last week, the extended Hart family, Andries Cronje with a number of male relatives and friends. The Fergusons were staying away, 'We're not strong enough yet, Anthea. All that awful rage.' The faces in the dim light looked greenish, as if their shock had drained away their blood.

That afternoon the witness's voice seemed at once louder but tiring. He had put on an extra-large blue tracksuit top over his white t-shirt. Dora Makken held her bag on her lap. Once when Joseph repeated a phrase – 'in each and every phone box was one person, in each and every one' – mechanically, as if he was rehearsing lines, she darted a look upwards, not at him. Her eyes rested on the moving blades of the fan, then dropped to the front row of the gallery where Anthea was sitting.

'I did not want to do wrong,' Joseph Makken was saying. 'I wanted to do the post office at 4.30 a.m.'

Anthea held Dora's gaze. Dora put an opened hand perpendicularly to the side of her neck like a shield, the side the raised mole was on. She angled her head as if to say, Listen. Listen hard. Anthea's vision blurred with tears.

The judge pursued the question of the timing of the limpet bomb.

'You say, Mr Makken, that you chose the fuse – the blade you say – the blade that allowed a maximum delay of twenty-five minutes before blast-off?'

'Yes.'

'However, the police report concerning the arms cache you used claims that there were in fact other fuses available. Other blades that should have given more time. Forty minutes, an hour, enough time to wait for a telephone, send a warning. What do you say to that?'

'I say there was only the red time-fuse and the yellow fuse that allows ten minutes. I chose the blade that gives the longest time. I wanted no lives to be taken. This is the basis of my self-respect as a soldier for freedom. I will not betray my military training. When I became a soldier I was not any more a kaffir, a half-breed, a thing. I know I should rather place myself in danger than expose civilians to injury. When I think of that what happened at South Clacton I am deeply sad. It looks like I am not able to control my racial conscience, I am no better than the security service and its death squads, burning people on fires like steaks. That's why I put myself in the way of being arrested. I did not flee the country because I want just to tell everyone, I am sorry I placed that bomb.'

'However,' said the senior state prosecutor riffling through a brown folder, 'the first state witness, the gardener at the safe house to which you went after the explosion, testifies that when you heard the news on the radio you expressed disappointment. You said, I quote, *Shit, six only*. You said more than twenty died as a result of the attack on the offices.'

'He was telling lies, in fact. In fact I was sorry. I mean, I was sorry those people had died. I don't know how to say it but I am happy to be on trial here, I am happy for my suffering if it can pay in any way, if this flesh of mine can pay. I say it now to all of you and to my mother sitting there. People lost their beloved son and daughters that day, I know it. The knowledge is fixed in me, in my bleeding heart. I myself will pay for the death of those people.'

The next morning – the second and last day of Joseph Makken's testimony – the crowd on the court building steps was noisier. For the first time since the trial began the sky was overcast. Wind ruffled and turned the browning leaves on the plane trees along the road. It would be the last rainstorm before winter, said the morning news. Andries Cronje wore a pink woollen hat pulled down on his forehead. He told a paper he wasn't planning to cut his hair or remove the hat – his daughter Luanne's favourite – 'till justice is done in this country and we blast reform.'

Anthea pressed herself into the crush, no hope of catching Dora. Dora would be chancing it to walk this way today. She thought she glimpsed ahead the bent silhouette of Duncan's soldier relative. The nylon shine of his medalled blazer. She looked again. Wrong, too tall. The crowd closed in behind the man.

A woman in a red rainjacket bumped against her. The crackle of a plastic hood, a pressure against her side.

'How are you, Miss Hardy?' Dora spoke without looking at her.

'All right I think.'

They were pushed forwards by the crowd.

'And you, Mrs Makken?' No courage to say more.

'Hard days, Miss Hardy. For me. Also for you.'

'Mrs Makken, I should just say how very sorry I am. By now you'll have received – '

'Yes. I was just going to thank you. What a surprise.'

'I'm so sorry. I realised too late it was thoughtless.'

A hand on her arm. Sunspotted skin, colour-mottled. So-called Coloured, said people. Freckled brown in fact.

'I liked what you did. This morning when Mr Moodey handed me your note I wanted to smile. I was smiling at myself for starting such a silly topic in the first place. And at you, for thinking we have lawns in our township that could get damaged. But most of all I liked the tune.

I like that tune usually but especially I like it for today. You chose well. I hear *He's a jolly good fellow* and I think of weddings, congratulations. I kept squeezing and playing that thing in the car on the way here. God knows, we need cheering up.'

The plane leaves drifting in the park crumbled into dust before they reached the ground. Leaf bits settled in a golden-brown fuzz on Mrs Makken's hair. She arranged her lunch on a starched dishcloth stretched on the grass: a paper plate of corned beef and piccalilli sandwiches, sliced tomatoes in a Tupperware dish, a Giant Bag of Cheezee Balls, bought coconut tarts, Marie Biscuits spread with butter, chocolate vermicelli, strawberry jam.

'You eat,' she directed. 'My treat. Good that I spotted you, my sister Bernice always packs a big lunch. Let's hope the rain holds off. It's easier to eat in the open than indoors, like that fancy venue in town.'

Anthea lay on the ground tracing her fingers along the segmented roots of the yellowing grass. She thought of centipede skeletons, of grasshopper carapaces. She looked at Dora Makken's bunioned little toes burrowing into the grass. In a heap to the side of their picnic lay Dora's shoes, their handbags, Anthea's tube of sun lotion, a Checkers bag that had carried the lunch, a small make-up mirror that might belong to either of them. Seeing Dora search, Anthea had fished a mirror out of her bag, may not have put it back.

She ate quietly because she didn't want to make noise in her skull, the interrupting crunch of piccalilli onions, of biscuit. She sucked on the tomato slices. Wanting to catch each one of Dora Makken's words she closed her eyes.

'One thing he always does.'

Dora was speaking in sudden runs which abruptly stopped. She seemed not to be directly addressing Anthea, talking more for her own record, making a connection with Joseph in her memory, but not ignoring Anthea's presence in doing so. Occasionally she glanced at her, caught her eye. She had arranged Marie Biscuits in a double row along her stretched-out legs. When she paused she ate a biscuit, another biscuit. She began at the knee end of the left row.

'One thing he always does is remember his sisters. My Joseph, my only living child. The other two died of epilepsy before they were six,

Monica and Desirée. He'll always remember their birthdays and when they died. He'll come to me at supper and put his hands on my shoulders and just say the name against my ear, quietly. Even when he was mostly away from us these last months, year, he sent a message. *Desirée* was what he'd written on the paper. Just *Desirée*, imagine that, on her death day.'

There was a muggy taste of Dora's kitchen folded inside the sandwiches. Humid cupboards, paraffin, something else. Anthea sniffed her sandwich, bit into the bread, avoiding the crunchy onion, taking in Dora's smell.

'One thing he always does, he warms me up. What'll I do without him this winter, that Joseph? On a cold morning I'll ask him to come stand here against my back when I'm stirring the *pap*. Even in winter with only a t-shirt on he'll beam out heat, he's that way. The minute I felt him kicking in my stomach I felt his glow. Then I was the one who warmed people up. It got to be a game in the family that winter. Sending me round with my belly to lie on each person's sleeping-place for a few minutes before bedtime, warm it up. My father Sam's bed and his wife's, that was his second wife, and my baby sister Bernice's mattress. And my uncle Gertie who boarded with us then and slept on the back stoep.'

Anthea rolled over on to her back. The press of her elbows on the grass had burnt a pink tracery of knotted roots and leaves into her skin. She tested the depth of the pattern with a finger.

'Some days, you know, I thought my skin will scald I was so hot with Joseph growing inside. The funny thing is, when I heard the news of him and the bomb, it was on the radio, how he was the one named, the opposite happened, I went stone cold. Stayed cold everywhere, the blood frozen in my veins. That shows doesn't it? How a family's linked by blood. Sanguinary, said the doctor from England at the clinic I went to, he's a sanguinary baby. I asked, What's that? Full of blood and good humour, she said. And that's how he turned out. A warm sunny child he always was.'

Full of blood and bloody, Anthea wanted to say aloud, but couldn't form the words.

'One thing he also always does, did, was practice his speeches in the yard like a singer starting up his voice. He would sing his sentences softly to the tune of songs we knew. He was good at speeches, his friends've told me. He spoke at all the student meetings in the area. He told them about people power. Before meetings I would hear him outside chanting the sentences, bits from Biko and the Charter, like practising chords. But other times he'd just sing, he'd sing to make me happy. Tunes I taught him as a baby that came down in the family from my father's mother, she had a full life.'

Dora slid her last few Marie Biscuits into a pile and put them on the spread cloth. She cleared her throat, pulled back her shoulders. As if preparing for a performance, Anthea thought, the mother as witness.

Dora sang

Berend Botje gaan uit varen,
Met een scheepje naar Zuid Laren.
De weg was recht, de weg was krom
Nooit komt Berend Botje weer om.

'We loved that one, Joe and I. It's an old Dutch song, a boy goes out sailing and never returns, difficult to do the Dutch right. When he was little we'd sing that song together. I'd be working in the house and he was playing outside on the stoep. Or he'd help me wring the washing. I like those old songs that are sad and strange, full of prophecy. Like this other one of my father's mother's, an English song from the time of the Afrikaner war.

When the Lion shall lose its strength,
And the Queen of England pine,
Our Harp shall sound sweet, sweet, at length
Beyond the Southern line.

She hummed the song a second time with her eyes shut.

'Joe didn't mind what he sang so long as he was singing. Freedom songs, *We Shall Overcome*, *Blowing in the Wind*, the rhymes I taught him. It might have put informers off his trail, I say to myself, that he was singing these strange songs in the back yard along with the struggle songs.'

They tidied up the lunch. Dora wrapped individually in grease-proof paper the left-over sandwiches, the biscuits, a coconut tart marked by two half-moon bites, Anthea's. She put the food in the Checkers bag.

'That was good,' said Anthea.

'No thanks,' said Dora. 'I enjoyed it myself. I enjoyed not eating in the café. What I wish is that I could eat Marie Biscuits when I appear in court. It'd help, that I'd be able to eat and maybe sing as well as talk.'

'Will you be appearing though? I thought, I didn't know anyone other than Joseph and – '

'You thought right. But that headmaster's speech last Friday gave defence counsel an idea. Joseph feels he can present his own main evidence, yes, but Mr Moodey's a quick thinker. He plans to submit a request to the judge that the court be adjourned. Three or so weeks, he'll suggest. This'll give time to collect more testimonials like the one the headmaster Bram Meintjies gave, more evidence of good character. If nothing else we hope these might help ease the sentence, soften the judge. Mr Moodey wants to approach the student counsellor at Joseph's school. And he wants me to speak. Even if it's biased, whatever I say will show here's a boy from a good nest, with a decent mother. A mother who can and wants to speak for him.'

They brushed crumbs from their skirts. Dora picked up a bit of broken biscuit, blew the grass off it and put it in her mouth. She chewed intently. Anthea thought she had never seen anyone eat so many biscuits in one sitting.

'Mr Moodey thinks the judge will agree, if only for appearance's sake, to create at least an impression of change in the courts. Look at the state of the trial right now, what it still says about justice in this country. Joseph's so-called defence speech damns him, the evidence he's given damns him. He pleads not guilty to murder, guilty to causing the explosion. All he's given a chance to say is how he did what he did.'

They set out across the park. Anthea checked her make-up mirror was stowed in her bag. Dora had taken the one lying in the grass.

'You know, one thing he always did, does, one thing he always does is he never says a lie to me. Never. My Joseph. Until this year of the bomb he always looked me in the eye, until then. Even when we had the quarrels over his studies. All these years he's been meant to be getting his matric exam, he always looked me in the eye when he spoke. I said I wanted him to go to school, I knew about his anger but I wanted him to learn. He was calling for boycotts against unequal education, he wouldn't do his homework. He had no chance to study, he said, he was organising protests. I said under-education was better than none, so he set himself against me for a time. I could see that, he didn't talk much. He was lost from me sometimes when his heart got committed to justice. But even then he never dropped his eyes and he never said a lie.

' "Tell me where you go at night," I said, "I lie awake and worry for you." He said, "I have to do this alone, ma, it's not good for you to know what I'm doing when I leave my bed in the early morning and go." He could disappear weeks. When he was not yet nineteen years old it started. Think what that is for a mother. Once he must've gone to another country for supplies, training. He came home with a new cotton shirt, *Made in China* label, but he never said what happened, never said a lie. Even now he says he did it and that's no lie. But, Anthea Hardy, he doesn't look at me. In front of me his mother, for what's he hanging his head?'

The blood of the dead, Anthea silently interjected, the shame of shed blood, all our loved ones' shared blood.

Dora wasn't waiting for a reply.

'In front of me, his mother Dora Makken, he has nothing to be ashamed of, he must hold up his head. Since he was sixteen I've known about his struggle. The fire that burns for justice in him burns in me. Like he says, people who feel the bite of atrocity will one day answer with atrocity. The country's still sick, I agree with that headmaster. Even if beaches and bars are open, it's early days yet, people are ailing inside still.'

They reached the road and its noise, Dora spoke up.

'Fact is, Joseph needn't be ashamed, in front of no one. The deaths pain us all but he mustn't be our scapegoat. The time I was allowed to visit him in prison, three days before the trial began, just twenty minutes they gave me, that day he managed to say some top people had noted his efforts. He was told. OK, the Movement has officially condemned what's happened, they've got to now, but he's heard on the quiet some big names don't blame him. Even taking into account, if you'll excuse me, the serious loss of life. It's been a cold shadow on this land, white pressing down on black, no one says it's over yet. Joseph was firing a warning shot, Stop the agony today. He needn't be ashamed before anyone, and that includes the fighters who call themselves true Africans, real Black. To them I say, who's born in this country and suffers for their skin and isn't oppressed? Joseph stands with all oppressed people in brotherhood.'

Anthea noticed the new strain in Dora's voice. She thought of the low black attendance at the trial. But wasn't this because the court had been shifted to the white suburbs? If they showed up, the official thinking was, Joseph's bloodthirsty supporters would be conspicuous. They would also have to travel a long way in.

She glanced over at Dora to read her expression but she was walking slightly ahead. Anthea quickened her pace. They began to fall into step. All the way from the park Dora had been in front talking mostly to herself, but now she seemed to slow down, they were easing into step, Dora's skirt swished against hers. They were walking along the footpath opposite the court buildings and Dora suddenly took her arm. Anthea gave it up readily. Today, after Dora's kindness about the squeaker button, she felt little of that earlier hunger to draw back, stare askance. Dora tugged her in closer and so there came a new settling and evening of the atmosphere between them. And still it was strange, awkwardly strange, because Dora must have some idea what she was thinking, what she couldn't not think.

If Joseph need feel no shame then why was he hanging his head?

There was his statement just before lunch. A partial repetition of how he ended yesterday, Anthea remembered. 'I am happy for my suffering if it can pay in any way. If this flesh of mine can pay. If ever I can cut off a piece of flesh of my own and give it to those who remain, I will do it with pleasure.'

Why would he be saying this, Anthea wondered, if as Dora claimed he need feel no shame?

In spite of herself she suddenly felt her skin goose-pimple, a sharp helpless spasm of distress, but Dora went on holding her arm, seemed to be leading her into a steady rhythm of steps like a dance. She was humming under her breath, the weird high-pitched tune about the lion and the harp. And it was as if they were magically drawn into a single strain of music that began to pull them down the street.

A radio station was playing a violin solo, Beethoven it could be, a filler before the two o'clock news. The music spread from an open van alongside, from a car creeping through the traffic, from another car parked nearby, its doors open. Dora's own high hum blended into the sound, a long pull of chords through which they moved.

Across the way they saw Mr Moodey in blue-tinted glasses scanning the road.

Dora gave Anthea's arm a last tight squeeze and let go.

'Joseph's rounding off his story this afternoon, Miss Hardy. Saying how he got to his safe house, sheltered there. Then Mr Moodey will make his submission, successfully I'm sure. Judges like to create at least the look of justice. Anyhow, whatever happens we're having a party in support of Joseph this weekend. Saturday night, a party for his friends. Now I see that his friends in this case doesn't really include you, but who knows when we'll meet again? If you like you're welcome to come.'

She reached into her handbag for the envelope Anthea had given her. Anthea could make out the fat shape of the squeaker button. Dora scribbled over her own name in Anthea's handwriting and wrote down a house number.

'There, take this. The township used to be an army barracks so everywhere looks exactly the same, prefabs divided into living quarters. Make sure you use a taxi if you come. A white woman driving alone – better not. Even if, as it's said, it's not a black but a Coloured, a soft black township. Maybe you'd like to see Joseph's house, hm, where he comes from? You think about it.'

Handing over the envelope she was already beginning to move off. *And so say all of us*, the squeaker button mumbled. A journalist with a camera closed in behind her.

'Mrs Makken, please, your son said he wanted to pay for his wrong. Do you have anything to say to that?'

Anthea saw her put her fingers to the side of her cheek, that shield gesture, *Listen*. A lanky black student in dreadlocks holding a placard picture of Joseph Makken, the mug-shot in the papers, shoved into the journalist's path. Three white men roughly pulled him back, his placard was trampled. Anthea had to step to one side to avoid the scuffle.

# 15

'Darling, I saw a Coloured lady waving good-bye to you at the car-park exit.'

Connie Hardy steered the car through the brick gateposts. The left-hand gatepost carried the sign, *Hardy Hut*. Frothy late-season dahlias fringed the driveway. Razor wire rioted like some wild creeper across the garden walls, the servant quarters, the garage roof.

'Coloured lady? That would've been Mrs Makken. We were talking earlier today,' Anthea said. To herself she wondered how it was her parents' razor wire always stayed so new-looking and stainless.

'Makken? Oh darling, you mean … ? You'll watch out, won't you? *Please.*'

Anthea snapped the car door shut. Her mother sat a while longer, then her head rose above the car roof.

'This one's got central locking, remember?' She beeped the alarm.

Their heels grated on the driveway gravel. A blue plastic earring flashed in the corner of Anthea's eye, Connie had put an arm gingerly around her waist. At the security grille across the front door stood her father waiting as if on duty. His stiff smile dishevelled the expression of peevish tiredness that usually accompanied his pacing around the house after work.

He patted her cheek in place of kissing her but then at a glance from her mother drew himself up and pressed his palms into her shoulders, bringing her slightly nearer. His smell clean like a new car's.

Her first visit home for dinner after the bomb and they were treating her like a convalescent. 'You've got to come over, darling, and let me feed you.' Her mother's hand now gripped across hers on the briefcase handle. Yes, Anthea thought, this must be how they saw her, unhappy, drooping, indecisive, as in need of guidance as earlier, at university, though it was a long distance away from how she now felt. Now, with what was happening at the trial, this growing sense of peace, learning to sit the process out day after day, making contact with Dora, each night jotting down what she'd found out, the Makkens' story, its strands and threads. Joseph Makken watching Rambo movies, Dora Makken's efforts to send him to school. Threads and patches, stitched little by little across the surface of her grief, till today, when she and Dora had talked at lunch.

'I'll put the briefcase in my old bedroom, mum, so's not to forget it.'

On her way through the hall she noticed the china vase of autumn daisies her mother had arranged on a side table beside a framed photograph of herself and Duncan. The picture taken at the back here, on the verandah shaded by the syringa tree, the two of them sitting close together holding glasses of orange squash. Their healthy adolescent ease, Anthea thought, almost American-looking. Respectful of the camera's authority Duncan had put a flat right hand formally on her knee. Anthea remembered hating that, wanting to twitch back.

She went up to the picture, she touched the daisies, flicked a smile at her mother.

'I'm glad you like it, love. I did it for you specially.'

Connie left a pause, then she said, 'Well, what does everyone say to us sitting straight down to dinner? Daddy's seen the news. While there's still a bit of light I'd like Anthea to have a look at the new diningroom curtains. They're yellower than the old ones, Honey Gold the shop said, but I don't know, is the colour too bright? Remember, they're on the sunny side of the house.'

'They're lovely, mum.'

'Of course they are,' said her father. He pulled out Anthea's chair, a favour he'd never offered before, scraping the legs slightly. 'Your mother knows exactly what she wants.'

'Yes I know you always say that, Stanley, but what I definitely know I did not want and should've foreseen was for this to be maid's day off.' A clatter as she distributed serving spoons. 'I wanted Elizabeth to do us something fancy and delicious, darling, to give you a little lift after your gruelling day in court, but instead all we have is this ragout. I had to use the leftover rump steak daddy and I had last night.' She laughed a breathy social laugh. 'We can see it as economy I suppose. Can't have new curtains without a bit of saving, can we?'

A brown sauce glistened under the Pyrex lid she was lifting.

'It looks delicious.'

'Marinaded sheep's head next.' Her father's tone never quite made the distinction between an awkward joke and a hurtful dig. 'Organs in tribal sauce just like the Africans.'

'What do you do for lunch, Anthea, while this trial thing's going on?' her mother chipped in, trying to drown him out. 'There's not much on offer in the vicinity of the court.'

'I have sandwiches in the park mostly.'

'Darling, really? Is that safe? I'm sorry to fuss but you'll see it's hard not to worry. Even your going to this trial every day, it does worry me. I've read somewhere, you might be interested, after torture, victims have the need to go up and apologise to their torturers, you know, for being victims. Stanley, when I picked Anthea up today she was talking to Mrs Makken. *Makken*, you know. She seemed to be saying 'bye nicely though, didn't she, love?'

'Still on with the protests, Anthea?' Her father's tongue clicked gummily against his ragouted palate. 'Any sensible person might've thought – '

'Stanley, not the time or place. Darling, ignore us, I'm sure we have no idea. We just want you to mend your life, be happy. Duncan was such a lovely gentle man, what a terrible loss.'

Anthea chewed, fixed her eyes on the three trout heads mounted on a wooden panel hanging behind her father's chair. Have you noticed, Duncan had once said, how those trout of your dad's *smirk*? She wanted now to smile but instead her throat seemed to close and her eyes burned. Wait, she told herself, this flurry'll pass, within minutes mum will offer more potatoes, sauce. In their dealings with her younger brother David and herself, her parents proceeded by way of these sudden bungled intrusions, after which they fell quickly back into the subdued griping that seemed to sustain their married life.

She squinted at the glare of evening light reflected off the polished table. Maybe the curtains didn't quite blend with the room decorations after all, she let herself think, that gay yellow against the embossed white wallpaper, the trouts' varnished gaping, the watercolour reproductions of English castles, the golfing shield on the dark sideboard. All this detail and hard gloss.

'It remains a great country to be happy in,' said her father also staring at the wall. 'Think of the many good things waiting at a young person's fingertips.'

'Which reminds me,' said her mother. 'I was talking to David yesterday, darling, our weekly call. He was saying he'd just bumped into that Charlie North, the head boy in your final year at school, remember, who invited you to the matric dance, and you said no? Well, he's also studying medicine now, obviously a few years further on than David, doing really well. Got a brand-new car.'

'Charlie North?' said Anthea. 'I hadn't thought of him in years. Is David all right?'

'He sent lots of love.'

Her mother nudged the salad bowl towards her, a cool glass arc along her forearm. As she helped herself to lettuce she felt Connie watching her, silently clearing her throat.

'Darling, you know I mean this in the nicest way possible, you know how we liked Duncan. But mightn't you start thinking about taking a break from your duties and troubles just occasionally? I mean, it's nearly three months since … You might try going out in a group of friends? Contact some people from university …'

'I'm busy, mum, really, I'm OK, not lonely.' The lettuce was sour. Anthea dragged it to the side of her plate. 'I know we haven't talked about it much, but what I'm doing's important to me, the trial and so on. The thing that happened with Duncan, it made a terrible break, it broke everything into pieces. But for me it sort of broke divisions too, social divisions. The way to get over things, I'm finding, is to think about those broken pieces, see how they fit together, maybe in a different way from before.'

'OK, we're trying to appreciate that, Anthea, but sorrow must be worked through, that's also important. Any counsellor will tell you this. And it does no harm to take time off. There must be people at work you could go out and relax with. Who's the nice man for example who sometimes takes phone messages? What does he do?'

'Arthur,' said Anthea. 'Arthur Naidoo, he's one of the senior journalists.'

'Naidoo?' her father said, 'You mean – '

'I'll get the pudding, it's your favourite,' said Connie. 'Apricot blanc-mange, remember?'

Anthea caught her mother twiddling her eyebrows at her father. She looked down quickly, instantly aware of having bumped into their shared open secret, the egg-shell etiquette of white people's race-group intimacy.

Skin, skin, skin, Dora Makken had exclaimed in the car.

'I won't have any, thank you mum. The meat was delicious.'

'No blancmange, darling? Are you sure?'

'No thanks.'

'I made it as a special treat.'

'Thanks so much, mum, but no, I can't.'

She folded her hands on her place mat. Her parents spooned up their blancmange. In the space offered by this silence she thought of what her mother had said. Charlie North, 'the Matric dance, and you said no', she'd forgotten completely. Charlie North, his bored grin and the special smile he reserved for teachers and the parents of friends. Slow, immensely caring. How he stared at girls' breasts when he talked to them.

The reason why she'd said no to Charlie North, she wondered if her mother also remembered this, remembered José da Silva. She smiled to herself. Olé José, her friends used to shriek in the girls' toilets, No way, José! Somewhere around their starting high school, José da Silva and his family had fled newly independent Mozambique in quest of the happy life still on offer to colonials further south. They had set up The Tuck Box, a corner shop close to the school selling cheap *Factory Fresh* cakes and chewing-gum, a venture that never embarrassed José. José da Silva, her first real boyfriend, which meant she let his tongue into her mouth. Tasting of onions. His mother did fried pig's heart and onions for breakfast. Anthea remembered loving the thick, strong smells in the flat behind the shop, she remembered the stuffy scent of the always unmade beds, so different from the clean of home. She had loved the shop itself, loved sitting behind the newspaper rack, cross-legged on the dusty floor with its faded Fanta stickers, holding hands with José and reading the comics.

She hadn't told her parents about him, they had found out from a teacher at a school sports day. 'Anthea seems very involved.'

'*Involved*, Anthea? What's this about? Who's this boy? Why haven't you told us about him?'

'He plays prop, mum, in the rugby team. You'll have seen him play.'

'Mostly I've only ever seen the other team in possession,' she remembered her father saying.

'But, darling, his *name*! Where does it come from? José da Silva? I mean – it looks *yellow*. It is yellow, isn't it?'

'They're originally Portuguese, mum. They lived up north years.'

'But darling!' Each of her mother's words like a sob. 'That means different, *yellow*. Are you watching yourself? There are such nice boys in your class.'

At that instant, drilling the toe of her shoe into the dust of the playing field, Anthea had felt a giving way inside her, as if a barrier was suddenly breaking, bringing an inrush of clean air – it was the first such awareness she could remember of her adult life. Her mother's comments had sliced through a surface in her mind, an enclosing skin like clingfilm that had wrapped her thoughts tight. That was suddenly cut through letting in an unnerving sense of new possibility and danger.

Not only white and black, but yellow too, these were the labels in people's heads, she had realised at that moment. You here, you there, and you a little further out again, skin difference marked by insult. Yellow José da Silva was from somewhere else. Anthea remembered her immediate disgust at her mother, for pointing to this, and at José, suddenly, because he smelt of onions and his mother couldn't afford a maid to wash the bed linen. And there was the disgust at herself too, that was unexpected, lasted longer, and which her new awareness only intensified. A disgust at noticing that what her mother had pointed to, she herself cared about, that she always liked to brush her teeth after kissing José. The skin-branding in existence everywhere was also present in her thoughts. Would Dora Makken leave a greasy patch on the car headrest? Not wanting to be yellow by association.

She and José hadn't lasted, of course, but not because of these new feelings. José had been a big-muscled grown-up boy, the only one in the class who shaved. He had dropped her for one of the assistants at the Tuck Shop not long after the sports day, a girl with a shoulder tattoo who offered a lot more than tongue-kissing. He had left school before the final exams.

'Speaking of school days,' Anthea said. She looked up from her place mat. 'Do you ever hear anything more of José da Silva? Do you remember him?' She tried unsuccessfully to add a laugh to her voice.

'Da Silva? Was there ever anyone called that in your class, darling? It doesn't sound right to me.'

Her father gave her a sideways wincing look, it could be a wink or a silencing. It seemed to beg, enough of this.

'If you're finished, Anthea, would you like a look at my new golf clubs? We got them on the Cape holiday. All-leather finish, an excellent driving iron. So excellent I could keep it under my bed, a weapon against intruders.'

He got up to pull back her chair. Now it was his turn to stretch his eyebrows at her mother.

She tried not to think what secret it was this time they were attempting to preserve.

# 16

*A second folded letter lies stowed beneath its companion under the old vellum lining of the odds-and-ends chest that stands on Dora's back stoep. In a corner of the letter a spider has woven a cocoon. The cocoon has never been disturbed. The letter has not been opened for nearly ninety years.*

Izinyanga Stationary Hospital<br>Sunday Jany 28th 1900

My dear Aunt Margaret

From you alone I cannot hide my present feelings. My last letter to you, on Monday, seems as if written a whole lifetime away. Since we arrived the work has been bloody and without respite and I am growing *so* downhearted.

Five days ago a vast new battle broke out along the English front in the hills to the west, a place called Spionkop. On the morning of our small team leaving Estcourt and setting up camp here, casualties, British, Irish, Russian, Boer, began pouring in by the hour. Until today the line of ambulance wagons still reached back into the hills. Our tiny hospital, a handful of bell-tents and sheds built on a treeless plain, would have been hard-pressed to deal with one quarter of this capacity.

What a ghastly horror war truly is. The air is permanently blood-red with the dust clouds stirred up by the shells and, now, the tramp of the English soldiers' retreating feet. Even today with the battle some days behind us, sporadic cannonading has continued to moan and knock in the valleys. The big guns – I can hardly bear to write this – tear off hands, arms, legs, pieces of torso. I have seen dislocated jaws, a head half-ripped from a body. An Estcourt butcher has come, under oath to preserve neutrality, as the exhausted orderlies cannot keep up with the amputations. How we have learned to admire the African ambulance drivers and Indian stretcher bearers, such fine inspired men, every day covering long miles of rocky terrain with their green canvas dhoolies. I have learned one native word since arriving here. It is *ngalimala*, injured.

The beleaguered civilians from the besieged town too are not spared – far from it. Long Tom, the enormous Boer gun, booms and hurls its makeshift shrapnel shells daily from the long hill to the east. I see the wounded cover their ears to withhold the sound and myself go to bed each night with a head-ache. Today I sat until seven, when she died, with a young Zulu woman from the town whose belly was quite sliced away by an exploding shell. I will never forget her face, that last convulsion and crumpling of the life within her. The baby she was holding was uninjured. I have him here beside me, the poor creature, fast asleep, wrapped in flannel against the shock.

To think the imperialists talk of the war as bringing progress and freedom to this country. Their lies are smoke screens, they are treacherous as the clayey dust that blurs our vision. Yet these same awful untruths also threaten to choke, I will confess, my own – our own – idealism.

In what ways, I ask myself, my petticoat stiff with the mingled bloods of many nations, in what ways does it help our Ireland to join the strike at tyranny when the enemy's power is as savage as this? Haters and hated I fear will blow up in a great conflagration. No matter how long it takes, no matter the cost, the Empire plans in the end to destroy to its foundations the opposition of these small farmers, as well as ours, their Irish supporters. Yes, the more I see the more I am convinced it is as their President says. The British will make an example of this country: they want the Boers' land, and the capitalists want its gold.

Certainly I need not have been concerned about having no

role to play – a role, that is, in the sense of offering immediate succour. On my second day I graduated from stopping wounds to assisting at the trepanning of an Australian's skull. Every 'free' moment is spent spongeing and turning sun-blistered, feverish men. As to the greater purpose however my confidence is fast waning. I recall the strengthening words of our poet William Yeats just before Christmas, that it is right to strive for 'the just cause of the Boers'. Yet there have been sleepless nights when I have doubted the possibility of a conclusive victory for liberty through physical force, whether here or elsewhere.

In this regard a Gujerati lawyer who works around the camp as a stretcher bearer, said something that drew my attention. Clad in its tattered motley of battlefield cast-offs – frock coats, cotton singlets, tweed trousers – it was his team brought in the dying Zulu woman. The lawyer's name is Mr Gandy and we sat talking one late afternoon over a can of Africa's khaki-coloured tea.

Oscillating his small poised head, he said that to counter tyranny on its own ground, by its own tactics, is doomed to ignominious defeat. Instead, he said – and being Hindoo *must* speak with authority – the tactics of passivity, universal compassion, healing, these are the weapons for the tyrannised. The war, he went on somewhat contradictorily, offers a 'golden opportunity' to demonstrate imperial loyalty, but to do so by rendering gentle assistance, by '*devastating* with service'. In discourse with him I was briefly heartened by having come here to nurse.

So on many occasions, dear Aunt, I feel entirely inadequate and useless, but do not ever doubt the justice of our shared cause of freedom or the courageous devotion of these noble Burgher patriots. A group of them were today brought to the prisoner of war tents on the one side of the camp, broad-chinned dazed-looking men one of whom, I noticed, was carrying an English novel in his pack. I ask myself what it means to feel such sympathy and yet to continue working under the neutral sign of the Red Cross.

Even among the English officers there is praise for Boer camouflage, their genius for hauling guns up difficult heights. They use, it's said, slatted barrels as wheels and the guns as axles. I do hear on good authority however that it is our very own Irish Brigade who most securely mount the big Boer cannon and calculate their elevation and range. You can imagine I am often comforted as well as amused by the thought of those gallant Mayo and Derry men camped in the hog-backed hills but a few miles away, daily pitching havoc into the British town!

I am sure I write so wildly, my dear Aunt, because of the discomposing effects of my exhaustion. Quite apart from the ruthlessness of the war, this cruel heat we are suffering would lower even an unweary spirit. A large spotted moth just flapped into my candle flame and crashed dying on to the page, scattering the dust of its unearthly furry feelers. I could not help feeling something like a tearful sympathy for it. How I do long to sit in conversation with you over an early tea and a fire, sharing toast and honey as we did so regularly last autumn. I thought of you early this morning when a rain storm plucked wild honey combs from the blue gum trees around the camp. Mr Gandy to whom I was then talking joined me in falling upon them in relief and glee.

My dear aunt I am always
Your faithful and loving
Kathleen

# 17

'We're all of us confused together.'

The elderly man was hunched over a cigarette held in a curled hand.

'All of us here, we carry the burden of the confused past. The foggy memories creep through our clogged veins.'

The man gave Anthea what seemed an assessing look. His face was dark against the burn of candles standing in earth-filled beer cartons on Dora's front-room windowsill.

'I say this to my neighbour Dora, time and again. But she has other things to think about. I say it as a comfort to her. She knows what I mean, she invited me today.'

He poured a glittering hoop of yellow liquid straight from a half-jack bottle into his mouth.

'You, Joseph Makken, Dora, we all carry the mixed-up past inside us.' He sniffed, wiped his mouth. 'We act alone, or that's what we think, but our communities and our parents' parents are gesturing through our hands.'

He cocked back his head, poured a second time, sniffed again.

'Look at me. My father was a drinker, like me. All the men in my family have been in the transport line of work. Me, I was a motor-bike messenger before I retired, like my dad. And my grandfather drove ox carts between Durban and the north, and his oupa before him too. My father's line has always been on the move.'

He drank again. This time he let his lips rest against the mouth of the bottle and gazed thoughtfully at the concrete floor.

They were sitting in an out-of-the-way position. Sounds of sudden laughter and the syncopated buzz of a small tape recorder came from the back stoep. When she had arrived not long ago Anthea had directed herself to this end of the row of chairs arranged along the side wall of the front room. A naked bulb blazed overhead, Dora was nowhere to be seen. On the table beside Anthea's chair stood an empty basin laced with the congealed froth of home-made beer.

As she sat down she had noticed a woman and a man whisper to each other and move off outside. She had seen shadowy figures at the back window cluster together, marking her arrival. Her whiteness attracting uneasy attention, as she might have guessed.

Joseph Makken's home ground. This place.

'A party at the Makkens'?' Arthur Naidoo had called earlier to talk about her return to full-time work this coming Monday, thought she might need acclimatising.

'Do you know what you're doing, Anthea? Your boyfriend's bomber's support party? If you could see me right now you'd see I'm shaking my head. Call if you want company getting there.'

The coloured taxi driver shook his head in his turn as he drew up at the end of the street running between the barracks buildings. She had paid him in advance. 'Sorry, madam, no further. That road, no thank you very much. Tsotsis live there, gangsters. You don't want to hang around.'

The elderly man came over moments after she had seated herself. He moved with speed despite a visible stiffness, age or arthritis. She had been fingering an empty glass, staring vacantly at the open front door opposite. Don't look at anyone, attract attention. Fastened to the door was a crude pencil drawing of a photograph, Joseph Makken as a young teenager, the same deep-set eyes as on the police identikit. Hooded eyes, said official reports.

As he drew up, lowered himself into the neighbouring chair, his joints clicking, the old man had seemed to pick up an ongoing conversation.

'It looks an accident, it can be explained. We're thrown together, it makes no sense, but it's history. History jumbling us together.'

She gave him the bottle of wine she had brought. He must, she thought, be a family member standing in as host. The wine was a light Cape riesling, carefully chosen, not that plain, not that smart.

He put the bottle on the table in the corner without so much as glancing at it. He had his own bottle. The one he was now again unscrewing. She felt his gaze resting on her.

'Miss, my life's been a long one. I've seen things in this world.' He rasped his throat clear. 'One thing I can say you young ones don't know. Is there anything now straight wasn't once bent? You ask Dora. Think of bones, bones in ditches, chucked in the veld. Who's to say who they belonged to? Black or white? white or brown?'

He stubbed his cigarette butt against the chair leg. The knuckles of his hand were swollen. He extracted and lit another cigarette. Lucky Strike.

A group of five people came through the front door and walked out to the back talking loudly. Two whites, two blacks, the fifth's face shadowed by a beret. Their passing dislodged one of the drawing-pins fastening Joseph's picture and a top corner of the paper flopped over. The picture was drawn on the reverse side of a bright red beer poster, Anthea saw. *Castle. The taste that's come to Life.*

The smell of porridge and humid cupboards steamed from the empty basin at her elbow. That taste saturating Dora's sandwiches, that was it, paraffin and home-made beer. She tried shifting away from the smell, her chair crunching against the old man's. Who took this as a signal. He exhaled into the room, leaned across.

'Yes, miss, what's now whole wasn't once a mess? Think of the hundred feelings that bring us here today. Forces pull us apart, crash us together, pull us again.'

His voice sank to a lulling, even, sing-song. He began to rock, his chin shrunk in and fixed.

'We carry those forces, that confused history, we ourselves. You think of what that means in this country, this cocked-up scrambled country where apartness goes on sitting and squatting in people's brains.'

She had been pinned down by the mad old man of the party, Anthea now perceived. The ancient mariner, compelled to speak. She put her finger-stained glass on the table. The whispering couple had returned indoors, their backs were towards them. A woman, a new arrival, studied the picture of Joseph, her hand leant against the loosened corner. No one likely to rescue her. She took a risk, she interrupted him.

She said, 'But where do we find that history? You said veins, you also said forces. Is history inside or outside us?'

Living up to his role, the old man took this as a cue to continue.

'It's been a long one, my life, miss,' he said. 'I've seen things I wouldn't've believed when I was a small boy in shorts. I've seen milk come in cartons and bread wrapped in plastic. I've seen friends become enemies and children sit in judgment on their parents – here in this township of ours. I've seen the Boer state's arch enemies stroll free as birds down our city streets. The years I've been a pharmacy messenger, riding my two-stroke with the tin box behind, I've seen the suburbs mushroom around this city and the big roads cut open the hills. Big roads that make it easy for vehicles with no number plates to go speeding through the night. I've seen what happens on early morning errands, yes, even now, since our miracle summer. I've seen the half-dead bodies dumped and bleeding in the fields. To attack an unarmed someone at dead of night and then leave them miles from help, that's something deep and complicated. There you've got the start of strange bones. Our ancestors, those Boers' ancestors did it different, with God's sun shining on the hands that held the rifle. I've seen many things.'

He drank, he stubbed out his cigarette.

'Everything's confused, but you see how it fits if you keep an eye open. You ask Dora. We Coloureds more than most, we know history isn't straight, we carry this mixed-up country inside us. Where's our tribe, our language? We claim whatever we can find. Hand-me-downs, off-cuts of this and that, bits of *taal*, other people's words. Unlawful mating as they say, it's in our skin, our names betray it. You haven't asked what I'm called so I'll tell you.'

His hand raised to shake hers, but arrested in mid-air. He bent closer.

'Gertie Maritz, Gert Maritz. A good strong Afrikaner name, or what do you think?' Dropping his voice, pulling back his suspended hand. 'So you see. The Boers our enemies were our friends sometimes, must've been. At dead of night. They warred with us, made love with us, those white Boers that us brown men like Joe Makken fight.'

A man in a crumpled shirt and a shiny polyester tie approached from the back door holding an opened bottle of sherry.

'Ja, John.'

'Gertie.'

Gertie mimed glugging motions and patted his pocket. The other man turned a questioning look on Anthea, swished the bottle. Her fingers had not touched the glass before warm sherry was splashing on her wrist.

'You look worried my friend – ,' Gertie turned to her again.

'Anthea,' she said. She took a mouthful of her drink.

The other man made an unsteady path back to the stoep door.

'Anthea my friend, you look worried, sad even. *Aikona*, try not to be. Keep a bright face. Everything I say will make sense, mark these words. What's blurred will be clear. We're all survivors here, carrying our cocked-up history with us. Like my grandfather, he could tell a story about mixedness. In the big war last century, what people call the Boer War, he worked as an ambulance man. He drove his ox cart between the battlefields and the main hospital camp up north of here. It was a thrown-together untidy place, that hospital, it suited him. He made friends there with a Canadian reporter, he met a troupe of black singers from America who'd got caught in the Boer siege entertaining the township. He went out with one of the girls, she'd been wounded, not seriously. The camp was meant to be neutral, but with that many people around under siege conditions, what's neutral? There were Australians and Indians there on the English side, Irish soldiers and Zulu trackers working on both sides. Years later my oupa heard that the Indian leader Gandhi put in time around there as a stretcher bearer, they must've worked together. Like I say, we try to disguise our past but who can do it? It jumbles us and we keep on going. You ask Dora about her sister Bernice's red hair.'

He wiped the white spittle thickening in the corners of his mouth and was suddenly silent.

Anthea waited. His eyelids drooped, he seemed to be resting. This gave a recess, a moment to look away. Something about the conversation had worked like an induction. She felt less obvious sitting here, letting her gaze begin to shift around the room, along the streaky whitewash, past the primus stove planted on an old Singer machine stand, beside it the food cupboard, its chicken-wire door hasped closed with a bent fork.

Joseph Makken's home ground: this place.

Now she slid her eyes around a big dresser covered in teddy-bear plastic, photo of a man in a panama hat stuck to its side, and into the dark space of the bedroom door, across the darker mound of the bed that bulked there. A white crocheted cover, three scatter-cushions neatly plumped into a pyramid, shadowy photograph portraits on the walls. She looked away again.

The ordinariness of it, this was what defeated and crazed her. This plain ordinariness, the irreproachable human plainness of Joseph Makken's home set out for all to see, its plainness and poverty exposed by its cleanliness. The chipped stove, the plastic-lined dresser, how rubbed they were, how they gleamed! How nakedly the furniture was queued up along the walls, the surfaces so reassuring, solid, clean and plain. So baldly plain. It became offensive to her. Through what process did this plainness become terror?

When shock cracks open an ordinary day?

The elderly man here talked about mixing. Where were those connections that he saw? She thought of a bomb in a sports bag. Two men drinking juice, Duncan wounded, smashed … Crossed paths in that case had meant explosion, merciless destruction, not a moment to run away. There was the sentence the *Times* court reporter yesterday had included in his résumé of the adjourned trial. *Foil-wrapped pik-'n'-mix toffees drifted on a pool of blood.* Duncan's blood. How did that ordinariness of sweets get mingled with terror?

'Confusion's not easy, though, is it, Anthea my friend?'

She stiffened. Gertie Maritz leaned in again. He was nearby, his pupils small and focused.

'It's real but not easy. You're asking yourself, nê, why's he telling me this? what's it about? So I'm telling you now. I'm telling you this because you need to hear it, it'll help. I saw you hanging about at the trial, I was there attending. I recognised you from the papers. You were in the one picture, the photo of the Ferguson funeral. Dora's my good friend, I'm an old friend of the family, so I've been following these things. I've got a scrapbook of cuttings. I see what I see, put two and two together. What I have to say I think you need to hear. You're here to hear it. We're all survivors, the relations of victims, Joe Makken's relations, here we are carrying our cocked-up history with us. In any woven cloth it's useless to look for a thread that hasn't taken the bend of the others. Nothing's whole wasn't once mucked. And vice versa.'

'You keep saying that.' Stunned by cheap sherry Anthea again broke through her caution.

'It's here inside me, that's why, and it's what you want to know. See, with Dora, she talks and doesn't talk, she's kind but tough. You ask something and she'll avoid the question. I can see why. She doesn't want to confuse things for herself, she's committed to Joseph. She wants to see Joe in this one way, a fighter, brave, and whole in heart. And that's what he is. That and more than that. What's ever straightforward, Bernice, hey, in this country?'

A woman in a tight lurex dress hitched a buttock on to the table corner beside Anthea. She was a slightly taller and younger image of Dora. Her hair a little reddish, Anthea checked, could be henna.

'Now ou Gertie,' she said, 'You're not boring the hell out of our guest here please? I've come to ask how she can sit buttonholed by ou Gertie at a strangers' party and still look cool.'

She offered a plate of brown bread sliced warm so that the chunks were sheeny moist at the core. On her arm balanced a bowl of red curried sauce.

'You try this,' Bernice said. 'Dip the bread. It's Dora's lucky meat sauce. She marinades the mutton in apricots and chili, two nights, and it always turns out nice.'

# 18

'Who is that one?' Bernice asks. 'There Dor, the white one in the jeans? Pointy face.'

The window frames the lit-up front room. Dora squints, who is that? The one ou Gertie Maritz is gabbing to? Skimpy body, blondey hair. Ah. Yes.

'Somebody from the trial, Bernice, from the other side. There's a story there I'll tell you.'

She gulps the wine punch Bernice has poured. It tastes of hardly anything, alcohol, easy. Bernice is a miracle-worker, knows what a person needs. She was up till one last night copying that big strong picture of Joseph stuck on the front door.

'Bernice, maybe you can go over some time and cut ou Gertie off?'

But Bernice is shouldering her way through the crowd on the stoep, heaped plates of food in her hands.

Dora drinks again.

Pointy face, said Bernice. Stretched by her strain, Dora thinks, remembers those cords pulled taut in Anthea Hardy's neck. She puts fingers to her own face, the baggy skin around her eyes. A party must be the right thing for her, that Anthea, she decides, take her out of herself, relax that driving will of hers for an evening. And she does deserve some relief, definitely, not missing a day of the trial, the pleading and desperation in her face. It's the best they can do for her, invite her here a few hours, though not so long as to make more demands. Dora's too tired for demands, can't face the effort it would cost, the drag on her, can't face even going over to see the girl now. She'll feel stronger later maybe, but can't face it right now. Longing for Joseph gripping her heart.

She drains her glass, licks the grainy sugar sediment off the rim.

Fancy though, she thinks, the girl coming all that way and then landing herself in a never-ending chat with ou Gertie Maritz. Gertie blabbing as usual, saying God knows what.

Dora pushes this thought away. Perched on a chair out here on the stoep the tape recorder is playing *Radio Juju* syncopated by a persistent squeak. It's the shoebox-size machine she got Joseph for his eighteenth birthday, second-hand, with a flip-up lid. Bought from none other than ou Gertie, a jumble-sale score he fixed up himself but without mending the squeak. That Gertie, a magician with machines and a devil for gossip, finger in every pie. Thinks he knows everything about everyone, and when he's drinking says exactly what that is.

A man pumps her hand. 'Hey Dora, your boy did well, considering.'

And another voice, 'Your Joe, he made us proud. Forget what people say. See how he gave his own speech, like a real leader.'

'So far so good, Dora. Amandla.'

She sits down on the edge of the stoep, cool cracked clay against her thighs. Somewhere beneath the gentle tide of wine that's washing through her arms and legs she can feel she's deeply exhausted, cumbersome with soul-weariness, sad beyond tears. She looks up and sees the Milky Way foaming like fireworks in the clear late autumn sky. A special show for Joey's party, wasted on him. Would he even have a window in there? she wonders. In that top-security section, would they give him a small high window that shows some stars?

People push in and gather round her, say what they have to say, kind pointless words, drift on, let her be. Bernice refills her glass and some time later makes her eat a plate of pap and gravy. Dora stays sitting on the stoep edge, her thighs clammy against the clay. The Milky Way swirls through the darkness.

Beyond the strip of light fanning from the house she sees her John standing astride a Cape apple box in the middle of the yard. He's talking to a woman in black leggings whom she doesn't know. There are so many people at this party she doesn't know, Joseph's friends from school, John and Bernice's friends. Bernice, it looks like, has invited the whole street.

She watches John for a while. So long since she stared at him hard and straight. That familiar sloppy laugh, just the same as when they first went out, to the Malabar Drive-In it was, to see *The African Queen*. And the sherry bottle sloshing in his hand, also just the same. She can tell he's comfortable with this strange woman. His free arm slides lightly around her neck. His hand, moving as he speaks, wants to chafe her breast.

*Brown as a berry, drunk as a lord, happy as Larry.*

How she coached Joseph, over how many years. Learn good speech, Joey, it'll open chances me and your dad never had. Think of my Jane Eyre, she was poor but lived on her learning. Fair can be foul and foul can be fair. Stand up for yourself and be decent. Proverbs are handles to speak with.

She walks over to the zinc laundry tubs at the left end of the stoep. Here in the shadows people will have trouble tracking her down. She can safely gaze into the party crowd and imagine it's Joseph across there, just hidden by a knot of heads. Those there are his hands slicing the air in conversation. Or he's emerging from round the house, like that young man who's now striding up the steps, bending to change the tape.

Juluka, the band run by the white man trying to do Zulu music. Heart-in-the-right-place songs that people like, but Dora prefers real folky tunes. Simon and Garfunkel now, that would be gentle, *Bridge over Troubled Waters.*

At a gathering like this, man but she misses Joseph. Joe at parties is such good company, never less than a good companion. Like when he mimes the pop tunes. He'd mime this make-as-if Zulu tune. He'd wind his lips round the words, pump his elbows, wiggle to the rhythm, all the while pressing beer on people, making sure everyone, his pa, Dora herself, everyone, was doing all right.

But without drink. Partly it's his discipline but also he doesn't need the boost. Since politics became his road the sullenness of his teenage years has lifted like mist. At the big party they had for his eighteenth birthday he hoicked the slouch hat heirloom off its hook on the wall in the front room, put it on with a flourish, Disney-style. Stone cold sober. Then did a jig that was half a Boer two-step and half some sort of mad Scottish reel out here on the stoep. Wearing the hat. Guests gathered round, unsure about clapping, laughing anyhow.

That hat, sticky with kitchen dust. Should have been taken down years ago. 'What are we doing with that thing anyway? A Boer hat?' said Joseph. 'So what if it's in the family?' Before this party today she hid it in the dresser, avoid questions. Too late to please him now.

Joseph in his top-security cell, and such good company at a party. 'Ma, you look tired, let me start collecting bottles. People'll take the hint.' Always watching out for her. Since the arrest friends have said there once was a girlfriend but he never brought anyone home. He looked after his ma, kept her feelings in mind. They said it was someone he visited just three streets away, 'a real chick, with Rasta hair'. But he never said a word about a girl.

And so she told that Anthea Hardy Joseph never slipped her a lie, Dora sighs. She leans her weight against the laundry-tubs. True's true, he didn't, he stayed quiet. A planned silence isn't a lie. To bring your girl to a party and have your mother see you kiss her mouth, touch another woman's breast – no, better stay quiet. *Brown as a berry quiet as a mouse.* Better not say too much about anything in case she worries and lies awake at night. Better to disappear for weeks to keep the family peace. And then come home and dance a jig on your birthday, make the world smile.

Keep quiet, keep the peace, make them smile. *Happy as Larry.* Meanwhile, plan a bomb. All on your own you secure the explosive, set the blade.

Dora feels the chill of the dew in the clay under her bare feet. People are filtering indoors. She pulls upright, supporting herself on the wooden odds-and-ends *kas* standing against the stoep wall, Sam's old chest, she hasn't cleaned it out in years.

'So there you are. Mind your head now.' Bernice stacks dirty plates on the running board of the tubs. 'I've been trying to find you, Dor. I met your white friend. She looks even more worried close up, worried and definitely quizzy.'

'She was still talking to Gertie?'

'She was, or he was talking to her, but she used me as an escape. She said about taxis.'

'She's on her way?'

'I think so. It's late, my sister Dora. Gertie has fallen asleep with a slab of bread in his hand and your sauce dripping on to his good trousers. Your friend said to tell you she was tired. And she liked your sauce.'

'She often says she's tired.'

'John has gone off with God knows who. As usual.'

Dora puts her head against Bernice's shoulder and feels Bernice's arms come round her, cushiony and enveloping.

'God knows, Bernice, God knows, but I can't get used to it. My brain – it can't do it. We have strangers at our party, we've got people talking to strangers about us at our party. And meanwhile our own boy is locked away.'

# 19

Tomorrow the everyday work of daily stories.

Anthea opened her green notebook. The kitchen bulb cast a blobby grey shadow of her folded hands on the white paper.

She read

*When shock cracked open an ordinary day.*
*But from the other side of the story.*

She rested her forehead on the page, against her folded hands. The pressure that had been building up in her temples these past weeks had tonight, on the way home from Dora's party, become almost unbearable, a deep-seated ache she couldn't now lose or forget. It pressed in on her, this sense of being held back from a suspicion, some phantom instinct of possibility.

*What it was that appeared from the other side of the story.*

She thought of going into work on Monday, the walk between the two rows of desks to her own desk, the PC quietly waiting there, and the pressure closed around her forehead like a forcing hand. The daily work of everyday stories, in all other ways welcome, but meantime there was this suspicion, this insistence, close by, here, weighted by the old man's words. A story from the other side. Untidy and pulled but densely woven, ravelling.

*There was this ordinary woman who opened her front door one day unsurprised to find her son named a bomber.*

Unsurprised.

Human ordinariness changed by terror. Terror settling into ordinariness.

History is jumbled, the old man said. You ask Dora. We warred with our enemies, loved them. We carry our cocked-up history inside us.

And *real Black*, Dora spat. Who's born in this country and suffers for their skin and isn't oppressed?

Somewhere within those half-concealing words Anthea felt this suddenly concentrated expectation, the complicated pull and stretch of this new story. A pull against what appeared to be. Somewhere in there was a pattern knotted together by a secret. She felt tears of weariness itch in her eyes.

*Writing the news, bringing it home to people, is what I have a mind to do.*

Now, when there was no time.

'You might think of a feature article.'

Arthur's call before yesterday's party was friendly but carried the force of a order.

'A research-based piece gives a way of getting used to things. You settle back into the nine-to-five schedule without having to go out and find your stories.'

She was summoned. Her generously extended part-time leave could be extended no longer. No longer, despite the adjournment of the trial? Arthur repeated her question as a statement. No, no longer. He must have been delegated to clarify this. The editors were toughening up even if still sympathetic. Yes, Arthur said, people were aware of her attendance at the trial, yes, but whatever came of it – personal reminiscence, reflections on political violence, probably all interesting – what came of it was a matter for her, not the paper. Her story, not theirs.

Dora's not hers, Anthea thought. Or, hers and Dora's.

'You know that, don't you?'

'What's that?'

'The *Times* has its own court reporter present at the trial.'

'Yes.'

She had to sit down to find the strength to continue the conversation.

So why not think about this feature? Arthur reasonably ended. Try to do a history of early magistrates in the province, a tale of local justice. It should dovetail neatly with her personal interests. She could use the Provincial Archives in town, the experience might be eye-opening, they were sitting on loads of untapped material down there. Write an anniversary article with a contemporary edge. It was, did she realise, nearly one hundred and fifty years since British colonial rule was established in the province, locking into place, so it was said, security and justice?

'So it was said,' Arthur repeated, wanting to coax her into laughing with him.

But her attention had drifted.

*Our cocked-up history inside us.*

'Call if you want company getting to the Makkens,' Arthur said. And said goodbye.

Anthea now wrote in her green notebook.

*I was searching for a pattern of events to help think about Duncan's death. I have muddled into something even more complicated, thicker. A difficult story snarled with trespass and concealment.*

*Why the Makkens carry that name.*

*Dora slips into and out of focus. She set distance between us, she made a connection. She invited me to her party, she ignored me there.*

*Our names betray it, Gertie Maritz said, you haven't asked what I'm called.*

*I checked the telephone book. Dora isn't in there. There are no Makkens in it.*

*Dora likes to chat about this and that, here and now. Her son, naturally her son. In spite of what she said about dealing with the general problem, she talks only about the particular. Her background, her history, she hardly touches. The topic the old man doesn't let rest she doesn't touch other than in her songs. In images and riddles he speaks of it, a confounding history, forbidden things. 'What's now whole wasn't once a mess?'*

*Dora's wistful song about a harp in the south.*

Anthea went over to the kettle, tested its weight, filled the plastic jug that stood beside the kettle, filled and switched on the kettle. She traced the cracks in the formica surface of the kitchen unit, the cracks raised and slightly opened by scabs of ingrained dirt.

She walked back to her notebook and tried two more sentences.

*One day an ordinary woman opened her front door unsurprised to meet that face she recognised. The anger that lived in her past had come to visit her again.*

She leant back from the page, her eyes narrowed. Then in front of the word *anger* she inserted *vengeful,* crossed it out. She began again to straighten, held still, bent over the page a second time. She changed *anger* to *danger* and added *strange,* looked at the phrase, scratched it out, and wrote *secret resistance,* small. *The secret resistance that lived in her past had come to visit her again.* Then she closed the book and made tea.

# 20

The defence counsel at the Makken trial, though obtaining the three weeks' adjournment they requested, did not finally secure the clemency of the judge, or so newspapers' editors observed. To respond to the nation's sense that the violence inflicted at Easter had been out of all proportion, to lance the boil of retaliatory expectation that festered in several circles, a crisp efficiency had been demanded of the court. The judge accepted the state's deposition concerning the admissibility of selected testimonials only of the accused's character. The school counsellor's reference pointing to Joseph Makken's habitual recalcitrance – 'a stubbornness and determination even in any small thing discussed' – was pronounced sufficient for the requirements of the case. Mrs Makken's prepared testimony on her son's behalf was ruled out. By eleven o'clock on that Monday morning of the reconvened trial the court withdrew to consider its evidence.

BOMBER GETS LIFE

The three words confronted Anthea as she walked down the shady arcade that led to the gate of the Provincial Archives. It had been another afternoon of research, sifting through the magistrates' files and personal documents of more than a hundred years ago. The headline sheets were thickly clothes-pegged to the door and roof of the news kiosk on the corner.

Can't be. Not this soon.

Her car keys scratching her fingers in her haste to pull them out of her bag.

In the office Arthur Naidoo leaned on his desk with his head planted in his hands, his small transistor turned to full volume. Dan, a sports journalist working late, sat stiffly opposite listening. Looking incomplete and somehow unsteady without her usual rattling trolley the tea-lady Gladys stumbled heavily up the aisle between the desks. Dan reached for her, they grabbed arms. At the far end of the room Robert Meyer and his secretary stood like sentries on either side of his office door, their faces exhausted with shock.

Arthur made space for Anthea to wheel up a chair.

'You'd think – to impose anything so severe, at this unsteady time – '

As the news signal sounded a sub-editor came running down the passage leading from the layout room. He held the headline sheet as if it were a sandwich board, his bare elbows two black eyes of ink. LAST YEAR, JUDGE SAYS, HE'D HAVE HUNG. The sub-editor raised his eyebrows miming a surprised question and glanced from face to face around the room.

Arthur's finger furrowed his lips.

The news reader sounded energetic. He could have been delivering a transport report, an upbeat update. All traffic around the city moving unobstructed.

'Joseph Makken, the accused in the Clacton bombing trial, has been found guilty on all six counts of murder as charged and on a seventh count of endangering the lives of others. The court's opinion was that the prosecution had established a case beyond all reasonable doubt for the deliberate and wilful murder of civilians. Even taking into account the winds of change moving through the country, the majority decision found no extenuating circumstances whatsoever. The court held that there was no factual evidence suggesting that the accused's state of mind might have been influenced in any way such as to reduce his moral blameworthiness. Summing up, the judge stressed that the culpability of the accused was established by his own admission.'

Arthur's palms came down flat on the desk, a smacking noise. The small radio shook and teetered. Anthea stretched to hold it still, Arthur took her hand. 'Culpable with regard to the explosion *only*,' he said. 'This is a throw-back. It was in their power to consider him a prisoner of war.' She felt him shaking.

The newsreader handed over to the station's court correspondent.

'Yes, Barry, what a day of high tension this has been. However the court's findings have really allowed us to expect nothing other than this sentence. From beginning to end, it was felt, the accused's evidence was improbable and his answers to the judge robotic and evasive. For example, he claimed first to want to hit the post office, then to have planned to telephone from it. But there's no evidence he was ever in the vicinity of the post office on the day in question. Passing sentence, the court conceded the continuing existence of troubles in our society that inevitably made an impact on an impressionable young person. However against this background they had to ask why the accused selected a supermarket at 11.10 a.m. in the morning, despite his express desire not to kill. Why not select eight at night, why not four a.m.? The detonator he used left no time to phone a warning. And once he realised a warning was impractical, he made no attempt to go back to disable the explosive. In short, the accused knew the home-made bomb he had put into operation in a crowded arcade on the day before the Easter long weekend would within thirty minutes kill and maim indiscriminately any number of people who happened to be in the area. Old or young, white or black, healthy or infirm.'

'And the upshot, James, is that Joseph Makken gets six life sentences?' the news reader striving to keep a finger on the story.

'Yes, the court was unanimously of that clear view.'

'And the public response? Do people have a sense of justice being done?'

'One thing that people in court have commented on in particular, Barry, is how everyone has acted as it were true to character. The judge, known to be one of the country's most pragmatic, was as to-the-point in his summary as he was in his questions to the accused. As for the victims' families, headed by Mr Andries Cronje seated in the front row, they remained impassive as the sentence was passed. Mrs Darlene Cross the daughter of Glenda Hart, alone appeared as far as I could see to smile and punch the air. The mother of the accused Dora Makken was equally grave and stoical as she has so incredibly been from the beginning of this for her so harrowing trial. Her head was bowed throughout the summing up. She made eye contact with her son only as he rose to present his final statement to the court following sentence.'

One thing he always does, Anthea remembered Dora saying, he warms me up. Some days I think my skin will scald when he comes to stand here against my back.

*If ever I can cut off a piece of flesh of my own and give it to those who remain.*

She felt a dampness on her arm. The tears could have been hers, could have been Arthur's. She rubbed her arm with her free hand. Arthur gripped her more tightly. Her throat hurt with this unexpected suppressed sobbing. Out of the corner of her eye she saw the sub-editor walk down the passage slapping at the wall divider with the flat of his hand. The sheet of headline paper crumpled under his arm.

'Ja, Barry, probably most remarkable was that final statement of Joseph Makken's. Obviously at the present time I cannot give the full details but I can reveal something of the drama I'm sure the entire court felt.'

Without a word Arthur switched abruptly to a coastal music station situated just beyond the state borders. Instead of the official evasion came, so clearly, the careful questioning accent Anthea at once recognised, those flat vowels. She looked up, suddenly dry-eyed.

'My son said,' said Dora Makken, and voices burring around her hushed. 'In his final statement from the dock my son said what he set out to do was strike a blow at the system. I quote. "In this country," he said, "for generations, we blacks and tyrannised cannot make things happen. We have no schools, no houses. The situation happens to us. I tried to help make things happen. The deaths caused were needless but not the action itself. There are hit men out there even now torturing my comrades. I have said I am sorry for the dead and the relatives of the dead. People say my insides are stone but this isn't true. I'm telling it again. I had not the intent to kill. The system is ruthless. Until all race suffering is lifted, we have to go on resisting the system with every day that goes. We will keep focused on that one purpose."'

There was a long pause. They heard a pulsing rush, traffic. Anthea thought of the court steps, the busy street running past, the bare plane trees lining it. Dora in her red blouse, her worn, lined eyes.

'My son says, "Our fight will continue till the empire of Babylon falls utterly."'

A low cry as of pain or jubilation tore from sections of crowd and was as suddenly swallowed.

When silence returned Mr Moodey was speaking.

'A boy intensely sympathetic, serious. All who know him say he helped people. He appears to have acted unlawfully because for him his people don't yet hold power.'

The reporter holding the microphone thought this of insufficient interest. Mr Moodey receded, a robust voice welled to the foreground, the senior state prosecutor.

'Culpability established by his own admission. Justice has after all been done.'

Arthur's grip on Anthea's hand now slackened. He looked at her with his thumb on the transistor off-switch, she nodded. The burning spot of the late sun was scorching concentric silver rings into the office windows. Arthur's face blazed with the radiance. Gladys had vanished, Dan began to pack up his things. Robert's door clicked shut and his secretary hurried past, her bag over her shoulder, a tissue pressed to her temples in a way that hid her eyes.

'Come for a drink,' said Arthur. 'I can't think what else to do. We could try one of those international bars on the Parade.'

Anthea opened her mouth and no sound came. The hurt in her throat, that same dry hurt as when Duncan … She swallowed hard, tried again.

'I want to, Arthur, but not today. Do you mind?'

He paused before saying, 'No. No, I'd understand.' He rolled the volume button on the silent radio. 'I'd like to talk to you some time though. About the trial, your thoughts. I wasn't very supportive of you at the time I don't think. We needed you back here. But God, you sat through it. I mean, you made it, you survived, through your grieving. I'd like to hear what you think now. It still can't be easy for you.'

Anthea stood up.

Arthur said, 'I go on thinking this was probably a justified act and a justified trial, but one that has turned into a totally predictable tragedy. Greater leniency would have been an act of such courage, a symbol of new trust.'

Anthea cupped her hand to the side of her face to block the sunlight.

'The situation's gone wider than that for me now,' she said. 'Maybe Joseph Makken's in fact lucky that the death penalty's under review. But I dare say I can't look at this thing as an isolated incident any longer, as one life sentence or a single bomb. There's more to it, a vast network of mixed-up causes and effects. As far as I can see I've hardly begun to understand it. Though it helps me generally, trying to.'

'Yes, I see that. Naturally the event must be seen in the broader context. A violent and unjust state breeds a violent society even years after it has itself died.'

'But possibly even broader than that, Arthur.' She put her red notebook on top of the green notebook in her briefcase. 'To me it looks more complicated, how can I say, not one situation of conflict only but something layered and knotty, almost patterned, *as if* destined? More so than I could've imagined. The past coming back to haunt us, sort of.'

She looked back from the door, gave an uncertain wave. He was still sitting, holding the transistor between his long palms, a man blessing.

There were two phone booths across the road from the newspaper offices. Two men with their hands in their jacket pockets stood waiting for the single phone in use. The other booth was vandalised, the phone unit levered away from the wall baring a thick bundle of green and blue wires. A young woman Anthea recognised as an office cleaner chatted noiselessly in her booth. The men shuffled. Anthea stepped in behind them. A Niknaks Bumper Bag wrapping blew across the pavement and flattened itself against the booth.

She had to speak to Dora. This was all she could think – speak to Dora. Say what? She didn't know. The killer to be given life, to give up his life, yes of course. Dora was the first to say it. He'll likely be badly hurt, she said. It had been a time of terror, of terror breeding terror; a bomb would have its retribution, as Dora knew. As the severe and unsmiling Andries Cronje knew. Justice is still white justice.

But even so the shock jammed Anthea's throat.

And gentle Duncan? Duncan who, avoiding all aggression, all intensity, had disappeared from her life for ever on the day of the bomb. What of him? Duncan? What of the ghostly voice that had now sheltered itself so familiarly in the back of her mind?

So he sits, she imagined Duncan saying, spreading open his soft, lightly freckled palms, So he sits for life. When last did any such penalty heal a conflict?

She had to speak to Dora, Dora large-breasted in the red hound's-tooth blouse, getting into her lawyer's car even now, leaving the court buildings behind her for good.

The woman in the phone booth hung up, the first man took her place. Anthea shifted forwards. She thought of that calculatedly long distance between the court buildings and the townships. She had time, time enough to let Dora know, well, only, It's me, calling to say I'm calling.

On the limited strength of what we've exchanged.

I wanted to say, How right you were. No, more than that. What I wanted to say was this, I wanted to say, Your sorrow, Dora Makken, has become my sorrow, our sorrow. I remember the first days after Duncan's death, after the bomb, that terrifying silent chill of my grief, and I think of you. Despite everything that might divide us, I think of you.

The sentence has come upon me as a great weight and I'm surprised at myself.

Calling to say I'm calling.

The two men did not take long. They spoke greetings, arrangements. The mouthpiece felt warm in Anthea's hand. She riffled through the buckled phone book, then jerked upright at her own oversight. *I checked the telephone book. There are no Makkens in it.* She flipped on to Moodey, ten Moodey numbers. David Moodey, was it? No, Daniel Moodey, the lawyer. The number rang four times, went dead, a disconnected phone.

She leaned against the booth door to open it. An early headline sheet – DROUGHT TOLL RISES – flattened itself against her legs. How could she get to Dora? Let her know, It's me. She felt in her handbag for the envelope with Dora's house number written on it, that bulge of the squeaker button. And so say all of us. She tightened her hand around the envelope choking the tune dead.

She walked the block to the taxi rank beside the city hall. Flowersellers were sluicing the pavement with the water left in their flower buckets. Dead carnations and chrysanthemums had been dumped on the canna-lily beds garlanding Queen Victoria's statue. Victoria scowled obesely at the pale-green evening sky. There were no taxis. Anthea waited. A mini-bus drew up, passengers pressed against the windows. As if by arrangement room was made for two flowersellers. There was no talk.

People everywhere will have heard the news by now, Anthea considered. Which meant a white woman in the townships wouldn't be welcome. She waited another half-hour. The last of the flowersellers walked off in a tight group, their scarved heads bowed like mourners. It grew dark and the wind freshened. There were no more taxis. It was as if the city had emptied itself, blacks leaving in their sorrow, whites out of fear. She walked back to the office car park, thought better of it and made again for the telephones.

'Yes. I'd like to send a postal telegram.'

'Address, madam?'

She pulled out the envelope. *For he's a jolly good fellow, And so say all of us.*

'The Coloured township, madam. And your message?'

'Your sorrow is our sorrow. New line. The harp shall sound sweet, sweet, at length. Anthea.'

'I will repeat, madam. "Your sorrow is our sorrow. The harp shall sound sweet, sweet, at length. That's two times sweet. A-N-T-H-E-A.".'

'And two separate lines.'

'Got that, madam. Fourteen words. Will you be paying by credit card?'

# 21

*Memoirs: Upon Retirement*

G.A. Ashworth
Senior Native Commissioner
Natal Province

[Stamped Provincial Archives Jan. 1920]

But to what end our efforts at upliftment and civilisation? This question, after 45 years and 7 months of government service, I remain unable to answer. Yet I begin this last portion of my memoirs with it, as upliftment was the primary objective towards which our energies were tirelessly bent throughout many wearying duties: encouraging the Natives to abandon their old habits of lazy indiscipline and to adopt our own approach to life. I will say in fact that it was not only the frustration arising from the few opportunities for advancement in government service, as I have already described, but the more general realisation of the futility of the work, that has made me now look forward with keen anticipation to my early retirement.

I might write at length about the red tape which has hampered me, as well as the Native backwardness which has, with predictable regularity, thrown obstacles in my path.

And yet memoirs are intended to divert one's descendants. I will summarise no further than this therefore. Throughout, my greatest distress has lain in the Natives' destructive disregard for all that one has done for them. When, some eighteen years ago, not very long after the formal end to the war, I assumed duty in the hilly district of northern Natal, for example, I began to implement as soon as possible the new colonial government's policy of reclaiming eroded land by fencing and tree-planting. And yet no sooner did the saplings grow to mature height than the local people cut them down for firewood, while the fence posts were removed almost as soon as fixed, for the same purpose.

Related to this in degree of frustration, without question the most demoralising aspect of the work, was the length of time one spent on the bench in one's capacity as Magistrate trying civil actions. Oh the endless repetitiveness and pettiness of this duty! The Regulations stipulate that any claim, however trivial, can be brought to Court, and, as the Native simply revels in litigation, these cases took up a vast number of one's days – days that one felt could so profitably have been spent otherwise. For instance, only last year I had before me a claim for £3, the value of 15 cooking pots which were 'despoiled by the defendant'. Both litigant and defendant were young women who fell to raging and shrieking at each other across the court room. Another claim before me involved a dispute over Native bride price which dated back to 1887. The extreme infirmity of the witnesses in this case meant that evidence had to be taken on commission, a mind-wearying and largely futile process.

There have been many other such frivolous cases, such as, again, one of the first I remember trying, brought by a young girl's parents against the man who they claimed had tampered with her against her will. It was a serious charge, but one can never take these tales at face-value. The claim in question eventually turned into one of spirit possession, for, after many inscrutable silences and refusals to name the accused, the litigants at last suggested that the girl might have 'seen' and 'felt' something rather than had an experience in reality. The accused was perhaps of a different world entirely, a devil or ghost, and resembled, so it was preposterously said, a man of a different race in appearance, an Indian or European. Thus rendered not only useless but suspect, the claim was thrown out, but not before any number of doubtless bogus witnesses had been gathered, and forms filled in. So days can go by dealing with this stuff, and meanwhile there is so much else that should be done for the benefit of Native people in order to train them to adopt our European code of diligent reason and civility. It was many years ago already when I first began to feel that the job was not worth the candle. I would be very glad when the time came, as it now at last has, for me to stop.

Belltane Farm
Vryheid District, Natal
July 1919

# 22

Anthea saw the skinny arthritic fingers bunched around a lit cigarette stub. She knew she recognised that hand, the green-and-yellow eyes, the half-jack bottle poking from a torn coat-pocket. She looked hard as the man edged crab-wise, his cigarette hand leading, across the grey carpet of the *Natal Times* reception room. The stewed smell of brandy reached her and she heard again his words, *our cocked-up history inside us.*

'It's an old Coloured man who won't give his name, Miss Hardy,' the receptionist's discreet telephone whisper. 'Doesn't look so right in the head. Be careful now.'

The sight of him took her breath.

Throughout that week following the sentence, images of the trial, single sharp images, had densely overlaid her thoughts. She saw the courtroom fan turning and rocking as it turned. She saw Dora's bag clamped in her lap, Joseph Makken's strained knuckles. It was as if the dead weight of her sadness could not shift these images. She went in to work as usual: she dealt with the morning's local stories. She spent the afternoon in the brown shadows of the Archives reading the magistrates' reports and journals from around the turn of the century. When justice was locked into place. She went at everything slowly; her walk was slow; she slotted coins into parking meters slowly, trying not to fumble. She went to bed before nine.

Duncan's cactus stood on the kitchen table. She switched it to the bedside table at night, to stand beside her glass of water, the dusty book of Yeats's letters, unopened since before the news of Duncan's death, a wallet folder of archive photocopies. Twice this week she had been for a drink with Arthur, Wednesday, Thursday, an hour each time. He had peach juice, she had a bottle of Castle. The second time he introduced her afterwards to the Ajmeri tea-room, 'cooks the greasiest bunny-chows in town'. They hadn't mentioned the trial. They had talked about family holidays, hers. The collapsed tents, the sunstroke. He said lightly his parents couldn't afford such luxuries. Living in a seaside city 'with this level of cuisine' was holiday enough.

But throughout their conversation, throughout the week, she was aware of the weight hanging heavy on her movements, her legs, her lips. She was aware of the drag of her hand across the pages of her notes.

The depression she knew was not about any particular loss – Duncan, the bomb dead. Or the other loss she could at last accept as a simple fact. The death of her idealism about violent opposition to a state of injustice. The accumulation of her weariness and sorrow had rather now been tamped down, impacted, by the news of the sentence – by the hopeless predictability of it, its smallness, at the very time when political leaders, poets, people on the street, were making gigantic gestures of hope. 'The new ketchup defeated me,' a Robben Island veteran had joked in a newspaper interview. 'That you can now squeeze the ketchup out, not have to shake and glug it, that's amazing.' After a twenty-five-year sentence a man spoke with this lightness, but a judge, as if without thinking, must make an uncompromising example of Joseph's act. And that meant danger, the trial swinging round once more the deathly cycle of retaliation and sorrowing, of mourning calling out further mourning, and weeping weeping.

Unless, no. Unless people ignored the old cycle, looked elsewhere. Unless a different script was possible, and not only among leaders and parties, but one to one. A different script *must* be possible. Each night before bed that week Anthea stood at her kitchen table with her green notebook lying in front of her, which remained closed. Unless. Unless there was a different pattern of connection; a web, not a cycle. A ravelling web, a thicker story, bigger pictures.

She saw Dora in the park put back her shoulders to sing the nursery songs she remembered from times when Joseph practised his speeches, the songs about harps in the south and paths of no return. She heard Joseph's words. *The situation happens to us. I tried to make things happen.* There was a hint there too, sharpening this new expectation.

Anthea repeated the statement to herself hearing Dora's faithful quoting. *Make things happen.* Make things happen by understanding otherwise. Throw a new pattern like a diviner scattering bones.

*Our cocked-up history inside us.*

His voice so close to her thoughts that the appearance of Gertie Maritz across the grey carpet in the reception room fazed her for the entire time it took him to approach.

And he looked different. She remembered him from Dora's party as wiry and animated, less creeping. And his eyes, under the bright bulb they hadn't then looked speckled. Pale green eyes, dark speckles, the pupil just a darker speckle than the rest.

Staring past her he took off his hat. He fingered what seemed to be the bottle in his coat pocket, but then produced a letter on filmy pink paper, held it out. Anthea supported her suddenly watery right wrist in her left hand and took it.

Dora's elongated up-and-down characters, big copperplate capitals, the writing on the envelope in her bag.

She sat down to read, Gertie stood over her.

16 July
Wentworth

Dear Anthea Hardy

I write to thank you kindly for your thoughtful telegram which reached me some days late. I am away from home, staying at a friend of a friend's house to escape unwanted newspaper attention. My sister is with me and a great strength.

I cannot say if we will have a chance ever to meet again but I do want you to know that I will remember you all my life for having been with me that time in the park when we had lunch and biscuits. You heard the testimony that the judge did not let me give.

These have been hard days for us all. Please know I include you when I say this. Our lawyer Mr Moodey hopes to present an appeal. I have doubts this will make any difference. Joseph is a good brave son.

I trust that our Gertie Maritz will deliver this to you in good order. You will remember him from Joseph's party. He seemed to know the newspaper was where you worked.

Yours sincerely
Dora Makken

Gertie stared at the first-page facsimile poster on the blue wall opposite. *3rd September 1945*

Dora gives, withholds. Anthea folded the letter along Dora's creases. Offers a finger, pulls back her hand.

'I'm not stopping,' Gertie said after a silence. 'I promised Dora not. Last time I said too much. It was the drink. She doesn't want me blabbing to every next person. I'm an old family friend that she relies on.'

Gives, withholds. Sends out Gertie, shuts him up.

But now an unexpected cunning tensed inside her. She glanced at her watch: there was time. She stood up feeling suddenly more cheerful, her movements quick and precise. Only set him talking, open a bottle, lend an ear. As soon as his voice absorbed him, shouldn't the rest follow? She'd clear the path, he'd drop his crumbs.

There'd be a way back to Dora in what he'd say, back to the complicated past he shared with her.

'I take an early lunch today. Do you mind if I walk out with you?'

'Miss, Dora wants me not to speak. Let that be understood.'

He put his hand into his pocket, he placed his feet close together.

'And think how it looks, you walking with me. A professional white woman, and me.'

'I'm a journalist,' Anthea smiled, 'I'm seen bothering all kinds of people for stories.'

She walked ahead. At the glass double-doors she waited. His halting shuffle coming up behind.

'We could have a *dop* together as we go. Since my boyfriend's accident I never go without a small bottle of some hard stuff in my case here.'

A lie. Take the risk.

'No true?' His narrowed gaze sliced the side of her face. 'Only those people in positions like yours can get up to those tricks.'

They stepped outside. There was a chilly wind cutting in from the sea. He tightened his scarf and doubled his coat across his chest.

'I'll tell you a secret though.' They began to walk. 'In my days as a pharmacy messenger I always kept a brandy bottle in my delivery box. Handy for emergencies. You never can tell with emergencies, they burst in.'

He chuckled humourlessly into his scarf. She fitted her steps to his slantwise gait, hooked her arms over her briefcase, hugged it to her. She steered them across the road past the telephone booths, the vandalised unit still dangling, around the block to the city hall, the benches flanking Queen Victoria.

'No thanks to the city planners for facing these seats towards the lady,' he sat down.

'She's not to your liking?'

'She's too big. She's in my view, gets into my sun. In real life she was a little lady, I know that.'

'You sometimes come here?'

As Gertie drew out his bottle Anthea placed her briefcase upright between her legs.

'Us retired folk meet on these benches. Now and then the police say to move on but not often. We don't bother anyone, it's too public here for whites, especially since the changes. See over there's one of my mates. I've got company so he's pretending not to greet.'

Anthea scanned around the statue, its yellow-stained pedestal and grassy circle. A wild-haired man cloaked in a sack was pacing the path between the canna-lily beds.

Gertie waited for her to produce her own bottle. She felt his watching, his interest. She fiddled with the catches on her brief case, she adjusted her collar. The cold wind. She motioned for him to go on. He took another look at her briefcase, then unscrewed his bottle.

'I'll tell you something about my mate over there you won't believe.' Gertie swallowed hard, then blew out sharply, shivering his lips. 'My mate there served in the big war against the Germans, in the desert up north. Carrying a message one night he got so close to the enemy lines he heard them talk. After that cannon fire knocked out his hearing. But has he ever been compensated? No never. Who'd have expected otherwise?'

He glanced at her fussing hands, then raised his bottle a second time.

'Man, in the winter the first dop of the day tastes even better than usual.'

She sat straight-backed. The tightness in her neck felt close to snapping.

'There's another mate I sometimes see here,' he said. 'Lurchy's his name. He was a POW in that same war. Up there in the old world, Italy, they had separate POW camps for the whites and the non-whites, surprise surprise. Nothing changes in this cocked-up warring world of ours. Joe Makken tried saying he was a POW and where'd it get him? But, *aikona*, there I go again. There you go talking rubbish, Dora'd say if she heard me.'

'But it's not rubbish, Mr Gertie. At Dora's party you told me what you say's real life stuff even if it's not easy. You said you were telling me things because I needed to hear them.'

'I was telling you rubbish,' he said sombrely. 'Ask Dora.'

'But I can't ask Dora. She's not around for me to ask and if she was she wouldn't say. And still what you tell me's important. Like what you said about everyone in this society being bound together somehow. You yourself keep saying that.'

'Miss Anthea, I also keep saying Dora wants me not to speak. Maybe we're all scrambled together but it's important at the same time to keep our history here inside, to ourselves. Dora's right when she says that. She was cross when I talked to you. I was hanging out our community life for all to stare at, she said. She's always cross when I drink. Her man's a drinker but he knows how, he keeps quiet, doesn't get in her way. Where people haven't had rights for all their history it's OK for them to protect the past. It's OK for them to choose to leave what's happened well alone. I told you too much.'

'You told me very little actually. Nothing but hints to get me thinking and guessing.'

He drew his lips in, pressed them tight.

Anthea leaned down. Now was the moment for the briefcase at last to be genuinely opened, the file to be slipped out. Lying on top of her notebooks and loose papers, *Reports of the Native Commission*. She snapped the case shut.

'Seeing as we are talking after a fashion, maybe you'd like a look at this. It's something I found not so long ago doing work for the newspaper. It reminded me of what you were saying at Dora's.'

Gertie faced forwards. Victoria's bulky petticoats.

'See, these are records of cases brought before Native Commissioners around the time of that Boer siege you mentioned, where your grandfather was present. There are reports of lobola disputes, quarrels over cattle, cooking pots.'

Anthea extracted photocopies from the file at random.

'Here, closer to our mark, is a compensation claim against property damage by shell fire. Also some pass infringements, incredibly, even during a siege.'

One by one she drew out the papers, posted them back in, tempting his curiosity. Gertie studied Victoria's shape.

'What especially interested me in regard to what you said was this. This report here. A case brought against a Captain Everett of Winterton by a woman who must have been black, as these are native reports, but her name is written as Sara Belle. She might've been one of those American singers you mentioned. Towards nightfall on 31st December 1899 Captain Everett is alleged to have approached this Sara Belle in the main street. You see here. With suspicious intent. A sister from the local convent vouched for the woman's moral rectitude.'

Tracing a finger along the neatly typewritten line.

'Like bride price disputes, cross-race misdemeanours are commonplace in these reports, also during the war. Here's another. The defendant in this case eventually pleaded spirit possession.'

Gertie knocked the ignored paper as he raised his bottle. His friend squinted at them round the edge of his rough cowl and Gertie waved. The man retreated into his hood, slid round behind the statue.

'So you see how right you were.' Speaking lamely in spite of her earlier energy, the courage of her scheme. 'It wasn't just a white man's situation. The Afrikaners' war was a black people's war too.'

'And so it is always, Miss Hardy, as I told you before. But I'm saying no more because I've promised Dora. You stop pushing me now. If I was you I'd take those reports back to your office and keep them there. Do with them what you were first going to. Nothing that's now mucked wasn't once mucked. If you're doing this paperwork to understand us better, approach Dora's family in some way, she won't let it happen, be warned.'

'You could look at it like this.' Anthea dropped the file into the case and clicked the catches shut. 'There's nothing to lose by pushing. There's no embargo on working through the Provincial Archives chasing my hints and guesses. Whatever I do it's not likely Dora and I'll meet again that easily. But if we do I may have something to show her. Stories from the past that share echoes with her own.'

Was it the right moment to let her eyes rest on the bottle placed on the ground beside him? She held out her hand. Please.

As if he had been waiting for this his arthritic fingers glided smoothly down and back.

The harsh burn of cheap brandy. She had to gasp. She sensed the intensifying of his speckled stare.

'My friend Miss Hardy, I've seen many things, but I've never seen such – such firmness as Dora's. Dora Makken won't meddle with what's done with. The Makkens don't like to deal with that stuff, and fair enough. The present holds enough suffering. She's had enough of trials and wars in her own lifetime. As for Joseph Makken, he once had a story that an ancestor of theirs, some great induna, fought the British in the Zulu War. It wasn't true of course, he was making it up, but that ancestor was a symbol for him, a banner he could fight under. And fair enough.'

Anthea heard his voice fall into the sing-song she'd been aiming for. Yes, *please*. Almost laughing in nervous relief she jammed her hands between her thighs, an arrested clap. He shook a cigarette out of the packet he carried in his breast pocket, Lucky Strike. Then he took a long pull from his bottle and handed it back to her.

'What Joseph really needed to do – I'm speaking as an old man now, I've seen many things. What he needed to do was look a generation further down, closer to us, to find a real-life big ancestor. There's a whole different scene there, one he wouldn't have wanted to touch. But wait my friend, I can feel the twitch in your fingers. I saw that paper in your journalist's briefcase begging to be filled. I'm saying no more than this. Then you'll take your case and leave me and go back to your office. We're painfully thrown together. You've also been hurt by this mad jumbled system that goes on jumbling and mucking us, and so I'll say this, no more than this. Remember, the past's inside us but we can do new things with it. Dora must know that, Joseph too.'

Pressing his clawed right hand against the back of the concrete bench Gertie pushed himself upright. He took his bottle, then held still, panting lightly, his extended arm propped. His skinny brown arm was an inch from her left ear, forcing her down. Touching her nowhere yet pushing her down. His stare grasping hers.

'And why do I say that? I say that because Dora Makken's father Sam was a Boer War baby, born during the war. His father was a decorated soldier from overseas, a white man. It was a mixing, something like what your reports there say. I know this because Sam once told me, when we were first mates together, often drunk. If he passed it to Dora, I've no idea, it's not a story that's easy to tell. This soldier you see, Sam's father, he followed the war, soldiers do, and we know nothing more of him, not even exactly what nation he went home to. But this much is known. It's more than anything your reports will teach and it's all I'll say. Another reason why Dora Makken resents the past. Now head off and never tell her I told you this. Sam Makken's father, Dora's oupa, fought in the war on the other side, the black-hating side, with the Boers. It was there, in the Afrikaner trenches, where the family tradition of sabotage began.'

## 23

*A letter written on good vellum paper, watermarked Bewley and Draper's, Dublin, is folded inside the front cover of a journal. The journal is stamped* Provincial Archives.

Izinyanga Stationary Hospital
Saturday March 3 1900

My very dear Aunt

How long it has been since my January letters! How many times I have tried in vain to send but one or two lines assuring you I remain well in body and certainly determined despite the dejected exhaustion last described. Wounds and diseases how-ever are no respecters of war or its fortunes. The past week has given many people reason to rejoice, yet our hospital work has been if anything more consuming, especially since a violent form of dysentery closed its grip on the camp.

Yes, three days ago the siege was lifted. Since then celebratory fireworks have not ceased to explode every night in the streets. You will doubtless have heard the news almost as soon as we did, for the besieged town has widely been seen as the keystone of Republican resistance. Queen Victoria herself telegrammed congratulations to us all.

The first sign of relief (if so it can be called) was the unmis-takeable presence of movement in the suffocating stillness of the land round about. Retreat, retreat! the cry came from the direction of the big gun's hill. And sure enough when I climbed the railway bridge, our lookout point, they were clearly visible. Across the still hot hills where for so many weeks they had lain unseen, the Boers in dark clusters were riding away to the north, moving with extraordinary speed. It was like an accelerated but utterly silent great trek, these stalwart commandos still looking powerful and free, or at least freely escaping, even in defeat.

As I gazed I almost felt the tears come. In the clear light the Afrikaners seemed so close, as if by walking rapidly in their direction I might easily join them, gaze at last into the stern ruddy faces of the men and of the women who have fought so fiercely at their side. I was not in any sense as moved when about five hours later, after a thunderstorm, two tired-looking squadrons of British infantry came splashing down the road that runs by the steaming manure heap that is our camp, and passed into the valley beyond with the fading light.

And yet it would have been difficult to ignore the electrical transport of relief running through the liberated town. Off-duty I was able to join the throngs bristling with Kodaks cheering on the pavements. For a few hours creed and colour were forgotten as Zulu scouts shook hands with English officers, and gaunt and convalescent garrison soldiers embraced their battle-worn fellows. Irish and German civilians, Imperial Light Horsemen, cattle-rustlers, nuns, storekeepers, any number of people, smiled and laughed together. Mr Singh, the coolie dhobi whose job it was to ring a bell and warn the town of oncoming bombs, was carried about on shoulders. There were guided tours to the bomb-shelters dug into the banks of the river. The now nearly world-famous hotelier Mr Grover distributed, in fun, platters of siege-fare, cubed and very dry horse-steak, going cheap.

Friday March 16th 1900

Dear Aunt, there I broke off, called to the sick bed of an elderly Italian lady from the town. She had been subsisting for some weeks on puddings made of violet face powder and green peaches. She has I am glad to say recovered. But is one of the few.

Two weeks on and a dreadful lot of sickness still surrounds us. For the rows upon rows of broken-down men we can do so little – little more than offer phenaticin and fan the coagulating black flies from their poor faces. The cartloads of the dead we transport to nearby battlefields where trenches not yet filled with fatalities are used as mass graves.

There is little opportunity for reflection yet thoughts on this war continue to wring my mind. Truth to tell, I have been so very involved with these thoughts that sleep, even when I do lie down, is elusive. At times it is the faces of the wounded distorted by their pain, I cannot forget these faces. At other times it is the smells, the oozing fluids of the dying, I feel that stickiness between my fingers.

I find some relief walking through the camp in the cool of midnight but dread to think this may draw comment. A doctor has prescribed chloroform, a few drops each evening. At least it blots my memory with short snatches of dreamless sleep.

My last letters expressed (ill-advisedly as you'll hear) a growing sympathy for the Boers alongside questions about force as a means to withstand force. However having now seen more of the progress of the war, my doubts, I can say with certainty, have been utterly vanquished.

What has been cruelly and improperly wrenched away can only be won back with aggression – with aggression and cunning. This I have now accepted, tho' with pain. Even considering the unequal spread of men and arms that marks this war, retaliation is required of the downtrodden, the inequality itself demands it. The English understand no other language but that of the sword and the gun. As regards our situation here, it is already noteworthy that the generals are asking questions about their ineptitude over so many months at breaking the Boer siege.

If you see fit to use these lines at an Irish Transvaal Committee meeting I would not object. I am no nationalist Brigader, yet reports from the front line help varnish a speech or sauce a resolution, as we know.

Their upper hand restored, there is no level to which the new victors do not stoop. Every day this week displaced farm folk, white and black, have crept into the camp, petrified at reports of house-burnings and evictions across the land. These are no mere rumours. A family arrived from over the Free State mountains three days ago. The last they had seen of their farm was a column of smoke against the evening sky, and a group of British soldiers driving their cattle before them.

There was also the poignant tale brought by a young African-looking woman bizarrely attired in a Boer hat and leather breeches who stumbled through our gates yesterday. She had walked for two days and nights from a farm in the Dundee district, in fear of her life and that of the child she says she is carrying. Severely dehydrated, she crept blindly into the bed we made her and woke late this morning, still croaky and somewhat distracted.

It appears that an advance guard of British troops battered their way into the homestead where she worked. The soldiers, she said in surprisingly good sing-song English, spent several hours pitching the household effects into the yard and carting off candlesticks and metal plate.

The scene she described inevitably reminded me of the evictions inflicted upon our own people in the West. Those magic lantern slides beamed on to the outdoor screen as part of the December protests. The old mother on a blanket on the ground. The family bed and the kitchen dresser standing in the rain.

The soldiers in this girl's case tried torching the place as well as looting, so she was considerably frightened. She was thinking of the child, 'the small soldier' she curiously says. She feared the British would discover the farm had been supplying Boer troops with food since their invasion in the spring.

And not only this. On certain nights her baas had given accommodation to soldiers on the Boer side, foreign soldiers with a song in their voice, she said. I knew at once she meant Irishmen, Brigaders. And one Brigader in particular, whose speech she has mimicked, whose name she now says she bears, this African woman. Talking here in my tent an hour ago she called herself 'Dollie Macken'.

And her *man*, I asked carefully, using the Boer word for husband, what of him? Had he escaped north? was he safe? He's a hero, she said curtly, of course he was safe. He'd ridden away into the hills with the retreating Boers but he'd fight his way back, smiling, to her. There was the happy smile he tossed over his shoulder, most brightly so when mounting his horse to ride into battle. She says she kept his smile 'tight' in her mind as she journeyed over battlefields still soft with the dead. And yes, of course he was safe, she repeated.

A piece of good news I can report is that the orphaned baby who slept beside me a month ago was sent out to nurse in a nearby Zulu village and is thriving. On depressed afternoons I have gone over to see him. The people receive me impassively but with goodwill.

The Belfast nurse Brid O'Donnell heard recently that, due to the vigilance of the censor, our January letters may well have been held up by the war office in Durban – this despite their heroic transportation in the black of night by native runners. If this is so – and indeed my words were rarely impartial – the letters will I trust eventually be returned to us. I intend to save them, and if the situation continues this letter also, as a record to show you once I am home. The Red Cross say, to my relief, that they keep volunteers' families informed of how their loved ones are faring.

I have loaned 'Dollie Macken' the wooden chest, your present, as well as a few pieces of my clothing. Please do not mind this. She arrived here with nothing. She plans to fill the chest with knitted goods for her baby.

Yours, with a full heart
Kathleen

# 24

'Joey.'

'Ma.'

'My Joey.'

'Ma, you look well. In the circumstance you look well.'

'We put on a strong face for you, Joey, at home. You know that. Me and Bernice, and John.'

'You were there in court, ma, every day.'

His fingertips pressed against where hers show white through the thick glass barrier. The bakelite phone he's using thinning his voice.

'Of course. Like I said before, Bernice was sorry but she couldn't come.'

'Ma, it's for me to be sorry. Sorry and at the same time happy I can pay even with my own life and flesh, ma. Pay to our final victory.'

'Yes Joey.'

'Try not to be sad for what's happened, ma. If you can think – think there are many things we must still sing for. We must go on singing until our people in Egypt all are free. All those songs we used to sing, I sing them in my cell.'

'Yes Joey.'

There is silence. He chews his lip. His bottom lip is a chain of purple sores moulded by this chewing.

'So it's maximum-security now. Up north. They must keep me safe.'

The fidgety prison officer sitting beside the reinforced door touches his uniform cuff to his sweaty forehead.

'It'll be harder for you to travel.'

'It'll be harder.'

'Friends can lend you money?'

'Maybe so, Joey. Bernice will I know.'

She presses her fingers so hard against his that her veins quiver across her bones.

'Anyway. Did I say I've got a new job?'

'Ironing again?'

'As well as. You'll like this. It's the hat counter at JH Dark's in the centre of town. They give these jobs to us brown blacks now. Two weeks already it's been. OK, so it's not my library assistant dream, but it's decent – decent pay. They thought your ma was respectable enough to sell hats at fancy prices to housewives off to church.'

'And when haven't you put on a good show, ma, all my life?'

'I wore a dress of Bernice's to the interview, off-white, hair combed down. Hoping they won't recognise me. And so far so good. The manager's from Poland, maybe she doesn't follow the news.'

'They pay OK?'

'We survive, hey Joey, in this cowered existence we lead. I forgot to say, we had a party for you when we were still in party mood, start of the adjournment. Masses came, half I didn't know, comrades of yours, Bernice's friends. John as usual found a special friend. There was even a white girl there, she knew Duncan Ferguson. You know, Duncan Ferguson.'

She waits a long second.

'I know, ma.'

When he nods, his face, twisted by the reinforced glass, seems to wobble.

'You say she came to the house?'

'She came, I let her come. She's working something out for herself. It was a party for you Joey, and we missed you. I missed you so badly.'

'Ma.'

'Ja.'

'Ma, I can't say … I'm sorry – I'm sorry this has been sore for you.'

He wipes his sweaty palms down the front of his khaki uniform, a familiar gesture. Then he puts his hands back up to hers. Holding back these tears binds a scarf of cramp around her neck. He presses his fingers more firmly against the glass, condensation haloes from his fingers.

'We support you, Joey, always. We must be proud of you.'

'Half-proud, ma. Those people, I didn't want to target them.'

'Time's nearly up now, Mrs Makken. Please say your goodbyes.'

It is as if a shutter drops across Joseph's face. His eyes grow glassy, almost sleepy. He pulls back.

'OK ma. Hamba kahle. Go well. And to Bernice and everyone, go well.'

'Proud, Joseph, proud.'

'Ma.'

'We're always thinking of you.'

'Ma, not proud until triumphant. Not fully proud.'

'Bye-bye, Joey. Bye-bye now.'

She can't bear it, it's not possible, she can't do it. But she goes on walking, evenly, steadily, a decent upstanding woman always, one foot in front of the other, through the reinforced steel door, and then another, along a narrow corridor ending in a double grille door, and then more corridors, first painted concrete, then tiled, then parqueted, one-two, one-two, *brown as a berry, proud as a peacock, ber-ry, pea-cock,* one-two, one-two. Until it's the open air and the brown-and-beige Slasto paving underfoot where other visitors mill round, and the jumpy prison officer, her escort, is bobbing and ducking at her elbow, doing his job within the new system, smiling his goodbye. Yes goodbye, her lips perform as they must. Good speech always, good sentences open doors, fair's foul, foul's fair, the body betrays the heart. Her womb feels emptied, split in two. Two, three. Monica, Desirée, Joseph. Who'll remember their birthdays now, Joseph? whisper against my ear?

She walks with raised shoulders, bent forwards. Bending eases the pain, shrinks it a little. She takes a taxi to the Technikon building that looks just like a caramel ice-cream wafer under this gentle afternoon light, then she walks all the way to the hat counter at JH Dark's, a one-hour walk, and she's back on time. A reliable decent woman. Three hours for urgent gallstone treatment, she told them. Can gallstones be treated in three hours? Hope for the best.

In the cloakroom she puts on Mrs Arnold's lipstick. She touches the red to her lips, then to her cheeks, lead questions away from her puffy eyes. She stashes a large bag of Cadbury's Chocolate Eclairs in the top drawer of the hat counter beside the credit card processor. She crams four sweets into her mouth at once, chews hugely, swallows. Eating as always strengthens and blankets the empty spaces inside. She leans on the counter, juts her elbows. Shrink that pain. 'Yes madam, can I help?' The body, the belly, betrays the heart.

Just before five o'clock the lady on haberdashery calls her to the phone.
'Yes?'
'Dora.'
Gertie's voice embraces her reassuringly. Thank God, thank God, it wasn't the prison. It wasn't an accident, a forced accident. He attacked an officer, he tripped in the toilet. As everyone knows, anything can happen. Under a life sentence he's in the grasp of their worst.
To escape the 24-hour lighting he accidentally died.
'Dora, sorry to disturb.'
'Yes, Gertie.'
'I'm downstairs from you, the call-box outside your main entrance. I need to show you something. I've seen many amazing things, but here's one of the most amazing.'
She can sense the mature brew of alcohol on his breath. The telephone unit is stapled to the wall behind a tall rack holding upright bolts of cloth. Thick winter cloth, fuzzy browns, blues. She leans against the rack, tucking her body in behind its height.
'Yes, Gertie. Are you behaving yourself there, Gertie?'
'Now, Dora, give me a minute, hear me out. I was just with that girl, you know, from your party, the journalist?'
'Anthea Hardy, yes, I know.'
'She called me. She's been trying to find me for several days. She's discovered something. Man, what an eye-opener, what a stunning thing. You won't believe it, Dora.'
She cups her hand over the mouthpiece, muffling her voice.
'Gertie, I told you don't walk that track. No talking. I can't take it. Anything of ours, it's not her business, it's not anyone's business.'
'*Aikona*, my sister, it's not what you're thinking, she did this by herself. She was doing work for the paper. It's all out of her own sussing this came up, nothing to do with me.'
'Whatever it is, I don't want to know it.'
'I'll just say it quickly, Dora. It's about your family, the Makkens, or

Mackens, spelt with a c. Joseph Macken, Irish hero of the Thukela, Dublin rebel in training, Dollie Macken of north Natal. Your family, ninety years ago.'

'No Gertie. No.'

'Dora, you've got to see it. I've got a copy here. A letter. There's a book too, a lady's journal, a beautiful red and green book from long ago – '

'Listen, I don't want to get angry. I'm just back from seeing Joe, I'm on a short fuse, you understand. It was the last time, Gertie, before they take him away, the last time to see him close to home. I'm in no mind to deal with schemes. I'm in no mood for this girl's funny business, or yours.'

'Let me finish, Dora.'

Gertie rattles coins into the phone. Dora peers between the bolts of cloth. No one in sight.

'I knew at the beginning she must be bad news, pushy, reminding me of everything I want to forget. I should've followed my feelings and steered clear. Don't upset me now, Gertie, at this time. I'm trying to hold down this job here, keep quiet, respectable.'

'But, Dora, don't you see what I'm saying? You don't see because you're not giving me a chance. If it's true what this girl has found out, if it fits and the connection works, it might help get our Joseph off the hook. I'm sorry, what's the word, it gets his sentence changed, commuted, he's declared a proper prisoner of war, an Irish-origin soldier. Your history can save him, if you can manage to piece it together, if the name fits right.'

'A customer announcement', the taped voice is gravelly, uncompromising. 'The store will be closing in five minutes.'

'Gertie, look, listen, I didn't catch your last words there. I don't want to know about this. It's time to go back to my counter now.'

'Off the hook, Dora,' Gertie is shouting, 'No life imprisonment, do you get me? If we can prove this. Joe and you aren't half-Boer so much as half-Irish, or a bit of Boer and a bit of Irish. How your Bernice got that red hair.'

# 25

*A green-and-red marbled notebook mottled with black damp and bound in frayed scarlet ribbon. Two letters folded inside the front cover, one dated 1900, written on broad sheets of browning vellum paper. The other letter, postmarked Dublin 1902, is in a different hand.*

KATHLEEN GORT'S JOURNAL

Friday September 15th 1899
Ireland

The blue sea air blowing over the cliffs here at Howth opens the heart and releases the spirit. I had forgotten its power. It is weeks since I was able to breathe like this, to stride and pant and fling my limbs. Weeks since the dreadful news came from India and Grandfather imprisoned himself with his savage grief behind his study door.

Before this sad summer I would not have thought myself capable of resenting bird song, the brilliance of light, the shrieks of children playing outdoors. I would not have thought myself capable of ferociously resenting these things. How many days did I not spend sitting in the dark heat of the curtained drawing room, the letter from the Government College in Bihar in its coarse grey envelope in my lap? In the mornings it was almost too difficult to leave my bed, my arms seemed too heavy to arrange my hair. From below, hour upon hour, came the rough coughing sounds of Grandfather's weeping.

Throughout we took our meals alone. Mrs Temple made custard tarts, stewed apple compotes, the softest fudges. She begged me to try a little oat broth, a pannikin of her own beef stew. Yet every mouthful tasted like mud, while Grandfather could not be prevailed upon to eat at all. His must have been a sympathetic affliction. Papa and Mother, wrote the Head Master of the College, died of a fever related to the famine sweeping northern India. Grandfather when I kissed him goodbye at Euston Station, felt as thin-boned and light as a cat. Only a year ago, when he travelled constantly between London and the Iberian Peninsula importing port wines, my arms reached but half-way round his ample waist.

So it was indeed an inspiration, Aunt Margaret's invitation to have me spend the winter with her here in Ireland. The smooth passage across from Holyhead three nights ago felt like a voyage into another country, a country of vivid blues and greens and strident seagulls, so distant from London's mourning and closed-up rooms.

In recognition of this new phase of my life, this sensation of expanded light, I have begun this journal. As seems fitting, a notebook purchased in Charing Cross Road here joins itself with the dark reliability of Bewley and Draper's good Irish ink. Sitting at Aunt Margaret's pen-pocked desk gazing out towards the cliffs, I catch myself at moments thinking I am not orphaned. Papa and Mother are alive, working thousands of miles away in India as they always did. But simultaneously I know I am cut loose from them. I am twenty-seven, abroad, freed into my own independent life.

How many times they appear to me still as I saw them last, saying farewell at Portsmouth five years ago. Mother in a full white blouse, Papa's long waving arm and long hand bannered high above the heads of the crowd on the steamer deck. I remember, year after year, the exhaustion of missing them. With each letter describing ghoulish festivals and spice-laden food they slipped further away into a veiled world I could not share with them. *The eerie, plangent cry of the chaukidar,* Mother wrote in a recent letter. I remember the phrase for its sugges-tiveness. Yet if the *chaukidar* is a bird or a flute or a man I have no idea. She had long ago quit explaining the Indian words.

I weep for them still, most nights, and yet feel strangely freed. I feel the youth and strength of my body, I feel I can travel far. Yesterday while Aunt was attending a meeting in town, I walked along the cliffs to Baily's lighthouse, reacquainting myself with once familiar caves and hollows. When I threw myself into the heather it sprang up against my back, just as it did when I played here as a child. I felt sure I could walk round all of Ireland without tiring.

Papa and Mother died within three days of each other and are buried together beside a *neem* tree. Mother I remember once pressed some *neem* leaves between the pages of a letter, three slender leaves that bore a thin sultry smell. Aunt Margaret says the *neem* must be the Indian willow.

Aunt continues to wear her mourning dresses but otherwise accommodates her grief in day-long work for political societies. When I was younger I remember being in awe of her loudness, her height and rangy frame. I was glad Grandfather rarely sent me over for holidays. Now I find myself fascinated. Though as a woman she may hold no committee office, she speaks everywhere against evictions in the West of Ireland and regularly composes articles for the press. The English Queen, she writes, is Satan on Earth. She cannot yet comprehend how Mother, her own younger sister Eileen, could have worked for the Empire by teaching in India with Papa. Her vehemence startles me but I am moved by what she says of the trouble people have here, and their pride in what is their own, their land, their songs and stories.

On Monday I will begin to teach myself to type-write. I agree with Aunt that it is 'good training if ever I want to be of practical use in the world', as a respectable young woman of limited means should be. She herself seems able to turn her hand to almost anything. On my first evening she welcomed me 'home, to your true home' with a fragrant stew of mutton and fresh peas. Last night she hinged the lid to a wooden chest for my belongings, that she bought second-hand and varnished herself. She is to be seen everywhere around Dublin on her stout

Lucania bicycle with its fan-shaped mud-guards, proudly riding like a rajah on an elephant.

If I gather up my courage I may attempt this somewhat perilous form of locomotion myself. A kind neighbour who brings us eggs has a bicycle left by her son when he departed for Canada. His photograph hangs in her front room between a chromo of the Sacred Heart and a faded picture of some nationalist hero, I believe Wolfe Tone.

Sunday October 1st 1899

Now I begin to understand a little of the force that so often trembles in Aunt Margaret's fingers. The talk on the streets is all of today's stirring gathering. Press head-lines around the world, Aunt's editor friend George Grierson tells us, are registering the shock waves. Despite beetling opposition, Ireland has declared itself in a loud voice for Republican freedom against imperial tyranny in Africa.

Last week I barely knew of their existence, this week I sense my life may change on their account. In the south of Africa a small nation called *Boers* or farmers (for they are but simple peasants living close to the land) are striking out to defend their independence, an independence which the Empire, brazenly interested in Transval gold, is intent on snatching from them. The English papers are filled with rant against these *Insolent primitives, Fit but to die!* War, they claim, will break out within days.

It was late last Friday night inaugurated my political education. Aunt Margaret returned from a pro-Transval meeting at the Celtic Literary Society, her shawl silvered with rain and her voice sharp with a sympathetic fury. For over an hour she restlessly paced the carpet before the fire till at last Mulcahy the ginger cat could bear it no longer and left the room in bristly indignation.

The Empire would grab the African mines no matter the cost, Aunt said, dishevelling her hair with wild gestures. Ireland as a small country should join the Boers in their efforts to hurl themselves against the great, to stand up for land, language, liberty! Differences of religion could hardly matter where solidarity was so pressing, so right. I did not know what to say to this. I begged her to take a little of the Bovril and buttered toast I had made. Yet I was glad she invited me to today's meeting, for, dull with two weeks of solitary type-writing, I was made excited and confused by her anger. Having spent so many years in London with the genteelly dogmatic Englishman who is dear Grandfather I cannot quite tell what is meant by clanging phrases such as 'dark tyrant' and 'enemy of freedom'. I have always heard that English traditions are for justice and the rule of law.

A little more light was shed at eleven today as the thousands gathered on the Quays before Custom House and the bright red, green, blue and white flag of the Transval Republic was unfurled. To witness a crowd express fellow feeling with a people so far distant makes a strange and powerful impression. I wonder at the suffering from which such angry identification must rise. Never before have I felt the press of so large a throng, of legs, arms, backs forced fast against one, the thrusting and tussling as of one body as the people strained forwards to hear the speakers.

Within moments of our arriving Aunt and I lost each other. As we craned about trying to catch sight of her friend George, a stocky man, the mass seemed suddenly to heave and engulf her. Left to fend for myself I found a position beside a lamppost not far from the Custom House steps, at which favourable vantage point I was soon joined by a tweed-jacketed young man with moist white cheeks like the skin on porridge. His incoherent shouting which began almost at once, continued throughout the two hours we stood there. He was completely silent only during the magnificent address made by a statuesque redhead with a great square jaw who is called Maud Gonne. Her low-toned voice carried through the crowd, touching me to the bones. 'The Boers are fighting for their freedom in the only way that freedom can be attained,' she cried. 'With guns! Meanwhile Ireland waits in slavery!' The canary in the tall enamelled cage standing at her feet, the Great Dane crouched beside her, became motionless as she chanted, the words flowing like music through her lips.

Even when she spoke more practically of the need to oppose Irish enlistment for the Empire, her rapt eyes were lifted above the heads of the crowd, unblinking in their determination. A boy with a liquorice stick hanging from his mouth had meanwhile left a black stain on my skirts. I write myself down a fool for having worn a clean pinafore to a public meeting yet at the time was unaware of his proximity. All freedom-loving women – Miss Gonne suddenly burst forth – should help the Boer cause by dissuading their husbands and sweethearts from joining up. No drop of Irish blood should be wasted in pursuit of the tyrant's wicked ends. Follow British Army recruiting sergeants into the public houses where their hoodwinking work is done! Then she took up the Transval flag and held it aloft crying, 'In the name of Ireland and independence!' The response was deafening. 'Up the Republic! Up, up! Up the Boers!'

It is an tremendous hypnotic power Miss Gonne has. Not until I was back on the train to Howth did I find the settledness of mind to stand back from the sound of her words and think about their substance. Slavery is an expression charged like a bomb, and as dangerous. And yet I have sufficiently attended to Aunt Margaret's talk of famine and hardship on the land to understand perhaps that the injustices Miss Gonne speaks of cannot be denied.

Aunt Margaret herself, who had reached home before me, was enthusiastic about the energy of the meeting, if rather circumspect concerning Miss Gonne. We set about preparing a plate of griddle cakes, filling the whole house with their warm collected fragrance. The promising poet William Yeats, Aunt said as we battered and buttered, was also to address the gathering but was sadly withheld at the last moment by a collapsed voice. I was interested to hear this. Since I arrived she has pressed me to read his dreamy *The Wind Among the Reeds*. He is, her friends say, the voice of Ireland restored to Greatness.

Later over tea, Aunt spoke at greater length about her society work, her hopes for this country. She described the first large meeting she ever attended, the protest at Queen Victoria's

Diamond Jubilee celebrations two years ago, a manifestation more incendiary than this one, she claims, though less practically useful. On that occasion the procession carried a black coffin inscribed *British Empire* which, when the police began to club heads, was dumped into the Liffey. Next, she said, her voice rising, the crowd streamed to Rutland Square to see, by arrangement with the Corporation workers, the illuminated Jubilee decorations all over Dublin snuff out. The single source of light remaining was from the large projector in the Square, as it beamed harrowing slides of eviction victims on to a vast white screen: scenes of mothers huddled over babies in the stinging rain, of broken dressers and tables piled higgledy-piggledy like bonfires in deserted yards.

All that month of June, Aunt Margaret remembers, she helped National Club wives embroider the numbers of the Irish famine dead on hundreds of black flags, white silk on black flags. The flags were distributed amongst the crowd. It was, she says, that painstaking figuring over her spirit lamp, stitching out the noughts of the thousands night after night, that pricked her indignation to breaking point. She confronted the Nationalists in their Club and asked them – all men, worn by their battle, used to each other and not to women – to give her work. She now has hopes that the fiery presence of Miss Gonne will improve the situation for us women. To date however, she adds sourly, Miss Gonne has disappointingly preferred to radiate the magnetism of her beauty quite unassisted.

As she spoke thus of women and our work, Aunt, who had been straightening the cuffs of her black blouse, suddenly leaned over and touched a cold hand to my temple. 'Ah, my dear girl, dear Kathleen,' she murmured. 'Here you are in my charge and I lead you into danger and uncertainty. Will our sweet Eileen who is so far away from us now, though always watching over us, forgive me for it?' But the set look in her eye belied the anxiety she was expressing. It is that look that most nearly captures the spirit of today.

That, and the image of households of Dublin women embroidering figures of famine dead in white on black cloth.

Wednesday October 25th 1899

My bicycling exercises – at which I am pleased to say I am much improved – have stood me in good stead these past few days. Each morning for over a week young friends and relatives of the newly formed Irish Transval, or is it Trans*vaal*? Committee have been sent out to distribute bright green anti-enlistment leaflets door to door.

The first day, the 16th, we began the venture on foot, radiating in pairs from the Celtic Society rooms where the pamphlets bearing their message, *England's Difficulty is Ireland's Opportunity*, are delivered hours before dawn. I was accompanied by a dark floppy-haired Theosophist named Malachy Lyons who seemed pleasant enough yet said hardly a word all day. Through the medium of tremulous smiles and furtive nods however he agreed with me that, while walking was advantageous for the hanging of posters, cycling would help us cover longer distances.

It must be because I am the only female member of the distributing team, and the bicycle is a protective getaway machine, that my proposal to the Committee, conveyed by Aunt, was quickly accepted. So, since Friday last, I take the train into town through the misty dawn light with the brewery workers and shop-girls, and report with my bicycle at the Committee's Headquarters in an Abbey Street so quiet my heels ring on the paving stones. Most remarkable is how, apart from the police who tear down our posters, we encounter so little opposition. In the street people's faces are nearly always eager and interested. There was for instance the shopkeeper today in Dame Street who asked for extra pamphlets for his sisters' sons, as well as a poster for his window. There was the clerk outside Bewley's last Monday who shook Malachy Lyons's hand and complimented us on a campaign that was 'both necessary and useful' to the nation. We had just hung a banner which shouted in large white letters *Enlisting in the English Army is Treason*.

A living energy against imperial England evidently fibrillates in the most unassuming passer-by, to me still so astonishingly. How disgraceful it now seems that, every Christmas when she came to Richmond to see Grandfather, the family would pooh-pooh Aunt Margaret when she spoke of the Irish 'electricity of opposition' to English rule. So we heard a few days ago that in far-off Johannesburg patriotic Irishmen working on the mines have formed themselves into a Brigade in order to defend the rights of the Afrikaner nation and their own against the Empire, 'their ancient foe'. For Boer and Irish freedom – as if in one fell swoop! Scorning British identity the soldiers have assumed honorary South African citizenship and will, it's said, ride to the Natal front within days.

Immediately this news came through, Maud Gonne began work on a Brigade flag to send to the heroic men. Yet, as she is so busy, much of the sewing has now fallen on Aunt, who slept over at the Celtic Society offices last night to finish tacking the gold-fringed green Dublin poplin. The flag is to carry a harp symbol which Miss Gonne has designed. It was simply staggering, says Aunt, to see her at work those first few hours, her fingers flurrying, blurred by their motion. To see the flitting of her eyes as she thought up new strategies even as she was faultlessly occupied with her tracing. Aunt does acidly wonder however whether Miss Gonne quickly became aware, as she herself now is, how easily poplin puckers when tightly sewn, consequently abandoning the true graft of flag work to others!

As I read back over these pages – written in so stretched and rushed a hand, not improved by the stiffness of type-writing – I can't but marvel at how my new political interests have become imprinted on my time. I no longer think as often as I used of Mother and Papa, though when I do a crueller head-ache than I ever experienced lays hands upon me and my vision quite collapses, revealing nothing but blackness and diamond-like chips of steel. At these times sleep alone can solve away my distress. My thoughts are of that untended grave, the weed-ridden mound, sodden and broken by monsoon rains.

Yet I also know that I am rivetted and increasingly convinced by what I have so far witnessed as regards the nationalists' activity. I remain woefully unlettered in politics, but, having reflected on this matter, am happy for the present to give the support I

can to efforts that mitigate what seems from all I hear to be a
gravely ill-matched war.

Next evening

Within a day of scribbling those last lines, my nascent conviction has been put to the test by the visit of William Gough, a
Belfast port wine merchant and long-time business associate of
Grandfather's. While attending to trading matters in London, he
met with Grandfather and, we suspect, was then sent over to see
us and make sure of my well-being.

As Aunt rarely entertains, Mr Gough's coming threw us into
a frenzy of stewing and pastry cutting, from which, to our surprise, we came out creditably with a dinner of beef and
Guinness pie and baked apple pudding served with yellow
cream. Our guest often stretched up and puffed his throat as he
ate in what we later concluded must have been gustatory satisfaction.

Far less satisfactory was the conversation at dinner, a long
disquisition on Boer Stupidity, Irish Disloyalty, and Imperial
Rightness from Mr Gough, interspersed with clipped remarks
from Aunt, bitten off out of politeness to Grandfather. A sampling. 'There's no such thing as Irish famine, in the sense of
widespread starvation,' Mr Gough began his pie, scooping med-
itatively into the gravy, 'If there is hardship in the West it is all
due to rent boycotts.' And Aunt Margaret, quiet as a faraway
noise, 'But you cannot deny Ireland has suffered through being
under England. And not poverty only but the extinction of her
distinctive nationality.' Then he, after a pause, as if primed to
test her, 'Yet nothing as regards that suffering was ever so severe
as to justify the present treasonous support of the Boers. The
Boers are a bloodthirsty and uncivilised people, a grossly
uncivilised people. They have not so much as a flowering shrub
near their houses. The trumpeted liberty of their republics rests
on the oppression of Africans who – were we aware? – may not
walk on the pavements, but only in the streets of Afrikaner
towns.' At which Aunt, 'How many times has England not used
the name, and the name only, of native causes, to oppose white

liberty in the Empire?'

'And yet,' returned the old man, his jowls sunk upon his chest, 'all the white countries of the Empire stand in solidarity with England at this time of crisis, excepting Ireland alone. It was not only thankless, it was perverse behaviour. Besides which, the Irish Brigade rumoured to be fighting on the Boer side were an undisciplined bunch who could barely ride, much use they'd be to our noble Burgher warriors.' This to the scraping of pudding plates and the gurgle of the Sauternes bottle, to which our guest was liberally helping himself, as no doubt befits a port wine trader.

We ended the meal in a silence so perfect it stickily magnified the sucking sounds made by the seats of Aunt's leather dining chairs, especially when the sitter is of generous girth. Mr Gough ordered his cab dreadfully early, before 10 p.m.

Aunt and I then fell to wondering whether Grandfather might not have connived with his friend to probe by provocation her suitability as a permanent companion. In which case, despite her restraint, she will have sadly failed. And yet, and so I will answer Grandfather, if there was a test here tonight then Mr Gough and his opinions suffered by it. There was too much of oily complacency in his tones, and too much of rant in his language. One needs walk the streets of Dublin but a day to encounter the people's instinctive sympathy for the South Africans.

The one happy consequence of the occasion is that it laid bare what I had not expected in Aunt, a deeply embedded vein of frivolity beneath her hardened political skin. In preparation for Mr Gough's visit she had her own seamstress make me a tea-gown using a delicate nun's veiling, a soft drifting fabric newly on sale at Clery's. Yesterday after pamphleting I fetched the finished dress myself and hardly knew what to say to the size of the parcel.

Aunt had me try on the gown as soon as I was home and, as I paraded through the house, showed me how to lift, swish and (seemingly effortlessly) curl my skirts to execute turns, for the gown, so light in appearance, is cumbersome to those not

coached in this art. 'And what of a little profligacy and spend-
ing!' she almost laughed when I protested, clapping her hands
in pleasure. 'I want you to have a fine gown. Politics must not
be allowed to weary the soul.' The draped whiteness now graces
my bed, and glimmers in the firelight.

Tuesday November 28th 1899

These are days of wind and freezing rain. Aunt and I have
put up the heavier curtains lined with brown velvet that used to
hang in their Donnybrook drawing-room when she and Mother
were children. 'When these were taken out each November my
darling Eileen would say we were being buried in earth,' Aunt
said. 'Buried like moles. She lived for the light, cowering always at
winter darkness, running coatless in the spring rain. I shouldn't
wonder that she went to India, so loving heat and light.'

The icy conditions have not been favourable for bicycle cam-
paigns, besides which we have covered most of the city twice
over. I have gone to see for myself the troops setting sail from
the North Wall Quay and am almost sure that the cheering on
these occasions has lost in volume and enthusiasm.

The Transvaal idea has hold, we think an increasingly firmer
and fiercer hold, in Dublin. A woman to whom I gave a leaflet
last week had the green, white and blue flag embroidered on her
collar and men everywhere wear Transvaal buttons in their hats.
Photographs of the Boer Generals are on sale in bread shops, in
haberdasheries: stern pictures of Cronje, Botha, De Wet, those
dark slow names. A limelight display of war pictures outside the
*Independent* offices is frequently the scene of fisticuffs between
Trinity students looking for trouble and equally excitable pro-
Boers. I have witnessed one or two of these outbreaks in the
company of my spiritualist fellow-pamphleteer Malachy Lyons.

I have little experience of young men but am sure there are
few quite so odd, and at the same time so self-reserved, as this
Malachy Lyons. My hours at the Committee offices are not
always regular, so I cannot tell how it is except by otherworldly
prompting that he runs into me whenever political trouble
occurs. He is seemingly able to anticipate it. I happen to be set-

ting out for the centre of town or the station, there is a noise of raised voices, perhaps the sound of striking and scraping hooves, I turn into a side street, and he is there with his strange shambling gait and spasmodic hand gestures, announcing himself only by a raised hat and a whispered 'Miss Gort'.

We have already walked many miles through Dublin together yet barely had what might be called a conversation. Out of shyness he will seldom allow his eyes to drop from the rooftops to meet one's own, and avoids replying to any sort of opener. To 'Changeable weather' he one day murmured 'Talisman evoking Lir'. Not wishing to prolong any misunderstanding, I was at a loss what to say next. This has become a standard response of his, an indecipherable aphorism thrown to the clouds.

He seeks, I have gathered bit by bit, a communion with the Forces of this country, to bring into being its Higher Destiny. He quotes Lionel Johnson and other writers to the effect that 'malign armed Angels' have fallen upon the nation, yet Irish Angels in the form of its heroes and poets will wrest back Her Flaming Sword. He himself has had a poem published in the *United Irishman*. Like thickly embroidered cloth, the verses are stiff with elaborate decoration.

He seems not in the least to notice me physically, but at those times when I am or feign to be absorbed elsewhere, I feel his sideways gaze upon my neck and face, and a pleasant tingle runs up my arms. Even so I do not know if my heart can be convinced by him. If Aunt has ever peered through the muddy Committee windows she will have seen me leaving Lower Abbey Street with him on many an afternoon, yet it is significant I cannot speak of him to her. I doubt she would identify him as the prophetic poetic voice which I know he feels is gathering strength within him.

However obscurely engaging he is, he seems always like an unmoored boat to be drifting away from that which most grounds me here in Dublin and gives a sense of purpose: the work against the war. As Malachy himself knows well, the higher forces do not distribute pamphlets; their magnetism does not animate tired fingers as we type-write letter after letter seeking subscriptions for our new venture, an ambulance corps to send out to Africa along with our fine-looking flag. Although this is tedious work, the ambulance will, we're told, be desperately welcome. Contrary to imperialists' expectations, the war will by no means be over by Christmas.

Such practicality is not served, even if hearts are lifted, by Malachy invoking the 'tearful Hosts of Eire', as happened yesterday on our way to the train station. By his enjoining her 'Ceremonial Harp' and 'Immemorial Horn' to 'tremble into passion', all the while gazing away over the rooftops and, slyly, at my cheek, my hair.

To tremble into passion. Some nights in bed – it is easier to write than think this – I do yearn for the touch he seems to suggest, sometimes it is as if my soul clenches with the desire. Even as my hand moves across this page it creates such agitation, I grow exceedingly warm. I think of fingers running across my face, I think of the back of a hand sliding lightly across my shoulders. I close my eyes and try to feel this, the face of the toucher I cannot properly see. He is not my Theosophist though he is dark, tall. He brings his body close but not so as to touch mine. It is the sliding hands that touch me and draw the blushes out of my flesh.

Monday December 18th 1899

It has been a week of exhilarating Afrikaner victories which ended yesterday in another dramatic demonstration against Empire and the war. Yet on this occasion, though I am made thoughtful, my emotions are less deeply scored. Aunt Margaret and the editor George Grierson, and Michael Davitt too, while unable to contain their excitement, have asked questions about the wisdom of the protest leaders in proceeding with the meeting once the police had banned it. An 'example of cowardice' had to be avoided at all costs, Miss Gonne told the Committee late last night, but she knew the crowd would be unarmed.

The debate boiled into the small hours and it was eventually a small group, including Miss Gonne, who in the early afternoon mounted the funeral brake that was to act as their speech platform. Their horses trotted briskly down to Custom House and there forced a path through the police cordon, the crowd giving the party a rapturous welcome. The roar carried right the way to O'Connell Bridge where Malachy Lyons and I had found a good position, one with a view of both the river and the street.

We could tell from the look of the policemen standing shoulder to shoulder all along the bridge that this seething down river was not to be the last of it. And within the hour Miss Gonne did predictably come riding by, her burning hair flowing like a Sidhe's, her face in transport. Yet her joy shocked me. As we joined the crowd rushing towards Trinity, the mounted police in mass formation behind us, pressing us, the horses blowing, I suddenly felt miserable and uncertain about such delight in struggle as Miss Gonne's, such wild love of conflict as if for its own sake. Had it been possible I might have turned back there and then, gone home to the fire, to tea.

College Green was a fairground display of waving Transvaal flags and a magic lantern screen, and still I felt overwhelmed. By this time the mass shouting was deafening, my growing headache buzzing so hard I feared it would quite disable me. It has been a time of great urgency and fatigue. Standing there trying to keep my balance I began to wonder whether we have been thinking as clearly about this war as we should. A man behind us set up a chant 'Mafeking has fallen!' (mistakenly as it happens) and the flag he and his companion were waving flapped across my face. As the green cloth covered my nose and mouth, tasting of starch, I had to gulp for breath. Men and women in the crowd were now running into shops for brooms, poles, oranges, loaves of bread, anything that might serve as a missile. Malachy with a vague sweet smile on his face pointed out a man who was waving a revolver wrested from a policeman on the steps of the Royal Bank. I knew then I had to find a way out. At an opportune moment, just as Horse Police reinforcements rode up bearing swords, I lost Malachy by leaning back into the crowd, then ducking. I trust he will have saved himself. It took over an hour of hard pushing and bumping but at last I reached

Amiens Street station where the train out to Howth was completely empty.

Now, although a day has passed, my dismay has not abated. For the first time in many months my head-ache has knocked me up completely, my limbs feel entirely soft and weak and the bruises inflicted by the crowd are a rich blue on my arms. Aunt has advised bed-rest, and it's in bed that I'm now writing, fortified by a glass of Bovril and whiskey she prepared before she set out. There'll surely be, after yesterday, much talk at the Committee rooms, much gloating self-defence. Many I know will judge the event a success, the long-hoped-for rousing of the easy-going Dublin people. I do feel a little ashamed of myself to be lying here, nursing my doubts and a weak head, but am relieved even so to have time to myself.

Perhaps it will straighten my thoughts if I set them out in plain sentences, as follows. After these many agitated weeks I feel, I cannot help feeling, that the Irish Transvaal resistance is in danger of forgetting the noble ideals with which it began. Yesterday's protest meeting was an angry sensation, it succeeded as a sensation, but what will people now do with their excess of rage and panic? They have broken windows, they have fought hand-to-hand with policemen … But what now?

We have pledged 'our help to the nation whose enemy is ours', so someone shouted into a brief silence during the protests. As we grow heated about how best to trip up the Empire, we lose sight, I think, of that pledge. We become as confused as is Malachy bound for his higher plane. In the Committee rooms these worries might well be shouted down, yet I am concerned that we move beyond the stage of single agitations, Ireland-only protests. There is more to be done, more work directed at the war itself. My hands long to take hold of some real labour beyond the typing of letters. The African energy that quivers in us must be channelled in some way.

That it has been a black week for England there is absolutely no doubt. On every front its attacks are reduced to hopeless disorder and the Boers have mastery – but for how long? Every day the British Army is reinforced. I have written this over a thousand times in our letters of subscription, *Let us address the fearful damage inflicted by this vile and unjust war.*

Last week we said goodbye to four Dublin nurses who left for Paris where, as part of the Committee's ambulance corps, they'll be equipped for Africa. I know there is subscription money left over to sponsor one or two more helpers. I ordered French passports for all four to travel out to the front. Would it be impossible to do the same for myself?

Friday December 29th 1899

My exact purpose remains indistinct but my plans are firmer. I travel to Natal with a detachment of the French Red Cross early in the New Year. Since Christmas our days have been frantic with accelerated preparation.

Christmas itself was quiet. We roasted a small chicken and all day feasted on fresh African peaches, the most beautiful globes, rosy golden as the sun, a gift to the Committee from the Transvaal representative in Paris. Grandfather sent over a Fortnum and Mason's pudding which I had all to myself. Aunt, out of patriotism, could not bring herself to eat it.

In a short note enclosed with his parcel Grandfather asked whether I continue happy in Ireland. It is the first time we have heard from him since Mr Gough's visit so I immediately and animatedly replied. Yet as he said little of his own state of mind I find myself in some perplexity as to how he will respond to my war plans. Aunt has offered to break the news once I am gone.

The cold has thrust its icy finger deeper in. My weakness has passed, but, wrapped in a woollen Indian shawl of Mother's, I cannot stop myself from shivering however close to the fire I sit. Thus chilled, I look upon those African peaches as a sign or a confirmation. The southern sun has radiated as far as Ireland to draw me down to its warmth, its war.

I have become in recent days a regular ward visitor at the City of Dublin Hospital. To look the part I bind my hair in a tight roll using the springy cotton rats Aunt has loaned me. The first time the effect was distinctly lopsided but my kind guide, the matron Elspeth Samuels, did not bat an eyelid.

Nursing will have to come mostly through watching, 'learning on the job' as they say, for the Women's Detachment of the local Red Cross have no time to train me. Yet I am glad of the neutral channel that their organisation offers. Accompanied by the small French ambulance I should be able to reach the front closest to the coast, along what's called the Tugella River. Once there I will be able more narrowly to assess the situation, to see where help is required. I have taught myself the spiral bandage, the reversed spiral, the figure of eight, I practice late at night with a first-aid handbook. At midnight I replace this with William Yeats – his yearning lines do so charge my blood. I walk before the fire in quest of warmth and I chant, *The wrong of unshapely things is a wrong too deep to be told.* The words move fluidly in time with pacing feet. My desire is to get the poems by heart, to travel with me as invisible singing companions.

Since I left him at College Green Malachy Lyons has chosen to keep away although he writes nearly every day. Yesterday he described a dream that has thrice visited him. In the dream, clad in sparkling yellow robes, I dance in slow measure through the stars of the Southern Cross.

In contrast my dear Aunt has kept almost entirely silent about my plans, though I am reassured by the practical help she is giving me. To my Essentials List for Africa she has already added many articles, and this not only by way of verbal suggestion, her big voice vibrating through the floorboards, but in kind. The wooden chest she herself hinged in September is piled full of Switzer's best cambric knickers she bought only today. 'Going cheap after Christmas,' she said.

From the years of correspondence with her sister Aunt knows a great deal about tropical protection. And again betrays her underlying sensitivity to appearance. 'Dear Eileen said a hot climate gives a tendency to greasiness even in the best complexions,' she slips a box of papier poudre between my blouses. I smile secretly at the thought of using, in the wilds of Africa, this middle-aged ladies' cosmetic aid.

But it wasn't until breakfast this morning that Aunt was for the first time more forthright about her feelings. She gripped my hand in hers and her words were crisp, I remember each one: 'I want you to be careful, Kathleen. I have heard Britain is arming Africans against the noble Boers. You understand, these are nothing but unchristian savages, Bush men. As strange as this may sound coming from me, I fear your idealism. There is little to which the English generals will not stoop, and women have always been the pawns in men's wars. I think of my responsibility to your parents' memory, our dear Eileen.'

She has shown me the draft of the letter to Grandfather she will post the day I embark for France. She cannot yet finish it. The letter begins in the broadest terms – *Kathleen and I oppose by every means ...* – but is, I am relieved to see, less obscurely anxious than were yesterday's remarks.

For the present there is little more to write. I am I dare say both expectant and relieved if also inevitably a little apprehensive. The New Century will set me afloat on uncharted waters – I am eager to discover however to what shores my voyaging may bring me. This past month has beset me with many doubts. Now, paradoxically, as I face uncertainty, I feel far surer what I am doing is right. I have the political will to effect some small change. I would not want that will to turn back on itself like a confined shoot and grow sick. Though I cannot yet say along with Miss Gonne that Liberty is never without the sacrifice of blood, I believe a strong symbol *for* freedom and *against* tyranny can be obtained from showing solidarity with the Boers – from showing solidarity and giving attention to the war's pain.

From the moment I made my decision to go to Africa my head-aches quite left me. I feel well and tolerably strong.

August 1900
Natal

Strangest of all the strange and distressing scenes I have witnessed in Africa is the stillness settled upon the hundreds clustered here together. The starving do not speak and cannot play. They stare at the bleak compound through dulled eyes, they sit.

Their silence is stranger even than the nightmarish contrast

made by this god-forsaken Umgeni encampment and the ver-
dant valley on the rim of which it is built. From a side barracks
we are able to see the white spume of the handsome waterfall at
the valley's head. We view it through an eight-foot-high fence of
barbed wire and iron plates, curiously enlaced.

In nearly five months I have not moved more than a mile
beyond the forbidding boundaries of this British centre of
refuge for Afrikaner women and children. The Boer name is
*konsentrasiekamp*. In late March I set out from Izinyanga hospital as the nursing assistant in charge of a group of refugees from
abandoned farms in the north of the colony, fondly hoping that
my presence might somehow ease their distresses. Though I had
not yet learned their language, privation I believed knows a
common tongue. And yet there was little even a seasoned nurse
could have done working on her own in an overcrowded cattle-
truck in the sweltering heat. We were three days in that truck
covering a distance of only 90 miles, and we had a single tin
drum of water between us.

But it was not a general sympathy only that moved me. My
interest had become tightly fastened upon the *enceinte* African
woman who had arrived starving in Izinyanga from the hills,
naming herself for an Irishman. Macken. As a Boer servant she
was consigned here along with the rest. I remember her vividly
as she first appeared to me, described in the letter to Aunt
Margaret I still have in my possession. A slight, starving dark
woman who, shockingly, spoke English with an unmistakeable
Irish music.

That special letter to Aunt is pressed here inside my journal,
stamped by the war censor in Durban, as were the other two
earlier letters, now stored deep down in Aunt's wooden chest,
under the lining. Like a chit giving assurance of payment, these
letters must stand in for the many months I have neglected this
book. There has been so little opportunity lately for the luxury
of writing, so little *place*, I have been it seems always hungry
and tired. Volunteer rations rarely exceed what the captive
women are given, for a reason that is disheartening but simple.
Though officially neutral we volunteer staff are considered sub-

tly compromised, indeed suspect, because of our sympathy. Our foraging schemes in the nearby town whether for ourselves or others are baulked at every turn. This means that the meat we now get is almost always green-tinged and spongy, our coffee like the sweepings of warehouse floors.

If I do have a moment to myself I prefer to sit quietly in the shade of one of our few trees, a scrubby mimosa wattle on the valley side of the barracks. The tree sheds a pungent dry perfume that masks the more noisome odours of the *kamp*. Occasionally I read the first pages of my journal and am left confounded at the individual represented there, her freshness of expression, her lightness of heart.

I came in part to assist her and others like her yet she has become my strength, my conversationist, this 'Dollie Macken' sporting her pro-Boer slouch hat and singing songs of Harps, Green Flags and Battle Spears, interspersed with local croons and clicks. She is housed with the other always-present African servants on the barren north side of the *kamp* where conditions, if that were possible, are even more inhospitable than on the Boer end closer to the meagre spring. Pleading her belly Dollie has contrived to secure slightly larger portions of tinned meat and maize bread than the other blacks, and is consequently quite sanguine, all things considered. She walks at large through the compound, her distended navel pointing through her ruched shift like an accusing finger. Before she became visibly gravid, her fine broad features and proud carriage found much favour among the British *kamp* administration. Her Irish loyalties however have remained quite set.

Almost every morning around six Dollie comes over to my tent to talk of things Irish and share my screwball coffee, which we make believe is stewed Irish tea. I assure her I am no authentic product of the island, but for her it is sufficient that I have lived there. I do not sing the Empire's praises so my heart must be in the right place. She asks me about country fairs, Dublin streets, Mayo hills, rain, families, feast days, the size of the rivers. Is there ever a cloudless day? And do I know such and such a song (humming a melody I rarely recognise)? But always she works round to talking of Irish men. Are they faithful and true? Is their sweetness of speech matched by a sweetness of spirit? Lamely I reply I do not know, I cannot tell. I only ever had the one male friend in Ireland and he a dreamer.

With her arms folded on her belly, she gives me a squinnying look. 'He said he would come back for me,' she says. 'The Afrikaners need help protecting their capital from the British, he said, they need the Irish to dynamite the railway bridges. But he said he'd come back for me, he'd never forget me. I had the mettle of a fighter. I thought he meant metal, like iron, till he explained. There were many more battles to fight for Ireland, he said. The nation sought determined hearts. Our son if we ever had one would be a soldier for freedom like himself.' It is as if she is defying me to dispute this.

'When he left he knew you were with child?' I ask. I have asked several times and each time comes the same reply. 'I know he sensed it. He placed his hand on my belly saying farewell. And he was smiling as he rode away. Some nights I feel him talking to me, to the child and to me, telling us not to be lonely, keep strong, he'll be back. When my spirits are low I repeat this to myself, *I have spread my dreams under your feet*. It's something he said.' 'That's a line from a poet,' I say. 'He is a poet and a soldier, and the songs he sings are poems.'

I myself no longer recite the Yeats I once had by heart. The words have grown too dream-heavy, I cannot breathe through them. Dollie has taught me instead a song she says her lover Joseph Macken taught her (on Thursday for the first time she spoke his name). It is a Brigade song for the Boers and from its mysterious measured quality I sense it comes from the Irish. As I walk the rows of hollowed eyes and cheeks distributing cups of saline against dysentery I cannot help whispering the words. Though disjointed they carry the power of cursing.

England was a Queen,
A Queen without sorrow,
But we will take from her,
Fiercely, her Crown.

That Queen that was beautiful
Will be tormented and darkened,
For she will get her reward
In that day, and her wage.

Her wage for the bones
That are whitening to-day,
Bones of the white man,
Bones of the black man.

Her wage for the blood
She poured out on the streams,
Blood of the white man,
Blood of the black man.

Her wage for those hearts
That she broke in the end,
Hearts of the white man,
Hearts of the black man.

I look into those hollowed eyes and see there is reason to curse the Famine Queen indeed. Every day enormous groups arrive here by train, weakened and tottering but under armed guard, to be housed in tents that are already overcrowded. The women give birth squatting upon stones.

The central *werf* or compound affords an eloquent symbol of our condition, remaining despite all our efforts a waste land of rubbish, a muddy quag after rain. To walk from the staff living quarters to the hospital tent is to stumble through a spilt and stinking kedgeree. Soiled bandages and dressings are mixed with medicine bottles, bully beef tins picked clean, upended latrine pails and human waste, a squashed dead bird.

In comparison to this the wounds of the soldiers at Izinyanga were almost more bearable, cleaner somehow. Nothing thrives but diseases, dysentery as usual, but now also an epidemic of measles. As I write I smell the thick sickly odour of the typhoid, the fever that took Mother and Papa, on my hands. It is a stench that I at times fancy must itself be infectious. All night long the high-pitched moaning of the feverish children mingles awfully with the sound of the wind sighing in the wire fence.

The African servants including Dollie have helped improvise corrugated iron huts covered with sacking to ease the over-crowding. Yet to the Boer women it is worse even than death to be housed 'like a Kaffir'. The punishment for refusing to use the huts is to be penned in a small wire enclosure open to the elements. This however they accept almost equably. I am I confess daily amazed at this aspect of the much-admired Boer stub-bornness. Far more hateful to them than any cattle-truck, I am told, was the British soldier's threat as they were driven from their homes, 'You'll marry Natives if you don't give in.' Dollie has heard the taunt, and shrugs ambiguously at their response. 'It's their nature,' she says. 'That's why I like my Irishman. The Boers fight so hard because they're full of themselves, full of their country. Like a possessive woman loves a man they love it, crushingly.' I recall what William Gough said of whites-only pavements in Afrikaner towns. I recall Dollie's song, *Blood of the white man, blood of the black man*. The one here, the one there.

The few papers we see begin to recognise the existence of the refuge camps, but to recognise in order to excuse. The Colonial Government is *morally bound, the homeless cannot be kept alive any other way*. 'We burn farms because they won't be subdued,' says Major Colville our *kamp* superintendent apparently with-out blenching, 'Once the women give in, the men will.' But as Dollie says, and she should know, who began by *sweeping* the countryside, who first starved the men? As in Ireland we can only speculate with dread as to the effect of such insults on the national soul.

There are days when even Dollie has trouble raising her spir-its. Like a sick thing she will creep away into the fetid hut she shares with twelve others. I have found her there curled on a mat, small and childlike despite her belly, her breathing laboured. The longing for her man, she explains, seems at times almost to paralyse her heart. I take her head in my lap, stroke her forehead a little, her glossy temples, her glossy tightly curled hair. Once, troubled yet secretly proud, she confided that her Joseph was a known frequenter of Johannesburg saloons, 'before we met.' My answer was to trace my fingers across her cheeks. I see clearly what charm an Irish Brigader with a quick and wandering eye might have found in these fine moulded features, the high domed forehead like an Egyptian princess's.

Over and again, as if delirious, she asks me to speak of Ireland, the same questions about country fairs, Dublin streets, rain. Do I know such and such a song? *The Curse of the Irish upon the Empire?* I merely repeat what I have already said.

Through a form of bush telegraph involving cross-fence gossip among the African servants and, as I surmise, night singing, Dollie has recently gathered some news of the war's progress. Over the past three months the Boers have been falling back steadily, herded from river to river across the northern veldt, she says, still 'keeping touch' with the enemy but unable to withhold their numbers. The British shelling runs up and down their river-bed defences like fingers on a concertina, she has heard, at Johannesburg sightseers came out on foot to see the battle. The details seem convincing enough.

The official *kamp* news is that the Republican leaders have fled into exile but this I suspect as a means of further demoralising us. Whatever the truth, it does seem to go hard for the Boers. 'So he said,' Dollie raves, half of what she says becoming a mix of African and Cape Dutch. 'Retreating east in winter the sun would be in their eyes. How would they see to shoot?'

Of the Irish soldiers themselves sadly there is little news. They are said to have laid dynamite at the Sand River, the Vet, at Brandfort, to have burned British railway stores. Of course, of course, she frets, her lover predicted that too, he was a born fighter and saboteur. He foretold systematic dynamiting, a Brigade skill. 'The war will last as long as there is a man, woman, or child left in the Transvaal', so the British should not smirk so fatly in their complacency. And if the Boers revive themselves, she cries, Joseph Macken will be there! He will fight his way smiling back to her across the mountains. So raving she casts herself from side to side, rolling her belly most alarmingly.

I try to speak of what might happen after the war in an effort to calm her. 'Not until every woman and child's dead,' she repeats, 'will the war end, so Joseph said.' 'But Dollie this is my fantasy. This is what I hope. I hope for a rapid end to the war. I see the barbed wire entanglements rolled back, the Empire humiliated. Peace. And you and the baby come to Ireland with me. In my fantasy we take a little house somewhere, we wait for your Brigader there.'

'But he said he would come back *here* to find me. I must wait for him *here* on *this* side of the mountains.' 'In that case I will stay and wait with you. We three will go back to your farm and await him.'

'You know it is not my farm,' she then says shortly from under lowered eyelids, and no more. We watch her belly ripple and toss with the 'small soldier's' kicking. She lets me place a hand on it, on her, the skin incredibly warm and taut.

And after a few moments begins her refrain again. 'He says our hills in the mist are like Irish hills. Is that so? Beautiful green hills but without dark people? It is strange to me. A country full of white people and yet suffering under oppression. Miss Kathleen, speak to me of Joseph's country.' I resort to telling her Aunt Margaret's story of the Jubilee protests, the black flags and the white stitchery. Sometimes I read from the entries in this journal, about the big events in Dublin, and she slaps her legs in delight. I recite the poem she so loves, *He wishes for the Cloths of Heaven*. Then she closes her eyes and seems at last to rest even as her belly billows like a sail. Her day must be close at hand.

To me though still remains the question what to do after the war. That is, if Dollie does not stay with me. Whatever might be the fortunes of the Boers, the hot denuding light of Africa is making me restless even in my exhaustion. I want to move on but cannot think where to. Aunt Margaret's letters describe with elation the successful tea-party protest against the Queen's visit to Dublin. She urges me to come home and recuperate. Yet somehow I can hardly think of going back to Ireland yet, not now, not alone. I would feel lost and incomplete.

It may well be I have not in me the material, the mettle or

metal, that makes a great resister. I have not the fire and conviction that sweeps a woman to the head of a crowd, a man to the cannon's mouth. My inclinations are at once more commonplace and more wilful. I want to choose responsibilities, not to be appointed to them. I tire of other people's quarrels, I lose their point. There will always be those in the thick of things who will know more and feel more than I do. My fingers seek not the chilly expanse of the invisible Ideal, but the gristle and scrape of the particular. I recall the old Italian lady during the siege who kept herself alive on face-powder puddings of her own devising. I think of the quiet Mr Gandy falling upon the wild honey combs at Izinyanga, how he loudly exclaimed at that sudden sweetness. I remember his watchword: to build as well as to destroy. I think of Dollie's dear face, her sheeny smooth skin. I think of a *neem* tree and a shared grave in Bihar. Was it but a year ago, but a year last week, that Mother and Papa died?

This is, to be sure, not the time to be thinking beyond the dreadful conditions that surround us. The war is, as Dollie reminds me, far from over. It has taken two weeks to write this entry and recent rumours are as she predicted, the Boers are reorganising as a guerrilla force. All we can do at present is await the birth of this child. I certainly do so with excitement. When it comes I hope to help care for it, if Dollie allows.

This week I sent away to Durban for blankets and a small mattress. My bed linen is already cut up for sheets. A parcel of clothes has arrived from Aunt Margaret (who fortunately won't be aware the child will be black). Dollie and I together have freshly lined the wooden chest I've loaned her with vellum paper to keep the fresh cotton things free from fish moths. Later, when the time is right, my presence may come in useful to make contact with the new family in Ireland. The arrival may not in the end be a small soldier, literally interpreted, but a mere girl. If he ever thinks back to the time with Dollie, it is difficult to tell how its disappointed father would feel about it then.

The huge African moths are as usual powdering their wing dust on my page. An owl hoots secretively in the mimosa tree, sounding very much like the owls at home in Howth. I should rest. Lately I have been feeling so knocked up and even more seedy than usual, full of aches and pains. Almost every afternoon gongs in with its head-ache and, though a tablespoon of chloroform reliably unfolds a mantle of sleep, it puts a harder fist into my temples the next day. Some nights I am wakened by my own screaming, convinced that shells are slamming through the top of my skull, that all the babies in my ward are dying. It must be extreme fatigue has brought me to this, I so badly need rest. The matron has prescribed green amara to relax my nerves and improve my appetite. If I do fall ill however, I must remember to tell the superintendent, my journal should be given to Dollie for safekeeping.

Dollie, I will write this out. This is for you, my friend. Take it as a keepsake. A memento, with love, and an identity document. A piece of Ireland to have and to hold in trust until the day you and your child travel there yourself and, I dream, take it home.

# 26

It was too early for hat sales, eight thirty, the escalator creaking into motion. Under the dull-white buzz of the neon a woman in a starched uniform feather-dusted.

'Exactly like you said,' Anthea almost hiccuping. 'What you said about the songs in your family coming down from the time of the war. But this journal, it like, adds bass to the tune, *hearing* and *seeing* the live connections.'

She leaned her elbows on the glass counter, the polished panels screeched. Trays of smooth, coloured ribbons, tortoise-shell clasps, butterfly grips and hat pins were spread out on display beneath.

'See here, your grandmother Dollie singing a song about harps. It must be the song you sang in the park. Or here.' Rifling through the cleanly photocopied pages. 'Here she is, teaching the Irish nurse, the diary-writer, another Irish song. *That Queen that was beautiful will be tormented and darkened.* It's mind-stopping, isn't it? – you don't know what to say. The day I found this, Dora, about Dollie and the singing, I could see nothing but haze. There I am, just reading in the Archives a little over a week ago, part of my job, and I bump into this book with its stained cover. OK, this is interesting I think, it's one of the few journals by a woman in the magistrates' papers. But I'm not expecting any kind of discovery. I say to myself, maybe the book was used as evidence in compensation trials, the trials held after the war when people finally wised up to the conditions in the camps, that's why it's here amongst these papers.'

Dora irritably puffed her cheeks. Anthea lifted up, crammed down more pages.

'Anyhow, I couldn't not read on. It was a break from the dry reports, a chance for a bit of exchange across the decades. Great, I think. Hours on I'm still reading. I began with the letters tucked inside the front cover. That was when this version of your name first hit me, *She calls herself Dollie Macken. This African woman. In a Boer hat.* But I wasn't going to make anything of it. A local black woman seduced by a white foreigner, it's a standard story, all over the papers I was reading. Except in this case she took his name.'

A hank of hair flopped across Anthea's eyes, long brown roots, scratchy white ends. Impatiently she snatched it back, looked across into Dora's bent forehead. Was she reading these heart-numbing lines along with her, she wondered anxiously. Would she not be compelled by this? The beads of sweat were pushing through the loose foundation powder on Dora's nose, she was that close. The dry granules pressed against the sweat.

'Then suddenly here she came, here, Dora, singing your song. Brave, spirited. In a place just a hundred miles up the highway. I had to come tell you, I had to find you. In the end thank God I found Gertie in one of his haunts around the city hall. Think what this means, I said to him, for Joseph, for you. Stumbling on this incredible chance, a chance of freedom forged through a legacy of freedom struggle.' Pausing to catch her breath. 'You and your Irish ancestors, them and the Afrikaners, an intertwined history of resistance.'

Dora cased up and down the carpeted passage that ran between the glass counters, swinging her head low. Anthea's eager elbows had rucked a photocopied sheet against a branched wire hatstand. Three soft red fedoras, popular this winter. Dora pressed the crackling sheet flat and rubbed its fold with the side of her hand. It was the copy of the journal's cover, grey and dark-grey squiggled lines, smudged mascara in a rain storm. Neat block-printing made thick with hard pressure. KATHLEEN GORT'S JOURNAL, Dora read. A woman not lacking in force.

'*A Legacy of Freedom.* That's how I might write it up, if you agree, *A Twisted Legacy.* You see, an article would help publicise the issue. *Life sentence upon foreign national*, something like that. Dora, you get how I couldn't stay away, don't you? You don't mind? I couldn't suppress, how can I say, these echoes. I keep thinking I'm holding my ear to the page like it was a shell and hearing the sea.'

'I have to go to the ladies, excuse me. Must get some water.'

'Take the copy of the letter with you, where Dollie Macken is mentioned. Why not have a look at it on your own?'

'You should be worried, Miss Hardy, what I might do with it there on my own, sneaking secret items into the toilets like I was shoplifting. I might flush it down the toilet for example. In fact, with half a chance I might decide to flush that whole folder down the toilet, or dump it in a bin. That would put a spanner in your works for a while, hold up your big case.'

Anthea turned white at the coldness in Dora's voice, blue veins flared in her forehead. She had expected a distance from her, even a feigned uninterest as she got used to the idea of how much had been found out. She had not expected this withering hostility.

'My case?' she said uneasily.

'Your efforts to discredit Joseph. So deep inside he was a delinquent Boer supporter all along. Or if not a delinquent Boer, some adventuring settler's offspring. Descendant of a troublesome bastard, a Boer mercenary and an untrustworthy Irishman. Just like any one of his black or white nationalist enemies might say. He screws up the freedom process because he's one twisted half-breed.'

'No, Mrs Makken! Give me more credit than that. OK, so I'm excited by this story, the links it makes. But I'm also excited because I really think we can use this to do something for Joseph.'

'Miss Hardy, who is this *we* who will so very kindly, big-heartedly, do something for my condemned son? What gives you the right to be part of that *we*? this right to be excited? Approaching my family story with its hidden sorrows and shame like a *discovery*. Setting out with hardly a moment's pause to convert it into an article for your paper, this story that I myself don't know the beginning or end of and don't anyhow want to touch. Mn? What gives you that right?'

Dora addressed the question at the empty air beside Anthea and noticed a customer at the scarves and gloves desk glancing over, moulding her perm with the long-distance help of the hat counter's oval mirror. Dora took hold of the papers, a surprisingly thick pile. Anthea braced herself, her mouth was cramped open. Dora tapped the papers together, snapped them across. She was torn between wishing the girl would simply exit, leave her here to her hard-won self-containment, and saying more, giving vent to these choked-in feelings. Let the unavoidable division between us rest, she wanted to shout, it won't disappear for all your worrying it.

'Can I help you, madam?' she asked the customer.

'Just looking. I was hoping you'd have some of the new stuff in, the spring collection.'

'Not yet, madam. Unavoidable delays, I'm afraid, the European side.'

The woman trailed her fingertips across the fedoras as she moved off. Dora slid the papers into the brown folder. Weary with disappointment, Anthea reached for the open flap, a completed transaction?

But Dora stepped back, keeping her hands on the folder. The long in-breath she took made Anthea want to hide her face.

'Miss Hardy, while we're about it, there's a few more things I must say. The first's this. I think you forget, you totally forget, that even if I don't like to shake them out to show the world, bits and pieces of this history you've discovered are half-familiar to me. Maybe, you know, I've heard something about my grandmother Dollie before today. I've heard about some of her misfortunes. This may be surprising seeing as her story happens to be partly my own, but yes – '

'Mrs Makken, *please*. Of course I'd not deny that. Of course your past, or some of it, is known to you. There was even a time when I thought you were trying to tell me more about it yourself. Our lunch in the park, that time. Maybe I was mistaken, but I thought you were letting me in just a fraction. All I've done now is shown how the background broadens. I've shown its crumbly detail, how full it is, or no, Kathleen Gort's journal has shown that. I've been the mechanism, I opened the book. You can look at it that way. I opened the book.'

A clatter of cups and saucers from the trellised tea shop, nine o'clock. Two white ladies padded past, their sibilant whispers.

'But what gave you that right, Anthea Hardy? This is my number one question. What gives you the cheek to come here and educate me about my own family? You, with everything that you stand for in my life? What let you go quizzing into our background? It must've taken hours of nosing to come up with this – this *find*.'

'Even so, that's genuinely what this is, Mrs Makken, a find. As much as I might want to claim this story as my own, I haven't conjured it. The journal was there in the Archives, the clues to your family story are in it. I couldn't believe the luck myself when I stumbled on them. As to what I stand for, well, my own personal involvement in this situation, yes, rather than keeping me out, it strongly pulled me further into the history. You'll remember me talking about trying to understand the fatality of the bomb. Wanting to see the broader picture, the linking pattern, even before the paper sent me to work on those documents. But then the connections began to unravel like magic. The record of it is in here – here, in my notebook.'

Stretching down to her brief case while keeping one hand splayed on the counter, eyes raised. Dora looked into those bloodshot whites, the request that was always still brimming in them.

She shook her head.

'OK then.' Anthea righted herself. 'Basically what I say there is this, just this. I was interested in the larger history because I wanted to see how we reached where we were. Something different from the usual black-and-white set-up, something more complicated. I threw a match, kind of, but after that things happened of their own accord. Like watching threads of veldfire join and flare in the hills at night, that's how it was, the patterns forming before my eyes by chance.'

'Chance plays a part, Miss Hardy, but you are a quizzer and a noser, you made chance happen. You found these papers, you sniffed them out. What made you keep looking at records from this particular time, the time of this war? What made you go on and on with them? You asked Gertie questions and matched them with what you found. He told you to stop but you took no notice. I told him to tell you from me, let's keep our history to ourselves. You went on kicking your way into our lives.'

'I had a sense of something difficult in your past, all right I admit that, I acted on that hunch.' Anthea talking to her feet, concentrated, not shame-faced, flecks of spittle marking the counter. 'After what happened at Easter I thought it would give me an understanding of my own changing feelings, how I hated injustice but how I'd come to hate violence also. It was important to see how we were related, not apart, mixed-up in a shared history. For the rest I was a spectator helping to piece things together, filling the gaps. Filling the gaps made things feel less empty.'

'But Miss Hardy, as you know, we're not here to assist you. Joseph's people aren't here to help you prop up your life.'

'I haven't forgotten your saying that. But then I also couldn't stop what I was doing. I mean it was breathtaking, the find – the finding. I was sure you'd have felt the same. There was the song you sang that day. I can't get it out of my mind. And then I find a trace of it here. And your name. How can I forget your name? And I find it here too. And other details, the poetry. I felt this book was talking to me. *He wishes for the Cloths of Heaven.* That poem Dollie likes is one I often read with Duncan.'

'No better than a spy,' Dora suddenly burst out, her eyes bulging, furious, as if the reason for her anger exceeded anything they'd yet touched on today. 'Excuse me for saying, but this is no better than State Security. Did you take the chance of coming to our party to poke around too, check out our photos while we're not looking? Maybe you even spot the Boer hat hanging on my wall. Ha, you think, another clue, another nail for the frame of my story, my big exciting discovery. I've got them, these Boer-hating bombers. See how crooked and fucked-up they are.'

'Mrs Makken, believe me, I don't know what you're talking about.' Anthea was still focused on her feet, her whole body slightly trembling, as though every part of her was set on keeping a balance along a narrow edge. She said, 'I saw no hat at your place. All I did at your party was talk to Gertie and he told me things without my asking. And you yourself invited me. There was also your letter after the verdict. *I will remember you all my life for that time in the park when we had biscuits,* that's what you said. I've not forgotten that. It made me feel in a way welcome.'

'But there wasn't a licence in it, Anthea Hardy. Being friendly to you in your grief didn't give permission to come and mess. It didn't give the right to close in – '

A slight tremor in the glass counter, the thin squeak of the panels. Dora had pinned the folder down with her fists. Anthea protectively clutched a flap corner, without pulling. A suspended tug-of-war that held, that held, till Dora straightened up and the folder jerked towards Anthea. The opened flap swished a slow fan of Kathleen Gort's writing on to the carpet.

With a faint wail Anthea dropped to the floor. Huddled over the raft of papers she looked very little, her back narrow and miserable. Dora moved around the counter, slowly walking her hands. Hand over hand, hand on Anthea's shoulder. She crouched down beside her. She found to her surprise that her anger had evaporated.

'Look, I'm sorry. I didn't mean for that to happen. Let me help you. It's days – days I haven't been myself. Sometimes you know I just can't bear it – keeping going. Joseph. What's hanging – '

She stopped abruptly. Her soft loose, cheek was almost against Anthea's face. Her arm sank from her shoulder to her back.

'I can't bear what's hanging over him, so excuse me. I won't say I'm not affected by this story, even I suppose by your effort turning it up. I mean, your effort, you, Duncan Ferguson's friend. You're right, a chance like this, it's strange – I don't know, it's got force. I'm not sure how I feel. My own flesh and blood, in here. It's almost like I recognise the handwriting.'

She drew out a page to look at it in full.

*She walks at large through the compound, her distended navel pointing through her ruched shift.*

Balanced together, their free arms stretching, gathering papers, they teetered. Anthea braced her feet, Dora pulled herself upright. Nine thirty. Her hand pat-patted across the counter, felt for the drawer handle, her bag of chocolate toffees, she crackled one open. Anthea squared the last loose papers. Dora took her by the arm, led her round the counter, to the corduroy-covered high stool there, pressed her down. Three Cadbury's Eclairs spread on her palm.

'Here, relax a minute, we both need it. Like I say, it's too much this, on top of everything else. It's meeting yourself in a different shape. As if you've got a twin somewhere back then, wearing clothes you recognise.'

The toffee sweet clamped Anthea's jaws. Her feet swung in space, the folder was flat on her lap and secure. She felt completely wrung-out, almost light-headed. Dora leaned on the counter stretching her back. She talked across to where Anthea had been standing, she unwrapped another Chocolate Eclair.

'That hat she's wearing, that most of all. As far back as I can remember we've owned a Boer hat, the one I mentioned, no idea where exactly it came from. Joseph hated it, I was embarrassed about it. The day of the party in fact I hid it away, haven't taken it out since. Sam my father said it belonged to someone in our family, a war hero. The time he wore the hat, Sam made a point of saying, the Boer was a freedom fighter too. But I got nervous when he talked that way.'

Dora chewed, switched the sweet to the other side of her mouth. Her cheek bellied.

'You see, being Coloured, Anthea, it's not easy. Everything feels like a hand-me-down, Second-hand Rose. Your name, your colour, leavings. Nothing's straight and simple. And you want it straight, you want it pure, simple as pie. Something you can take hold of, not a messy muddle, a bit of Boer hat or Irish soldier to add in with the rest. And the vomity stink of betrayal – just *everywhere*. I mean, what about this devil-may-care soldier Macken inside here?' Tapping the folder on Anthea's lap. 'Did he ever come back to own his child? Bet one hundred bucks he didn't. Same old story.'

'We don't really know.' Anthea tugged her molars apart. 'There's a letter here you haven't seen yet. It gives an impression of how Dollie fared later.'

'Hey but your stubbornness, see, it gets to me, Anthea Hardy. You go on and on looking for answers, and so damn seriously, no matter what walls you knock against, no matter what breaks in the process.'

Anthea was raising the folder flap, Dora pressed it closed. She faced forwards again.

'Like I said, this is my story, parts of it, believe it or not, I might just know a bit about. My father Sam's mother now, this Dollie Makken. He remembered she herself spelled the name with two k's, she would've picked up some schooling in the households where she worked maybe, some grounding in English, some letters. Anyhow she died long before I was born, 1912 or 1913, Sam said. She died of exposure one cold winter's night, lying beside a road cradling him. He was still a boy then, big but still a boy. They'd been dispossessed by the new natives' land act along with millions of others. Calmly living on a farm somewhere north of here, then suddenly kicked out. A concentration camp survivor, but it didn't matter, the new act said get out. She sang him to sleep, that night like all nights. Sam remembered it well. She sang *Berend Botje*, the song about the boy who went out sailing and never returned. When he woke they were crusted with frost.'

Dora scrubbed her face with her palms, cleared her throat.

'After that Sam came here to the big city. Worked as an errand boy in the Indian market and around the docks. Before long he ran into Gertie. Even in those days Gertie knew everyone and gave him a stoep to sleep on. Hard times. Sam never said much about it but he did remember those songs. His mother singing him those songs out on the road.'

Four schoolgirls filed by. Some secret truancy stamped tense smiles on their lip-iced lips. A woman stepped off the escalator, shaking a wet umbrella.

'That's the important part of the story for us, you see,' said Dora. 'The act of native dispossession. Four in five people lost their land. That's where we date ourselves from, that's our anger. Coloureds were better treated, yes, but Dollie was black, looked black. The rest of the history, we put it behind us, don't hear it. It's too confusing, gets in our road.'

Under the neon Anthea Hardy's face was sickly.

'Looks like it could be too wet to go outside for my coffee break.' Dora watched the woman with the umbrella. 'Morning storm, unusual for this time of year. Maybe you want to wait here a bit longer? Have another sweet.'

'No thanks. I should probably go. Should've been at work half an hour ago.'

She did not move from the stool. Dora stretched her back, leaned on her elbows. Now, with the help of the sweeties, she felt the mood between them lifting. And she enjoyed being the one to talk. The counter creaked. Anthea shifted on her stool.

'Did you have any idea about the concentration camp then, Dora, alongside what you were saying about Dollie's story?'

'Not before today no, or I don't remember Sam mentioning it.'

'But that shows, don't you think, how we could link things up, what you know, what I know? Truly I didn't want to come here to tell you your story. But I did hope we could give it shape, working together. I mean – ' Anthea ironed the purple-and-gold sweet wrapping with a thumb-nail, folded it double, folded it again. 'I mean, it's just as much a source of anger, isn't it? Your grandmother imprisoned for no real reason in the camp. That, and the later dispossession? We could match those stories. Both times mistreated, shoved to the side, but trying to keep going.'

If Anthea reached out she could touch the back of Dora's neck, the one mole there. *Her glossy skin, her glossy tightly curled hair.* A pink comb had worked itself loose from Dora's bun. She saw the coiled knot of a fatty fingerprint on the plastic rim. The glimpse of that ordinary, medium-sized fingerprint was sharply moving. She thought of Dora rushing to get ready in the morning just as she herself rushed, hurriedly doing her hair while making a cup of tea. Suddenly she thought of Duncan also, of Duncan stretched on the floor with his Walkman morning and evening, superquiet, disturbing no one, ever, his foot silently beating the rhythm of his music.

Ten o'clock. A customer's watch alarm beeping.

'Dora, please listen, I really do think there's a way of helping the situation.' Anthea spoke carefully, choosing her words. 'If we sat down and tried to piece together Dollie's story from what you know and from the threads we have here. If we read and reread this book and spent some time and thought about what we'd read, called her story up out of your memory and these fragments. It really would help the cause, the case, your appeal against his sentence. And as part of that, yes, I could sketch something for the paper, a reconstruction of Dollie's life. A story that would connect you and Joseph to a family, a people in another land, a story reconciling people. Imagine it.'

A man browsed the hats, combing his rain-damp hair with a hand. He sneaked a look at himself in the mirror, pursed his lips, whitened his cheekbones. Anthea dropped her voice.

'To put it as bluntly as possible. If we proved him, as it were, a foreign national, if we could prove foreign connections, chances are it could release him, you ask Mr Moodey. At the very best it could get him extradited, but at least his sentence might be commuted. We could get him ten years, fifteen, instead of a life sentence.'

Release him. So Duncan would have said it, Anthea thought to herself. He'd have said it lightly, without prejudice. Release him. Release. How airy and freed this word made her feel.

A little-finger tap, then a soft thud-thud-thud. Dora rolled her fingers across the glass counter. Right hand, left hand. She spread the fingers, examined her nails, prised away a granule of dirt. Raspberry

Sundae polish didn't cover, and needed an overhaul. Ever since the trial, try to look the part.

The sigh shook her shoulders.

'I wonder what happened to that diary-writer in the end.' Her voice so low Anthea had to bend forwards from her stool. 'That Kathleen, seems a decent enough person. She didn't need to do what she did.'

'She went back to Ireland, I think. Like I said, there's a clue in the letter you haven't seen. A letter to Dollie herself, from an Irish nationalist.'

The file was open before Dora could turn.

'Keep this to read in your own time. It might help make up your mind. The letter was stored in the book along with the other one. It makes me think, you know, that Dollie owned the journal at some point. Perhaps kept it in her wooden chest. Until one day, moving on, she left it behind.'

'The book maybe but not the chest,' said Dora. 'I'd say we've got that *kas* at home. It's very likely the one, a wooden chest like that letter says. Sam passed it down to me, it travelled everywhere with him as a young man. When he was little Joseph stood it on the back stoep and used it as a stage to sing me his songs.'

She slid the photocopy into her drawer under the bag of Chocolate Eclairs, closed the drawer.

'Always the performer,' she said swivelling the counter mirror. She tightened her bun. Her gaze met placidly with Anthea's in the reflection.

# 27

Wearing his blue-tinted sunglasses indoors Daniel Moodey puts through the telephone call. 'Maximum-security prison. Yes.' Dora sidles the lengths of his office walls. She studies the pictures and certificates she already knows so well from previous meetings. Mr Moodey follows her round, whipping the telephone cord as he manoeuvres across it. No, she motions him away, Don't want to sit down. She peers as if newly short-sighted. Inside the knotted rigging of a skeleton ship at the Cape of Storms she sees for the first time the ghost of a shouting face. Behind the door is a Rainbow Chicken calendar, a photo touched up to look like a painting of three pink-white children balancing on a farm fence.

'You're through, Dora.'

'Mevrou Makken. *Maak seker nou*, make sure please to stick to the matter in hand.'

An official voice claiming the treacherous kinship of language, of *taal*. Our brown siblings in sin.

'Hello?'

'Hello hello.'

His greeting thrown across mountains, slipping along streaks of cirrus. An ocean of electric tappings and flacking stretching between them.

'Talk ma, I can hear you.'

'Joey, Joey.'

'What is it, ma?'

A fluke find, turned-up-just-like-that, she explains, finger tracing the silver medallion on one of Mr Moodey's certificates. A Dollie, must be Sam's Dollie – your great grandma, *ouma grootjie*. The names and places match like hand in glove. She tries to remember a convincing detail, yes, a head to fit our heirloom hat, a chest to hold a book. Ja, the self-same *kas* as on the back stoep. The past growing noisy, that's how she sees it, opening out like the stuck folds of an old concertina. Sam always made a point of saying it, you know Joey, the Boer used to be a freedom fighter too.

'So what are you asking, ma?'

'Nothing. Except, what do you think?'

'About being whiter than we knew?'

'Irish.'

'Ja. Black Irish.'

'Joseph, it could get your sentence shifted. They want me to help put together a piece of the family history from the scraps I know.' She glances over at Daniel Moodey watching her. 'Establish as convincingly as possible the Macken to Makken connection, that's what they say.'

'Tell what you know about us?'

'Tell what I know about Dollie's life, about Sam. Patch up, fill in.'

'What's the white woman's interest in this? Who's she? Why's she doing this?'

'She's a researcher, Joe. Miss Anthea Hardy. Obviously making this find has grabbed her imagination. She'll be writing it up. For the appeal to be a success a write-up'll be helpful.'

'She got anything to do with the one at the party? That one you mentioned, the white?'

Why does she fold her free hand into her armpit? *Cross my heart, hope to die.* He'll work it out anyway, makes no odds. But right this minute she doesn't want to say more. She's so far in already, that Anthea Hardy, her intentions shaping and squeezing the air between them.

'She's involved specifically in this project, Joey. Mr Moodey says it's worth a try.'

Mr Moodey is cracking his knuckles, snapping his neck, diamond-shaped window reflections semaphoring in his sunglasses.

'Ma, if you want it, if you want. Irishmen have died for their freedom, I know this. I said I would pay with my suffering, my black flesh and my blood. Yesterday I was a black terrorist. Tomorrow – '

A clacking turbulence.

'Yes, Joseph. Tomorrow?'

'A half-Irishman sentenced for half a life. A half-breed freedom fighter and no fucking freedom.'

The hiccuping laughter, crossed with static, suddenly cuts out.

Mr Moodey twists the phone out of her clenched hands.

'What was his feeling, Dora?'

'I think he said, he must've said, go ahead.'

She finds there are tears of relief cooling her cheeks, relief that the call is over, they've got this far, herself and Joseph – and Anthea Hardy. She dabs the tears with a tissue and straightens her back, finds she can do this, it's not as difficult as it was. The disquiet that's been breaking her inside is easing, as if a gap, a wound, is beginning to knit.

# 28

Province Hotel
Cavendish Row

Monday April 7th 1902

Dear Dorothy Macken (if I may)

I write having heard much from the men of the Irish Brigade, including Major MacBride, and now from the nurse Miss Kathleen Gort also, of the wonderful support you and your friends in Natal Colony gave my countrymen during the recent War. They have spoken warmly of the rustic hospitality and fine home cooking which sustained them so indispensably during their early battles.

In recent days we of the National Convention here in Ireland have been deeply grieved to receive news of the imminent peace to which the still-resisting Boers are being driven like hunted deer. We have heard how Lord Kitchener is strangling your hearts with farm-burnings and barbed wire camps.

But we know also that your spirit will remain undaunted, one day to rise again.

War is a black infamy, but even worse is the ravening autocracy of which the Empire that is our joint enemy is the ultimate expression. We were so proud of our regiment and our ambulance detachment when they took a stand alongside your forces. We continue to hold the example of your military courage before us. Of guerrilla swiftness and sabotage by noiseless stealth we know our Brigade had much to learn from your commandos. But probably their most important lesson of all was this, Freedom will never be won by words!

A balm to our sorrowing is Kathleen Gort's news of your son Shagan and of his well-being. He is the child, if so we might christen him, of our brave nationalist alliance across the Atlantic Sea. Joseph Macken along with the rest of the Brigade safeguarded Ireland's honour at a time of great need. Your son is the fulfilment of that honour.

If ever I am blessed with a son in the years that lie ahead I know I too will name him Shagan.

Miss Gort tells us you seek news of Joseph Macken. We hear only that he arrived in Trieste from Africa some while ago and then left for America to raise money for Ireland. No more. I am sorry for this. I think what you must be suffering and wish with all my heart I could spare it you for no one deserves this pain less than you do. I too have sorrowed greatly through a sad episode of love. I know so well how useless it is when people say as they always do, And with your eyes open you married him.

It may perhaps help you when you hear that Joseph Macken like others of the Brigade has not yet been to see even his family. Were he, despite his Boer citizenship, to set foot on Irish soil, his brave actions in Africa will have laid him open to an indictment for high treason. Yet, if ever there is word of him, we will be sure to write to you.

Your material suffering we will attempt at once to remedy. You must try to leave the deathly concentration camp as soon as you are able. I enclose a small cheque for £10, a gift from the patriotic group the Daughters of Erin. This is to tide you over until we are able to make more formal arrangements.

Miss Gort herself, you will be pleased to learn, has recovered much of her strength since returning to Ireland. Twice during the fever, so fatal to so many, that finally brought her low in Capetown, she fell into a sleep from which no one thought she would wake. Thereafter she was confined to her bed for many months, a virtual prisoner in an Imperial hospital known for its fine oleander gardens and its unfriendliness. Her aunt is now overjoyed to have her back in her care.

About ten days ago, the night after Miss Gort brought the news of your quest and showed us the grass bangle she says you made her, I had a strange dream in which I saw you. I saw you all in white, a white hood with a plaited wreath of white roses, and a light about you. There was a child leaning against you wearing white also, and you held a jewelled chalice and in the other hand a jewelled sword, and on this hand gleamed a ring carved all of diamonds, and you were smiling.

From this vision I hope I am right to conclude that you are well at least in spirit. Who knows how things are? We are all living out a pattern of destiny and must find our peace within it.

I believe you are much interested in our Irish songs. One day perhaps it will be possible for you to visit us and to see the beautiful hills where our songs are made.

I also enclose with this letter an embroidered symbol I have crafted to mark your connection with us. I was recently in a nationalist play in a small theatre here in town and was able to embroider during the rehearsal. The symbol shows the intertwined flags of the Irish Brigade and the Transvaal Republic folded into a circle that may be either a Celtic cross or the sparkling ring of my dream.

I remain
Very sincerely your supporter and sympathiser
Maud Gonne

# 29

Arthur and Anthea discovered the ripe avocados at a pavement stall on Mgeni beach after a walk in a high wind. Though it was late in the season for avocados, one or two of the fruit in the box were still green and just beginning to soften, the stone knocking in its closed yellow cave of buttery flesh.

They drove back to her flat. His first time there. She dumped her keys, her handbag, her folder with its copy of Kathleen Gort's journal, on the kitchen table and he turned silently in the livingroom, rolling on his heels, not ready to sit down. All these bare walls, he looked around, these untouched boxes of books, this anonymity, and yet threaded through this the surprisingly near scent of her, her bare skin, her towel hung on the back of a chair. No pictures of Duncan Ferguson, he checked, aware of an uncertain excitement. In the bedroom maybe? The box of avocado pears lay flat on his arms, their hard green shine.

'Arthur, here, come into the kitchen. There's a way of preparing avocados I'd like to show you, a kind of avocado mousse.'

Her fingers curved round the mottled pear she had pointed out at the beach.

'I experimented this to perfection as a bored teenager. For a dream treat you need lemon jelly, but lemon juice and cream should be all right.'

She cut open the fruit and pulped the flesh in her hands. 'So incredibly soft.' Her sideways glance at him suddenly faltering. 'Why don't you make coffee? The things are over there.'

The white rope of cream coiled into the mixing bowl.

'The secret is to keep the lemon separate from the cream. The lemon goes in with the avocado, then a rasping of onion, there, that's it, now the cream and pepper, a touch of ginger.'

His head bent over the coffee mugs, a frown unsettling his forehead. 'We forgot bread,' he said.

'We could eat it straight from the bowl.'

Her lips closed stickily around the root of her middle finger. Her hair glistened with crystallised sea-spray. They looked at each other with a new, unguarded interest. She saw how the blue evening light streaked the bent ridge of his nose.

'Something wonderful like this, that's local, makes me think about that nurse, Kathleen Gort, that it's a pity she didn't have more pleasure when she visited. She lived in the torrid zones and as far as we know never tasted avocado, mango, dived into warm breakers … '

'She wrote about what was important to her. She found the wild honey in the rain storm.'

'And the pleasure of stroking Dollie's head.'

His mouth, eyes, near. That mass of thick dark hair she'd always noticed about him, just here. She could trace the creamy avocado across his lips by dipping her finger, lifting it to his mouth.

He sat at the table and pulled her down beside him. She began to reach for a spoon, he took her wrist.

'Anthea, you're very deep inside this Makken affair.'

'To state the obvious, yes. And getting deeper.'

'Yes, and getting deeper, that's what troubles me. You're very involved, and being so involved, you're vulnerable. Your liberal sympathies and your sympathetic grief could easily be manipulated. I'm speaking as your friend – as someone who feels warm towards you.'

His smile opened his long face.

'Excited by you too.'

They were holding hands, watching their fingers, their own, the other's, interlinking. Not indistinguishable, Anthea thought, not like holding hands with Duncan. Your fingers or mine? they'd say, now you see me, now you don't. This stubborn fact of skin, skin difference, her skin lightening, Arthur's darkening by contrast. Getting used to the fact of skin these past months had meant gradually getting closer in, to Dora, to Arthur, like this. Winding herself deeper in, Arthur's fingers between her fingers, skin on skin. Knitting into him even while thinking, not thinking, Duncan's skin. Duncan's torn-up, fragile skin.

Arthur said, 'What I've been wanting to say for a while, Anthea, is take good care.'

'I appreciate that. But seriously, I don't think the situation as involving as you say.' She pressed her fingers into the spaces between his. 'For a long time Dora has avoided contact. She's still reluctant to see me. For her I remain a kind of victim, or related to a victim, that's a good reason to resent me. As for my role, I've become a message-carrier, a go-between – between the past and the present. I'd like to encourage Dora to help me reconstruct Dollie Makken's story. Right now it's the blank space in our hoped-for network of links and connections between Europe and Africa, then and now, between the different warring sides. Once it's filled we have the case for an appeal. We'll be able to present Joseph Makken, Irish descendant.'

'And you're saying all this is not embroiling? You're simply standing outside your web of connections tweaking the threads?'

'Yes and no. Outside the web because this isn't my family. Inside, happily inside, because I'm part of an evolving context. That living history of jumbled causes I once mentioned, it's emerging around us.'

'Which confirms my worries. You began as a facilitator, Anthea, OK, but now, being interested and vulnerable, you could rapidly become drawn in, a piece of Dora's story. I worry what your connection with her might persuade her to do, mount a big campaign, get the foreign media's interest. You've got to ask yourself, who's in control here. Who's holding the pen?'

The harsh scrape of her chair. She made a thin shape against the light, the palm trees outside framing her head like a bizarrely lavish garland.

She spoke out of a face in shadow, her hands hinged on the edge of the sink.

'I'm hoping Dora'll help me tell Dollie's story, that's all. I don't know what else you could be suggesting. All Dora herself keeps saying is back off, you're interfering. And, in fact, rather than this hurting less, with time it only seems to hurt more. I like her, I'd have liked to have met her outside of our sadness.'

'Anthea, Anthea.' He stood up and moved towards her, wanting to rub that scribble of white hair from her forehead. 'I intend this in the best way possible, as a warning. These past few weeks, I've kept realising, I've kept wanting to say … I mean, I see how close the events of Easter still are to you, so this could seem like getting in the way. But even so, I just want to say, you mean a lot to me.'

Drawing the side of his hand lightly across her eyebrows, her nose, the arc of her collarbone under her thin shirt.

'I wouldn't be honest to myself and to you if I didn't say this. Much as I'm sympathetic to her, I wonder if Dora won't interfere *back*. You've made yourself available, you seem to want to be her friend. She could try to use you, perhaps even without realising it herself. She may weave misleading fabrications into what she says about Dollie. She may suggest greater loss and neglect than she has evidence for, to plead greater restitution. Thicker bandages for deeper wounds.'

'That's not how she is.'

'I know. Dora's a decent woman but she loves her son. She'll do anything for him.'

He dipped a finger into the bowl of avocado cream, took her hands, and painted a pale green vein on the narrow flank of one of her arms, then on the other. A sticky thread which he lifted with his tongue, licked up each soft length from the wrist, pressed his mouth into her elbow hollows.

Anthea felt a long-held tension stretch and soften inside her. A pain behind her eyes was leaking away. What he was saying was becoming a rhythm of breaths against her skin. He knelt down and she put her wetted arms around his neck. His head came against her breasts and his hands around her hips.

'It may seem ridiculous but I've had what I can only call jealous worries.' His breath warming her skin. 'Some days when you're away in the Archives, I worry that Dora might be trying to set up something between you and Joseph. A relationship between you two, I mean, what an ideal failsafe in any appeal against his sentence. See, the bomber has a partner, and what a partner. How tightly this wouldn't knot you into the Makken story.'

'If that were so,' she smiled ironically, holding his gaze, at last running her fingers across his head, through his hair, 'Then you've acted in time.'

She slid down beside him and kissed his mouth.

# 30

It takes fifteen minutes to mount the three flights of stairs to Anthea Hardy's flat, pausing on each landing, the concrete slapping up against Dora's feet, her lungs quivering like imprisoned birds, the folded letters in her hand turning squashy with sweat. Everything seems to want either to squeeze in upon her or to burst outwards. Anthea's face peering from her open doorway is an expanding cloud of dancing silver lights.

The kitchen is all avocado. There's a bowl-full on the table beside a potted cactus, a basin of crusted green paste in the sink. The wet compost smell of rotting avocado fills the air. Dora puts her sleeve to her mouth. The avocados crowd upon each other in the fruit bowl, too alive, taut with overripeness. The green globe of the cactus is a bristling pear.

She wonders how it is she's suddenly sitting. How did she get from the door to here? Today time is broken by gaps, patches of no memory, tired breathing, tired footsteps. Silly to have walked all the way here, up that hill, then the stairs, that strain on the heart. When there's already quite enough to be sweating about, the stress of all she's agreed to, this morning's discovery on top of everything else.

She can't exactly remember what she's been doing since that moment early this morning rummaging through the odds-and-ends *kas* on the back stoep. Getting ready to come here to Anthea's she had the first good look inside that chest in years, it held so much of the past. She turned up the speckled slabs of Bernice's laundry soap, a knot of shoe-rags and odd socks and a kid's knitted scarf, Monica's? she recognised the snowflake pattern, and rummaged deeper down under a motorbike manual, a clattering of Joseph's old matchbox cars, and then

saw the writing that she recognised, beginning to sweat. KATHLEEN
GORT. PERSONAL ESSENTIALS FOR AFRICA. That neat block-printing,
now paying her a visit too. A yellowed scrap of time keeping itself to
itself for how long, out here on the stoep? She leant further into the
chest, pulled back a dog-eared corner of Kathleen's lining, and then
another, thinner-paper, layer, and saw the two letters folded there, just
as the journal said, the same thick yellowed paper as the List, and the
same writing. Her heart, she felt, almost struggling to beat, her vision
dissolved into these daubs of light. History shaping into a circle, making good.

She reaches for the coffee mug on Anthea's table. *Duncan*, a red
joined-up-writing stencil looped right the way round. The letters blur-
ring as she stares, a small ring of fire.

'Maybe you'd like a drink after all, Dora? Some water? You said –'

'No thanks. Please no. I was just looking. At the design. The writing
on the mug.'

Behind her drifting veil of silver stars the girl is flushed as usual,
excited probably, bitter with deodorant. A bite-sized mark like a burn,
an angry mouth, on her neck.

Probably a good thing too, if that means a boyfriend. Try to lose herself a little, Dora said it once before.

Anthea opens a green notebook to its blank back page. Her fingers
lie lightly on the buttons of a small tape recorder. In the other palm is
the tiniest cassette Dora has ever seen.

'How do you want to do this? Timed sessions? Or shall we talk till
you want to stop? You say. I'm your note-taker. In the fridge is cold
water, chocolate, biscuits. Take whatever you want.'

'I don't want to tape yet,' says Dora.

'You want to talk?'

In silence Dora opens her hand, the two letters lying there moulded
like shells by her moist fingers.

'They were stored in the *kas* just as we're told in the journal,' she
says. 'More of Kathleen Gort's letters home. Early war news, how close
to the African struggle she feels. I knew you'd want to see them.'

When Anthea picks up the folded papers she is shaking uncontrol-
lably. The letters move in her hands as if alive.

'Anything about Dollie?'

'Not that I could see. They hadn't yet met at the time these were written. But then I've not properly read. You read them later.'

Anthea slides the letters between her trembling palms, longingly, as though they were lucky dice.

'Later?'

'Yes, later. I think we'll have reading later and taping later. Right now we must think about Dollie. Finding those letters fixed something for me, turned it around in my head. I'm sure now what to do, I want to think about Dollie's voice. For that even Kathleen Gort can't help me. I need to sit and feel her voice inside.'

The tape-recorder drops into Anthea's bag, a dull clunk. She slips the letters, reluctantly, gently, one by one, into the middle of her notebook.

Dora says, 'I read that other letter too, several times, the lady nationalist's. It made me sorry. I don't know how much she cared. I don't think she got it that Dollie was African. Kathleen Gort must've kept it back.'

'Yes,' Anthea says. 'I think Maud Gonne was probably stuck in her own sorrows, which she mentions. She did try to get in touch.'

Dora presses her hands against her eyes, drags the palms down her cheeks. One hand edges across the table towards the letters in Anthea's notebook as though to make sure of their existence. She just touches the protruding corner of a folded page. Her breathing is uneven and loud.

She says, 'Wouldn't a word-processor make this quicker?'

'And noisier.'

'But Anthea Hardy, this can't be me only, not at first anyway. I know just bits, you've read that whole diary. I can't manage more than a page now and again. I feel choked, like suffocated, when I do more.'

'I've made notes that might help us, here in the middle of this green book. Life on a Boer farm for a black house servant. What the Brigade was up to in Natal. Eventually we can draw on these new letters, we can scan these images on to your view of events, like showing several slides simultaneously. Then we'll go to my office, write it up, see what we have.'

'It was a hardworking life,' says Dora, 'For a sharp-boned restless young woman. Orphaned young. Her son remembered her sharp bones jabbing him when he rested against her, he remembered her solitariness. It was a life broken open by the visit of the red-haired stranger.'

'Yes,' Anthea says.

She writes, *the wonderful visit of the red-haired stranger.* She feels very warm, as if the top of her head and fingertips are radiating heat. Can they do this? she thinks, she and Dora, will they stay the course? How long can they survive on the thin fuel of their disconnected sorrow, their unsteady trust?

Behind her pressed eyelids Dora sees the outlines of the kitchen etched in pink, silver lights dancing everywhere, in wreaths, in wraiths, in braids of writing. Wreaths of silver stars. *A plaited wreath of white roses, and a light about you,* she remembers. A dark wraith in a shining veil. *The rumble of their Irish voices,* wrote Kathleen Gort, *lifted my heart.*

The dead coming home to roost.

# 31

*As told by Dora and Anthea, and written into Anthea's notebook*

When the big guns began rolling down the railway line that
runs through the third pasture, their barrels pointing south,
that was very strange. Wonderful also was the sight of Mevrouw
huddled with us under the kitchen table, praying aloud, Bet
echoing her. And the explosions too, they were strange, the
sound of cannon fire ripping the air like it was cloth, so that the
battle three valleys away seemed just next door.

But to me there was little so astonishing, little so wonderful,
as the visit to the farm of the smiling red man.

The short red man with his hair the colour of June sunsets,
the colour of our blood-red clay, leading the horse he could
barely ride to the back door. Beating his sjambok handle against
his thigh to a silent tune in his head.

I had never seen so pink a man.

And his eyes so blue they looked faded white. Though they
smiled at me.

At me especially.

At night when I sing myself to sleep that is the picture I see.
Out here on the road in the cold, cast out of our home, the land
we've worked for ten years, holding our son Sam's head in my
lap, heavy against my hip-bone, that is the picture. The bright
red man with his strange eyes wearing a Boer slouch hat and a
bit of purple veld flower stuck in the brim. His sideways smile

as he said slowly to Bet the head kitchen *meid*, 'Would you ladies refuse a thirsty man a cup of coffee?'

And beside him another man, Matthew Finn his friend, who was silent in my memory, but stood alongside, Bet always reminded me, stood alongside him, tall, freckled, and also grinning.

Their chorus, 'We are Irishmen fighting in the service of the Republican government. The government has annexed these hills but will allow neither robbery nor plunder of farms. What we take will be entered upon a list and a receipt given.'

The rain running in sheets across their cheeks.

And naturally, because we were hardly grown women yet, we were giggling, giggling and wiping our eyes, even at the official talk, spoken in such an unfamiliar tongue, and us mainly used to our homely mix of English and Dutch and our own other words.

The little red man's left cheek crinkling at me, and his foot tapping, while the other made pleasant talk.

Saying it was the flag hung on the front gate that invited them in. The white sheet we had dyed green, red, blue, with Marta the house *meid* and Mevrouw Bester's help, pig spinach, beetroot, mulberry, in blotchy blocks.

Our home-stewed *Vierkleur*.

We nodded and did not say it wasn't until yesterday's news of the English retreat from Dundee in the freezing rain that we took the shop-bought Union Jack off the gatepost and began boiling spinach and dipping the sheet. We glanced at each other and did not say there were British soldiers here at this same stable door only last week, Tommies full of big talk of 'thrashing Boojer and Kroojer'. How our mountains are hardly mountains, nothing like 'the Himaleeyas up at Simla'.

We did not say but I could tell from Bet's laughter she liked these ones more.

They were talkers, their speech was kind, their faces were loose. Their khaki shirts looked slept-in but they didn't seem to mind. They were on an adventure and so far the luck was going their way.

Bet slid the stable-door bolt open but already I had dragged the kettle on to the coals.

There is no sympathy for Britain in my heart.

(And for that matter little for the Boers either.)

The soldiers stretched their wet boots towards the stove. They shook the wetness from their hair, the droplets blazing in the firelight. They said that last Friday, the same rainy day we were huddling here together, the British fired on their own men and lost hundreds capturing a rocky hill at Dundee. The men were mainly conscripted Irishmen marching into battle with pipes alight, the hill the Boers abandoned anyway.

We had to lean in close to catch the tune of their talk, so lop-sided was it to our ears, harmonious but gargled.

That day of the Dundee battle, they said, they themselves were pressing the British left flank but didn't get in deep enough. Lost in the mist, they smiled, a botch. But even so they'd captured a crowd of Tommies hiding behind rocks. They were conscripted Irishmen again, Dubliners, whom they and their Republican friends had packed off to Pretoria, though not without first saying, That'll teach you whose side you fight on.

Luck oh Mother of God yes, was going their way, they said. They were out to hit England wherever they could. And this was the best coffee they'd tasted this side of the border.

It was at that moment Mevrouw cocked her head round the door and smiled to hear them. In her soft strained English she welcomed the two 'liberators' to 'the land of her forefathers', and hoped her household, indicating us, would make them feel at home. But even as she did so, her people mistrusting all strangers, she cast a sharp eye over their guns and boots.

We took her welcome as our invitation. We set about mixing a sweet batter for poffertjes, that they called griddle cakes, 'but these are fatter and pointier than those at home', and ate them dripping with honey three at a time.

His left cheek crinkling at me.

Until after a silence he said, his eyes on me and not only on my face, 'And what do you girls do up here in the country for amusement?'

'On Saturday afternoons we sit in the shadow of the pink stone wall by the wattle plantation and sew,' said Bet. 'Crotchet sometimes too, sing to each other. Xhosa and Zulu songs, Dutch songs.'

And he, 'Yes?'

'Well other times there's work, plenty of work.'

And she went on to say how we both began as scullery maids here on Pieter Bester's farm Doornkop, she, Bet, a few years before me. Talking fast because these soldiers' faces were so open and friendly. So when Dollie Zwartman over there, pointing a finger shiny with butter, when Dollie, she said, was still learning to scour floors, she herself was made water carrier. And when I, Dorothy Zwartman, was water carrier, she, Bet, was already laundry *meid*, though Dollie being an orphan always got the milk and sugar treatment, sugar for her porridge, milk for her coffee. So we were never exactly in step in our promotion. Never equally treated, even though she was the older and the paler one. No one scolded Dollie for dreaming, and she, Bet, always had to carry more water.

She smiled teasingly when she said this but I knew she smiled through invisible tears, for Mevrouw was often harsh with Bet, and punished her when it was I who was slow.

He still looking at me.

So I said, 'I like to see the silver fingers of water close around a cotton sheet in the laundry. When I rinse clothes, I think of what my mother said. The weight of water a laundry woman has to carry is as nothing compared to the beauty of its wetness.'

And he, slapping his hands laughingly against his still-sopping trousers, 'But amusement? What do you girls do for amusement?'

'We've been down to Ladysmith the once,' I said, 'To see the singing troupe from America. They were a native troupe, black men and women, but smartly dressed. The master gave us three days off and an ox cart to travel down to see them.'

'Gave *you*,' Bet said as I blushed for having forgotten. That time she was kept home for burning Mevrouw's Sunday bodice with the hot press.

She shuffled the third batch of poffertjes on to the soldier's plates, her voice flinty.

'Some weekends we sit in our rooms and drink with the boys from down the farm. Though Dorothy here being so young usually prefers her bed.'

'Well then,' my soldier said, his friend stretching his arms in a way that suggested leaving, 'you've lived here a while?'

'Nearly all my life,' Bet began to say, but it was me he was addressing. 'Here and on a neighbouring farm —' she said, and noticed Matthew Finn unlatch the door.

She slipped into the pantry to get their wet coats.

And now no one was there but us. The room had fallen suddenly silent though my skull was roaring with the beating in my chest. I gave him the cup of water he asked for, to wash down the cakes, and felt the enamel heat up as he took it. My hand resting on the cup, my fingers scorching.

No one there but us. Eye to eye, he no taller than I.

'So you're a local girl?'

'No, not exactly.' Looking at the ground, no longer able to bear the flicker in his gaze.

'My mother's people belonged to a Basotho mountain clan, so she said,' I began, surprised at this ease of talking to a stranger. 'She came from the blue hills beyond the Free State, but who knows, some said her father was her mother's baas. Master,' I translated for him, 'A European master.' As he smiled knowingly and whispered, 'Three years I've lived on the Rand.'

'Well, poverty visited the homestead and she ended up on the mines, a hotel laundry maid but proud, and bitter in her pride, long before I was born,' I took the cup from him, which was still warm.

'Then we may have laid eyes on each other before today,' he said stepping closer. 'And maybe I recognise you. I've been welcomed at many of the hotel bars on the mines, O'Reilly's, Parnell's Green Duck Saloon. It was in O'Reilly's bar we organised the first Irish national society on the Reef. It was in the saloon bar on Pritchard Street our leader John MacBride recruited our countrymen for this war. Lay England by the heels, he told us, Do your duty and strike hard, for we cannot yet do so at home.'

The red man himself almost cheering to tell of it.

'It was from Pritchard Street we set out for Pretoria to meet the President,' he said. 'And from there we came down here by train.'

I prepared to scald the dishcloths in the wooden trough beside the back door. Again I shifted the kettle to the hottest part of the fire, talking and working at once was a way of avoiding his look.

'I would have been too young to remember you,' I said. 'My mother brought me here three, nearly four years ago. She smelt trouble coming. She said the mines were cursed because the whole world wanted them. Zululand, the country my father came from, would be safer. He had been a miner, a migrant to the mines, but I never knew him. His name wasn't Zwartman. That was the name my mother gave me, Dollie Zwartman.'

'And I was a mine worker also,' he said. Smiling so warmly I had to dig the heel of my hand into my middle under my apron. 'We were mechanics on the mine railway, my companion Matthew and I. Which is why we come in useful for the Boers on this Natal invasion. Clever with machines like big guns, me and the rest of the Irish Brigade. Clever with machines and dynamite.'

'My mother and I,' I said, the words still flowing, 'my mother and I reached Natal Colony but got no further. We didn't make Zululand. She died on the road, spitting blood, she was tired beyond endurance. We'd walked from the Reef. Ten days it took, two to get over the mountains. We saw the sea from the mountains it was so clear a day, and then she died. I came to the first farm I could find, this one here, and they buried my mother and took me in. It was good of them. The Besters have no children themselves, their servants are their children. And who can say what we would've done if we'd reached Zululand? My mother didn't know my father so well, let stand his people. My parents were together no more than a few days.'

'The fiercest loves can be the briefest,' he said close behind me.

Breath needling my ear.

I slapped a dishcloth flat on the running board.

'A lie if there ever was one,' I cried, and must have cried loudly because Bet opened the pantry door with a start.

'I was a burden to my mother all my life,' I said.

Bet swung the heavy coats across his arm and took the dishcloths from my hands, shooting me a questioning look.

'The strength of you Africans, men and women, is beyond compare,' he said.

A wave of blood ran from my heart into my face.

'There were seven thousand Zulu miners came down a week ago from the Rand,' he continued, 'expelled by the mines and walking to Natal, walking and starving. At the border the generals commandeered them to drag the heavy Boer guns across the passes. And they did.'

'We heard of that,' Bet through tightened lips. 'There are days when we know not what to think of the Boers.'

And he, his speech coming up from the back of his throat, 'But I hope you'll think softly of the Irish. The Irish like the Boers are a small nation fighting for freedom. With the Boers we've a common foe.'

'A common foe makes strange bedfellows,' Bet said primly.

'Ah bedfellows,' he returned. 'If it's beds and bedfellows we're speaking of – '

But the horses were stamping at the door.

He put out his hand so I must dodge back or take it, and said, 'Dollie Zwartman, Joseph Macken, Transvaal State Artillery.'

I had taken his hand, small, fleshy-red, hot. His pink sunburned mouth smiling.

And he was gone, scrambling his way into the saddle, an ibis cawing and wheeling overhead.

An hour before, before the war reached our back yard in the form of these two men, I had not heard of Ireland, nor been anywhere but the mines. Yet that minute holding his hand, his sunburned mouth so nearby I could see the spider-web patterns on the flaking skin, that minute I knew his life would touch my life, that his spirit would run in my veins.

Handing back the dishcloths, Bet said, 'Dollie, be careful. We don't know where they come from. That one with the eyes – somehow, I don't know, I've the feeling *hij smaak jou*. He could take liberties.'

*Hij smaak jou. He tastes you, he wants to taste you.*

And I, feeling myself blushing, 'But Bet! Only to you I cannot say I do not like him. Did you see his smile? Did you see how he shrugs into his coat? Like liquid. And how he says my name? As if he was rocking me. Dol-lie Zwart-man.'

I was looking out at the driving rain but then twisted round, quick enough to see Bet's stretched-open mouth.

'Dorothy, he's a white man.'

'A red man, a white man. Not all of them are the same.'

'I'd forgotten. Your white grandfather.'

At which I scowled and turned back to the scalding.

But scowls did not last long between us. Bet and I depended on each other, just the same as did the soldiers in their commandos. Besides it was thanks to her, her persistence and her scheming with Marta and Mevrouw, that some weeks later we set out on a visit down south, to where the Tommies were besieged. It was she helped encourage Baas Piet's growing excitement about the Boer campaign and the power of their cannon.

'And to think of foreigners, outlanders, mounting the guns,' she said, 'Irishmen.'

The baas might be brushing his hat in the front room, scraping the horses' hooves in the yard.

'To hell!' he finally cried, 'If it's not my wife it's my servants, nagging. Let's go to see this show.'

By which time, a month later, the war had become a picnic.

The exercise frame taken from the abandoned British gymnasium at Dundee, that was our biggest piece of loot and made a fine clothes horse. But Baas Piet had also hauled away from the surrendered town not only brass trumpets and regimental colours, but crates of tinned food and boxes of fruit, a bounty that set us gawping in wonder. For weeks, our skin glowing, we feasted on Norwegian fish and New Zealand mutton, and from the Cape the sweetest peaches and pears.

Baas Piet, giving me a quilted sleeping-bag that no one else wanted, had said, 'An army so loaded down with goods cannot win this war.'

Shaking his head but his eyes twinkling.

All that month I had slept with the sleeping-bag rolled lengthwise along the side of my bed, the nights still being cold. And every morning Bet laughed to see how I held it twined in my arms.

'Dollie,' she said, 'He is a mere roisterer and not to be trusted. When we go to the battlefield you'll see then.'

But it was a different story we heard at the Boer sangars this side of Ladysmith.

We travelled down by Glencoe Junction and the trampled banks of the Waschbank River, and in the evening camped beside a muddy stream not far from Pepworth Hill. The only signs of the war's presence seemed the few broken rifles scattered amongst the brown rocks.

But then at dawn we saw the holiday spectacle flickering through the trees downstream. A host of families with children, ponies, dogs, wagons, had come to visit the war also. The sky that day was bright with soft clouds and the breeze gentle and, though firing could occasionally be heard, the atmosphere was as of a festival. Everywhere cloths were spread on the sand, and cake and fruit laid out, and Baas Piet wore his braces hanging at his sides. A Pretoria man sitting on an ant-heap nearby cleaning his rifle offered dops of Cape Smoke brandy wine to all passers-by.

It was he who said, 'The State Artillery? By happy chance, they're just beyond the next rocky scarp. Where you see the aloe.'

In new white-cotton pinafores, Dundee plunder, Bet and I were turning our feet in the direction of his pointing, when this same soldier said, 'So you know our local heroes?'

And he began to tell those milling round, about the last battle before the siege, here at Modderspruit. How after a fierce artillery duel the British had been driven back in confusion, their troops scattered, their mules stampeding. How those heroic Irishmen, our own October friends, had clinched the day.

Thing was, he related, Bet and I forcing our way closer, the British never expected the forty-pounders to be installed on mountains. On forts, yes, but not on mountains. Yet, verily, there they were, he pointed up the hill ahead. The men of the Irish Brigade and the State Artillery with their oxen and small tribe of natives had hauled the big guns to the top of grassy Pepworth Hill, and there they had stayed all morning, blasting away at the British infantry through the lingering haze.

But a few days after we fed the two of them at the farm.

For the first hours, the soldier said, the Artillery met with heavy weather. 'Over there on Lang Kop I have difficulty holding this Mauser here still, so much does the ground round about shake with the fury. The British're concentrating all their fire on that hill.'

And then, towards noon, a Boer corporal came roaring over to a group of the Irish who lay behind boulders covering the flank of the hill. There was John MacBride there, and Patrick Savage, and fearless Joseph Macken, and the Keating brothers, and poor Colm Lovely too, who was later badly wounded.

Bet and I looked at each other.

'Ammunition for Long Tom!' cried the corporal, 'It's about all gone. New levers! More shells!' The Irish boys jumped to their feet. 'Ready, Ready!' And within moments were racing across the line of fire to the depot below.

The Republic's renewed blasting, the Pretoria man told us, had the discouraging effect upon the English that forced them to give up the day. Drag their own guns back to Ladysmith and invest the town.

Boers came over from miles around to meet the brave Irishmen, shake them by the hand, share the stock of beer they'd seized from an abandoned farmhouse that very afternoon.

The brave Irishmen. My cool red Irishman. How carelessly he shrugged when we at last ran into him, crying, 'We've heard what you did! What a splendid show!'

He was lying under an acacia tree nursing his gun. To the tree was lashed a faded green flag, that we had tracked down.

At first however, as we hopped from rock to rock to reach the tree, I asked Bet in a whisper if she thought he must be very surprised to see us, so empty was his face as he watched us coming up the slope, his cheek resting on a mound of earth, a stick of grass in his mouth. But then Bet unwrapped her cloth and spread out a fresh batch of griddle cakes, and he looked over at me and smiled, suddenly, bright as a fanfare, tapping his one boot against the other.

'Dollie Zwartman.' He sang the sounds, singing as I had been singing his name and my own name while scrubbing the kitchen floor, and washing up, and scraping tripe, every day this past month.

Then three other Irish Brigaders came up, hailed by him, to partake of Bet's treat. They boasted of 'ragging' the English town with cannon fire, aiming for the ridiculous little fairground turret of the town hall, you could almost see it over there between the trees, with its asparagus-headed dome. They explained how the British naval guns were no match for the heavy Transvaal cannon. And as if to order came a tiny pop somewhere behind the next hill, followed by a lazy puff of smoke, then nothing.

They spoke also of the slow days, the boredom of besieging, the horseback rides, the dozing in the sun chewing dried sausage. Boasting of the ease of battle, it seemed, but uneasily. By night, they said, they exchanged pleasantries with the British sentries. Cork men, Roscommon men, why fight for the enemy? they shouted, Come home! By day they got up to tricks, built scarecrows operated like puppets, that they set to dancing and so drew fusillades from the English lines. Mostly wide of the mark.

Joseph Macken raised a middle finger in the direction of the town.

Spitting, 'So much for Lord Kitchener.'

At that, Bet later told me, she heard a soldier seated behind her murmur venomously, on an undertone, 'Oh Kitchener please, maintain your siege. Keep safe, oh do not touch, our lovely fleshpots on the Reef.' Looking hard at Joseph Macken as he did so. 'Is a siege not a fine time to take French leave and seek out the kind hostesses on the mines?'

But I did not hear any such words, though I was sitting right beside Joseph.

After a while a circle of quiet formed around us, with his smile shining at the centre of it, and I noticed everyone had melted away, Bet included, and his hand was resting beside mine on the ground. The crystals of sweat shining in the copper hair on his forearm. And I became aware of his singing.

When the Lion shall lose its strength,
And the Queen of England pine,
The Harp shall sound sweet, sweet, at length
Beyond the Southern line.

He was singing these lines over and over, till my skin felt cold with their ringing magic and my arm shivered against his. Then he looked into my face, his eyes pouring into mine like lamp-light through mist, and, humming in the back of his throat, he lowered his voice and chose a still darker and more powerful song.

England was a Queen,
A Queen without sorrow,
But we will take from her,
Fiercely, her Crown.

That Queen that was beautiful
Will be tormented and darkened,
For she will get her reward
In that day, and her wage.

Her wage for the bones
That are whitening to-day,
Bones of the white man,
Bones of the black man.

And I murmured, 'You too. You too know the heaviness of a charm.'

But as he was singing he may not have heard me.

'Is it possible to fight without song? To love without song?' He took my hand between both of his. 'Without poetry, how would the nation charge its spirit?'

I held his fingers tight and thought of the Zulu impis at Isandhlwana, my father's people, singing and stamping their way to victory against the British, just a generation ago. The land still soaked in their blood and their chanting.

I began to hum, following the rhythms of his voice.

From his pocket he pulled a folded paper, thumbed to greyness, and from it read,

Had I the heavens' embroidered cloths,
Of light and night and the half-light,
I would spread the cloths under your feet.

At which I put up my hand to touch his hair, thick and springy like my own, red as fresh blood.

And Bet's voice came crackling through the trees, 'Dollie, Dollie, we're late!'

He spoke against my ear, where for thirty days, since he had stood beside me in the kitchen, I had felt his breath stroking my skin.

'Next time we meet, Dollie Zwartman, you wonderful creature of half-light, I will kiss your lips till you bruise.'

Then I at last had the courage to reach into my pocket and give him the ring I had made. Finely plaited clay baked to a hard sheen in the oven, a skill I have. To fit exactly his little finger.

And he set his own Boer hat with its floppy brim upon my head.

'You may need it,' he said. 'Walking in this god-damned sun.'

The sun does not hurt me but I wore that hat every day following, till long after my flight from the farm.

Throughout that month of December I went about hoping the soft days and leisurely nights of the siege would tempt Joseph Macken to make the two-days' ride to return the courtesy of our visit. But then we heard that the British were massing south of the great Thukela River, their searchlights flickering Morse signals on the clouds at night. And to the north, people said, the Boers were cunningly digging themselves into the river's serrated red banks and laying wire in its channels. So cunningly that the land looked uninhabited and unbroken, but was teeming with horses and men.

A week before Christmas the calm split. Up through swirling dust in neat columns came the British, solid sheets of smokeless fire cut them down in blocks. Within a day the Pondo transport driver brought the news to Dundee, but Bet had already guessed it. There is a nerve inside her feels the shifts in the air and hummings in the land.

She put her hand to the earth. 'I find hundreds of fallen. But our men are safe.'

So we waited, thinking, if not the joy of victory, then Christmas might draw an unroofed soldier to a hearth-side and a roasting goose. And we were right. Although the heat was so great that the bird dried as soon as plucked and our tinned Christmas pudding, more Dundee loot, was warmed on the yard stones in the sun.

After the final basting of the goose I went that Christmas morning to walk in the wattle plantation, trying without luck to find a breeze. I was watching the sunlight make twinkling stars in the branches overhead when suddenly a white bird with great raised wings seemed to flare at my feet like a flame and surge up through the trees.

I screamed, I felt it was the passing of a spirit, a bird of omen, the land was so filled with the dying, the dead. And then he was there, my soldier, cradling my head against his chest, before I knew it. Wandering out to find me he heard my scream, rushed through the rough ghwarrie bush to clasp me to him.

My hand closed round the plaited ring on his little finger and we kissed.

And I felt the chip in the ring. The moment our lips touched I felt it.

During the battle, he explained, a rock in his path. He had thrown himself into a trench and cracked his hand on a rock. To foil the enemy, he said, they were hourly shifting the guns up and down the zigzag Boer lines. They were having to run bent double behind walls of boulders and sandbags. He threw himself down and chipped his ring.

But Matthew Finn up at the house gave Bet another story. It was when Joseph Macken was thrown from his horse in the thick of battle that it happened, he said. Thrown while riding to capture the ten English field-guns abandoned on the plain. A Boer soldier had to slide his horse across to protect him. Both men got away without a mark, but for a damaged ring.

I twisted the ring halfway round his finger to hide the chip. So as not to feel its sorrow.

In the hot dark of the kitchen he later showed me his battle souvenir. The cast-iron sight of one of the captured cannons, stamped *Birmingham* in raised letters. Which I guessed, but was mistaken, he wanted to give me as a keepsake.

Holding me to him, the souvenir in his hand, spiky against my back, he gazed out of the blue window.

'Christmas and no frost and chill. Beggars belief,' he said, and put the polished sight back in his saddlebag.

Then he and Matthew Finn went sweating into the front room to eat their Christmas goose with Baas Piet and Mevrouw, for the two were war heroes now, not strangers, despite their unfamiliar talk. Bet and I waited at table, and Baas Piet brought out the ten-year-old port wine to toast them with their pudding.

Afterwards they came to eat a second dinner with us amongst the lengthening shadows of the yard. Or we ate, and they drank whiskey milk punches and fed us. Joseph shredding the meat with his teeth, sliding it into my mouth. Licking his fingers and painting my lips in goose grease and spittle.

Nightfall, the secret signal between me and Bet, seemed to come rapidly then. She cleared the plates and in the ruddy darkness I led him by the hand across the yard and into my tiny room and there his Christmas present lay spread on the bed. A charmed *pelsjas*, a native patchwork skin-jacket such as I had seen Boer commandants wear, and had copied myself.

Many midnights, nine candles'-worth, had gone into its making. Cut from kudu flank hide for strength and also speed, it was cross-stitched to a leopard lining for ferocity. For cunning I had fringed the edges with baboon tail and then, humming his song, hemmed in dog's teeth and a dog's paw, for loyalty.

'Easy-easy with the dog,' Bet said. 'I knew a woman put too much of that into her man's coat when he left for the mines, and nine months later she gave birth to puppies.'

At the last, when the coat was almost ready, I sewed a precious shred of lion skin into the left lapel, over the heart, keeping a narrow ribbon of the same for myself. The skin was bought from the sangoma below great Mpati Hill, the best and most expensive sangoma I knew. It was she who had treated the garment also, and sung over it, and given me bitter apple berries to place at my door to protect me, and pronounced the jacket safe.

A charmed jacket to keep my lover faithful and safe.

I draped it over his shoulders and watched for what I had long awaited. The charm enfold him. The liquid slide of his arms into the shining skins, faithful and safe. And then I blew out the candle and unclasped my collar, drew my pinafore and dress down over my hips and stood before him naked. He put his hands to my breasts. His charmed red hands, burning. And the skins of loyalty and cunning swung about us.

When I am cold and alone, like now – cold and alone but for the sleeping body of my child, my *ngane*, in my lap – I imagine I feel him still. I feel still the nuzzling bluntness of our loving there on the narrow bed, our knuckles, knees, butting. I feel my fists in his back, the big thick muscles there. How he rubbed, nosed, nuzzled, made low whimpering noises like a feeding baby. And I was glad of it, the clumsy butting gentleness of that loving, as he was my very first.

At dawn I rose to sponge my blood from his jacket. Which we then wrapped carefully to fit into his pack. The morning was again hot, too hot for skins, and a charm must not be overworn and so worn thin.

He raised his arms to adjust his reins and the sweat was black on his chest.

It was then I saw the furled green flag folded across his saddle-bag.

He said patting it, 'That's mine to look after during this Christmas recess.'

And I, 'It's an honour.'

'An honour indeed, but not the highest honour,' he said smiling. 'For now we have a new flag, a crisp new flag of green Irish poplin sewn for us by women of Dublin. From Dublin and Marseilles it came by boat all the way via Zanzibar to Lorenzo Marques. We received it the day before yesterday, the day before Christmas, and held a ceremony at our camp. Ah Dollie you should have seen it! In twos and threes the lads went up to kiss it, their Erin's banner, and the tears of their homesickness and pride fell thick upon it.'

He gripped my arm, 'My darling, are you well?'

I had stumbled at his words and a foul sickness held my throat.

The lads went up to kiss. The Irishwomen's stitchery.

And from my jealousy I knew, even in my hour of claiming him, that I would as quickly lose him also. But two days back he had kissed this symbol, a charm made by other women's hands. Two days before I could lap him in my skins.

From then on, without break, a foreboding shadowed my yearning to see him. Twice in the new year, though he sent word with the transport driver that he would come, I doubted his word and he did not appear. I asked Bet to test the air in the way she had and she said she felt nothing, only the weight of renewed preparation, artillery scoring the countryside, men on the march, British soldiers. And Boers measuring their manoeuvres, as Joseph said they did, according to the movements of the British spy balloons.

And every night I lay awake in bed practising his songs and the rhythms of his voice. Holding between my breasts the ribbon of lion skin cut from his coat. And every morning was surprised to find the nail marks. Deep cuts I had scratched into my chest.

But the third time he sent word I knew he must come. The coat had its powers. So I slipped into the front room where the bookcase was, that I knew well from Mondays when I helped Marta to dust. There were the three bibles, a book of psalms, the English cookbook. I carried the cookbook into the kitchen under my pinafore and asked Bet to help me read it. She had been educated by the children's governess at her first household, a Scottish family near Vryheid. I had my letters from my mother alone.

'I want,' I said, 'a thick strong food to give my man the feeling of home inside him. Something he can take into battle, and eat when he needs to, thinking of me.'

Bet, turning the pages, sighed a deep sigh, refusing to see my look of love. But I ignored this. Bet had spent all that Christmas night talking and only talking to Matthew Finn about his Irish sweetheart back home, the neat way she had of fitting her head under his chin. There was a reason for Bet's dullness, so I said nothing.

And before long the secrecy infected her also. She was making *pap* for the night meal and every time she crossed the kitchen, took pots to the sink, she like me made sure to put a hand inside the pantry, reach into jars, finger tins, her step quick. In my apron pocket I soon collected currants and raisins, a screw-paper of flour, the crusts of yesterday's bread rough with the pap off Bet's hands.

I put the meal before Mevrouw and Baas Piet at table, their heads were still bowed in prayer, and now I was off duty, laying my captured food on a bench in the yard. Currants, crusts, flour, which I shook up together in an old biscuit tin. Bet came swaying through the lit square of the kitchen door with a tray. A jug of milk. An egg-cup of treacle. A small basin of good yellow suet off the farm. I mixed again, singing. Singing Joseph's songs about Harps and Queens, winding them into tunes my mother had sung me in her minefield sculleries. *Ngane*, listen to my song.

Murmuring and singing, Good yellow fat, fat of cattle, silky as flesh. Raisins, fruit of our soil, soil he defends. Black skin, black as treacle, and white milk, white as he – his white stomach, his armpits white against the sun-weals where his secret red hair sprouts.

I folded and pressed the mixture together, rolled it over and over with my fists, pressing down with the power of my love for him, the weight of my love. The weight he will feel, my short red soldier, when he carries this pudding with him into the trenches, heavy as a stone.

Then I wrapped the dough in a fresh muslin cloth bleached that morning in the sun, and Bet and I boiled it. Three hours we boiled it. At ten o'clock I went down to the wattle plantation to gather more wood for the fire. And at eleven o'clock once again. And at twelve as I was lifting the saucepan from the stove I heard the footsteps striking the yard stones.

Five Brigaders led by an African groom and Joseph among them, the five richly breathing brandy they had taken in the Glencoe hotel.

Till three, when Baas Piet came out in his nightgown to send them to bed, they sat in the yard and sang songs of home, special songs written for them in the Irish papers, that made them laugh.

And I stood up against the doorframe of my room waiting and, from his bench in the yard, the African groom cried out in his dreams.

When at last my love came to me he stretched out on the bed in his boots without saying a word and fell straight to sleep, the candle still lit. So I eased myself down quietly beside him. The rest of that night I lay close beside him listening to him breathe, staring into the white-blue glaze of his half-open eyes in the candlelight.

And in the morning there was the pudding standing cool and sweet-smelling in a basin on the kitchen table. Cool enough to wrap in paper and put in his saddlebag, safe beside his folded jacket.

This was the pudding he carried with him into the great battle of Spionkop, as I later heard. The last time I ever saw him he made sure to tell me the pudding kept him strong during the long hours of that battle, and tasted sweet until the last morsel, shared with a wounded Russian as night fell.

Now he swung into his saddle, more nimbly than I had ever seen him manage it and none the worse for the brandy. He kissed me wetly. As he rode off with his companions they were singing one of their songs from the revelry of the night before. A song into which they had taken turns to weave their own names, drinking after every verse.

> Our brave Boers fight for home and kin,
> Our fathers did the same,
> Against the Saxon robber horde,
> We hate and curse the name.
> They robbed us of our homes and lands,
> Our deeds and names they blacken.
> Strike home! Strike deep for vengeance,
> God Bless you, Joseph Macken!

It was as well they had that time of merriment together for, as the summer aged, the fortunes of war were rapidly changing. Each night the moon burned more yellowly in the sky, looked more like the sun, and each morning the cicadas yelled more scornfully in the trees. Bet felt the changes in her skull bones, a throbbing ache that I too began to sense, the onrolling shudder and moan of the British guns.

The troops entered the farm that early afternoon by sniping, running up unseen through the wattle plantation. The youngest ploughboy had been playing by the pink stone wall and was wounded in the leg. Carelessly putting him to one side, they then torched the plantation, and Mevrouw's plum orchard also, and came into the yard with fixed bayonets.

By the time Mevrouw was led from the house she was already praying out loud. Praying and singing *Jesus, Rots vir my geslaan, Laat my nie verloren gaan!* Let me not be lost! and calling Baas Piet's name, fruitlessly. Baas Piet, as the soldiers must have known, had set out before sunrise for Dundee to confirm at the hotel the rumours we'd been hearing, the worrying rumours of retreat. Despite recent victories, Boer retreat.

Watching Mevrouw weep and sing we stood with our backs to the shady side of the yard wall, Bet and I and Marta the house *meid*. Quiet as posts. Shaded black servants whom the soldiers busy ransacking the house ignored.

It was a scene as in a dream, the inside things piling up there in the thick sunlight. First the soldiers dragged out the big family bedstead, and the wooden bible box Mevrouw brought from her home when she married, and the nightmeal brass candlesticks, and the Delft rack with the plates already broken. I saw there in the brightness as if stripped bare the knots in the wood that I knew well from cleaning, and the fluffy grey crevices between the bed spindles where I had forgotten to dust.

Next came the old hallway settle and the enamel stove, the soldiers panting to carry it, Mevrouw's geese honking at their feet. A kneading trough, the scalding trough. The bookcase seesawing across a stone, spilling its bibles one by one. The piano, Baas Piet's looted collection of British army trumpets, the painted case clock, a drool of dried goose dropping streaked down the side. The kitchen cupboard with its ball feet, which sprang open when it was set down, showing Baas's meat drying inside. At which a soldier twisted his lips and said Boojer food stank, he wouldn't feed it to his dog, but Mevrouw was weeping too loudly to have heard.

Now the soldiers were showing impatience, glancing over at the officer in charge, and at Mevrouw's noise, and back again, twisting their rifles in their hands.

The sudden cracking of a fallen mirror their signal.

The soldier standing beside the piano drove the butt of his

rifle through the lid and under cover of its clanging another put a stone through the kitchen window. The whole party then burst into a nervous boyish laughter and, laughing, fell to a wholesale hammering and smashing as though to level every bit of furniture to the ground.

When the yelling of the officer brought them to a halt. 'Straw!' he bellowed, 'Kindling!'

I crossed my arms over my front and braced my shoulders, defending my young, hugging my small soldier to me. Even that morning Bet had sat pressing cold spoons against my temples, shaking her head as I retched and cherished my belly, its growing roundness my new comfort. A reminder of my lover's reality, his warm butting presence inside me, right here inside.

An African bearer ran up from the plantation with a smoking pile of branches.

Seeing him Mevrouw began screaming. She threw herself before the officer and tore open her bodice, '*Ag Meneer, skiet my*. Shoot me, shoot me, we've nothing to live for if our farm's burnt.'

The officer averted his eyes.

'The best plea for mercy,' he said, 'is hold your tongue. This is happening because you people don't give in. Hold your tongue and we will take care the Kaffirs do not get you when you reach Durban.'

At which Mevrouw jammed her hand into her mouth and rocked herself, her eyes roving wildly round the yard. It was then that she seemed for the first time to catch sight of the three of us, Marta, Bet and me standing against the yard wall. And she spat. Despite many years of maternal kindness she cast us a look that was pure spitting curse, that said, God damn you Kaffirs to the deepest pit of hell. And fainted clean away.

In the agitation that followed the soldiers ordered us to assist, and Bet and Marta hurried forwards, and so in their case Mevrouw's bad luck curse soon took effect. As Mevrouw was carried slumped to a waiting farm-cart, the officer herded the two in behind her, holding his gun aloft. By then orange flames were already fringing the kitchen window, and the corrugated-iron roof of the homestead was screaming and snapping in the heat.

The last two soldiers bolted coughing from the smoking back door clutching pieces of pilfered metal plate to their chests, the younger one wearing Mevrouw's Sunday shift like a turban.

I ran in their wake, my hands laid upon my belly, and then, ducking round the privy wall, veered off in the direction of the smouldering plantation, rightly guessing the English would not double back, but head instead for the main road.

There in the hollow beside the pink stone wall that I knew well from sewing afternoons with Bet, I crouched waiting. I heard the soldiers' boots crunch down the driveway track, I heard the sounds of weeping. Women's weeping and crying out. I may have heard Bet scream good-bye. Weeping a little myself I crouched waiting where Joseph had found me once before. For although there had by now been many lonely nights when I had waited for him in vain, when I couldn't help thinking of Bet's overheard rumours – the white fleshpots of the big city, those kind hostesses of the mines – yet crouched in my hollow I wept only a little at my abandonment. On this first evening wept only a little, because I knew the Boers were retreating this way, across the mountains, and he must return to see me. The charm must work at least one more time.

And around midnight, his hour, it did.

The fronds of his skin jacket marking a spiky silhouette against a sky white with stars.

To call me he was singing his song, *The Harp shall sound sweet, sweet, at length.* I fell in with his tune as he approached.

There was another man with him I saw, who waited on horseback out on the track holding Joseph's horse.

The smoke wafting from the blackened farmhouse.

At first we did nothing but hold hands, not talking. On a mud trough heated but left whole by the fire, we sat close together and I stroked his fingers and after a while we kissed. I noticed at once his ring was gone but it did not occur to me to say anything of it. We kissed and I placed his hand on my belly as we did so, and again I did not think to speak. We were speaking without speech, so I felt.

Then came the whistle of his companion. Joseph grasped me tight.

His voice was low and echoey like it was coming through a mask of sleep.

He said, 'Dollie, my own Dollie Macken, for so you are, my faithful love, more faithful and tender than any woman I've ever known. My dear Dollie, this isn't farewell, there can be no farewell between us. But I do fear that many months will come in which we won't see each other. The Boer army has been disastrously scattered and though I know in my heart it will regroup, I want to make sure of your safety, as you once did of mine.'

He took my head in his hands, rubbed my cheek against his lion-lined lapel.

To which I pressed my lips, at the same instant closing my free hand around the bit of lion skin in my pocket.

From his bag he drew one of his own shirts and a pair of Boer leather breeches.

Wear these, was his instruction, these and the hat you now have on. Keep to the valleys, follow the setting sun. And take this package of dried meat and biscuits also. In two or three days you should reach Ladysmith. To the south of the town is a Red Cross camp, and then further down-river another larger hospital – go there. We passed the area only yesterday evening covering the Boer retreat. It's the safest place to be for anyone suspected of giving support to the Boers. Go there, wait there.

He dropped his voice to a whisper.

'Wait for me there, my dearest love, keep strong, and don't be lonely.'

His hand cupped across my navel. I felt him smiling in the dark as if we shared a secret.

Hand-in-hand we walked over to where his horse and companion stood waiting, and for the last time he leaned in to kiss me. His lips wet, cracked.

Within earshot of the other man he said, 'I want you to take good care. Walk striding like a man. The British baulk at nothing. They are arming Kaffirs and inciting them against Boer women.'

*Kaffirs.* My body jolted in his arms. I do not know that he noticed.

*You wonderful creature of half-light,* was what he once had said.

Over the long months of war, had my colour faded from his memory? my face from his mind?

We stood within the shadow of his horse and still I kept silent. As when, in a dream, the urgency is to speak, I could not move my lips.

And must have been shivering.

He was saying, 'Here Dollie, my beautiful faithful Dollie, take this blanket. Don't fall ill. Isn't there something left around about the house we might find to warm you?'

Pressing against him I detained him one last time.

'Remember, I have my British Army sleeping-bag.'

The bag which was doubtless but a wisp of ash in the ruin of my room.

He laid his hand on my left breast.

'I'd take you with me,' he said, 'but cannot. We are soldiers in a permanent war for Ireland. Oh my love, keep with you a memory of this hand of mine, so that when you are lonely, you might think I am touching your heart.'

His companion cleared his throat.

Joseph Macken bent down from the saddle, smiling.

Breath needling my ear.

'I will share your bed in paradise.'

They diminished into the darkness, the stars blazing whitely where they had stood.

Had I the heavens' embroidered cloths,
I would spread the cloths under your feet.

I spoke his words how he might have said them, low and echoey. And as though my chant had conjured him back, I seemed to feel his voice passing by me, his spirit brushing past me, warm and ruddy, smiling, 'I have spread my dreams under your feet.'

Joseph, my cloths, my dreams, under your feet, I answered, stretching my hands to the stars that hid him from sight.

Then, doing as he had bidden, I changed out of my skirt and petticoat and into his leather trousers. The lion skin I put safe in the front pocket, where it knuckled into my belly. Leaving my own clothes folded in the hollow behind the stone wall, I turned my back on the dawn already paling along the horizon, and began to walk.

And it was as if his wish for my safety, and my love for our child inside me, quickened my limbs. I walked striding all that day and into the starlit night. Around midnight I crossed the railway line between Dundee and Ladysmith and then lay down under a bush, resting my head on my hat. His hat.

Chanting to myself, I have spread my dreams, my cloths, my dreams, under your feet.

But when I awoke the second morning pocked with sand, the chill of the earth had frozen me to the bone, and I knew my hope was dying. I looked up through thorny branches into a sky still grey with night and it felt as though my life was being torn out of me through the chest. Bet was taken and the farm was burned and I was left desolate. Joseph Macken had left me. He had ridden away over those mountains to the east and I, his Kaffir woman, was left here in this valley of death, where the corpses of horses lay pointing stiff legs to the clouds. A creature of half-light. But for the new life beating inside me, I was numb to the core and my arms and legs dragged heavy with cold.

Somehow I must have got up that morning, walked on. Somehow, a day or so later, I do not remember how, I reached the warming fire, the sheet smoothed by gentle hands, a canvas roof marked with a Red Cross, as Joseph had described. Luck must still have led me, I had kept my fingers clutched around the lion skin in my pocket. Luck accompanied me and took bodily form in the brown-eyed nurse who sat beside my stretcher bed and, while stroking my forehead, said she came from Ireland and would help me.

I asked her to press harder so I might feel her fingers through the numbness of my skin.

A puppet moves, can waltz and even somersault, but does not flinch if you prick it. Even so was I through the six months that lay ahead. A jigging puppet issued with a refuge camp number, a night soil bucket and one blanket, carrying a great belly. A clumsy jointed figure not unlike that scarecrow erected by Joseph's Brigade in the trenches outside Ladysmith to goad the English into useless fire.

Yet, though its heart felt dead, there was much to animate this puppet. All through our time in that war hospital, all through our trek south and the hungry days in the tented concentration camp that followed, there was my expanding interest in the baby, my small Irish soldier, and the nurse Kathleen's keen hope for it and her kind concern. And there was the baby itself growing big and healthy, and every day sinking its head deeper into my bones, making its way towards birth.

There may also have been the message brought by the peddlar who in the middle of winter visited that camp which for the next two years would be my home. I like to think at least there was a secret message brought by the peddlar of hair-dyes, ostrich feather fans, second-hand postcards and bits of old paper. I was sure there was a message buried somewhere in the handwritten notice tucked into the side pouch of his khaki pack. He carried the notice folded in rough paper, a Dublin-printed songsheet. Two words on that songsheet at once struck my eye, *God Bless*. This was a seal in itself.

The talk in the camp was that I, the nurse's *meid*, was a friend to disloyal Irishmen, so the peddlar came to the refuse trench behind the latrine huts to unwrap the message with me in private.

The notice was addressed, *United Irishman, Dublin*.

*Border River, Portuguese Frontier.*
*We of the Irish Brigade would hereby let it be known that, although we have fought bravely from frontier to frontier alongside our liberty-loving brothers-in-arms, we have now been driven to a*

*standstill through lack of horses and guns. Believing they have*
*much to learn from our friends' guerrilla tactics, individual mem-*
*bers of the Brigade have the desire to continue the fight against the*
*Empire, the Kingdom of Babylon, Ireland's foe. As a group how-*
*ever we can be of no further use to the Republic and must sadly*
*take our leave. More we cannot say, other than that this country*
*will remain forever in our hearts.*

> *Though many a sigh and tear it cost*
> *For those who rose at Freedom's call,*
> *'Tis better to have fought and lost*
> *Than never to have fought at all.*
> *Power to God's People!*

First I tried reading the writing myself, then three times
asked the *smous* to speak it for me. Listening, holding the songsheet on my front, I heard in his reading the hollow voices of
tired men, but that may have been because the peddlar was
himself cold and tired. Then I asked if I might keep the songsheet, the songsheet only. I liked the paper's greasy well-
thumbed feel.

*God Bless you, Joseph Macken!*

The notice I thought had been written at a great distance
although the rolling verse could have carried the force of
Joseph's rhythmic voice.

After payment of a flannel blouse and a linen skirt, presents
the nurse Kathleen had made me, the peddlar agreed to my
request.

That well-thumbed songsheet lay under my straw bolster
many weeks, until the night I awoke crying out, drenched by the
spilled waters of my coming child. Drenched and splitting open
with a pain that seemed to break my hips in two.

Throughout that night and until the late afternoon the nurse
Kathleen sat with me in the hospital tent, cross-legged on the
galvanised-iron floor, stroking my forehead. But, while it was
her arm I wrenched, it was Joseph's face I saw when I closed my
eyes.

'No. No. No. No.'

In the evening I returned to my hut with a child whose hair was the colour of June sunsets, the colour of our blood-red clay, and found the bedclothes had been changed, and the bolster replaced and the songsheet taken. I lay down with my baby beside me and for the first time in six months felt my limbs were no longer numb, although my tongue remained dank with sorrow.

I put the child to my breast and whispered to him his name, Sam. This I thought, though I was mistaken, was Irish for John.

Samuel, the name of a prophet.

# 32

After three meetings at the flat, Anthea and Dora decide to try the township as an alternative venue for talking through Dollie's life. Anthea arrives in her Fiat and Dora, her sea-green headscarf pointing and crooking like a windsock, waits for her at the corner shop, 'Always best you travel our street with a darkie in tow.' Bearing large alarm warnings alongside On Sale notices the barred shop looks closed and inaccessible, but Dora has not been put off by this. In her arms purchases gleam like perspex jewellery: a litre of creme soda, oranges, a bottle of ketchup.

She side-steps into the car and pats Anthea's knee in greeting, 'You OK?' Dust blows in cinnamon streamers through the hot winter air and Anthea's spirits, delighted at Dora's touch, lift like a leaf. They have been keeping strictly to their programme of producing Dollie's story, each time diligently filling the tape with the help of the notebook, but, despite their hard work, with each one of these meetings the atmosphere has felt steadily less forced and watchful, steadily lighter. And with this opening, beginning with the two of them paired in the front seats of the car as during their first conversation, it looks, Anthea hopes so much it looks like, feels like, a growing collaboration.

At the front door Dora pauses before pushing aside the security grille. She meets Anthea's eyes, 'Welcome to our house. I'd not taken the chance to say that before.'

As at every other meeting there are few preliminaries, a glass of water, biscuits offered but refused, Anthea rewinding the tape so they can remind themselves of what Dora last said. However today Dora is from the outset finding their task more of an effort than before, more so even than on the first occasion when Kathleen Gort's two early letters drew the sweat from her palms. Now she is frequently stumbling, pausing for long moments, breathing hard. 'Dollie's coming child,' she says faltering, 'Yes, my *ngane*, my coming child.'

She holds her fingers to her eyes, presses them to her throat as if troubled by a blocked cough. Anthea is seated at the table against the wall where the beer basin stood during the party, her feet propped on the Makkens' wooden *kas*, shining with a fresh coat of varnish. 'In honour of your guest,' Dora said Bernice had said. 'She dragged the *kas* in from the stoep last weekend and got down to making it look nice. It's been how many years in the open air?'

Now Dora is tracking her way round the perimeters of the room like a cat new to a house, painstakingly, gingerly taking the corners, as if walking on glass. 'Yes no, ja nee,' she keeps saying, reaching for thoughts she hasn't quite got the measure of. The figure of Dollie again looks fuzzy to her, she's covered up like she was the first time, wrapped in a shimmering vagueness like the blur of a migraine.

'No, I can't think what would've happened then. *God Bless you, Joseph Macken*. Yes no, I'm thinking now, I'm thinking hard of her, I want to feel her voice again. *God Bless …*'

The turning sprockets of the tape softly whistle in Anthea's lap. Outside, the sun, perfectly round, stares through the dust clouds like a bloody eyeball. Inside, but for Dora's pacing, things are equally still, in their place, lined up against the sides of the room, clean as ever, the bedroom door shut, its handle polished. Curiously though, the ironed-out neatness of Dora's small prefab no longer troubles Anthea. These surfaces wiped clean, shipshape, it's how Dora manages her torn life. Almost, Anthea finds, the plainness is now soothing.

'What must have happened once Dollie got out of the camp,' she prompts.

'But I don't know, Anthea, jislaaik.' Dora faces the empty space on the wall, a pale circle, where the family hat used to hang. She studies the photo of Joseph in his smart high school uniform standing beside the orange jug and glasses set on the dresser, the photo taken in a studio nearly ten years ago, yes it must have been then, his cheeks so smooth and round. 'I don't know Anthea. I don't know more than what I hope, what Dollie might've done. I mean, we're on shaky ground here, it's our make-believe, how I'm choosing to think of her. There's always been the family rumour about the foreign fighting man, Sam the war baby, all of that. But after Sam's birth, and before Dollie gets back north, to the farm where he grew up, it's empty space, it's guessing. What she maybe did or maybe didn't do. We're talking chances here. If Joseph ever came back, though likely not, if she managed OK once the nurse was taken sick and left. If she ever got back in touch, if she ever got back at him.'

'Got back at him,' Anthea repeats staring out at the sun suspended in the window. 'Struck back,' she says faintly.

'I say lunch,' Dora cuts in and Anthea looks up startled. 'I say we need energy to go any further, something like, well, what do you say to piccalilli on bread, Marie Biscuits? Oranges after?'

They prepare the food beside the sink, facing the window on to the back yard, the laundry hanging out on the washing line, newspaper shreds and shopping packets blown up against the fence.

'Shouldn't have done my whites on a dusty day like today,' Dora follows Anthea's eyes. 'Plus that red t-shirt got in with the rest and washed a pink colour through the lot.'

Anthea notices the puckered lines of a silk-screened slogan on the inside-out front of the red garment. Those shirts she helped print at university, she remembers, those shirts which until Easter time still hung on her own washing line.

'That's Joseph's shirt of course,' Dora says, 'But I wear it now when I do cleaning. John was drinking here with friends last night. I had to tidy before you came, told John he can go somewhere else for the day. Try Gertie's, I said, he's always game for *dopping*.'

'Maybe I could borrow it?' Anthea suddenly finds herself blurting, blushing. 'Like, I don't know, I've never met Joseph, only seen him in court, but I feel – what we're doing's so concerned with him. I think I'd like to try wearing something of his.' She feels the blush flaming across her forehead, down to her throat. *Take a mother's advice*, Dora's old warning echoes through her, *Watch the sun*.

'Anyhow,' she stumbles on, talking now because she can't take back her words, because, well yes, she must mean what she's saying. 'As part of our appeal it might be an idea to get t-shirts done, or badges, my friend Arthur even suggested it. Recycle our Free Mandela pins to say Free Makken. Free All Remaining Political Prisoners.'

'Anthea, girl, relax,' says Dora. 'It's OK. You can have the shirt.'

Anthea gapes in surprise at Dora wiping her hands unfussed on her apron.

'No, I don't see why you can't have Joe's t-shirt to wear. That is, if you don't mind how my big tummy has stretched it. And you can stop looking so shocked. I haven't forgotten how you barged into our lives, no, how I hated it, but now, putting it fairly and squarely, that's the situation. You're inside our lives, that's the way it is, and maybe now I don't mind too much.'

The garment she gives her is still a little damp to the touch, smells of sunshine and dust. 'Put it on.'

Anthea draws the shirt over the green cotton dress she's wearing. *Forwards ever*, says the slogan.

Dora tugs the shirt down at the back, tweaks the sides, smooths the whorled creases.

'There you are.'

Almost natural, the awareness glances through Dora, she feels the chafe of the cotton tingle in her palm. It's the t-shirt Joseph wore whenever he led a meeting. She gives Anthea's shoulders another smooth. And yes, it feels almost completely natural, a close touch given without forethought, like neatening a child of her own. It's as if Monica or Desirée was standing there … Yes, she thinks, that would be about right, as if Desirée, Anthea exactly as old as Desirée would have been now.

Without warning her heart feels suddenly filled out, closer to whole. It's like forgiveness must feel, she thinks, the relief of forgiveness – if there was anything about this situation she had to forgive. Here's the girl, within arm's length, within reach, and she, Dora, doesn't mind. She has touched her warmly, closely, and what she said was right, her annoyed anger has dissolved away. She reaches inside her memory checking, but, no, it's gone, the resentment's gone, a wound that's closed. Looking at Anthea standing here in Joseph's shirt, she barely sees the living victim, the walking reminder of this year's awful pain. She stands back and sees a young woman who's embarrassed and pleased with herself all at once, the same age as her second-born would have been, blushing like a silly thing.

'There you are then,' she says again.

Anthea smiles at her, hungrily drawing in Dora's touch. She runs it through her body, drawing in its distinctness, its definite warmth. *I asked her to press harder so I might feel her fingers through the numbness of my skin.*

Dora puts Anthea's plate of food on the table. She herself remains standing, her sandwiches untouched. She leans on the bottom half of the back stable-door gazing outside.

'I've been thinking, Anthea,' she says at last, 'about this work of ours, how difficult it is, how difficult sometimes to find Dollie's voice. We've got a long way together, of course, but as far as the track Dollie walked goes, we're now moving outside of Kathleen's book, outside the help she can give. So I've been thinking that what we maybe now need is a change of scene, a better change of scene than what this township here gives us. I think I definitely need this, to go away for a while, a week, maybe longer. I don't know, Dollie's voice, like I said, it comes and goes. I try to feel it inside, and then I do, and then it's gone again. I need time away from this house, I think, everything around me. It weighs heavily on me, this story, Dollie's hurt. Patching together a history doesn't improve much, I sometimes think, elastoplasting a family doesn't heal the past. There are times after we've been taping when I feel really bad, really sick and weak. Anger isn't sorted out by being passed on down to us, being gone over, that's what I keep finding. We've nothing to pay back Dollie's loss.'

'But everything we put into creating this history, Dora, will have its return. We think through the heartache eventually to let it go. Every time we meet we talk our way towards Joseph's possible release.'

'Maybe yes, but the price is high. As I say, we've nothing to pay back Dollie's loss.'

'Why not try going back to my notebook, the letters?' Anthea frowns, made anxious by what Dora's saying: they were managing together so well. 'There may be more pointers you can follow ... '

'No,' Dora crouches down in front of her, puts her hands on her shoulders, and again the touch is firm and warming even though her arms seem to be shaking. 'No, I've gone through those letters enough, I've finished them up. A change of scene is as good as a holiday, so I was wondering – I was wondering, can't your paper find money for me to go off somewhere? These things happen, fact-finding missions, isn't that what they call it? I mean it. As part of writing up our story, let me travel somewhere else. You could even join me, after a while. Why don't I, say, go somewhere Dollie or Kathleen Gort might've gone, turn up more details for our work? Let me be alone with Dollie, Anthea, prove I can do it. I think this is what I need.'

Anthea's hands are folded across Dora's where they lie on her shoulders, her sun-soaked red t-shirt. Her forehead feels the round of Dora's forehead, the tough bone and hot skin, pressed against her own. For moments they remain hunched in this embrace, Dora rocking her forehead against hers.

'I'll see what I can do.'

Dora hunkers back. Anthea, feeling dizzy, buffeted by emotion, can't do more, can't move.

'God bless you, Anthea.'

Dora drags her palms down her cheeks, feeling the skin give, settle back, like pulled nylon.

# 33

*As told by Dora and written into Anthea's notebook*

Shifting my small soldier on to my back, shrugging him round by stages, I took a last look about me. There were the mud-stained bell-tents in rows, the wattle-and-daub huts to the side, the rutted walkways. I walked round to the back of my hut, stood one last time in the spinach patch I had made there, its bristly border, mealies on three sides, sweet-reed on the fourth. Beyond, still clearly visible between the mealie stalks though now filled in, was the refuse trench where once I had the conversation with the *smous*, the peddlar of hair-dyes and fans and bits of old paper.

Bending to remove a stone from my shoe I took a last look at my hut, the camp round about, my home these two years, my only home. Then I Dollie Makken turned on my heel. Making sure one last time my small Sam's back was securely packed into the sling of my blanket, his buttocks snug against my palms.

I began my walk to the main gate.

Around me lay silence, a silence pulled taut like a drum skin, the breathing silence of people watching and suspicious, all women. Two uneven lines of women sitting in front of their tents, looking up from their tasks, a torn apron, a nit-infested head, a plate of dried mealie cobs, looking up unmoved, their eyes shaded by the half-circle shadows of their poke bonnet brims. An everyday scene but today extraordinary. This was the morning of my departure, and the faces said nothing. I would be the first, white or black, to be leaving the camp, but the set mouths, the shadowed eyes, showed neither anger nor regret. So, the petted black, the sick Irishwoman's darling, was getting out before them. So. The Lord alone knew the Afrikaner was the most oppressed of peoples.

So. And yet I walked there as one they knew. For nearly two years, from the time the nurse Kathleen was invalided home with enteric, I had worked as their wash-house cleaner and unpaid washerwoman, my *ngane* slung heavy on my back. Many of these women wore shifts and collars I had pounded white, lived in huts I had built, built even when with child, Kathleen herself once begging this. 'Dollie, we should lend these down-trodden Boers a hand. As best we can. They love their freedom as well as you and I.'

Loved their freedom but sat before their huts now, and the bell-tents I had helped patch, with their gaunt and liverish children clinging to their skirts, and turned their faces away as I passed, and hissed through their teeth.

The Kaffir *meid* getting out before them.

With the nurse's wooden *kas* balanced on a roll of checked cloth on my head, I passed slowly through that hissing silence and tried as I passed to look each woman in the face, tried to find the shaded eyes beneath the draggled linen bonnet, but saw only the tight lips and hard-bitten lines of their resentment. Even the young woman in her starched collar whose laundry I had weekly done, who had advised I put cold cream on my skin to prevent the sun from burning me darker, even she faced away. Every night they both had dysentery, I had washed and rocked her baby, but sitting before her patched tent she now faced away and turned the child away also.

Not a single woman in that long double row meeting my gaze.

For the Lord alone knew the Englishman was black-hearted and weak enough to let the Kaffir go free before the Boer.

# 34

*God Bless you, Joseph Macken.*

Dora drags her palms down her cheeks, feeling the skin give, settle back. The sun grinds the hot heel of its hand into the ground. She is sitting on the lowest concrete step of the National Library in the frondy shade of a cycad and feels the soles of her good shoes sink away into the softening tar. The noon heat has emptied the Cape Town pavements of all but a somnolent beggar and an ice-cream trader with his cap over his face. A rising breeze crackles the leaves in the trees.

A change of scene, she said, and Anthea's newspaper bought the idea, literally paid money for it. Robert the editor, so very polite and gentlemanly on the phone, remarked that Dollie's Story, set up as a highlighted attachment to Anthea's feature, would certainly pull in readers. 'Here *and* abroad' he said, 'Joseph's fortunes changing in line with a changing country. If he's freed it'll make the *Times*'s history. By all means take this trip.'

Dora's glad of his support, because till now the facts she was hoping to hunt out have proved stubbornly hard to get. This morning she began on the Table Bay harbour records, to check if possible when the nurse Kathleen sailed, when Joseph Macken might have disembarked, if he came this way at all and not via the East Coast, the route he followed leaving. But the tiny writing in the harbour ledgers and registers resembles nothing so much as up-and-down brown scratches, spider tracks, fading and strangely odourless, she dug her nose into the spine to check, thought the past would carry a spiciness, the smell of turmeric and pollen. After an hour or two she left early to get herself a cooldrink.

For definite I'll find more flesh for the bones of the story, she said to

Robert on the phone, to Anthea at the airport waving goodbye. For definite – but the flesh so far is still mostly of her own devising.

A party of schoolchildren files down Government Avenue on their way to the Cathedral, their teacher immaculate in a white suit, unflustered by the heat. Dora likes her cool efficient stride, her easy self-assurance. She likes that wherever she turns in this city she picks up whiffs of intonation she recognises, encounters faces built along the lines of her own, wide cheekbones, blunt noses, and faces moreover that look like they own the place. She's probably even more of a chance hybrid than most, what did she tell Anthea, offspring of a mercenary bastard and a black *meid*? – but still she feels there are no apologies to make here, on these streets where the country's fateful mixing first began.

Brown flesh on mixed bones.

To make up for the lack of facts she's working hard on the tapes, she's trying to produce a picture of Dollie's voice in her mind, and for this the change of scene definitely has helped. Nearly the whole of this past weekend she's spent with Dollie Makken. She's roosted in the quiet guest room up against the mountainside, a B & B run by whites – she's never stayed in a white home before, smart as the Arnolds', must be a sign of the times. Nearly a whole two days and nights she's spent with Dollie Makken and the cassette recorder, talking out Dollie's heartache, feeling her pain and her resistance tightening her own chest. The soft stuff, the glances exchanged with her Irish lover, the gifts and the visits, she and Anthea mostly covered back home. But the anguish which cut into Dollie's love, and her efforts to escape that anguish, this matter she has saved for herself alone. Here alone she's dreaming of Dollie Macken wreathed in stars, radiating rage and light.

In the B & B room she works at the dressing table, Chocolate Eclairs stowed in the overnight purse at her elbow. She talks with her lips close to the warming plastic of the cassette as if it was a baby's ear. With her eyes closed. To bring Dollie to mind, imagine her face as she, Dora, speaks. Like Bernice's, she imagines, but thinner, blacker, more fixed and bony.

How it was for a pregnant woman to shelter alone in a blasted landscape. The heavy sky bleak as the end of the world.

Every so often, forgetting herself, she catches sight of her reflection in the dressing table mirror, a washed-out no-makeup blotch, her shoulders looking saggy with what? tiredness, the weight of the past? She runs a finger along the swollen bags under her eyes, the deep lines round her mouth, feeling disgruntled with herself. The mirror's at least furry with dust, she thinks, you can't see yourself that clearly, they need a cleaning woman like Grace. Put a hand to the glass and it leaves a clean imprint, bits of tired eye and nostril peering through the finger marks. She thinks of the Arnolds' shiny house, of Mrs Arnold's tired voice.

'Enjoy your holiday now, Martha,' Mrs Arnold said only Monday last week, the last day ironing, sighing as if the very thought of holidays fatigued her. 'Don't do anything I wouldn't do.' Thinking, like they do at JH Dark's, she's off to a relative somewhere, cousins in the north, in Mafikeng.

'But Martha, are you sure you can afford it?' Mrs Arnold's afterthought, her tongue tip resting in the Cupid crook of her lip. 'I mean, your hourly rate isn't exactly … '

There's a campaign fund for my son, Dora should have said. This far from home it's safe to think it. Perhaps you don't know, she should have said, There's a campaign to reduce his sentence, release him maybe, the *Times* has adopted the case. He was, is, you see, the Clacton bomber.

But instead she took the extra twenty rand Mrs Arnold was offering, giving a curtsy-bob so tense it made her kneecaps throb.

Once, yesterday, with the cassette machine slid snugly into her new leather handbag like a letter in an envelope, the bag a holiday present from Anthea, she tried taking the tape with her on a walk around the city centre. In a coffee bar and on street corners she stopped to murmur into the machine. Never mind the traffic sounds, the noise of people's conversations, pigeons flapping, the general hubbub, this would be a warm-up for later, back at the B & B. 'The Kaffir *meid* getting out before the Boers.' Talking above the street cries of brown people talking a lot like herself.

*Hubbub, hugger-mugger, hullabaloo.* Dora picks a pellet of softened tar off her shoe sole, checks the time, nearly end of the Library lunch hour. *Hubbub, hullabaloo.* That was a word-list in the Standard Nine Reader, she remembers, the one propped there on the dresser at home between the varnished bricks, beside the orange jug and glasses set and Joseph's high school picture. *Hugger-mugger*. The Reader and the photo and the jug and glasses standing there at home, looked after by Bernice and maybe John even now, surprising thought, as she's sitting here having her mango drink, watching lunchtime strollers drift by.

*Hugger-mugger, hullabaloo.* Words arranged in a shaded column on the page. Result, she has to watch not to confuse them.

African street traders, Halaal butchers, minarets and Victorian statues and pillars, hubbub together.

On that same walk yesterday she went over to look at the Parliament Buildings across the avenue from where she's sitting now. She walked alongside the spiky fence gazing across the hydrangea bushes at those vast white pillars, at authority making its weight felt, so soon to change hands.

How would Joseph've rated this as a target? she wondered, walking another length of the fence. Would the structure be too big, too propped up with security? In its heyday, the old days, though, it would certainly – yes certainly … And then she gulped dry-mouthed, sure, sure she'd just glimpsed him, the Old Man himself. The Old Man and two companions in black suits walking out of the decorated gate and turning in the direction of town. Must be. That tall back and grey head, couldn't mistake them, the back unbowed by the years of breaking stones, turning in the direction of town as if on a casual afternoon walk. She quickened her step, shoved through a group of tourists – 'Mind where you're going, lady' – tripped, righted herself, broke into a trot. She wanted to catch him up, see him up closer. She wanted to say something, say what? 'How many years haven't I wanted to meet you in the flesh'? To introduce herself, Yes, it's Dora Makken, the Clacton mother? Or no, maybe not that, because she'd like to hear his 'It's a pleasure – ' lightly spoken over joined hands, as if she was just anybody, a domestic worker, an assistant in a department store.

But by the time she had unknotted herself from a second group of ambling tourists, Mandela, if it was him, had dropped out of sight.

She was left panting, silver lights dancing across her vision. *A wreath of silver stars, and a light about you.*

2.10, they're late re-opening, she checks the time again, gets up to test the Library's unbudging brass door handle. The crashing-crushing sound of empty bottles being swept up and heaped together comes from the park café across the avenue hedge. A mistake to have waited out the hour and not had lunch, she thinks, her stomach feeling bloated and tight with hunger. She reaches into her bag for the toast wrapped in a napkin she saved from her B & B breakfast. Can't resist that lifetime's habit, a bit of cost-cutting, even with all expenses paid.

She eats and puffs the crumbs off her lips, extracts her compact mirror, pats on more face powder, lipstick, a smudge of blush, kisses her red mouth to herself in the mirror. She straightens her collar, a nice subdued dress this, a soft camel, Truworths, brown collar and cuffs, and Bernice's press-stud belt the one accessory.

It's when she gets up to walk down the avenue towards town, can't see the point of waiting any longer, that the unexpected spin of excitement hits her. A whirr, a gulp. Yes. It's not the hunger or the heat, not that only, or remembering that glimpse of the Old Man's grizzled head, that felt so real even if she only imagined it. It's that she knows suddenly she's almost done it, she can make it, she doesn't need the harbour records or any kind of document to do it. She can make it to the end of Dollie's story, alone, unassisted. She can see the pattern. By talking all weekend long she can now see clearly the pathway of Dollie's life, it's stored there on the tape and in her head, a completing story, she's gathering, has gathered it in. Dollie cooking sewing aching for her love. Her long walk across country to the moment of giving birth, Dora's own father Sam Makken's birth, then her brave journey, so Dora imagines it, towards liberty. She's pulling Dollie's life towards those moments, the birth and the release working together like a drawstring gathering the life's folds. Who'd have thought she'd manage that? Pulling a voice out of the silence of the past?

Grandmother Dollie, singing her songs of harps and flags in the south.

She can't remember a sensation like this, not recently. Like winning a competition, must be like, this fizzing inside. Like putting your new baby to your breast, or meeting Madiba properly, in the flesh, face to face. The last time she felt like this, when was it? Joe's surprise Christmas present, those OK Bazaar chocolates? Joey watching closely, making sure she wasn't disappointed, and her scalp feeling hot on top with the pleasure.

Dollie Makken stretched her hands up to the blazing night sky, Dora thinks back. *A ring of white stars, and a light about you,* that letter said. Her head wreathed in light, as if floating, and her back unbroken.

'Pardon please, was that left you said? Sharp left? I'm looking for the docks. Was that straight on you said?'

No harbour records but the harbour itself, she decides. She decides she wants to reach the docks, get as close to the sea as possible. She wants to stand and look out across the water, feel the breeze in her hair at the very shoreline where the country's black and white first met, first fatefully mixed. Where Dollie would certainly have walked had she ever come to this city, coaxed to visit, say, by a convalescing Kathleen Gort. Wouldn't Dollie have aimed for the quays also, the fresh salty air, the suddenly searing cries of the gulls? Among the colonial pillars and statues and these overshadowing buildings, wouldn't she have felt unsettled, have darted in haste for the quays, the open sea views, her child on her back? Peering out at the faint, watery horizon where her Joseph had disappeared, from where he must one day return?

A plane makes a low flight path overhead, the vibration buzzes in Dora's teeth, runs up across her skull bones. She feels the worn paving stones underfoot cave in the middle like flopped pastry, tipping back her heels.

Anger, dear Anthea, she says out loud but under her breath, walking straight along, Anger I said isn't sorted out by being passed on. But now I don't know, I'm not as sure as I was, feeling this excitement, imagining Dollie's movements, her sharp-eyed, bony face. Yesterday's bitterness doesn't soothe us today? No, I'm not so sure. Isn't it rather the first shock that hurts so badly? Moulding shapes you partially recognise and partially don't choose to see, out of the muddle of the past, isn't it this that hits so hard? Think of Sam, should be Sean, Shagan, who never knew his father, the soldier hero his mother sometimes mentioned, murmuring. And his soldier father probably had no idea of him. Could've had no idea, unless, say, nurse Kathleen had told him. Unless Dollie herself had troubled to trouble him, her bruised love darkening to anger. Think of his face turning sick with alarm at the news. Which was hardly possible, was it? Where Dollie was daily sinking into daydreams, so Sam remembered. Remembered dragging at her skirt, Mama come back! Talk to me!

Sam my son, listen, this is a tune a brave rebel once taught me. He sang it before he went into battle. I learned it off him before he rode away to wage more wars.

And Dollie's mouth twisted in hurt. In useless hurt?

Dora walks several blocks, not turning left or right. The shadows between the buildings are growing cooler and bluer but she can't yet smell the sea. Sweat begins to break out across her forehead and in her neck, settles in the fold under her breasts, beneath Bernice's press-stud belt. She loosens the belt a notch. *Brown-as-a-berry-proud-as-a-peacock*, she says to herself, walking to the pace of that proverbs chant she once taught Joseph, *proud-as-a-peacock-drunk-as-a-lord*. She feels her inner thighs and knees chafing together.

*Ma, why a lord?* said sharp young Joseph on the sofa learning his lessons. *As in Lord God?*

And Dollie's lover's God, she thinks, what part might he've ever played? 'God is a waltzer and loves a trinity,' she remembers Sam saying when her and Bernice were small, handing out sweeties when he got home from work, after mama left with a man from up the street. 'Here, one for each hand, and one for your mouth. Never forget, the powers of your soul are three, will, sense, and a hungry belly, so my own mother said.' That one passing mention of formal belief. That, and *the heaven's embroidered cloths*, Sam's favourite poem.

And Samuel, the name of a prophet.

A wind has sprung up and begins to batter at her, winding her hemline round her knees. She lowers her head into it, hefts her handbag higher on to her hip. The docks must be closer. When she stops at the next red pedestrian light her breath is coming quickly and now suddenly she feels very done in, very unsteady. She leans against a blue plastic litterbin. Everything for a moment feels crashingly unreal, it's all impossible, Dollie's survival, Joseph's release, impossible and pointless her own presence here in this strange city, the Mother City the whites call it, what a young mother indeed. Joseph's life transformed by a half-made-up story – is this possible? Joe Makken the freedom fighter freed from his own past by the past? the Irish-origin black man made over, half-reborn?

Joe Makken, Joseph Macken, she repeats to herself, panting. She pulls herself upright and crosses the street. God Bless you, Joseph Makken, Joseph Macken. Joseph Macken, my Irish oupa. Yes, what of him? she asks herself. What of Joseph Macken, Dollie's carefree lover? Wouldn't he have got off scot-free and unscarred in the end? Scot-free, married to an Irishwoman perhaps? He had that quick and tricksy eye, and he loved his nation. When at last he returned to Ireland amidst general rejoicing, she imagines, wouldn't he have taken to himself a woman of his own tribe? And then wouldn't they have moved into a square white house like she's seen in Anthea's books, in the shadow of a rainy hill? Maybe he had more children, another boy, *For Joseph Macken a first-born son*. And the years would have passed. But every now and again there'd have been moments surely, damp winter evenings, when his muscles would have ached for battle, when he'd cradle his Mauser that always stood against the mantlepiece, and pull his listening son towards him?

How it was to level this at the Englishman, son. How it was to creep through the undergrowth without noise. Yes daddy, how was it daddy? You must keep one eye on the ground, look out for loose twigs, crumbling stones. Think of cunning as well as speed, so the Boers taught us. Dynamiting bridges means speed and skill, they said, ambush is mainly cunning.

Yes daddy yes, you creep forwards, one eye on the ground, and you put the explosive beside the British blockhouse, and when you run over your head come their bullets.

Yes, the English bullets zipping, the father'd say. And my head uncovered because I'd given my hat to a friend. There were comrades whose hats were peppered with bullet holes, but I was lucky because I was protected. I had a special jacket, a patchwork jacket made of the skins of all the beasts of the veldt and powerfully magical that a local woman sewed me. That jacket sent harm elsewhere as if it was invisible armour.

And where's it now, daddy, your magical coat? Let me see it, daddy, please let me see.

I put it away, son, it's buried. I shredded it and cast it into the sea, I put it on the fire. I had to have rid of it, its magic was for battle only and outside of battle it was too strong, so it's gone.

Sore. A jerk pulls through Dora's body, twisting her neck, just as if she's about to fall asleep. The effect of walking along daydreaming, her mouth hanging open, most likely looking dumb.

And now she hears the seagulls screaming overhead. The wind is yelling round her ears, knocking the street rubbish against her ankles. She continues down the wide boulevard with sharpened intent, breathing hard, feeling the square of the cassette recorder with its nearly full-up tape dig into her hip. Take it gently, she urges herself, *Tread softly on my dreams*. Gently, softly, it's a tough wind this, a wind with teeth in it, Sam would say, strips nerves. It makes her feel bare to things, as if she's on the brink of some kind of fall or fever. She watches her feet. Imagine, crumpling with headache, chest-pain, in the middle of this unfamiliar city, too awful to think.

A circle of heads fringing her blurred vision, a wreath of faces. A finger on her stuttering pulse.

'Name please, missus, what's your name? Where was it you were going?'

'I wanted to see the open sea. That's Makken with two k's. Where my grandfather came from.'

On both sides the buildings have dwindled down to foundation works. The road runs straight on for the distance of a city block, then narrows to a muddy track. She follows it. She's on a vast open stretch of graded ground, a land reclamation project. In the distance she sees heaps of rubble, cranes, new dock works, and beyond that the filmiest blue line of ocean. She half-closes her eyes to the wind and walks on.

# 35

*As told by Dora and processed into Anthea's pc*

With the nurse's wooden *kas* balanced on the roll of checked cloth on my head, and Sam on my back wearing his father's hat, I walked that long avenue of silent Boer women on my way out of the camp. I walked placing my feet with care, glancing to left and right, left and right, and not a single one of them met my gaze.

Not a single one but for the woman with the square open face waiting at the very last tent close to the gate, standing drying her hands on her apron, whose name the others spoke in lowered voices: Klasina Hendriks, still wearing her dead son's bandolier. The Boer Peril, so the camp superintendent called her. She was the one who had accompanied her *man* to the battle of Spionkop, the others whispered, who had helped dig his gun emplacement, after he had once come home to her in a lather of funk. 'What, you would cower in my kitchen rather than die in a free grave as our first-born died? Come, let us go, we fight till we die.'

And it was she, she alone among the Boer women, who had helped treat Sam when he was stricken with the measles. She had carried him to her own tent and laid a poultice on his eyes and chest that she made of cow's liver and bread dough, and spread soft goat's dung on his lips to draw out the rash. When the dough rose we would know the fever had gone into it, she said, and so it happened. The dough rose, the dung dried into powder, and Sam awoke cool.

Klasina Hendriks's lips curling now to see me. She knew, as we all knew, that an early exit ticket bore a high price. Her mouth curled thinly and it may have been she was cursing me, and the Irish nurse for spoiling me, but there was reason to think otherwise, as I remembered.

That midnight her teenage daughter took a fit and I went round to her tent with a candle. When I put the candle in her hands then, for the first time, I saw her smile or, to picture it more clearly, she gave a grim narrow grin, that thin curl of her lips. 'These civilised British deny us light and you a Kaffir gives a candle. It's an ill-sorted world, *dis alles deurmekaar*. To fight a satanic war we make bargains with the devil himself.'

Remembering this I sent her now, from the side of my face, a smile and, smiling, seemed to see, still from the corner of my eye as I moved towards the gate, how she pushed back her bonnet brim so the sun shone full on her eyes. How her hand rested there in the air, the muscular hand wide open, as if bidding Godspeed.

And the top bar of the gate was pressing against my front, the dusty grassland stretching beyond, and a rifle poked into my shoulder.

Though he saw the weight I was carrying the Coloured guard at the gate thought little of prodding at me, almost my breast, with his rifle barrel. 'Stop woman! Back! Where do you think you're going?' Two white policemen running up from behind the guard hut at his cries.

I said, 'I am headed for the coast. To Port Natal. There, at the harbour office, I will seek my family.' Seesawing on splayed feet till I again stood stable. Praying to small Sam slumped along my spine, Don't wake.

And now the whites too were plucking and jerking at me, 'Back, back, no one leaves without a pass. Where's your permission?

But I was prepared. I squared my shoulders, I had the measure of my foemen. The quiet work of this war rested in the hands of us black servants, I knew what I was doing. Because of our spying talents both sides should long ago have started to watch their backs.

'I've been here two years, and have kept order and obeyed rules, but now there is talk of peace and a big new colony for all and I am leaving.'

Drawing from my bodice the Irishwomen's ten-pound note folded small, nicely toasted by my skin. In my palm I showed it them, just an instant, slightly cupping my fingers so the paper was visible to none but their eyes. And as suddenly as it was slipped out it had disappeared. The Coloured guard was pulling his rifle back from where it had waggled about my breasts, and the gate swung wide.

I was walking down the wagon track to the main road, the toes of my Irish boots puffing up the soft dust, and I heard, dying down as I walked away, the argument break out between the two whites over who and how much, and the Coloured standing over them, stiffly on duty.

# 36

*Talk of peace and a big new country for all.*

Dora stands on the steel-reinforced edge of a new concrete quay. Just below the surface of the water a seal slides past, a skim of brown current. The wind clinks in the rigging of a pair of fishing boats, presses against her front, pulls through her hair. She's not sure if she's meant to be here, this far along the deserted new quay, not too far from the open water, but if no one minds she'll stay out a while longer. She walks a small distance further along, taking care around an oily puddle shiny with rainbows.

Somewhere out in the harbour, beyond the next crook in the quay wall, she hears what sounds like singing, the tune coming and going with the wind. It's a male voice, she dare say, sweet, catchy, she likes it, a pleasing echoey sweetness tossed here and away in the air.

She edges closer to the quay side, peers out to listen, stretches, steps into a puddle after all, damn. Not watching her feet. Her pantihose instantly soaked and strangling the toes of her left foot. She looks around. A coil of cable, a pile of chain links, and there, further down, a squat brown postbox. Surprising. Must be a last-call spot, a last ditch for passing sailors, Antarctic travellers, lovesick fishermen going out to sea, to drop off a word of goodbye. She could hop-shuffle over, lean there to work the toes free.

And must be right about the postbox, how it's the end of a track. *Now the time has come to say good-bye.* She's holding on to the brown top, pulling at the toe of her wet pantihose and she sees it. Just to the side of and in line with where she's standing, the small cast-iron statue of a man, a kind of memorial, facing the open sea. The two short uprights, postbox and statue, looking almost twinned, mounted on their identical pebbly-concrete supports. The statue though is thinner and frailer by comparison, the mannikin wearing an overshadowing hat and a double bandolier out of proportion to his size.

She bends to read the plaque. Definitely a memorial, someone who didn't get a message back. She sees, *Ireland in Africa*. The wind smashes at her ears a moment, rips away.

*15.7.1871 – 10.1.1902*
*Permanent soldier for Ireland in Africa.*
*Tragically Lost at the Cape of Storms.*
*'Be Thou Faithful Unto Death,*
*And I will Give Thee a Crown of Life.'*
*Rev 2:10*

Dora shoves her toes deep into her shoes and stands legs apart, concentrating on keeping her balance. *Ireland in Africa!* Even here, bumping into one of these Irish soldiers even here! She reaches into her bag for a pencil, hand shaking. Even here, a stroke of luck? These rebels thick on the ground, here as at home? The details, she must write the details down somewhere, try her temporary National Library card, an Irish soldier's dates, b. d., clasped neatly around the turn of the century. The pencil wobbles as she presses down. An Irish soldier in Africa, see how it materialises, some flesh for the bones of Dollie's story. A rebel soldier lost at sea – yes, she can build on that. Doesn't this give her a destination, a point she can move towards and fasten her story on? She clicks her bag closed.

And now she sees him, a bent shape bobbing out in the harbour, that singer in a yellow waterproof fishing from a tiny power-boat. A ludicrously tiny boat, a tiny outboard motor, and just a hook and a line.

As she approaches the quay edge he is reeling in a fish. A dark blue swell urges him closer in and he catches sight of her, waves hugely, just as if he's been waiting all day for her to show up.

'Four fish exactly,' he shouts, 'More than enough for a meal! Four good snoek. And they say this isn't fishing weather.'

So pleased with things, so welcoming, Dora can't help waving back, calling hello.

But the wind stops her voice at her lips. He bends to attend to his line. She waits a moment longer, holding down her flapping collar, squinting into the low sun. Then she turns away and as she does so becomes aware her smile is still fixed on her face, taking her by surprise. The first time in nearly half a year, since before that nightmare Easter, she's felt so easy, so quiet at heart. Smiling she swivels on her heel, and lands her toes in a puddle, a deep one this time, sloshy with oil, and chuckles out loud.

The wind throwing a line of the man's song against her ear. It's as if he spoke right here, she imagines, lips brushing her ear-lobe, breath on her skin.

*All that is finished, let it fade.*

And it must be a magical, godblessed day indeed, because there, coming down the quay towards her, waving, is a medium-tall figure in a red shirt, Joseph's height. A t-shirt just like Joseph's. Dora gasps, and as quickly pushes away the wild hope that suddenly leapt inside her. The figure is waving in response to her smile, she recognises that long arm and wrist, it's Anthea, one and the same, Anthea waving, smiling back. And yes of course she did say, Dora remembers, that she'd fly down later this week for a day or two, see how things were shaping up, if she could justify the trip to the *Times*.

'What are you doing trespassing on a security zone?' Anthea mimicks an officer's compressed vowels, 'There remain no-go areas in this country, madam.'

Dora feels Anthea's arms close around her – or, no, her own probably enfolded her first, it doesn't matter, she's laughing as Anthea scolds her, it's such a nice surprise to see her, tell her the news.

'You know what I've seen? You don't know, something so wonderful! First I thought I saw the Old Man himself, walking through town, and then, another thing again and also incredible, I saw this memorial statue, *For Ireland in Africa* it was called, back there. Come, it's not far, I want to show you. It sort of supports all our work.'

But Anthea is dragging her in the opposite direction.

'No, Dora, no, I mean it, no way are we going back there. This is a security zone for a purpose, there were red warning signs at the harbour entrance, the way I came. These are building works that they've hardly yet completed. Look how empty the place is. Who knows if the whole quay isn't unstable? No way am I walking on, we've got to go back.'

Dora lets herself be guided along the concrete quay, around a shed, a pyramid of cement bags, across the graded mud flat. She rummages in her bag. Where's that Library card, those details she wrote down? Show Anthea this if nothing else. But she can't find it, can't find the pencil either, did she drop them, waving to the singing man? She looks round, wants to catch a final glimpse of the sea, assure herself of its reality at least, but Anthea has led her out of sight of the water.

*All that is finished let it fade,* Dora repeats to herself, *What's finished, sink and fade* —

'I looked for you in the Library reading room,' Anthea's saying, 'but they told me you weren't back from lunch. Then, who knows why? I took a walk down here. They said you were consulting the harbour records. I thought of Dollie making for the harbour to find Joseph so I wandered down.'

'A good thing,' Dora says, trying to smile. 'Maybe you saved me from another brush with the law.'

They're standing facing each other in the middle of this space of bare earth, the mud clods crunchy under their shoes, salt crystals frothing in the cracks between the clods, and the late afternoon sky so clear it seems clotted with blueness.

To herself Dora thinks, Glad. Security zones aside, she's glad to see Anthea, that she made it down here, walking Dollie's track. She's glad to be able to tell her, 'You know, it helped, coming here. The trip I think was fruitful. I've just about talked my way to the end.'

She reaches into her still-gaping bag, pulls out the cassette recorder, her cassettes. Chocolate Eclairs and Crimson Smoulder lipstick tumble on to the dry mud.

'Here, you try this on for size. Three whole tapes and one in process, the last of the story to come, just about to come. And I want to try and put the very end of it down on paper for you to see back home.'

Anthea kneels down beside Dora to pick up the spilled things. There are tears running down her cheeks.

'I've nothing for you in return,' she says. 'I've hardly written a thing since you left. My version of the feature article is a rougher-than-rough draft. An Extraordinary Legacy of Freedom, I'm still calling it. An Extraordinary Legacy of Twisted Freedoms.' She flaps her hands against her dusty knees. The cassette recorder is snibbed under her arm. 'Things have worked out differently for us. Here I've been certain I'm on to something, a big story, a pattern of connections and chances, but the deeper I've looked, the more complicated everything's got, and the less I've written.'

'It helped me being here,' says Dora, 'In this city of mixed beginnings. I've felt I was, I don't know, finding Dollie's way of things, her, what was it? – her charm?'

They straighten up. A twist of Dora's shoulders suddenly brings her face hugely close to Anthea's, snippets of light are swimming across her eyeballs.

'Look, there is something you can do for me in return,' Dora says. 'Something I'd like you to do quite soon.'

'Anything.'

'No, not anything, Anthea,' Dora pats her arms affectionately and draws her closer in, close enough to feel her suddenly relax and then again stiffen as she says, 'Not anything, my always-so-eager young friend, but one definite thing, one very important connection I want you to make. You in that red shirt, I want you to go and visit Joseph at maximum security. I want you to tell him what we've been up to. I want him to hear from you how far we've got.'

'*Me?*'

Anthea's thoughts are spinning. The wind has died down, it's suddenly very still. The snippets of light in Dora's eyes seem to drift out into the blue air like sparkles, like shattering glass. *Anger and confusion,* she remembers in shocked code, *Anger and confusion,* her lover's broken body, his intact briefcase, the sparkling harbour lights. A confusion of fright and intense interest spins through her. She thinks, *Clacton bomber,* she thinks, *Dora's son.*

'Yes, I want you to go.' Dora is shaking her arms, pulling back her attention. 'After all it was your idea in the first place, this feature story, it's only right that you inform him where we've got. I'd like that. And I think you two might even find a few things in common. Like your stubbornness maybe. At the end of the day it's for your stubbornness that I think I probably admire you both.'

# 37

DOLLIE MAKKEN'S STORY IV

*As told by Dora and processed into Anthea's pc*

Making my way down the dock at Port Natal, down the line of
troop ships, small Sam slumped on my back, I had never before
felt air quite like it, wet as soaked flannel, hot as hot, stinking of
old salt and fish. And Sam's sweat, my own sweat, creeping like
red ants down my back.

It was towards the end of the line I saw him, his burnt face a
beacon, the young soldier standing away from his group. He
was smoking and leaning on a crutch, the cranes high above his
head swinging exhausted artillery on to the waiting ships, and
his red cheek creased like a currant.

'Dublin Fusiliers? What's left of them is down that way,' the
harbour official had pointed. Pointed after payment of the
nurse Kathleen's green-lined silk umbrella, because first he had
clapped his door shut in my face and I had to knock and stubbornly knock till he emerged roaring, 'There's only one set of
savages worse than you Kaffirs and that's the Boers.'

I followed him as he pounded in the direction of the Jetty
Tea Room, pleading, 'Tell me only, my master, my baas, if you
know of Irishmen going home. There are such quantities of
troops and equipment and rolling trollies about I cannot tell for
myself.'

And besides I feared to catch the soldiers' searching eyes.

'Yes, missus, maybe.' The red-faced Fusilier now held

Kathleen's tortoise-shell comb up to the light. Spots of filtered sunshine flashed gold across his cheeks, his sun-puckered eyelids. 'For this I might do it. This as well as the brush. For these two I'll carry your message home, your message and your parcel.'

Kathleen Gort's last present to me, that golden-and-brown brush and comb. Grey as death she had leaned from the ox-cart that would transport her to the hospital ship and then to Capetown. The points of her skull poking through her papery skin, the pattern of her bones like the Röntgen pictures I once had seen in the Red Cross operating tent. In my arms she placed her torn white evening dress and the tortoise-shell set, her breath stinking of bile.

'Take these, Dollie, they're all I've left. Buy yourself and Baby something useful. Food. Meat and eggs. And here, have my journal book also. For safe-keeping, an assurance we'll one day again be in touch.'

Weeping in sighing gasps and kissing my cheeks, my forehead, so that the thick salt of her tears puckered my skin, making it itch.

Baby Sam liked to watch the sun's lights dance through that shining comb so I had kept it and the brush and the gift of the fine dress till now, till the last, when I had nothing else left to trade. Not even the small mattress which Kathleen had ordered specially from Port Natal, from down here, before his birth. Not even the carved frame holding the photograph which she had done by the camp schoolmaster, Kathleen in her nurse's uniform with the white veil. Those things I had exchanged in January, in March, for Maggi chicken broth, for Benger's Food and powdered eggs, and astringent yellow bush herbs when the dysentery was rife.

So I had nothing to trade except things that could not be given away, only given back. Three things chiefly. The *kas*, her first present to me, and her journal book stored inside it, that was two things, and the third was the strip of lion skin saved from Joseph Macken's charmed coat, the strip balding now and slick from too much stroking. From day to day the book and the bit of skin had been feeling lighter in my hands, seemed to be lifting, pulling away, straining to return to whom they belonged. The chest meanwhile, which also held our blanket and my pair of Boer cracker trousers, only felt heavier, the three days' walk to the coast balancing it had left a spongy bruise on my crown.

'And you'll take the message along with this book parcel all the way to the city of Dublin?' Trying to read the soldier's face as I spoke. 'You'll take it to the street that I tell you? You come from Ireland, don't you?'

'Irish born and bred, missus, county Wicklow, sure as you're standing there and your son's handsome.' The soldier patting his green embroidered waistband as if showing off a full stomach. He pointed to the troopship the *Catalonia* lying at anchor alongside, 'Returning home at last. Should've been invalided months ago, with this bad leg.'

Which, though he propped his knee on his crutch, he did not pat.

'Then I must ask you one more thing.' Forcing an echo of my love's music into my own voice to sweeten my request. 'I must ask you to *write* the message also.'

At which he jigged his bad leg on the crutch, making as if to think of other things, and then said, 'For that I would need more payment again, a little more payment. It's difficult for me to sit down and write.'

In protest Sam woke with a squawk and fixed his uncanny blue-grey eyes in gloomy dismay on the stranger.

'I have nothing more to give away, except things without beauty. This wooden chest. This book which will make up the parcel you'll carry, which isn't mine to give.'

'You have your pretty white dress.'

'But it's the one dress I own.'

Stepping back in dread lest he might try to touch it. Kathleen's tea-gown as she called it, once a pure cloudy white, was much reduced now, grubby too, its lovely downy fullness stripped to make poultice bags, mosquito masks, bandages.

'Missus, for me to write your message and then to carry and

deliver your book parcel, the price is your white dress.'

'Then I'll say no parcel, I will keep the book. Carry the message only, and please can we write it now.'

A pair of monkeys chattered at us from a warehouse roof.

'To carry the message the price is the comb and brush set in my pocket, that my sweetheart will greatly prize,' said the soldier. 'To write the message I must have your gown. It will be her wedding dress.'

Pushing his point home he gave a jump to his crutch as if it were a stilt, his knee propped on the wooden strut, and yelped horribly at the pain. Small Sam in reply broke into a woebegone weeping, digging his fingers into my breast, and suddenly I could take no more. I wanted rid of my encumbrances, my weights and ties, I wanted rid.

'You can have it, I will give it!' Calling above the sound of Sam's shrieking. 'It's yours, I agree, it's yours. Just write the letter as I say, put into my message what I say, and then I will go behind that wall, and change into this pair of leather trousers, this and my bodice are all the clothing I've left. Just convey the letter to Dublin, the letter and its contents, this souvenir of lion skin. Agree to take it to the street I tell you, Lower Abbey Street it's called, and I'll give you the gown and we'll be done.'

The journal book, I suddenly knew, was too much of a heaviness to return to where it belonged. Differently from the wooden *kas* though, it was heavy because so blackly scratched and scraped with the marks of Kathleen's long-past hopes. Her reading aloud before she left had given even to me an ache, the strain of too much longing. Reaching her after her long illness, the writing would, I feared, drop like a night-time ambush upon her.

And if it did so it would fix her attention away from my letter, and it was my letter I wanted read.

The letter carrying the last powers of my charm to him for whom that charm was intended. To my red man with his careless eyes. The skin working out a special fulfilment of its magic, though one I had never intended to send.

'Done,' the soldier said offering his hand. Which I did not take.

I tore two sheets of paper from the back of the journal. One I folded and made into a boat and gave the boat to Sam, 'Play there in those puddles, and don't get wet.' The second paper I spread on top of the *kas*, then held the *kas* at elbow height so the soldier might write without stooping, leaning on his crutch. The pen and the ink he took from the canvas pouch at his side.

'Dear nurse Kathleen,' I said. Standing there in the white dress, the Irish bride-to-be's stripped-down white dress, the hem hanging limp with the moist heat, I looked past the rattling crane engines and the crates hanging in space, past the ships' cables and the green headland, out to the gauzy glimpse of ocean beyond, and for the second time in my life thought my heart was being wrenched through my ribs, screeching like a pulled root. In my right fist was the lion skin, mangy with handling, that I had kept both as my last weapon and my antidote. The sting in my tail and the pincer to draw the thorn from my flesh. That skin that I now wrung so hard I thought it might tear in two and the shreds fly away on the breeze.

Close up the charm, send it home.

'Dear nurse and friend Kathleen. You will know the moment you get this that I won't be joining you in Ireland like once you hoped. I heard in a letter from a colleague that you are recovering your health. This made me glad. You were always a staunch and generous friend to me. It was after I received the letter that I was able to leave the camp with our small Sam. Maybe our hearts and lands will be strengthened by our suffering, else where would we be?

'To find a place in this world for the child and myself, this is what I now desire almost to the point of sickness. I have thought we might travel back to the farm Doornkop as it is country I know well. Like we did at the camp we might plant a plot for ourselves in an unnoticed corner and make a small living, who knows, the land needs tending. Many Boer farms are now standing derelict and, though the English say us Africans must be released to our former masters, I cannot be sure when if at all the Besters will return. My own need is to keep to myself – it's a plan not far from your own fantasy of our taking together a little house. I long now to be satisfied with this simple existence of mine, with my own healed heart and my love for this child. Above all I want this love to fill the empty spaces in my life, so I am writing to ask you, in friendship, to do for me one last thing.

'Folded with this letter comes a piece of lion skin, the shred of a special coat I once sewed for him of whom I many times spoke. I find I can keep hold of it no longer, it hurts me even to touch it. Him of whom I spoke once said there could be no farewell between the two of us, between him and me, which promise has long since turned into untruth, my dreams trodden under his feet. Unless the skins of loyalty and cunning are kept darned together by love, this is my belief, the force that has gone into the sewing begins to strangle. The garment burns not only the skin but the flesh and heart within.

'So, in memory of the friendship you bore me, I am asking you now to send this fragment on to the man to whom it rightly belongs. It must be returned. Joseph Macken will come home to Ireland one day. When you hear he has, send this to him and let him know our love was fruitful.

'Dollie Makken.'

'Macken? The Irish name Macken?' The soldier teasingly wrinkled his nose at me while writing the name.

Then he took the skin from me, lightly between his fingers as though it might infect or burn him also, and placed it and the letter in a red tin decorated with a gold medallion and a label, *The Queen's New Year Chocolate.*

His look and the tenderness of his touch brought sweat to my forehead so I called my Sam and when he came up hurtling, jamming his small head hard against my thigh, I said, 'That's right. Makken, with two k's. The world is an ill-sorted place. I will go now and bring your dress.'

With Sam running before me exclaiming, 'A man, my mama's a man!' we left the docks soon after. The soldier's eyes scorching a hole in my back and the *kas* again riding high on my head.

But we didn't get far that day. I felt weary, my burden was heavy, the streets seemed busy and too wide and long. By giving up the charm it felt that late afternoon as if I had surrendered my last lungful of breath, everything I had wanted, my hope and also my regret. Hereafter, I knew, I would be a different somebody. A slighter sourer person, withheld, without trust, but well-cured as was leather, sun-baked, tough.

I settled us down to sleep that night on the pavement beside Harvey Greenacres General Store, my back against the stone wall – it would not be our first nor our last night in the open. Once I was briefly woken by a group of revellers singing as one man *For We are Jolly Good Fellows*. Singing and embracing they hung a banner across the store front that smelt boldly of new paint and clean sheets. In the morning I could read it. I looked up from my hard bed to see the banner shouting British victory and the bunting flapping everywhere in the streets.

Then, with the dew still clinging wet to Sam's blanket and lying dark upon his father's hat, I made my way to the railway station where the great galvanised iron roof was ringing with the noise of detraining troops. Our destination was opposite to theirs however, we were going north, to the mountains, my first train journey since arriving at the camp more than two years before.

In exchange for a ticket the white man at the desk accepted the nurse Kathleen's journal. The paper was good and strong, I said, and the second half of the book blank. 'I am to return to my master and lack the fare.' Not meeting his eye.

He ran the paper across his thumb, looking at me with unmasked curiosity as if for the first time in his life he was meeting with a chancer or a thief in a woman's shape.

'The peace office, used to be the war office, is tracing scattered families, soldiers and non-combatants lost in action. Documents of war can be useful to their work.'

It was in this way I heard for certain peace had at last indeed come, the amity of gold and grain and grape they called it, as though these things could spring from the land without the help of people's sweat. But it was not because of the peace but because of having shed the skins of my past life, all the shreds that clung to my past love, including the nurse Kathleen's writ-

ing, most of it, that, walking down the platform to the brown
Third-Class carriage, I felt lighter and somewhat freed. I
removed a stone from my boot that looked like a devil's thorn,
and began to chant softly to myself.

That Queen that was beautiful
Will be tormented and darkened,
For she will get her reward
In that day, and her wage.

Her wage for those hearts
That were cracked in the end,
Heart of the black man,
Heart of the black *meid*.

At this Sam, toddling at my side, shot me a sudden close
bright look like a question, and I wondered whether he could be
remembering the song from long ago, from before he was born,
though confusedly. When the cursing chant mingled with the
churn of the blood in my womb.

Those intent pale eyes in his brown face, that light in them.
The eyes pouring into mine.

I caught him up in my arms, we were at Third Class, just
behind the engine, and at the same moment the train whistled
and a cloud of steam and smut poured over us, making him
cough and cry.

'Time to leave, small Sam.' Almost blinded by the smoke I
stumbled but righted myself. 'Here, I will sing you another
rhyme, a lighter one. First the one about the lion, then the one
about the heavens and the stars.'

But 'Nanana' Sam cried, as I wound through the carriage trying to balance the chest on my head, the child on my hip, and
not to knock the passengers crowded there.

'Quiet now, Sam, quiet. No more. Tomorrow all this will be
behind us. Quiet, quiet.'

I twisted in beside a woman whose bare arms were slick with
the mounting heat. Then I whispered into Sam's ear, suddenly

sure he would understand me. I clucked and whispered over and over, 'Tomorrow all this will be behind us. What's finished let it wither, let it die.'

# 38

*What he thought*

So this is ma's white friend, Madonna blonde hair with frizz, doesn't look well, bile-yellow face under these fluorescent lights. The city-slicker suit not improving the effect. Like she's on the way to some place but feeling fucking sick doing it. Fucking sick or just shit scared.

What's she trying to prove anyway, dressing up for the no-windows smog of a maximum-security visiting room, thick with the guard's non-stop Camel Plain? And sneaking a look at me now and again through the fogged-up glass. I catch her doing this because I'm staring level like the gravel, not about to miss a thing. Here comes the look again, flicking over my uniform and up and down, up to my five-o'clock shadow, not bad for 2 pm, down to my hands folded here on the table. She's on to my hands. Check out those killer's hands but not so's to make it obvious. Any invisible blood stains? And those fingers, fingers like triggers, the finger that set that red time-fuse. Those nails ground to pulp. *Readers, he bites his nails to the quick.*

But do I need this? Don't like it, don't need it, interrogation by Supasoft curiosity. As if a polite face-to-face can bring us closer. What we need's a fed-up Fuck You, spat out, on both sides, and no thanks for the memories. What's happened, happened, can't take it away, some people's lives were rocked. But the bigger picture, Joey, said ma. My son, I'm trying to see the bigger story, the family history expanding. When ma was in here the last time, her visit before going away. Showing off a new green travel-coat, fitted her well. The picture expanding, Joseph, it takes your breath away, said ma. Think of it as the kiss of life for our family story. It lifts us out of ourselves, OK, but then makes us more ourselves. Lifting where? Expanding to what, ma? I wanted to say but didn't. It pains me, talk that aims high but goes nowhere. Expanding – shit. I'm focused here inside myself. Another story, not my business. The struggle's where we've always been. I'll tell you myself, Ms Journalist, I'll say it from the horse's mouth, the day I'm out of here, till this Babylon falls, till no one screws or braais a black person for their blackness ever again, I renew the fight. Reconciliation – that's a polite word for nothing-left-to-gain.

But that new coat and ma looking big-shouldered and dead right inside it, I wished admiring it I can help her with it somehow, like buy some of the outfit, that coat and handbag like a bloody satchel she says Ms Journalist got her. The way ma smiles, cracking her face open, when I give her a present. When I got her presents and chocolates, before. There's one advantage to being an expanding half-Irish black man and getting out of here. Spoil ma, plus carry on resisting. Carry on resisting, plus spoil ma, plus maybe if I'm lucky find a woman, that'll be the best or second-best score of all.

The white journalist quickly goggling at me again. So, I ease open my hands. So, Ms, ma mentioned the last time she was here, on her way to her holiday, that you'd found someone, a new man. Whispered the news glancing quickly left and right, doesn't mind a gossip but knows what people say. A new boyfriend, a dark Indian actually, she whispered. 'And a good thing too. Make her let go of herself a bit. You know what also? I think she deserves it.' What, ma, growing and expanding again? The black lover shows open-mindedness? A nice reward for all her sweet sympathy?

'Joey, take it easy.' Ma softly patting my hand held against the glass, just like the ma she is. 'What I'm saying is, she's all right, let her do her thing. I don't mind if she gets lucky.'

But I pull back, Crap.

There's something here I want to say.

'I see her colour wherever I look, ma,' I say. 'And I see our own colour, everywhere. I can't not see colour. Our colour is still the issue, whatever the politicians are talking.'

Then I stop because it's ma's last visit and she wants it special and that means gentle. I don't say what I meant to, that being with whites, around white skin, still gets me down. Thinking of the half-white skin wrapped around me, it can get me down. Like now. This woman's white eyes. How they're glassy even when they're moving round, how they look boiled, empty, at the same time amazed. What was that? the stare says. No, nothing to do with me. Just now when she glanced up I thought of – The eyes blue like that. Baby eyes even when yelling, '*Fokken moer*. Your instructor, man. His name! Are you deaf? Your handler's name. Who gave the word go?' My head kicked to the side, against the bed, the doorpost, but keeping my mouth shut. My brains crashing against the wall that is my locked mouth.

Nothing to do with me.

Patting the glass again, ma said, 'What I meant was that she would've been lonely, you know, after what happened. She's not a bad person, I see this now, and so, fine, she's got this friend. Look hey, do it for me, Joey, you're a good boy. Some time soon agree to see her. She can get visiting rights. She's involved with us now, we can't help it, she's helping your case. Do it for me, son. This story means a new starting-point, it means uncovering memories we can own.'

Starting-point for who? I wanted to ask. Can ask her sitting there now. You in the out-of-place suit. Who's got the new starting-point here, who's beginning fresh? What've you been trying to persuade my mother, you with your teeth biting and wringing your lips? And that closed notebook in your white-knuckle fists. Anxious, so much you want to be accepted. And the jacket lapels hanging slackly down, flat, over your small tits, must be. Definitely small. Mind you, from where I'm sitting, any tits are pretty OK, beggars aren't choosers. How long now since I held a woman? Must be a year, months. Lindi who lived in Snyman Road three streets from ma's, more than a year ago, before Easter. Not counting the one in Ixopo, behind the bar, no name, just that night. Ten days before that Easter. Pulled my hand on to her breast, big quiet eyes. So long since I touched a breast. Touch – think of that. Think, if the guard – If there was a space under the security glass, space for holding hands.

But that's rubbish – who can deal with it? Like in some sort of crazy TV. The bomber and his kind-of victim. The half-victim, so to say, and the half-breed terrorist, fondling. Sitting eyeball to eyeball, but who will make the first move, give the hidden wink? In another world. That finger of yours, you think, that primed the mine. My own arm bent and squeezed under the glass partition, the glass cutting in, my hand on your heart, around your breast, your living flesh and blood. If I can pay with this black flesh of mine. In another world.

Crazy rubbish. But not so crazy as us trying to talk, struggling to find the words, what words, that can break this silence. *Ma. OK. Chocolates,* that's neutral. *Friend?* Where do we start? What's done I did. Didn't mean to get him, him exactly, your dead boyfriend, ex-boyfriend. If he'd run in to buy you, or his ma, chocolates at the OK Bazaar over the road, if he'd stopped to give that beggar there some change – but crazy to talk this talk. Maybe today I wouldn't do it, or would do something different, knowing the pain – but crazy. With what's behind us it's less mad to touch than to have talk. Expanding talk and stories going where?

Nowhere I can think of.

The way it is, you see, ma's friend, is this way. If I get out of here I'm either a new somebody, a rebel I don't recognise, that's your plan, or otherwise it's amnesty for all, an amnesty based on careful swapping, every remaining political prisoner counted in, including the diehards and crazies. Them 1, Us 1 – any idiot white madman, him for me. Either I'm a dyed-in-the-wool Irishman, like-grandoupa-like-great-grandson, let me laugh here a minute, or we all walk free like Nelson, there are rumours you hear. And if you ask me, though you won't, we're neither of us in a position to ask, the last's more possible. Rumours inside have their grain of truth. Warders get friendly, prisoners whisper. Many prison doors have already opened, so many veteran fighters are sitting in their armchairs at home. If you ask me, I'm safe here for a while, and then my Movement claims me back, the freed Clacton bomber is a symbol of the changing future, and I walk out of here under the dazzling blue sky. My prison doors open, and the dusty grassland is shining yellow all around, and the blessings of my Boer prison-warder are raining down on my head. Us and the Boers, you check, have piles of business left to do, they've years of explaining yet to do, hours of counting how many they themselves have smashed to pieces. I say it from the horse's mouth, truth is stranger than any story. The tallest of tall stories turn out real.

*What she thought*

How long haven't I been wondering how he'd look, up close? Just

265

there. Close enough to reach out and touch, almost, if there weren't the partition. A warp in the glass so that when I shift my gaze his head seems to float free of his body. His stare piercing the cigarette haze, a hard, pointed stare looking into me, bedroom eyes I'd say if I didn't think better. Almost bedroom eyes, definitely not cold, and narrow shoulders, not much of a warrior, and sweat on his neck. When I looked down from the courtroom gallery, that sweat on his neck.

Surprised I don't shiver.

Did he shiver, even just the once, a sudden ghost sliding across his grave, on his way out of the Superette? A shiver, so that for a moment he almost choked, gave a grainy cough, while having his bun and juice. While keeping the bomb dead still in the sports bag.

Feel suddenly cold but I don't shiver, don't want to, want to hold steady, not look away.

That broad, shiny nose and wavy hairline, identical to Dora's. Funny how I like that, feel closer in. Like mother like son.

Else wouldn't look twice.

If I saw him in the canteen at work, say, wouldn't meet his eye, couldn't risk it. If I'd smile and then nothing, get nothing in return, I'd feel a fool, guilty for trying in the first place. The traditions that separate us, woman and man, white woman, black man, even without what's happened. Even with Arthur's face now showing me, his caresses and gestures now showing me slowly how to read the lines and movements in dark skin – I wouldn't look twice.

His closed, shut-down stare. Staring into the face of his prejudice. What he sitting so close, just there but so closed, must think of me? A hate figure, would it be, or just nothing? That interfering journalist with her notebook, or a vacant space? Can't think what would be worse.

*People say my insides are stone but this is not true,* Joseph Makken said. *I nearly had to laugh it felt so bad.*

Learning to read the lines and sensations in blackness. Sniff behind Arthur's ear and find it smells of just soap. Soap and skin, a bit of wax. That pulse working the skin just under Joseph's left ear, I can see it clearly from here. Think of touching the place, the nudge of his blood under my finger. *Now my heart is sore, my bleeding heart.*

And if we tried talking, to get over these hard stares and throw-back phrases? If I said, it was stupid to bring this notebook along, sorry, it makes demands. If I said, might it help to say, lately there's been nothing in it? Genuine, I've added nothing to it just lately. Since Dora left with the tapes, haven't really put down a thing.

If I said, your mother asked me to tell you she's reaching the end of her side of the story. When I get back home after this I'll sit down, listen to what she's given me, and begin writing it up. It'll be up to me to add – what can I add? When I write up this interview later, what do I say?

For a man with a reputation for destruction Joseph Makken is a great deal smaller and lighter than one might have thought.

Our hearts have been sore, our bleeding hearts.

Carrying the bomb along did Joseph Makken not list over? Looking at him one imagines him walking slightly askew, moving determinedly but unevenly into that shopping arcade. I see him pass the airline offices sweating, it's a hot day. I see a line of plastic shopping trollies, he shifts past them, one shoulder raised, a controlled hurry. There's a charity box at the Superette entrance in the shape of a blue-eyed girl with a caliper. Then I see nothing. I see a white space. Nothing I say now relates to then.

*Duncan* – a word.

That pulse under his skin.

My ravelling notes wind down into this openness of white paper.

What can I add? is it for me to say?

Do you have enough to eat? What do you do to pass the time? Study for your matric, your mother said. Or do you stare at the wall? Pick your nose, think about your dreams? Why the characters in your dreams have their faces turned away – so I imagine it – the blind backs of their heads. Your broad nose greasy with raised white spots.

To think that I never thought. How blackheads look on black skin. White.

Slowly we're arriving at different selves.

That I never before could think – how it was to plant that bomb. *You must have been sick to the stomach.* That I never thought of those burger wrappings concealing a half-eaten bun.

What can I say?

Here's what I've found, interknit snarled-up lives. But won't your ma have said that anyway?

What I can say.

How're you keeping?

*What they said*

'How are you keeping?'

'No OK. Taking everything into account.'

'Your mother's still on holiday.'

'She's on holiday. I got a postcard. She's OK.'

'I saw her down there last week. Said she's OK.'

'She's not letting on but she's probably enjoying herself. Time to be on her own.'

'She'll be on the beach this week, so she said. She said she's learning to be a tourist for the first time in her life.'

'You found my mother something to fill up her time, that was good. I must say this, it was a good thing, so thank you. It took her mind off me.'

'The family story's coming alive for her.'

'Maybe. That's what she says, sometimes. It's not the same for me. My resistance continues. Their oppression continues, but in more secret, twisted ways.'

'You still say that?'

'I still say that, me, one of the last of the system's prisoners of war, is that what you mean? I must keep my mouth shut? What I say is, what I'd say anywhere is, let the fight for freedom break out again and again.'

'They were saying that then too, during the Boer War, with the same kind of fixity.'

'That's true, OK. Bitter and true. And, OK, you can be bitter, you have every right. You've every right to hate me. I hate the state for doing what they've done. People still are poisoned and shot, the die-hards and their police friends still kill and torture, and the authorities turn a blind eye. For that to end, that's still my struggle.'

'End in blood.'

'If you want. See, there's nothing of what's gone on we can take back, can't do it. Things happened to us, I tried to make things happen. When I heard the story you were making I thought, no, that's shit. It lifts responsibility from my shoulders, to have rebellion in the blood, chip off the old block. I'm sorry for the deaths but always I'm responsible. But now hearing you I think, ja, there's a point in there somewhere. Striking back is my life, my life-blood, what did you say, fixity? I share this with anyone who loves freedom. Somehow maybe Boer warfare helped make me, a half-breed freedom fighter with one clean goal.'

'Time moves on though, people are changing. There are different arguments, a new state to work out … '

'People change, OK, it happens. And when one day this kingdom of race-hatred finally collapses, every bit of it, the rays of new freedom will break out like spears, like divining rods in flame across the dazzling blue-as-blue sky. And we'll use them for new ends, push-start the vehicle of peace. But resistance itself, then, now, it can't end.'

'So you were saying.'

'You're not writing anything down.'

'No, I'm trying to listen.'

'Ja, you listen. You can listen well, ma says. It's funny, I never thought ma'd chose a friend like you. White, young as me.'

'Sometimes the world turns upside down. Bossy, too, I'm sure she's said, stubborn.'

'And revolutionary, after all. A revolutionary. Convincing my ma of your plans, you turned her world upside down.'

'If you say so. A terrorist, a revolutionary – It doesn't feel right to want to laugh.'

'You want to laugh?'

'I never thought – I never thought I would, here, talking … '

'So weird things happen. Do you want to hear something else that happened? I've been saving it but now's maybe the time. A story for your book, you can write it down. Your ears will burn.'

'I'm listening.'

'You write it down, then tell my ma. So far I can't tell her.'

'I'm writing.'

'When I was hiding in the safe house in Ladysmith, it happened then. Before they caught me. I keep wanting to forget this but I can't. It was in that safe house in Ladysmith. There was another comrade there resting, he wasn't well in the head. He was fighting up north years, there were demons in his dreams. So one day this woman comes round selling live chickens. She has cataracts, eyes that look half-dead, but still it's like she sees us. Later she's in touch with our contact person. She's an *izinyanga*, she tells him.'

'*Izinyanga?*'

'Ja. She tells him she has medicine to give us, *muti* for fear, medicine for craziness, whatever we want. As if she can feel how we feel she comes back to see us uninvited. Uninvited, make sure you write that. She offers this grey powder in an Eno's Fruit Salts bottle, not cheap. We take it, a spoonful, and for me it does nothing, but my comrade says he feels better and the next morning he disappears. We don't get news from him again, it's like him and his demons have melted into the air. Then, a day or so before the police find me, I hear. Another comrade of ours gets the word. How the *izinyanga* in the area are digging down into the war graves. Ladysmith, like you know, is thick with those Anglo–Boer graves. How they're trying to reach the powerful bones, the jaw and arm bones of the dead soldiers, whatever side. How they crush the bones and mix the powder into medicine to make our warriors strong. You not going to write this down?'

'I don't – I wouldn't know where to begin.'

'They crush the old bones and make them into medicine to give us spirit, begin there. When I hear this I let myself out of the safe house just about choking on my own spit. It's the evening before they catch me. I let myself out after sunset but nearly not caring who sees me. I walk up the koppie that was pointed to me, I find the mass grave, the turned red earth marking the place, the white stones and crosses, one uncovered white bone shining in the light that there still is, the ghwarrie bush shooting out of the earth like an alive force. Out of the place where the heads lie. And that bone looking so fresh in the half-light that – see, I just can't move, can't get off the mountain till the moon comes out, can't stop thinking – who knows what spies saw me then?'

'How can I write this?'

'I tasted those bones, but not knowing.'

'I can't bear to think. It could've been – '

'It could've been anyone but it made no difference. The next morning and I was taken.'

'And if you're now reprieved, freed?'

'That's not for me to say.'

'It would be like magic, almost. The story coming alive, if you see what I mean, the bones living through you – '

'I see what you mean. I said your ears would burn.'

'And you?'

'I'm burning. You see how it's in my blood.'

# 39

Anthea and Arthur sit waiting on the velour settee in the Naidoos' livingroom, twining and untwining their fingers, drinking cane spirit and Coke between kisses. They are waiting for Dora and Bernice to arrive, possibly with Gertie in tow. Arthur's mother is making biryani and has banned them from the kitchen. The smell of seasoned chicken hangs heavy in the air.

'Don't care who comes as long as it's the main players in this Makken story.' It was Arthur's idea to have the party. Yesterday at lunchtime he called over to Anthea's desk. 'We must toast how far we've got. Drink to the success of those paragraphs shimmering there on your screen.'

'We'll bring the *dops*,' Bernice said on the phone, 'Irish whiskey even, and snacks. Mince pies for the season. Dora's favourites, Marie Biscuits, a giant box of Romany Creams. Why not make a big party?'

Arthur raises a preliminary toast.

'For you're a jolly good fellow,' he whispers against Anthea's lips.

She doesn't respond. She pauses, preoccupied, lifts her glass but doesn't drink. This party has meant her first invitation to Arthur's house, his family's home. At the door his mother greeted her smiling, but with dropped and wary eyes. Behind her, in the hallway, the unexpected presence of an outsize Christmas tree flashed with gold and crimson lights.

'So you say that's not a shrine?' Anthea says, staring out over Arthur's shoulder at a display cabinet opposite.

'No, my wonderful culturally-aware girlfriend, no. That's my ma's ornament collection, don't let her hear your talk about shrines. She's been collecting those bronze dishes and incense holders and things for years. The Sacred Heart squeezed in with the rest shouldn't confuse you. The family's been Christian for more than a century, since before your war.'

'Christian?'

'Forcibly christianised on arriving at these beautiful green shores. Which probably means, my Anthea, that if you and I ever wanted to marry there'd be few impediments, not in the religious sphere anyway.'

'Did you say marry? Now that's fast-forwarding.'

'It flashed into my mind. I do happen, if you haven't noticed it yet, to be crazy about you.'

'But I could hold you to it. To marrying.'

'In that case why not make the announcement here at the party? No time like the present. Think how Dora'd smile.'

'But never forgetting she's the focus of all this. We could also choose another occasion maybe? I for one … I could use more time.'

She has suddenly to sit up, turn away, though keeping her body held against Arthur's, tears closing the back of her throat. Yes, she coaxes herself, think of that name, let it come, the talk of marriage loosened it. Think it, *Duncan*. Of course. Duncan, the non-guest at this party. Time passing so rapidly over his memory now, greying it over. Since Arthur – Arthur who likes to talk, touch, yet somehow, she sees with hindsight, somehow more readily accepts her own need for silence or space apart – her empty pages – than ever did the silent and solitary Duncan. 'So gloomy, my girlfriend?' he'd say. 'Remember I'm the one who's introverted here.' Not disloyal to think this. That necessarily absent friend. If he was here, in this room soon to be full of talk, lights and party laughter, he'd find a way of leaving early, slip away without a word, waving a voiceless goodbye at the door.

She swallows, her throat aching. Duncan, always defined by his silences, his not-being-there. It is his absence has brought her here today, delivered her into this changing life. What was it those poets she once studied claimed: Rage burns us at last beyond strife and defeat, into intenser, sweeter worlds? And so it perhaps is, so it's worked out. Beyond rage, yes, an intenser world …

Arthur nudges the bag carrying her notebooks over to her side of the settee but instead of looking for a tissue she feels inside the crackling plastic for the envelope Dora sent on the last day of her Cape holiday, the letter arrived at the flat this morning. National Library letter-head paper, folded into fours, handwriting on the reverse. Two-and-a-half closely written pages.

'I should take a look at this before she arrives. Something for my notebook, my scrapbook, she says here a little unflatteringly, something she did herself. To fill up those empty pages, she writes. *What we've done has lifted us out of ourselves, Anthea, and has returned us to ourselves.*'

'You could read it aloud. Take my mind off the tantalising prospect of marriage. But stay sitting here and have me hold you.'

Anthea spreads the paper open on her knees. She reads, *December 1903. Dear Dollie.* Then she freezes round-mouthed. Her eyes run down the page, she turns the next page, glances at the third. She sits back and buries her face in the paper, swept by waves of relief, shock, hope. She coughs to free the tears still wet and tight in her throat and begins to laugh.

She says, 'Dora's done it! This isn't a scrapbook piece at all, it's an end for Dollie's story. What we've done eventually returns us to ourselves, she said. She's somehow got there, like she said she would. She's sewn in the loose threads, she's done it.'

# 40

*As conceived by Dora and transferred into Anthea's notebook*

Dublin
December 1903

Dear Dollie

I am extremely loath to open old wounds, yet a time of severe
worry has pressed me to make this appeal to you. Your anger I
am sure still is just, but my strong hope is that, even so, you will
harken to this distress. Find it in you, dear Dollie, to come to
the assistance of the honourable soldier and mutual friend who
is sickening now almost to death.

How well I recall the fate that once cruelly assailed you, the
relentless way in which missile after missile was hurled at your
breast. But on each occasion, I also remember, your spirit
rushed to staunch the cruel wound undaunted. We both of us
know what devotion means and the pain it exacts, we know also
the importance of a forgiving heart, and, moreover, of a nation
restored to pride. Knowing this I pray you will look kindly upon
this plea.

Since we parted, dear Dollie, I have thought so often of our
morning coffees in the *kamp*, our talk of things Irish, how we
made believe and chatted about the little Sean-to-be. Please,
remembering this, would you respond to this request as soon as

ever you can. The situation we confront here is unutterably sad. Here too we face a bleak prospect – a bereft national cause, a new family abandoned to its fate. The spirit of our countryman is tortured and sinking even as I write.

As you will clearly recollect, it was something over a year ago that you sent, via the Celtic Society, a token to the man who is your former lover. You wrote that the cherished object was rightfully his and therefore you could no longer be its custodian, *you could keep hold of it no longer*. Now, as we discover, nor can he.

He received the token in person, as chance would have it, having come home in defiance of British jurisdiction not four days before the soldier delivered it (dropping it off under cover of darkness, too fearful to show his face to patriots). After that visit Joseph Macken disappeared again from our view until about ten months later when his new wife wrote to us at the Society in some considerable trouble.

Joseph's senses, she told us, seemed lately to have left him. He walked every night in his sleep, muttering like a man possessed, he plucked ceaselessly at his clothing. He had made several attempts to strip himself naked even in broad daylight and in a public place and sought to bathe, or at least immerse parts of his body – hands, feet and head – in water, several times a day. At first she had thought it was the horror of battle still boiling up his mind, but now, since seeing him repeatedly wring a certain object while sleep-walking, she had started to suspect otherwise. The object was a dirty hairy thing like an animal's tail, or so she gathered for he would not allow her to see it. He growled at her if she so much as mentioned it, 'Not you too.' He had it stored in the English chocolate tin it came in, which she had effected to hide, thinking this might bring some improvement, but the months had gone by and there was no change. The larger her new baby grew in her womb, the stranger Joseph became to her, the more hostile to a loving word. So strange and hostile was he indeed that she was now convinced his soul had been bewitched. In recent days, with the baby's birth imminent, a red-and-black fan-shaped cloud had been flaring over their roof, growing larger by the hour, whereas round about, even in the next field, the weather was perfectly fine. Frightened to death that some force, some African spectre, would snatch her child at the very moment of birth she begged us now in God's name to come to their rescue. We had consigned the token to them, could we find some way to remove its malign force?

Immediately, it was about a month ago, my aunt and I travelled together by train to see them, trusting to the strength that lies in numbers. We were met with a heart-rending situation – an ailing newborn, a frantic mother and the father still sadly distracted. He himself linked his condition to the animal skin but would say no more as to what its precise effects might be, other than to growl, Curses, a contagion of curses, which we do believe might be close to the truth.

The truth we fear, Dollie, is that the skin, signifying to him your bitterness, conveyed to him at the same time a physical torment. I know from my own experience of continuing bodily weakness how once-diseased flesh or infected bone may hold stored-up for years the fevers which have afflicted or excited it. When in Africa, I heard whisper, too, of the deadly poison of the Euphorbia tree's milky resin, a poison which when administered by a practitioner may invisibly taint arrows, stones, and also skin. Forgive these wild surmises, dearest, as I am sure you will, they spring from a deep uneasiness, a chilling dread of the mind-fever or brain torture which causes the patient now, at the time of writing, to bathe nightly in the freezing sea – to cleanse himself thoroughly he says, to wash his agony away. Every late evening, we hear, he insists upon diving off the high rocks in the bay, relying on the waves to carry him to shore. It is very evident that one of these dives will some night soon be his last; it is hardly possible that he make the New Year.

If these speculations in any sense approach what might be the case, I beg, Dollie, that you show mercy. Joseph Macken refuses to allow us to take the token from him. He is fastened to his torture, yet so desperately needs release. Therefore we ask ourselves, would not some word from you help draw out the charm? Could you not write to say the past is behind us? We might then show him, in private, the letter. Or if this is too much to ask, could you not send a single clean page, a sign of forgiveness, on which you might have made an identifying mark, or simply pressed your soft hand?

That your Irish soldier has now suffered deeply on your account I can assure you. I trust it was a great and lasting pain indeed that drove you to take this extreme measure. Different beliefs are as we know but lenses through which to look at Truth, yet do think, dear Dollie, this destructive magic is a glass that darkens you, it shadows your shining face. I would also remind you of all that Joseph has sacrificed for his country, and with what courage. Long ago he swore himself a soldier in a permanent war for Ireland's liberty; of her living sons he has served her like few others. Judging from the unwearying grinding of tyranny's boot, I know there will be more and even more important battles for him to fight. If he should perish, who then will bear the arms he bore so bravely in Africa? If he should be taken from us, who will carry on his song?

Till I hear from you, Dollie, I remain
Sincerely in your debt
Kathleen Gort


Do you have a photograph of the small Sean that you might send along with your reply? Does he, as I imagine, still have that burning red hair? – KG